"A brilliant, funny, inspired, and courageous first novel from a gifted and psychologically wise young writer. In this Israeli landscape, the psalmist is a woman, and listening to her psalms, we hear a different and riveting truth. Kadish's characters have entered my life."

—Carol Gilligan, author of *In a Different Voice*

"Rachel Kadish has written a book that's wise beyond the years of most Americans. From the opening page, her novel brilliantly braids history, religion, family, and eros. I was moved by it, and very impressed."

—Russell Banks, author of *Affliction* and *Cloudspitter*

"Every first novel should be like this one: deeply imagined, deeply felt, and—as a result—deeply involving. I gave myself up to Rachel Kadish, and was not disappointed. She carries the reader along like a great river, never stopping until she's reached the mighty ocean."

—Gish Jen, author of *Mona in the Promised Land* and *Who's Irish?*

"*From a Sealed Room* is politically astute, emotionally honest, and displays all the technical mastery of a mature writer. The most assured debut I've read in years."

—Caryl Phillips, author of *The Nature of Blood*

"Kadish is a formidable new talent. Her courage, integrity, and rich imagination transform the world of the reader . . . a passionate, seductive song that will echo in the reader's memory for years to come."

—Susan Power, author of *The Grass Dancer*

"An extraordinary new writer."
—Brian Morton, author of *Starting Out in the Evening*
and *The Dylanist*

"A strong, ambitious novel, filled with vigorous and distinct voices and a generous, alert narrative intelligence."
—*San Francisco Chronicle Book Review*

"Tensions, layered and complex, are adroitly teased out . . . an intelligent and moving recreation of the ways, distinctive and universal, that different generations in different culutres understand civilization and its discontents."
—*Forward*

"This is a wise novel with many gifts to give . . . as Kadish's book reminds us, redemption and peace do not come easily."
—*The Boston Book Review*

"What makes this book so rich and historically resonant is the skill and boldness with which Kadish weaves the intersecting stories of three women representing three generations of this country . . . a talented writer."
—*Chicago Tribune*

From a Sealed Room

RACHEL KADISH

Rachel Kadish

B
BERKLEY BOOKS, NEW YORK

FROM A SEALED ROOM

A Berkley Book / published by arrangement with
the author

PRINTING HISTORY
G. P. Putnam's Sons edition / October 1998
Berkley trade paperback edition / September 2000

A portion of this novel appeared, in different form, in *Bomb*.

The quotation of Rabbi Zalman Schachter-Shalomi on page v
is from Rodger Kamenetz's *The Jew in the Lotus*.

The Penguin Putnam Inc. World Wide Web site address is
http://www.penguinputnam.com

ISBN: 0-425-17641-X

BERKLEY®
Berkley Books are published by The Berkley Publishing Group,
a division of Penguin Putnam Inc., 375 Hudson Street,
New York, New York 10014.
BERKLEY and the "B" design are trademarks
belonging to Pengtuin Putnam Inc.

They say not a blade of grass grows without an angel saying, "Grow, grow, grow."
—Talmudic teaching, as rendered by Rabbi Zalman Schachter-Shalomi

I cannot adequately express my gratitude to the angels who urged the growth of this book and of its author. Much of the novel was written in rich communities of family, friends, teachers, and fellow writers; their faith and encouragement made all the difference.

I am grateful to the Corporation of Yaddo and the MacDowell Colony for the precious gift of time; to the Mrs. Giles Whiting Foundation, the Rona Jaffe Foundation, and the Barbara Deming Memorial Fund for their support; and to the Mary Ingraham Bunting Institute, for a life-changing year.

I owe a debt to my cousin Yaron Galai, who patiently answered not only the questions I asked, but those I did not know enough to ask.

My thanks as well to Faith Sale, Aimée Taub, and Anna Jardine for their dedication, and Gail Hochman and Marianne Merola for making it all happen.

For my family
near and far

Most people interviewed perceived that the defenses were there to protect them, and nobody expressed a wish that they be removed.

—CAMILO JOSÉ VERGARA, *The New American Ghetto*

For the sky is large and tears are small
Close your eyes every first rain
And think of me.

—MAX GAT-MOR, "The Last Summer"
(song performed at a 1995 memorial
service for Yitzhak Rabin)

Part One

1

Long after the war was over they made love in the sealed room, she on top of him and he with his hands pressed in the flesh of her hips, and no more missiles hurtling through the night sky. She had been wondering for some time whether her love for Nachum had not faded beyond her ability to recall it, and now, in this room with its windows still edged with tape to ward off chemical death, its shelf piled with boxes of baking soda and gauze pads to make into poultices for chemical burns, and its corners cluttered with Ariela's dolls and books to distract the girl from too much fear, Tami could not feel a whisper of love for this man who had been her husband for twenty-one years.

It was their son Dov's room that they had sealed when this war had begun. Under one of the windows was a wooden desk, and pictures of coral reefs cut from scuba-diving magazines decorated the wall above a low chest of drawers. On the floor under the single bed were Dov's high school yearbook and a snapshot of a girl Tami did not recognize. The rest of Dov's things Tami and Nachum had piled into his closet. "When your commander next gives you weekend leave, we'll help you sort it out," Nachum told Dov over the telephone, and laughed at a response Tami could not hear.

They had chosen this room because its two small windows made it the easiest to seal. Tami and Nachum had made a game of the sealing for Ariela, who concentrated cross-legged over the slow chewing progress of her plastic-handled scissors. Tami trimmed the mangled ends of the tape before standing on the desk to stick the strips to the window frames. Nachum curled streamers out of purple ribbon, and while Ariela watched, they decorated her gas mask. They saved their good humor for the child; they gave Tami's mother, Fanya, their bedroom because it was the most comfortable, and spread their own necessities on the dresser and sills of the sealed room. To each other they barely spoke. The American cousin telephoned to ask once more: Was there anything they needed, anything she could send them?

With the double mattress on the floor beside the single bed, they could all gather in the room on the nights when the sirens rose one after another to merge and wail across the sky. Tami and Nachum, tumbled to opposite sides of the mattress, woke into a firmament of sound. They blinked into the darkness as the Silent Station came alive, its nightlong static broken by the voice of the radio announcer repeating instructions in language after language. Ariela's wild knock at the door was followed a few minutes later by the appearance of Fanya in her long cotton nightgown, hair freshly combed. Outside, sirens pinioned the sky. Still breathing deeply from his sleep, Nachum shut the door and sealed its edges in the dark. He rolled himself up onto Dov's single bed, Fanya and Ariela joined Tami on the mattress on the floor, and they unpacked their masks, the purple streamers on Ariela's crushed by the brown plastic case. The first nights of sirens they had been too alert for quiet, so they sang the songs Ariela had learned in school, and played the games suggested over the radio. Fanya could think of more words spelled with the letters in "Saddam Hussein" than Tami and Nachum and Ariela combined, and as they waited for the all-clear to be called for their sector they moved on to Bush and Baker, Shamir and Levi and Netanyahu. Fanya won every time.

After the all-clear they put their masks aside, and Nachum began snoring almost immediately. Lying on the mattress, Tami felt the woman and the girl on either side of her shifting as they passed into sleep. Fanya rested a lilac-smelling hand on Tami's shoulder. It was more to brace herself than to embrace, Tami knew, but she was entranced by the unfamiliar touch all the same. She held as still as she could, so as not to jar her mother's hand, and she hugged Ariela's sweet small body to her. It seemed to Tami that the three of them were something simple, like animals in a burrow. It passed through her mind that they would never leave this room of half-shadows and silent urgency, daily clutter and slow layered breathing. Tami thought she had never felt so close to understanding who she was.

On the nights when there were no sirens and the Silent Station was quiet, Fanya sighed from down the hall and Ariela breathed softly in her bedroom. Tami and Nachum stayed alone in the sealed room. They reached for each other and they listened to the static on the radio.

The war was over; they slept in the sealed room now only as a temporary arrangement. After the cease-fire and the dancing in the streets, when they had returned to the apartment, they had opened one window partially. Nachum ripped off tape and paint together, letting in the cold, wet night air. Jerusalem was bursting in fireworks all around them. Tami's head ached from the waves of sound. Out on the street she had held tight to Ariela's hand, while Fanya threw herself into the dance steps and glared at the ever rougher crowd and somewhere in an inner circle Nachum jostled shoulders with the workers from his shop. Back in the apartment at last, Tami tucked Ariela into bed to the accompaniment of shouts and whistles. Outside the window, explosions lit the sky. When Dov next came home they would finish removing the tape, repaint the window frames, take the baking soda off the shelf and replace it with Dov's magazines. Only a few days more and Fanya would pack her bag and return to Tel Aviv, Tami and Nachum would return to their bedroom. But for now the room remained as it was. The noise from the street all but obscured the sound of the telephone: the American cousin calling to congratulate them for enduring, her voice brimming with relief.

Because their sleeping in the room was only temporary, Tami and Nachum did not bother with screening the sun from their eyes but let the shutter stay open instead, all day and all night, until a bird nested in the pulley's track and they could not have closed it if they had wanted to. Ariela's hair ribbons lay forgotten under the bed; Nachum's papers from the electronics shop, graphs and charts and technical magazines, were strewn about the floor. The view of the botanical gardens and the road to the Knesset building looked in on them continuously. Long rectangles of light stretched across the mattress. On the rim of the Valley of the Cross stood buildings of thumbnail-colored stone, hardened planes whittled against the pale-blue sky.

"Tami, *shalom,* it's Yael."

"Yael!" Tami settled on one of the kitchen chairs. "How are you?"

"Me, I'm fine. You're the one who disappears off the face of the earth for days at a time. What do you do with yourself?"

"You know what I do with myself. I work."

"What, three afternoons a week? Four? So what's this nonsense, 'work'? I tell you, Tami, if I didn't chase after you I'd never see you. During the war I understood—everybody was going mad in their own house. But it's three weeks since cease-fire and I still don't see you around. A human being doesn't spend so much time alone, it's not normal. And don't argue with me, because you know it's true. Even in the army you were like this, if we hadn't been roommates we never would have spoken. And believe me, back then it was work too. Tell me, what do you hear from Dov?"

Tami drew a deep breath. "Fine, he's fine."

"Fine? He can't say more than 'fine'? My Benny is in Dov's same unit, and he can't get over telling me the craziness they put them through in their training."

"Yes, well. Of course he talks about that."

"Benny says Dov is considering trying out for officer, is it true?"

"Mm," Tami agreed.

"Dov would be excellent. Benny says the commander already picked him as a favorite."

Tami lifted a cooling hand to her cheek. "Nachum spoke with him last night, Nachum would know the latest stories."

For a moment Yael was silent. "Dov still doesn't speak to you?"

"I don't want to talk about it, Yael."

"But what on earth does he think you ever did wrong to him?"

"Tell me about Yoram's new job."

"Oh, this job of Yoram's!" Yael's laughter was full of grievance and pleasure. "This job and this new schedule of his are wonderful, so wonderful they will kill him and the rest of us within a year. But who can complain? At least the new salary helps with the overdraft." She sighed heartily. "So tell me, how is Fanya? Has she found some man to follow her to the ends of the earth yet this week?"

"I don't know," Tami answered. "She's been out almost constantly since the end of the war."

"Good for her. The SCUDs flushed a lot of sociable people from Tel Aviv, maybe our guests will improve the nightlife here before they leave us. How long is she staying?"

"Who knows—she planned to return to Tel Aviv two weeks ago already."

"She's probably out singing at all the cultured folks' soirees. Charming them silly as usual."

"I told you, I hardly see her. She's out all the time. I don't have that many friends in Jerusalem, and I live here." Tami caught the bitterness in her voice, too late.

"And why should that bother you?" Yael shot back. "Be happy she's up and about. Many people Tanya's age aren't so lucky."

"I didn't say I wasn't happy," Tami replied. "Of course I'm happy."

It was Dov that Tami thought about during the stifling afternoons of green printed forms and heavily resealed boxes. She stamped packages "Cleared" or "Suspicious," she sipped cup after cup of Turkish coffee, and she imagined her son's wind-chapped face. He had Nachum's face, that same wide nose and square jaw, the dark eyes that could brim with amusement. And he was broad like Nachum; the two looked more similar every year. The hesitant boy with upturned nose and thin arms existed only in her memory. Even the muscles of Dov's face seemed hardened now, his freckles long since faded.

"I said I don't feel like explaining." Dov had cut her off the previous evening on the telephone.

"I was just wondering what your unit is doing, that's all. I just wondered what's new." She fingered the telephone cord. "Is the training very difficult?"

"It's fine."

Tami heard a noise outside, the squeal of a bus slowing to a halt across the street. "Do you like your unit?" she murmured.

"Yes."

"Oh. So . . ." Her fingers were woven in the cord. Unbidden, the list ran in her mind: see to Ariela's bath, put her to bed, ask Nachum about the broken kitchen clock. "Have a good week," she said.

There was silence on the line. Tami heard the bus door opening and closing, then the laboring of the engine as the bus started up the hill. "Dov?" She searched into the clicking on the line.

Time after time she reached for one memory that would explain to her when the change had begun, but there was nothing to tell her precisely when it had happened. She knew only that at some point, as she had nodded to his account of some planned scout activity, she turned to find disappointment in the eyes of her eleven-year-old son. Another time, later, there was accusation: Dov's fists tight at his sides, his voice strident. *Aren't you listening to anything I say? Don't you care about anything?* She did not remember what she had replied, what assurance she had offered as she stared out the window, trying to retain what she had been musing about while he had been talking. Something, it seemed, about the way the trees in Jerusalem grew differently from those in Haifa or in Tel Aviv.

Only last month Nachum had remarked that Dov was growing into quite a man. "He substituted for Moti in the shop this Friday, and do you know, he was answering customers' electronics questions with no training but correctly. The boy has a brain in his head," Nachum said with a trace of awe.

Once it had been possible to pacify Dov, to salve his hurt with light words. Until he began to repeat the words back to her. She would blush with shame. For a time she told herself that his scorn for her must pass, that he would understand that even though she somehow could not concentrate on his rambling stories through to their finish, the rhythm of his voice soothed her and she wanted only for it to continue.

That last year when he was in high school, there were days when she thought she would do anything to break through the disdain on his face. Standing over the stove, foolish unstoppable tears rolling down her cheeks and hissing in the pan of sweet onions, Tami searched for something to hold him, to make him turn to her and say anything at all. "Tell me what you think I did wrong," she said once, his reactionless face more than she could stand. "You used to smile at me." She heard the quaver in her voice and could not stop it, so instead she fell silent. Dov walked into the living room without answering her. Through the kitchen doorway she watched him pick up a newspaper and cast it back to the table with barely a glance. Nachum, leafing through a magazine on the sofa, looked up and lowered his glasses. "Dov," he said.

Dov stared down at the day-old copy of *Ma'ariv.*

"Dov," Nachum repeated. "Dov. *Noodnik.* Come here."

With a sour expression, Dov stepped toward the couch. "What?"

Nachum doubled over and scooped something from the floor. The soccer ball hit Dov in the chest, hard, but his hands shot up and caught it. Tami held her breath. Nachum was laughing, and Dov was laughing too.

"So you're learning something even if you never go to school when you're supposed to. At least you're learning how to catch a soccer ball."

"I am, I'm better than you are now." Dov lifted his chin in that new way of his and looked at his father.

"You're better than your father, says who?"

"You want to go to Sacher Park and I'll show you?"

Nachum was on his feet, the magazine left open on the sofa. "Let's pick up Rafi and his father and we'll be two against two."

They passed through the kitchen without a word to Tami, who was cutting tomatoes at the table. She listened to their voices fading down the stairs.

When, last summer, Dov had seen her with the man from the greengrocer's, she had known that his contempt for her was now assured, and that it was all her fault that her son did not love her. She had tried telling him later that there was nothing to what he had seen. Nothing had happened, she would never do such a thing to Nachum or to him or to Ariela. But her words made no difference; he only averted his eyes from her.

And now he was doing his army service. Late at night, in her son's sealed bedroom, she worried that he would be reckless. He would play ringleader as he always did, and this time he would get himself hurt. In her mind he lay on a stretcher, his bruised face coated with dust. "Why did you do something so stupid?" his commander begged, and Dov answered with a last, pained breath, "Because I hate my mother." But then she thought, No. Why would he trouble himself to do something so dramatic for her sake?

At night, when they had finished with their abrupt love and Nachum slept beside her, Tami looked around the sealed room in the dim light at the things that belonged to her son, the desk where he stacked his magazines, the bed where he had slept, and she knew that he had seen the depths of her selfishness and there was nothing she could do.

When Rafi called that afternoon, Tami kept him on the telephone well after she told him Dov was not home.

"And how is your training?" she asked him for the third time.

"Training . . . training is training. My commander, Oded, he likes to tell stories about his family. The other day, we're standing at attention, one and a half hours we're standing at attention while he tells stories about his great-uncle. He's a joker, and tough too, but he's good to us. The hike we did yesterday had some of the guys crying into their canteens, but at the end Oded flagged a truck hauling oranges to Tel Aviv and the driver broke open a crate for us."

"And your unit? And the food?"

"Let me tell you about the food. I see olives in my sleep."

"Olives?" Tami echoed, and let his energetic response wash over her.

Rafi was the only one of Dov's friends who did not make Tami nervous. When he came to the door he spoke to Tami instead of right away asking for Dov; he teased her, opening the refrigerator to look for a snack without asking, and played with Ariela with a seriousness that made Tami smile. "The girls get crushes on Dov. And me? They want to be my friend, they like to hug me," he told Tami. She smiled her warmest smile at him when he told her this, although she dismissed his words without a second thought—she could not see any problem, there didn't seem to be any real couples anyway. Just one group of them, doing everything together, unable to be apart for an instant. When Dov was in high school and had missed classes for paratrooper tryouts, the phone rang a dozen times on the same afternoon. "It's Dafna," a voice informed when Tami answered the first call, and while she tried to connect the name with a face, Dafna went on. "A few of us wanted to pick up Dov from his tryouts. If you could just tell us where they're being held?" After the third call, Tami began telling Dov's friends that he had been picked up, picked up ten times over already. Privately she wondered, Didn't they have anything better to do with their time than drive for six hours?

And now they were all in the army. Together or separated, they still seemed to Tami an unbreachable whole. When Dov returned to Jerusalem for a weekend, Tami knew his entrance would be followed within hours by Rafi's knock at the door. The two of them were a center of activity: the apartment vibrated with outlandish insults, a soccer ball flew between hands, and the telephone rang without cease, familiar voices asking brusquely for Dov or Rafi.

"So I'm convinced that the *ramatkal* loves olives and has brainwashed his staff." Rafi clucked his disapproval. "Either that, or it's an army experiment to determine the psychological effects of olive saturation on—"

"Rafi," she interrupted. "What about Dov?"

"What about him?" Rafi stalled. "He hates olives too."

"I mean his plans."

Rafi was selecting his words with care. "Dov is one terrific soldier."

"But do you think he'll go to university after his three years? Nachum says he'd be an excellent student. Or is he planning to be an officer?"

"All I know is, the commander likes him. So it will be up to Dov whether to stay in the army."

"Then he wants to be an officer? But for a few years, Rafi, or for his career?" Her pulse raced, although she could not have said exactly why.

"I didn't say he's decided." She could see Rafi fidgeting as clearly as if he sat before her, his skinny frame angled against the sofa's back, one heel propped on the coffee table. "He'll choose well. He'll choose whichever path makes even more girls chase him, of that I'm sure. Don't worry about Dov." There was a brief pause. Then Rafi's voice took on its usual tone of mischief. "He'll choose well, of course he will, he has such wonderful parents."

The sound of the dairy truck unloading at the market boomed from up the street. It was the store's first full restocking since the missiles had stopped, and women waited outside the doors with their shopping baskets.

"Jerusalem is delightful," Fanya said. She stood beside Tami in the kitchen, peering into the pot on the stove. "How is it I forgot all this time? Tell me, Tami, how could I forget?"

"Maybe you should come visit more often, you won't forget."

"Don't be fresh." Fanya stepped to the window and looked down into the street.

It seemed to Tami that she had been sincere. She tucked a strand of hair behind one ear and stirred the heavy-smelling stew — something she had looked up in the "From Europe" section of a cookbook because Fanya would not eat the spicy salads Tami bought at Mahane Yehuda or the frozen *mellawach* she fried for Ariela's lunch.

Already the sun was past its height, and Tami chided herself for the morning wasted. As usual, Fanya had risen shortly after dawn and talked cheerfully over breakfast, mapping out her plans for the day while Ariela rubbed the sleep from her eyes. Making her exit as Tami braided Ariela's hair, Fanya promised that she would have walked more of Jerusalem than all the fancy tour guides combined by the time Ariela's short school day was through. Ariela giggled.

When the afternoon heat had settled into the neighborhood, Fanya returned to Wolfson Street, climbed the steps to Tami's apartment, and retreated to the bedroom with a satisfied smile. While Fanya napped inside, Tami sat on the balcony and watched Ariela playing on the street below. Watched, and waited for Fanya to rise. Tami had not spent so much time with her mother in years. It made her excited and nervous, so that she sometimes slipped and repeated herself, or forgot what it was that had brought her to the hall closet; Ariela would have to remind her that she had come to get Grandmother's sweater.

Now Fanya was leaning out the kitchen window, standing on her toes with stockinged calves peeking from the back of a tailored skirt. Tami had the impulse to pull her from the sill as she would Ariela. Instead she stirred the pot. "What are you doing this afternoon?" she asked.

"Watercolor class." Fanya spoke out the window. She had enrolled in a four-week painting class at the YMCA, a short bus ride from Tami's apartment. "Why not?" she had explained to Tami. "As long as I'm already in Jerusalem, I may as well see some life here."

"Anything after that?" Tami asked.

"After that, a walk in the Jerusalem Forest with Shmuel Roseman."

"Him again?"

Fanya pulled herself into the kitchen and brushed her elbows. "Yes, him again. He's a nice fellow, you know, poor thing."

They were all nice fellows and all poor things, these men who discovered Fanya wherever she went. Elderly widowers from Hungary or Germany, and once one from France who called Fanya every afternoon for weeks with long descriptions of the delights of her chin, her eyes, her complexion, before she finally advised him to take his affections elsewhere. Fanya accepted their invitations and their flowers and compliments until she grew tired of them. "That one was a sweet man," she said of each, and gave no other explanation. As for Shmuel Roseman, Tami had known him for years; he was in his seventies, from Prague. In the mornings he sat in the back of the jeweler's shop on Aza Street and repaired watches. He squinted for hours at wheels and pins far smaller than the tips of his fingers. On the rare occasions when Fanya ran errands with Tami and they stopped at his shop, he pushed aside the thick magnifying lens that jutted down from the strap across his forehead and blinked his heavy-lidded eyes at Fanya in adoration. "Your mother is a remarkable woman," he would tell Tami when next she came alone to the shop, and repeat it in a murmer as he held a tiny piece of metal to the light. "A remarkable woman." Tami imagined him trailing behind Fanya along the paths of the Jerusalem Forest, out of breath and in love, while Fanya pointed out sights and paused now and again as if on a whim. Letting him catch his breath just enough, but not completely, before setting off up another steep incline.

Popularity came effortlessly to Fanya. Since Tami's father had died, twenty-five years before, Fanya had taught singing twice a week to a group of old women at the Arts House in Tel Aviv. Each year her speech was more clipped and each year she was closer in age to her students, but to the women she led through warm-up trills and winding Stradella arias Fanya was still a miracle: seventy-two years old and as graceful and poised as they had always wished to be. She was delicate, her Dutch-accented Hebrew impeccable, her hair dyed a shade of honey blond that perfectly complemented her keen blue eyes.

"You'll never guess what nonsense the American instructor was spouting the other day in class," Fanya said. "He insisted America was the source of some of the greatest inventiveness in watercolor. I mean, for heaven's sake, Tami. Of course that one woman in New Mexico had some talent, but *Los Angeles?* Don't tell me it can compare to Paris for one instant. America is well and good, in its place. But really, now."

Tami was ladling some of the stew into a second pot; it might cook faster in smaller lots, and she was impatient with the rising heat of the kitchen. "Did you say anything to him?"

"I asked him, didn't he think he might be overstating the case for American art? And he replied that I ought to give America a chance, maybe Europe will find it has something to learn." Fanya tittered. "I told him he's a misguided young man, but a charming fellow all the same. Americans never lose that optimism, do they?"

"What's so bad about liking American painting?"

"Nothing's so bad, Tami, it's just—" She made a helpless gesture. "I suppose you would have to know something about Americans."

Tami flinched. "I do know something about Americans, I studied English in high school, remember? You said then that English was foolishness, a waste of time, remember? America, the upstart country with no culture and a cowboy language?"

"Now, I never said everything about Americans was bad, only that they might temper their pride somewhat to match their accomplishments, don't you think?" Fanya crossed to the mirror in the hallway and patted her hair into place. "Our cousin Hope is proof, of course, that America has its merits. Mind you, I've never understood her love for politics. Still, she's a refined woman in her own way. But Tami. When you understand Europe you'll know what culture means." Fanya smiled into the mirror. "For example, did I mention I'm going to the Waldmans' this evening? I'm to sing for their guests, and Lila is going to accompany me on piano."

"I thought the Waldmans had left Jerusalem for good."

"Oh, no—that was just an extended vacation they took. In Paris." Fanya shot a pointed look at Tami, who grimaced at what was coming. "Some people have the sense to take vacations in proper places. Not like your father. *I* wanted to go to London, but no, it had to be Palestine for your father."

Tami struck a match to light the second burner. In her mind played the litany she knew so well she hardly noticed any longer whether Fanya actually recited it.

It was August 1939 when Fanya and Daniel Gutman came to Mandate Palestine from Amsterdam on their honeymoon. When the news of the war in Europe reached them they decided to extend their stay into the fall. And then, only temporarily, until matters in Europe calmed, into the winter and spring. "Of all places to be stranded, we had to be in Palestine," Fanya had told Tami over and again. "Rough and mosquito-infested, a barbarous place, and it still is. We could have been stuck in Argentina, or Canada even, someplace with a hint of civilization. But instead, Palestine. And that, Tami, is how your kind came to this country, not because it was the Garden of Eden, mind you, and don't let your Zionist friends tell you otherwise."

Fanya and Daniel Gutman stayed and the country changed around them, each year more clamorous with broken Europeans and straight-standing pioneers; native-born Jews and Muslims jostling alongside immigrants from every direction; living languages, dying languages, and one, long dormant, now rebirthed by an unbreakable force of collective stubbornness. The new state was sealed north, east, and south by hostile borders and washed on the west by the merciful Mediterranean—the sea into which its children dove as if into the arms of complete freedom and from which they learned the audacity they made their trademark, and into which Fanya never stepped after she saw a jellyfish floating in its waters.

Tami's friends had always envied her her mother. "Fanya doesn't cling, she has such flair," they marveled, and Tami had to agree with them. "What I wouldn't do for a mother who was with it enough to be my friend," her classmate Hanna said, Hanna whose mother spoke only Yiddish at home and punched dough with thick fists, and who would not let Hanna go out in the evenings without jacket and hat. Tami had never been able to make her mother the friend everyone thought she was, and she felt sure it was her own fault—something she, in her clumsiness, had forgotten to do. There were the moments of conspiracy, when her mother grabbed her arm and asked about some new fashion or about the boys in her scout troop. Tami would stammer a response, but it was never enough to hold her mother's attention. "Live for the moment," her mother told her once, after a long silence, and Tami turned the words over in her head for days afterward. But these instants of heart-pounding attention were brief, and Fanya's moods evaporated without warning. After her father's death, Tami would find her mother sitting motionless in a dark room. Fanya stared out the window that overlooked the shore, a scarf wrapped dramatically around her throat. Once, when Tami came close and Fanya could not avoid looking at her, she lifted a piece of Tami's short pale-brown hair and let it fall. "It's a pity you inherited your father's hair and not mine," she said, and turned once more to the gray waves outside.

Some years after Tami's father died, Fanya began to insist that Tami call her by her first name. "You're a big girl now, you don't need a little-girl word for me," Fanya said. But Tami saw how her mother blushed when she, a teenager, called her "Mother" in public. She could not call her mother Fanya; she called her nothing instead. She watched Fanya become skittish, and coquettish without warning; she saw how her mother would not greet even Nachum without first checking her makeup in the mirror and straightening her skirt.

Cursing her own inattention, Tami ran a spoon across the scorched stew at the bottom of one pot. She turned off the flame. "Tell me again what the American instructor said. I didn't hear the first time."

Fanya smiled brightly at Tami. "Never mind, there's no need to get excited, it doesn't matter. Now, how is Ariela doing in school?"

"Fine, she does fine." Tami combined the contents of the two pots, dropped the emptied one into the sink and let the water ring against its charred bottom. The rush of steam caressed her arms and briefly obscured her view of her mother.

"I mean, does she have friends?"

Tami shut the tap, wiped her cheeks with the backs of her hands, and crossed to the window. On the street, Ariela was pulling another girl in a wagon. "Of course she has friends."

"Mm." Fanya picked a piece of lint from her blouse.

Tami waited, but her mother did not continue.

"Why? Why don't you think she has friends?"

"I just wondered. She's very quiet," Fanya said. "Like you."

Below the window, the glossy crown of Ariela's head, with its narrow, precise part, filled Tami with hopelessness. She thought she knew how her daughter would feel in a few years, eyeing her own face in the mirror with disappointment.

"Should I expect you back for dinner?" she asked.

"Oh, don't bother about dinner for me." Fanya glanced warily at the one pot remaining on the stove, its contents a leaden mass. "I'm sure the Waldmans can come up with something for a hungry entertainer."

"It would be no trouble."

Fanya looked at Tami, puzzled. "Really, Tami, the Waldmans will give me dinner."

Nachum's breakfast was always the same, a container of yogurt with hyssop mixed in and a pita to dip into it, a crisp cucumber, and a glass of watered-down mango juice, which he stirred noisily with a spoon. Tami slid a bag of milk into the plastic holder and snipped off a corner with the heavy kitchen scissors. Ariela was seated at the table, eating a new kind of American cereal with chocolate flavoring that colored the milk brown on contact. Tami watched Nachum finish his juice and set his glass in the sink. She caught her breath.

"Maybe we'll go see a movie tonight, Nachum? Yael tells me *Ghost* is good. We haven't gone out in so long."

"All right, so we'll go."

"Do you want to?"

"Sure."

"I heard it's sad. Yael said it made her cry."

Nachum groaned. *"Yael.* What's to cry about? A movie is a movie. It's not real. *We're* real. Right, Ariela?"

"Right." Ariela spoke through a mouthful of cereal.

"If you don't want to see the movie just say so," Tami said.

"Tami, do what you want. If you tell me we're going to a movie, we'll go to a movie. I'm happy." He bent and kissed Ariela on her forehead, and shook his head at Tami as at a child. "I have to go."

"Nachum." Tami's voice stopped him at the door. "What do you hear from Dov?"

He stood with his hand on the knob. "Same as we all hear. He's doing fine."

"But is he going to enter the officer training course?"

"I don't know. I know they want him to."

Tami hesitated. "Do you think he should?"

Nachum tilted his head, as if giving the matter serious consideration for the first time. "If he wants to be an officer a few extra years or even to stay in the army long-term, then he ought to. He seems to like it. It's not a bad life. And it's not as if he can escape reserve duty either way— any way you look at it, we're all in the army, all the time." Nachum stood motionless before the door. "Of course, it can be a dangerous life. I suppose I thought he might go on to university after his three years." He pushed open the door, and spoke carefully: "Really, Tami. About the movie. I'm happy to go."

The psychiatrist on the radio that morning had said that nights in sealed rooms could be traumatizing, and that in the weeks after the war parents should watch for stress in their children, signs of which included loss of appetite or inability to sleep. Tami woke from an uneasy slumber in the middle of the night and scuffled down the hallway to check on Ariela. She was sleeping, holding her favorite stuffed bear to her chest. Tami wandered into the kitchen and poured herself a glass of water. She listened to the apartment's night sounds: the drip of a bathroom faucet, Nachum's snores from the floor of Dov's room, the rattle of the refrigerator as it turned itself off.

It was not that she wanted Fanya to leave. The longer Fanya stayed, the longer Tami wanted her to stay, as if something that had never been might yet be retrieved. Tami had not spoken with her mother on a daily basis in years; Fanya did not call her daughter every morning, as other mothers did. She called only when she had a story to tell, or when a particularly triumphant evening's singing left her flushed and restless for an audience. Tami knew that on those occasions she was little to her mother but a willing listener. Still, she stayed on the telephone until Fanya was through. With a thin satisfaction Tami registered the contented sigh that meant her mother's story was over, and knew she had not retained half of it. *You can have my time,* she caught herself thinking, *but that's all it will be.* A miserable curse she cast at her mother: *I'll be here, but I won't really be here.*

But now there was something that made Tami want to listen closely. Or rather, there had been, on those nights when the sirens brought her mother to her door. Those nights after Nachum had reached for her through the yet static-filled silence, brushing a hand over the mound of her stomach and over her nipples, which felt instantly tight, as though her body had been waiting for him without her knowledge. Those nights when they made love and fell asleep side by side but not touching, and their sleep was broken by a steady voice on the radio rising and falling with the awaited announcement. On those nights, the flutter of Ariela's hands against the door was a prelude to Fanya's sudden appearance in the grainy light—as if Fanya had come to rescue Tami from a childhood nightmare, although Tami was certain she had not cried out.

Every few days Fanya made some motion to leave. She began to gather the cosmetics she had spread over the dresser top in Tami and Nachum's bedroom, or she asked for the telephone number of a taxi company for the Jerusalem–Tel Aviv route.

"Stay as long as you like, and leave when you like," Tami said as if she did not care. She wanted her mother to stay, to stay a long while, although she did not know why. The longer Fanya stayed to enjoy her postwar freedom, the more alone Tami felt.

Nachum made no mention of Fanya's presence, and he did not seem to mind sleeping on the mattress in Dov's room. His silence unsettled Tami, and several weeks after the cease-fire she asked whether he thought it was time for Fanya to go back to Tel Aviv. Nachum smiled his broad weathered smile and said only, "She'll leave when she feels steady enough."

"But don't you mind sleeping on the floor?" Tami insisted.

"Fanya won't stay forever, she doesn't like to be in the way. Right now she's out seeing Jerusalem and it makes her happy, *nu,* so what's the harm?"

She had never understood Nachum's patience, the slow, easy manner that won him confidences and friends in places where he did not even look for them. She was grateful, this time, that he did not complain about Fanya's staying on. Yet it made Tami want to rage sometimes, how effortlessly he passed through life. Long ago, this way of his had charmed her, but now it made her feel alien to Nachum and alien to herself, untrustworthy because she wound herself in knots while Nachum continued at his same steady pace, never hurrying, and the world slowed to accommodate him. He was late for everything and apologized with a smile; he never turned away a question or a request on the street, and when he lagged because of it people shook their heads and laughed. "That's Nachum," they said. "Nachum can get away with anything." Friends at the post office let him go to the head of hourlong lines, the last bus of the night slowed to let him on as it pulled away. Next to Nachum, Tami felt methodical and ineffectual.

Still, she accepted his tolerance of Fanya with relief. "All right, if you want her to stay," she told Nachum, "then it's fine with me too." And when Nachum left to join the conversation humming elsewhere in the apartment, she went down the hallway. Carefully she straightened Fanya's toiletries on the dresser, adjusting each item with care: powders and creams, and a single slender bottle of perfume. She stood for a while, then, in the silent bedroom. By the time Tami followed Nachum into the living room, he was seated in his favorite chair, holding court.

"Once," Nachum was addressing the three men in the living room: Moti and Yoni from the electronics shop, and Shmuel Roseman, who, Tami thought, was the only one who hadn't heard Nachum's stories half a dozen times already. Tami made herself busy with some linens she'd taken off the line that morning. She fingered a sloppily folded tablecloth and waited, despite herself, to hear which story it would be. "Once, when I was twenty-one, I had just gotten my first apartment. It was here in Jerusalem, a few months before Tami and I married. I had moved all my things into the place, but the telephone company said I had to wait for a line. Wait and wait and wait again. Every day that I was free, it was me going to the secretary at the telephone company and telling her I had no telephone, and she chewing gum and saying, well, that's a shame, because the only person who can get me a line is her superior, and he's on vacation abroad and she can't contact him until he returns."

Nachum leaned forward, inviting his audience to join him in a secret. "I said to her, 'But the telephone company is government-owned. The telephone company is the government, *nu,* what do you mean you don't have a superior in the country?' She said, 'Complain to the government, then, I'm supposed to be on my lunch break already anyway.'

"And I said to myself, 'You don't have a superior in the country? We'll see about this.' So that afternoon I went to a pay telephone." Nachum made a swift motion as if picking up a receiver. "I called the operator and told her, 'Quick, put me directly through to the office of the president of Israel.' The secretary in the president's office sounded suspicious, she wanted to know if it was important, and I said, 'Oh yes, it's very important.' And the secretary hesitated and then she said, 'Because the president isn't in, but if it's urgent I can get him on the field telephone. He's on a tour of the Jordanian border with the commander-in-chief, the *ramatkal,* you understand.' So I said of course I understood, of course it was important, would Nachum Shachar call if it wasn't important? And the secretary didn't know what to say to that. So she connected me to the *ramatkal's* field telephone, and over the static—I had to shout so he could hear me—I said to the president of Israel, 'Hello, this is Nachum Shachar, I just called to say good day, and do you know by the way why it is I'm calling from a pay telephone?' And there was no answer, so of course I had to explain the whole situation to him, how as our appointed leader he might be interested to know that the national telephone company hadn't seen fit yet to give me a line. And when I'd finished saying that, he didn't say anything for a minute. We both listened to the telephone crackling and whining, he and I." This was Nachum's favorite part of the story, and Moti and Yoni nodded encouragement. " 'Shachar,' " Nachum said in the raspy voice of the president, " 'Shachar, you are a thorn in my rear end.' " Nachum smiled and cracked a sunflower seed between his teeth, sucked out the inside and picked the shell halves delicately off his tongue with quick fingers.

"And within an hour my apartment had a dial tone. Of course I immediately called our president to thank him, *nu*, don't let anyone say I
don't have manners, but apparently he'd left a very clear message with
his secretary that he was not to be disturbed again. Even for Nachum
Shachar." While the men laughed, Nachum winked and reached for the
bowl of seeds.

Jerusalem bloomed that spring in muted colors. The rainfall had not
been enough, the Galilee was low, and the lilacs in Liberty Bell Park
gave only a hint of scent. Tami, walking home from the post office
along the edge of the Valley of the Cross, watched two soldiers flag
down a friend on Herzog Street, shouting that they needed a lift to the
central bus station. Along the sidewalk hurried an Arab flower-vendor
with her pan balanced on her head, making her way, Tami supposed, to
a better street corner, where the pre-Sabbath rush might relieve her of
her wilting stems. In the valley outside the monastery stood one of the
black-robed monks, conversing with an elderly tourist in a long yellow
skirt. Tami passed through the concrete tunnel and out onto the tree-
shaded path.

Dov would be at home. He had arrived in Jerusalem the previous afternoon on a bus from the north, toting his soldier's bag and his gun.
His face was sunburnt, slower to change expression, marked from too
much coffee, too many cigarettes, too little sleep. He was thinner too,
and hoarse, and favored his right leg when he walked. When he spoke
it was in a vocabulary of acronyms and slang. Even Nachum had to ask
him what he meant by some of the phrases he threw about as casually
as he dropped the Glilon onto his bed. Tami concentrated on his laundry: uniforms matted with dust and sweat, pierced by splinters.

They were chuckling in the kitchen, Dov and Nachum, and Rafi,
who nodded with mock formality at Tami's entrance. Rafi had lost
weight as well, and his eyes were bloodshot from lack of sleep, but his
grin hadn't changed. Tami felt herself smile back with gratitude.

"I'll just be a minute," Tami told them. She was changing her clothes
at the other end of the apartment when she heard a call from Nachum,
something about taking the boys down to the shop. The door slammed
and there was silence. Tami came into the kitchen buttoning her shirt.
On the table was a pile of photographs. Gingerly she sat in the seat her
husband had occupied.

The first photographs were of Dov and some other boys in uniform, looking serious as they leaned against one another and against their guns jammed into the ground. The next pictures showed lithe uniformed figures bent over a pile of gear on the hard-packed dirt. Then a picture of an airplane overhead, and then three of parachutes in the air, figures dangling from them, something dizzying about the angle of the shots that Tami could not place. She tried to find Dov in the photographs, but all the jumpers looked alike, stick figures hanging by strings from taut canopies. A picture of a billowing parachute that filled the field of the camera startled Tami, and when she came to the shots of Dov's face grimacing at close range, his features pushed up by the force of the air, his eyes slitted in laughter against the wind and his arms extended to hold the camera in front of him, she realized: He had sneaked his camera on a jump.

In the quiet kitchen, she stared at the proof of her son's cleverness. The photographs were glossy and smooth, she could get no purchase on them, and so they fell through her hold like water.

She had known Nachum, of course, when she'd started her own army service; she had known him growing up, in Tel Aviv. Nachum had attended the high school in the next neighborhood. Whatever the local scout troop's activity, he was always one of the leaders, arranging hikes or carpools or rendezvous points on the beach for midnight bonfires. They had never spoken, but Tami, like everyone else, knew Nachum's comically raised eyebrows and his endless ideas. Because he surely did not know her, she found vague reasons to disparage him in the privacy of her mind. She participated from time to time in the troop's activities, but mostly she ignored the invitations to movies or picnics that Nachum and his friends passed out after meetings.

When they had met at the laundry counter of the Negev tank base to which they had both been assigned, he did not recognize her. But he was quick with an invitation to a gathering that evening at the shed, where sodas and coffee were sold until after eleven, and the soda vendor left his radio propped on the stony ground so they could sit on the plastic benches and listen to American rock and Israeli news. Tami brought Yael with her that first night, and again the second, but she came alone the third.

She had not had a boyfriend before, unless she counted Aryeh, who used to walk her home from school with an arm across her shoulders while she, flushed, stared fixedly ahead. Fanya had not deemed any of the boys at school good enough for her, and Tami had not resisted her mother's judgments.

She was quiet with Nachum, and thought he would soon lose interest in her. The girls she had seen him with in the scout troop had been loud and free with their opinions, long-haired and tall: the sort to pick their way to the front of the hiking column and lead the group through the dry, bone-colored chutes of a wadi. While Tami herself trailed behind, running her fingertips over the slippery, water-smoothed stone that made the hikers' voices echo out into the blue sky beyond.

She was surprised when Nachum told her that he admired her quietness. "I've never met anyone like you," he said, and she felt a surge of unfamiliar pride. They had been dating for months before they slept together; Nachum seemed to enjoy being courtly with her, as if she were a breed apart from the sharp-tongued daughters of Tel Aviv whose signatures and scrawled remembrances Tami had discovered on his folded high school diploma.

They had been given the day off from their training. Nachum borrowed a jeep, and they drove, first on the highway and then off, over a rocky plain, until they were deep in the desert. They got out of the jeep and Nachum spread a tarpaulin on the hard ground. They would build a fire, make coffee, scout the area before settling in for the night—Nachum's ideas—but first they sat.

They took off their boots and stuffed their socks inside, and moving on hands and knees to keep the tarpaulin from blowing away, they anchored each corner of the crackling cloth. Nachum kissed her, and Tami smiled at him and looked away. Around them, the hills were dark against the fading sky. There was no sound of motors, of voices or animals or anything save the breeze against the side of the jeep.

"Are you comfortable?" he asked, and she nodded, too full of the desert and the wind and the last glow off the stones to answer. They watched the sunset spread and sink over the hills to the west. In the east, above the Jordanian border and the dim plains beyond, stars began to emerge.

Nachum had his eyes half closed, and the last of the light cast a faint shadow at the base of his throat. Tami thought to herself that he looked the way they were supposed to look, the way she had always wanted to look—dark-haired and strong-featured, suntanned and unafraid. She imagined the two of them free, wandering the hills as easily as the night animals; as unquestioning as long-ago, miracle-stunned men and women who knew that this was their home. It was what her mother would never understand: the Israel that had always eluded Tami herself, yet that at this very moment seemed closer to her grasp than ever before.

She told Nachum about her reassignment to the base communications office and about Yael's new boyfriend, and he appeared to listen. He took her hand, caressed it between his warm, dry palms, and pushed her gently down onto the tarpaulin. He began to undress her, and without a word she mirrored his actions. They lay on the unyielding ground, soundless in the cool and silent desert air, under a sky so black and thickly clustered that she could reach out past his back as he moved into her and fill the spaces between her fingers with stars.

The radio newscaster said that a near-fatal road accident had occurred outside Jerusalem. Drivers were admonished not to use cellular telephones while in motion. In other news, tourism was recovering slowly since the war. The airlines could not fill their flights; four out of five Americans believed Israel was a "hazardous destination."

Shmuel Roseman sat in the living room. Fanya was in the bedroom getting ready for their picnic; Shmuel had convinced her to relinquish her wristwatch for cleaning, and now, sitting in slacks and jacket opposite Tami, he spread the watch parts out on the coffee table.

"Poor Fanya, the war was so hard for her," he said, his expression laden with sympathy. Making a thoughtful O with his lips, he strapped his magnifying lens into place. With one eye distorted by the thick glass, he appeared to Tami to be weeping, only with a sorrow too great for regular tears, so that the eye itself had no choice but to waver and melt into a luminous blur. His other eye, squeezed nearly shut, seemed sturdily intent on the work at hand.

Tami watched him manipulate the tiny springs. She had hardly slept the night before, and she was mesmerized by the grace of his thick fingers. Then she realized what he had said. She turned off the radio and laughed sharply. "What about the rest of us?"

"You?" Shmuel spoke without lifting his gaze from his work. "You native-borns survive, it doesn't touch you. And old men like me, what does it matter for us, anyway? But Fanya, she's not used to these things."

"My mother has lived in this country longer than I've been alive."

Nudging a part gently back into place, Shmuel Roseman looked at Tami pityingly. "You don't understand. She's more sensitive than you are."

"Sensitive? During the SCUD attacks you think we weren't sensitive enough? We should have talked poetry and sung arias those nights in Dov's room, maybe?" Tami tried unsuccessfully to control the spite in her voice. "You Europeans think nothing matters except hearts and flowers and love."

"Who said anything about love?"

"You did, you with your art and culture and love." She was becoming irritable and confused; she had lost track of her point. She wished that Fanya would come out, so Shmuel Roseman would leave.

"Love, what kind of love can you have in a sealed room?" He lifted his eyepiece to stare at her.

"I don't know," she mumbled.

"Of course you don't," Shmuel answered, snapping the face of the watch back into place. "Not even Houdini knew. True love," he said conspiratorially, "comes in a forest. The Jerusalem Forest. On a picnic. On a Wednesday afternoon." He smiled a faraway smile. "Fresh air, that's what's needed for love. You can't have love without fresh air."

Tami's head hurt. "Maybe that's only what you think."

"It's what I know. Love in a sealed room? *Feh.* That would be no kind of love. What your mother and I have, now that's love. She doesn't know it yet, but she will soon."

"What's all this talk?" Fanya stood in the doorway, freshly made up and wearing light-green pants and a white sweater.

"We were just saying how lovely you look today." Shmuel beamed up at her.

"Oh?" Fanya arched her brows and smiled. "As long as you're staying out of trouble."

"You can be certain of that." Shmuel rose and, removing the strap from his head, winked at Tami. He crossed to the doorway and tucked Fanya's arm under his elbow. "We'll be going, then," he said. "You have a good afternoon."

It was Yael on the telephone. Tami dried her hands on a dish towel and sat at the kitchen table.

"Tami, you must be so proud of Dov, Benny tells me he's decided to train as an officer. You know that's no small thing for a paratrooping unit. He'll have his work cut out for him."

"I *am* proud," Tami said.

"Our boys, an unstoppable team, right? To tell you the truth, the training they have to do terrifies me. Benny came home last week shivering, they had been camping in the rain, and after a hot bath his temperature was still too low, Tami, let me tell you, I was frightened. I almost called his commander, but Benny would have hated me for it. I try not to ask. I guess it's better for the mothers not to know, right?"

There was a long pause. Yael spoke again. "Don't tell me you didn't know about Dov's decision."

"Yael, I don't want to—"

"All right, it's all right. So he didn't tell you, it's no big deal. It's not." Yael inhaled steeply, then let out her breath. "You'll see, Tami. The army will change them, grow them up. It will be good."

It had been *hamsin* when Dov's hatred for her became irrevocable, a day when the air felt thick and heavy with demands. The sky was white and merged with the light-colored buildings on the hills beyond the Valley of the Cross. It hurt to look across the valley; it hurt to look at anything beyond arm's reach.

Nachum had returned from reserve duty the previous evening. Tami stayed up half the night before his return, cooking in the relentless heat, making shnitzel, tomato-eggplant salad, kibbeh, and lemon-and-strawberry mousse for dessert. She knew it was nothing compared with what some of the other women in the building did for a homecoming dinner; she had never liked to fuss in the kitchen, and avoided her co-workers' weekly conversations about how many and which dishes they were planning for Friday night. But this time Tami lined the kitchen with cookbooks. She worked with the grim determination that Nachum's return would chase away the loneliness she had not been able to contain lately, so that sometimes at the office she stared at familiar forms as if she had never seen them before.

They ate the meal in silence. Nachum was exhausted, and close-mouthed about exercises in the heat and dust. He ate some of everything and took extra helpings of mousse, and while Tami was washing dishes he fell asleep at the table with Ariela in his lap. "Nachum," Tami said, and he opened his eyes, set Ariela on the floor, and walked to the bedroom without a word. When Tami entered moments later, he was asleep.

The next morning, when Tami awoke, her head throbbing with the heat, Nachum had already left for the shop. In her T-shirt and underwear she shuffled into the kitchen and, eyes half closed, took a glass out of the cabinet. The sponge she had used to wash dishes the previous night was so dry she could have snapped it in two, and her eyes filled with tears as she opened the tap and let cool water splash into the glass.

She dressed carefully to go to the greengrocer's. She wore her blue tank top and brown shorts, and the sandals with the leather straps that cut into her ankles when she walked. Before leaving the apartment, she reached into the back of a dresser drawer and pulled out a bottle of perfume, one Fanya had left behind on a visit years before and Tami had never bothered to return. She dabbed some on her wrists.

The greengrocer's smelled of sour milk and overripe fruit. Behind the register a girl painted her nails, and in the doorway a boy stood talking to the girl and leaning on a push-broom that he did not seem intent on pushing anywhere. Tami circled the store, filling her basket. She picked up carrots, juices—peach for Ariela, mango for Nachum—pitas in a blue plastic bag, a package of cheese, and four heavy bags of milk, and still she did not see him.

When she took her basket to the counter, the girl was gone; he stood in her place, smiling at her with those black eyes that had so many times sent Tami's own gaze fleeing to the littered floor.

His name was Nissim. For years he had rung up her groceries, helped her find misshelved cans of soup, and told her what she owed with a soft smile that made her blush. He was dark-skinned, Sephardic, at least ten years younger than she. He kept accounts in his head, and dismissed her apologies on those occasions when she did not have enough money with her. "You're a good customer, you always pay your bill, so who needs to write it down?" he said. "When a woman like you says she'll pay, she'll pay." He would offer to carry her groceries to the apartment for her. She had always refused.

"Will that be all?" he asked her now.

"Yes, thank you." She met his eyes and then looked away, fidgeting with her purse. "And could you bring the groceries to my apartment for me? They're heavy, and I'm not feeling so well today."

"Of course," he said, as if he did not know what she meant.

She sat in the apartment waiting for him; she thought to herself that this was crazy. She was the mother of two children, one already grown. Her stomach was flabby and pale, she had not worn her bikini to the beach in more summers than she could remember. Here she was, waiting for her Nissim from the greengrocer's to climb the stairs to her apartment. It was ridiculous; she would not answer the door when he came.

The doorbell rang, and she jumped, froze for a moment, then, cursing herself, unlocked the door. He was out of breath from the stairs, and he walked past her and set the box of groceries on the kitchen table with a thump.

"Thank you, Nissim." She fingered the money she had counted out in advance. She could hear her heartbeat.

He waited. She took a pitcher from the refrigerator and poured him a glass of cold water. She thrust it into his hands. "Here," she said.

They stood on opposite sides of the narrow kitchen table, and she watched his Adam's apple rise and fall as he swallowed.

When he had finished he placed the glass on the table. "Thank you," he said.

In one hand she clutched the money she owed him. Before she could hesitate, she lifted her other hand and brushed her palm against his tight dark curls, and at the same moment that she registered the shock on his face and realized she had made a terrible mistake, the door banged open and Dov was staring at the two of them from across the kitchen.

She dropped her hand and Nissim turned and fled, clattering down the stairs in his sandals without the money she still clutched in her hand. "Dov," she said, but her son turned and left the apartment without a word. The door closed so gently behind him that she held her breath to hear it, and the heat that filled the kitchen in the silence that followed told her everything.

They made a quiet Passover together that year, after the winter rains were over. Nachum and Dov raced together through the words of the Haggadah, making a game of their speed-reading at the dining room table while Tami and her mother carried in the dishes and Ariela chewed on carrot sticks. Nachum paused only once, at a passage about deliverance from slavery, to tweak Ariela's chin. "And what do you think that means this year, Ariela?"

"It means no more gas masks!" she shouted, and Nachum laughed and let her have a sip of wine from his cup. "That's my girl," he said more than once during dinner, and rested a hand on her head. Ariela had retreated into her usual silence, her excitement at the praise discernible only in the pink crest of her cheeks.

After the holiday they drove Fanya back to Tel Aviv. "Jerusalem is wearing on me," she had told Tami the week before. "No decent cafés at all. Not to mention all the religious fanatics spilling into the modern neighborhoods. Those black hats make me itch."

Once in her own apartment, Fanya shook out pillows and opened windows. Tami cleaned the refrigerator.

"Tami," Fanya said, stepping into the kitchen. Her forehead was uncharacteristically creased. "Hold on to that Nachum of yours."

"What do you mean?" Tami straightened, a wad of paper towels in her hand.

"I mean what I said, hold on to him."

"There's nothing wrong between us."

Fanya pursed her lips, and the thought flitted through Tami's mind that her mother looked worried.

"Did I say there was something wrong?" Fanya asked.

"So what do you mean, then?"

Fanya studied the back of her left hand, then looked Tami directly in the eyes. "I'm your mother, that's all."

Tami's face was growing hot with confusion. "What about Shmuel Roseman?" she accused.

"What about him?"

"Aren't you going to hold on to *him*?"

Fanya gave a light laugh. "Oh, who knows, Tami? Who knows, does that really matter? Shmuel Roseman falls in love easily, and he'll fall out of love easily."

"But he said—"

"He said what?"

"He said." Tami shook her head. "He said love was . . ." She stopped; she could not remember what it was that he had said.

"Shmuel Roseman is a sweet man." Fanya smiled. "But what makes you think he knows anything about love?"

"It's just that—"

Fanya turned for the living room. "What does it matter, Tami? Why does it matter to you so much. Don't break your head about these things."

They had moved back into their bedroom, but Nachum's graphs and magazines stayed in the sealed room, and some nights he fell asleep over his work. When Tami woke him and he had stumbled down the hall, she might sit on her son's bed for a while before returning to their bedroom. Sometimes she fell asleep, and in the morning woke, curled on Dov's bed, to the sound of Nachum mixing his mango juice in the kitchen doorway.

Still they reached for each other at night, less often but with that same detached intensity, like two young people who had not yet realized that time was not something that could be snatched and prevented from passing. She wondered whether Nachum saw someone on the overnight trips he took to Tel Aviv for business, but she did not ask. And she knew, after all, that he did not. He would never be as weak as she, to try something like that. It was only she who had somehow fallen into a crack in this great collective society; only she who had somehow, for all her effort, never understood what everyone else seemed to know intuitively. Lying awake next to Nachum one night, she reflected with a start of guilt that it had been years since she had smiled at his capers. A petty punishment, she saw, for his failure to do the one thing she had trusted him with all her heart to do: make her be like everyone else.

Hamsin again, and the dripping laundry that Tami had strung from the balcony before waking Ariela was stiff and gritty with dust by the time the girl left for school. Tami filled the tub with cool water and stripped off her T-shirt and underwear to sit in it for a few minutes before leaving for the office. She left a note on the refrigerator door for Ariela with instructions not to go out to play until she had had three full glasses of water, no cheating. Writing the note gave her satisfaction. At least Ariela still listened.

Nachum was tight-lipped when he dropped the evening paper on the kitchen table. He sat down and, resting his elbows on the table, pushed his face into his hands as though trying to seal his eyes shut by force. "Did you hear?" he asked.

"Hear what?"

"Three soldiers died in a training accident in the Negev. Dehydrated."

Dov was in the desert for more training this week; Tami had been trying not to think about him in this heat, going along with whatever craziness his commander ordered.

"Didn't the officers know to—"

"One of them was Rafi," Nachum interrupted her.

"Rafi?"

Nachum did not answer or remove his hands from his face.

She grabbed the newspaper from the tabletop. On the front page were the pictures of three boys. She recognized the photograph of Rafi from Dov's high school yearbook. He was grinning from the depthless paper.

"Oh." Tami said. She lowered herself into the chair next to Nachum. "Does Dov know?"

"Who knows? Who knows where he is? It must be on the radio by now."

The two of them sat without moving and without touching until the kitchen was dark.

They came unsummoned to the apartment that night, dozens of Dov's former classmates in uniform who had been allowed to leave their bases to make the trip to Jerusalem. Guns cluttered the sealed room, covered the bed and spilled onto the floor. Once the weapons were inside Dov's room, Nachum locked the door, and the girls held Ariela on their laps in the living room so she wouldn't go near. They sat in the living room in silence, the *hamsin* hanging in the air. No one spoke. Tami put out cups and a pitcher of water, and her son's friends— those same friends who for years had treated her like a road sign on the way to Dov—thanked her quietly. She stepped through the room, patting a girl's hair, brushing a hand over a boy's dusty uniformed shoulder, wanting to touch them all, as if her touch could heal, or at least hold them in place so that they would not disappear. No one moved.

When Dov pushed open the front door, they stared at him: perhaps, now that he had come, there would be an answer. After removing the key from the lock, he turned in the hallway and, instead of entering the living room, walked to his room. He took the single key from its hook on the wall and opened the door.

From the hallway, Tami could see the guns piled on his bed. Dov stood motionless. Then he rested his own gun against one wall of his room and stepped out. He closed the door behind him, locked it without a sound, and walked into the living room. One of the girls, whom Tami now recognized from the photograph on the floor in Dov's room, came over to him. Tears ran down her cheeks as she hugged him hard. Dov's arms clasped her waist, but Tami could see that he was not reacting to her; he was only staring at the wall beyond the girl's back.

The telephone rang.

"*Shalom,* Tami, I heard." It was Fanya. "Is Dov with you?"

"Yes." Tami felt feverish at the sound of her mother's voice. Her mouth was dry, she held on to the wall for support. "They've given him three days' leave."

"I don't believe it, I don't believe they could allow something so stupid to happen. A bullet I understand, a bomb, but the sun? They should have known what can happen out there, they should never have them train during a *hamsin* as bad as this one. Even if they force them to drink, it's still not enough in heat like this."

"You're right."

"I hear there's going to be a military investigation. Three boys, dead like that, just like that, it's not to be believed. But they'll investigate, they'll get to why and how and when and what happened. Does Dov know there's going to be an investigation?"

"What?"

"Does he know yet?"

Tami's head felt so heavy she could barely hold it up. "I don't think this is the time."

"Let me talk to him," Fanya said.

A protest formed in Tami's mind, but she found herself unable to utter it. Who was she to judge, who was she to protect her son?

She watched Dov hold the receiver to his ear. "Yes, I know," he answered Fanya, and then, "Just a few minutes ago." There was a long silence, at the end of which Dov opened his mouth and seemed ready to speak, but then only nodded and hung up. He walked out of the kitchen without looking at Tami.

From the balcony Tami watched them pass down the street, arms and heads pressed together, gathering strength on their way to the apartment on Radak Street where they would find Rafi's parents and sister. Only Dov walked alone, stepping straight ahead and ignoring anyone who approached him. Nachum was putting Ariela to bed. "But why did they let Rafi go out in *hamsin* without drinking enough?" Tami heard her daughter ask for the third time that night, but she did not hear Nachum's reply. She went into Dov's room; it was strangely empty, its door ajar. Dov had remembered to lock his gun in the living room cabinet, and there was nothing on the floor but some of Nachum's papers and the yearbook still open under the bed. Tami collected the papers and carried them into the living room. She closed the yearbook and put it on the shelf over Dov's desk. She folded the letter the American cousin had written to Fanya but generously addressed to Tami as well: dense pages of stilted Hebrew about another world; policies and progress and someone named Rodney King. Tami slipped the letter back into its envelope.

This time when the telephone rang it was Yael. She spoke quietly. "I hear something like this and I get so frightened. Tomorrow it could be my Benny, war or no war. I know about losing people in wars, Tami, you know my uncle died in 'seventy-three, but these accidents, these accidents, Tami, are something else entirely."

The next day and the day after, Dov sat in his room and refused to eat or to answer the telephone. Nachum tried to talk to him, but Dov only turned his back. "Come on outside," Nachum attempted, the soccer ball cradled against his chest. "We'll play, just you and me. As slow as you want."

Dov's passing glance at Nachum was condemning in its indifference. "No, Abba," he said. And when Nachum came out of the boy's room there was such a look of bewilderment in his eyes that Tami felt sorry for him and vindicated at the same time. She followed him through the living room, where he let the soccer ball roll out of one hand and onto the sofa. She followed him out to the balcony and watched him brace himself against the railing with both hands and look down through the glare of sun and dust onto the street. For the first time since she had known him he seemed lonely, and she was ashamed of the sudden tenderness she felt. She hesitated, then reached out and rubbed his shoulders. He patted her hand absently before going back into the apartment.

The third night was relentless; the forecaster said the heat had spent itself, but the *hamsin* did not break. Nachum took Ariela out for ice cream and a movie; he thought she needed extra attention. Tami agreed without a word.

She sat on the balcony in the sagging plastic chair. She had show-ered again, turning her face up into the cool stream of water. Already, sweat prickled at the back of her neck through her wet hair. She watched the moths circle the light bulb that dangled above her. Framed in a window across the street, a woman combed the hair of a girl who sat between her knees. In the blackness of the Valley of the Cross, a light burned in an upper room of the monastery, and a few pieces of the monks' laundry could be seen, white underclothes and long, dark robes bobbing on the line. On the hill, near the gates to the Knesset build-ing, a driver honked his horn.

From inside the apartment Tami heard a muffled sound that re-peated twice and then, after a pause, again. Rising slowly, she wrapped her robe more snugly around herself, then pushed aside the curtain and stepped in.

In the sealed room, Dov stood motionless. His hair was matted and his uniform hung on his body. Blood laced over the knuckles of his right fist in spidery-thin lines and dripped onto the floor.

"Oh, God." Tami stepped forward to touch his hand. He pulled it away.

In the wall, beneath the taped and unshuttered window, was a ragged hole, plaster chipping from its edges. Tami gazed at it; she expected somehow to find cool night air pouring into the room at last, bringing with it stars, the smell of eucalyptus. But Dov's fist had only knocked away the plaster, only smashed the surface and exposed the concrete behind.

"Leave me alone," Dov said, and when Tami did not speak or move he looked at her with eyes full of hate. "Leave me alone," he shouted.

She stood barefoot, staring at the spots of blood on the cool tile floor, and a sudden fury blew through her. What right had he to look at her that way? As if she had chosen for the world to be the way it was, as if she had ordered the wars and the terrorism, the dust wind and the desert with its patches of black sand that heated like furnaces and killed boys without warning. The rage that gripped her now, making her hands tremble and her jaw ache, was a comfortable rage; it was a collective, inevitable, irrefutable rage, so complete it absolved her of whatever she alone had done. What right had he? As if she had chosen this path for them, as if she had chosen that they live clinging to each other's bodies and the soil and the here and now, lest someone catch them without their roots deep in each other and all would be lost, with no second chances.

Looking at the soldier before her, she saw that his hand was damaged and ugly, and the sight tightened her throat until it burned.

"What's wrong with you?" she shouted into the quiet apartment. "What's wrong with you? Did you think you'd punch through? Did you think you could? Did you?"

She waited for an answer, her feet trembling on the stone tiles. Dov was sobbing softly with his head bent to his chest. His hands hung loose at his sides.

It was the simplest of steps that carried her forward, as easy and unwilled as a heartbeat. She held him, held his lean battered body, and she felt herself becoming something huge and primal and ancient.

He cried into her shoulder, he held her tightly, he did not let her go.

Part Two

2

The sun is burning the street. Burning the pale-veined buildings. There is pounding too, pounding like a fever on the head. Today the blacks are hammering. Over apartment doorways, on balconies, they fix their cardboard signs. Blinding signs, yellow signs, signs swaying above drizzling laundry. Yellow rectangles flash brightness at me like the shock of a newsbulb: sudden daylight sears the heart.

But I will not be fooled. I have no use for such signs.

I should not have gone out with the sun so strong, I should have waited. Until the vegetable man pulled down his awnings, the toothless Arab women turned for home, unsold wildflowers balanced on their heads. But today I was distracted by so many things. A moth fluttering against the ceiling, the sound of a car horn, an unfamiliar step in the stairwell. The path of the sun across the sky escaped me today, tricked me into venturing outside before it was time.

Four of the blacks, pale like parchment and squinting in this ugly Jerusalem light, are stringing a banner across the street. It is the same as the signs, this banner: red sunrise reaching across yellow background, sharp lettering that blinds the opened eye. My bag is filled with the groceries I will need so not to step onto the sun-beaten street for another week. I walk faster, my arms burning from the weight of this cabbage and this borscht, potatoes and powdered pea soup. Sour cream in a plastic tub. My knees hit the grocery bag at every step, signs catch the glare and turn it back on me. I squeeze my eyes shut, but there are holes in the pavement and children who throw pebbles in the yards, and these things *are not to be trusted, so I open my eyes to slits and watch. I walk past the blacks as fast as I can without looking at them or at their yellow twisting message. They do not glance at me, only shout directions to other blacks on ladders or greetings to those tying signs to the tops of battered cars.*

I have no use for blacks and they have none for me.

My arms feel like two stones and I draw the bag closer to my belly. I will not forget again, next week I will not forget about the sun, I make up sun-remembering rhymes. Crowding heat, song of beet.

Vision withers at my feet.

The pathway to my building beckons at last. An overgrown green, even in this dry season it is shaded and waits to receive me. The heat makes me weep but I am almost there, I have reached the pathway and now the forgiving shadows of the overhang, I drop my bag inside the entryway. I gasp like a fish, touch the rough plaster wall and try to drive the sun from my brain. I think cool water thoughts.

The postman is here. Gleeful gossip, he rubs his beardless chin and speaks smooth braids of words. About an American moving into the apartment building this afternoon. Just this afternoon, he informs me. Very polite for an American. A student, visiting Israel. Of all weeks, such a shame she should arrive now. Isn't it simply terrible, the racket these religious people make hammering those signs?

I hide myself in the corner and this man at last smiles a weary smile and leaves me be. He is on the garden path, then gone.

And now the rug peddler begins his calls. His Arab words are the mesh cast through the neighborhood, they gather the driving daylight to some faraway place. Rolled carpet over his bent shoulder, his strange words invite the bending of the sky, cooling air of evening.

I marry my whisper to his cry.

Soon the burning sun will leave this Jerusalem street, there will be cool dark and clouds running faint overhead. Soon only the mute stones of the buildings will give this neighborhood their quivering light that is like moonlight. Soon the day will turn its glare from this city, soon. Soon the cool jewel night, the blown flown night. The night that settles into the heart like water in a ditch, sinking at last, bringing sleep.

An American. *So many years it has been since I longed to see one of their faces.*

I turn and climb the stairs.

∞

Moving to this neighborhood was Gil's idea.

Emek Refaim. My dictionary translates the name as "Valley of Ghosts." Which might have made me superstitious about moving here—except for the way the Jerusalem sun claps down on your shoulders like a weight each time you step outside. It seems to me it would take a pretty stubborn ghost to survive in this climate.

I try to picture some obstinate spirit, shimmying through the alleys of the neighborhood. Throwing its feeble shadow against the sun-warmed rock, flitting between the bars of garden gates, whispering into the flowering caper bushes. But after all, the most determined ghost would still be too flimsy to last. At the thought of my imaginary spirit perishing, struck down by the Jerusalem heat, I even feel a bit sad.

Gil leans against the bare wall of the living room. "Maya. *Ghosts?*" His eyes tease. "Must be nice to be an American. Americans have no real worries, they get to invent." He pushes off the wall and steps behind me. I face him, but he moves behind me once more and his breath whispers against the back of my neck. *"Whoo, whoo,"* he calls.

"You don't sound like a ghost," I say, but he has me in his arms and tickles me until, my ribs aching, I admit that his sound effect was perfect, that all ghosts haunt with Israeli accents, that there is no one who could have done it better. Only then do the lines of his face waver, and break into his all-engulfing smile.

Gil's joy is like an unpredictable tide, sweeping his pale freckled face without warning. Sweeping me along with him into a fit of laughter. Gil is tall, his body bony and restless, and as he tells me where we will put the furniture I bend my neck and touch my forehead to the hollow of his chest, nodding to the rumbling rise and fall of his voice.

Emek Refaim is thirty minutes by foot southwest of the Old City, twenty-five west of the Promenade, a quiet dip in the hills of Jerusalem. The bustle of the city center is only half a dozen bus stops away, but here in the valley the streets curve around one another and those other parts of Jerusalem seem much farther away, more like rumored destinations than real places.

April 10, 1993

Mom,

I read what you wrote in your last letter about Gil, and taking things slowly. I know I'm young. But as you said, it's my life and my decision.

And I'm sure if you met him you'd agree this is right. You're always talking about the importance of commitment to something you believe in. I came to Israel this semester because I have always wanted to learn about this country. I guess one commitment leads to another—I knew the minute I met Gil that he was the person for me. You once said you thought I'd never care for something outside myself. Actually, I do. I'm in love.

As for my schoolwork, don't worry. Moving out of the dorms doesn't mean I'm going to neglect classes. I'll take the bus back to Mount Scopus every day, and I think I'll study more without the distractions of dorm life. Besides, Gil and I have agreed to speak only Hebrew in our apartment, which is good although it's hard for me. And hard for him, too. He says my American pronunciation hurts his ears.

I *am* planning on calling your cousin Tami, by the way. I have the number, and I promise I'll do it soon. It's just that things have been busy.

You said in your letter you're trying out some new programs at the Center. What's going on? I hope you'll write to me about it. I really do want to know.

Maya

The day Gil and I met was the day he'd gotten word of his job at a new gallery in Yemin Moshe. One of the students at Hebrew University was giving a party that night. Gil came because he felt like celebrating, even though he rarely went to student parties anymore—not since leaving the art program. He likes to say that his old classmates aren't particularly *evolved*.

But that night there was a party and he went. I was there with my dormitory roommate, Orit, who had announced her mission of introducing me to so many Israelis that I would have more friends here than in America. Since the gray February morning when I had arrived from New York and braved the drafty Mount Scopus hallways with my dorm assignment card in hand, Orit had taken it upon herself to be my guide to Hebrew University. Wherever we went she would summon other students. "Maya is here to study for the semester," she would inform them, twisting her dark curls into a rope and flinging it over one shoulder. "Be nice to her, make her at home. Show her some good Israeli manners." I waited beside her with an overready smile meant to communicate all that my shaky Hebrew could not.

At the party that night, Orit's friends applauded her invitation. They motioned for me to join them on the tattered sofa, and promised a display of their best manners. After bowing elaborately and calling for silence, Orit's chemistry lab partner, Magen, screwed his eyes back and stuck two french fries up his nose.

A blond-haired student named Shulamit eyed Magen's contortions with disgust. "There goes all the foreign aid," she said.

"Where are your priorities?" Orit wagged a finger. "Hell with the foreign aid. Be nice to Maya, be nice to all the Americans, or we'll never get a McDonald's in Jerusalem." Grinning, she patted my knee as if I were a new and prized possession. "McDonald's, that's all Israel needs for what ails it. The soldiers and diplomats have been handling matters wrong all along. I've heard that no two countries with McDonald's have ever gone to war with each other. Who knew peace could be so simple?"

Later, when the conversation had narrowed to an intense debate over some classroom gossip and the heat in my cheeks had begun to fade, Shulamit turned to me. "Why *do* you people want to see Israel?" While I struggled to frame an answer in Hebrew, she leaned close, elbows propped on her knees, and continued in stilted English. "This is what I never understand. I know you are Jewish. Still, why not go to France, where people can eat dinner at one a.m. and the restaurant stays open all night? Why not go to New York, a real city? That is where I would go."

I shifted against the spongy cushions of an armchair and looked at her. She had a smooth face, dark unwavering eyes, and a strong oval jaw which, I guessed, wasted no effort holding back opinions. A familiar hopelessness settled in my chest. After two weeks around Israelis, I still couldn't help feeling deferential. They all seemed to have something I lacked. Confidence, maybe. But something else too: authenticity. This college student, only one or two years older than I, had already been a soldier. She lived in a world of practical choices, she knew what it took to seize a corner of the world and push.

During the weeks I'd lived in Israel, everything American about me had begun to appear irrelevant. My dance-troupe friends and our shopping sprees, my university with its scores of extracurricular activities ("Bell-ringing clubs?" Orit echoed in disbelief). Drinking contests, the friends on the hockey team who head-butted campus lamps until the plastic sconces came loose and they could take them home to wear as space helmets. The academic advisor pushing her glasses higher on her nose, shaking her head over *one of the biggest discrepancies between ability and achievement in all my years of.* In America, I didn't have to think about life and death and sacrifice, or even my French history midterm. In America, I chose to think about dance routines instead. I chose not to attend the local political rallies my mother called from New York to notify me about or, on my infrequent trips to Brooklyn, to join the volunteers stuffing envelopes in her apartment through the night. Instead, I stepped between piles of flyers, nudged envelopes out of the way with my feet, and pulled the telephone into the bathroom for privacy.

"Suit yourself," my mother said. And I understood, from the way her eyes flicked past me as she said it, that she wasn't going to bother with me anymore. She pushed a lock of hair off her forehead and pointed a new volunteer toward the brochures for the Center for Community Renewal. Another volunteer handed her a slice of pizza. She took a bite, then set the rest aside and picked up a stack of flyers. "If you're not going to help, then just stay out of the way, Maya."

"I want to see Israel," I told Shulamit in Hebrew. "I want to understand the country and the history and the politics."

She was silent. At first I thought she was considering what I'd said; then I realized she was simply puzzling out my accent. She shrugged: Why was I wasting her time if I wasn't going to give a real reason?

Orit had disappeared, and there was no other help in sight. "It's that I want to . . ." I searched for the proper words in Hebrew or even English. Shulamit's gaze drifted with boredom. "I need to understand Israel, because all my life—"

"Go to Australia," Magen called out. He put his hands behind his head and reclined, fry-less, on the sofa. "Go to Greece and camp out on the beach. Go to a country where there's room to turn around and scratch your rear end. Israel is tiny, Israel—"

"Israel is the size of Magen's dick," someone said from across the room. "It's that small. Could you believe such a thing possible?"

The others hooted, confirming my understanding of the slang. I blushed.

Grinning, Magen went on the attack. "I didn't know you were such a right-winger, Yossi. Because clearly you mean Greater Israel." Magen gestured broadly. Shulamit groaned her annoyance. "Oh, yes. Greater Israel it is. In fact, we'll need some further territorial expansion, even more than the rightest of the right demand. We'll need to expand even beyond the West Bank. You're talking an Israel the size of the Soviet Union, may it rest in peace."

"May it burn in hell," said a low-voiced student. His Hebrew was heavy, Russian-accented. There were some nods of acknowledgment from the others.

I sank back in my chair, grateful to have been forgotten. Thinking of my resolution to pay close attention to discussions of politics, I blinked at these former soldiers. They were passing a bowl of pretzels; someone was calling for ice cream bars. I wondered what my mother would make of this mode of political conversation. I wondered whether anyone would notice if I didn't say a word for the rest of the evening.

The Thinker, my friend Ina called me. That was back at school in Purchase. Ina said I was quirkier than anybody she knew and she'd never understand me. One minute I was flirting up a storm with the guys in the dance group, the next I sat on the sidelines looking desolate.

It wasn't that I was thinking about anything in particular at those parties. It was just that sometimes, even around my best friends, I drifted wide. I accepted the drink thrust into my hands by the stranger working the keg, slipped onto a bench and sat between beer cup and wall. Then my friends were a noisy stream glinting and flashing in the near distance. I watched them windmill their arms at the ceiling in imitation of the new dance director's tantrums and, as conversation lulled, sling them across one another's shoulders. Sipping warm beer and letting the barely diminished cup hang from my hand, I found myself teary with affection for this loudmouthed group. I loved these friends so much it was absurd; I would have done anything for them. Sometimes I wished they would ask. I would stand, step forward. Offer everything I had. But I knew, in the end, that I wasn't truly one of them. I couldn't have said what was wrong with me, only that I was different. Somehow I couldn't take life as lightly as they seemed to.

So when the blaring music stopped for the DJ's break and my friends wandered by to ask which problem of the universe I was solving now, I offered a laugh to show I meant no harm. I wrinkled my nose at my warm beer, set the cup down, and popped off the bench. "If the universe is relying on me," I assured them, "it's in deep trouble."

In Purchase, at least I could slip back into the group, join Ina in exaggerating the effort of pulling our feet off the beer-sticky floor, until the mime became a stamping, whooping dance. Here in Jerusalem, I kept my voice soft—speaking too loud might cause the Hebrew words to tumble out upside down. Here in Jerusalem I crept past others' laughter with the hope that no one would call attention to my uncertain Hebrew, my uncertain spirits, my shaky grasp on this strange and clamoring country. I sank hard into the armchair's embrace, wary of the roving conversation that might at any moment turn on me and find me unprepared.

When I finally retreated to the kitchen on the pretense of looking for some ice, a lanky stranger was standing alone in the room, leaning against the stove and drinking a glass of ice water. He looked at me, then nodded in greeting.

"*Shalom,*" I stuttered. I had dropped my cautious smile on entering the kitchen. Now my cheeks ached with the effort of resuming it.

He said nothing. But the motion of his hand began as a gesture of dismissal toward the living room, swept on to indicate where I should sit at the kitchen table, and ended with a raking of his tousled red hair. I could almost see the arc of his movement hanging in the air, even though his hands, large and corded with veins, now rested at his sides. I thought, as I sat, of a Calder mobile I'd seen near Purchase. I thought: He moves like he's not creating shapes in the air, but showing me ones that already exist.

From the living room rose a wave of laughter. In the kitchen it was quiet. A newspaper was spread on the table, and on it was a pair of eyeglasses. The lenses magnified part of a headline, and the letters were slanted and beautiful.

Regarding me as though nothing I said could surprise him, he waited for me to speak. And before I even opened my mouth, I knew that, unlike other people, he would listen and wouldn't just let things roll off him.

Speaking Hebrew into that silence was as easy as falling. "It's just for one semester, but it's important to me," I told him. "My mother was here years ago, and it made such a big impression she almost moved here. She used to tell stories about Israel, but I never paid attention. Now I want to learn."

"That's perfectly right," he said. "You should."

Three weeks later, when he asked me to move in with him, I said yes on the spot. As I walked back to my dorm to tell Orit, I could hardly suppress a grin. For the first time since arriving in Jerusalem, I looked passing Israelis square in the eye. I, too, could be confident and unquestioning. I could act in the world, follow my heart. See here, I thought, I *can* be bold.

April 16, 1993

Maya,

I've read your last several letters closely, and I want to tell you I'm happy for you and Gil. It seems you've finally found yourself a place and a person you care about.

To know you're on your own two feet and will make a way for yourself in the world, this satisfies me more than I can explain.

I'm sure living with Gil is a good way for you to learn the language and culture. And I trust that Emek Refaim is a pleasant neighborhood. I hope you'll write to me about it. I have high hopes for this "semester abroad" of yours. Just one bit of advice—remember to study. You've gone to learn about another country. Don't waste your time in discos, which, as you know, are only imitations of the shallowest of American culture. A new country is a new start. A chance not to repeat the mistakes you made in your first years of college.

I don't mean to start another fight, only to tell you what I think is best.

I trust you'll call Tami as soon as you can. Perhaps the next time you take a break from your studies and your touring and traveling. By now they're all probably wondering what happened to you. Tami is sometimes a bit thorny, if I remember right, but my visit to Israel was many years ago, and since then I've corresponded mostly with

Tami's mother, Fanya. In any event, I know you'll enjoy meeting them.

Everything here is all right. The children at the Center are flourishing, just last week they put on a variety show for a fund-raiser. We made more than $300, and the children voted to put the money into the recreation hall.

I've been back to my full-time schedule for several weeks and feeling fine. There's no need for worry. Dr. Green says the chemotherapy is going phenomenally well.

I'll look forward to receiving another letter from you.

Your Mother

P.S. Remember to see the whole of Israel, not just Jerusalem. Travel, learn from the people you meet. It's a beautiful country. It's many years since I've been there, but as you must know, I hold those memories dear.

The day after Gil told me we had an apartment, I climbed a chair and retrieved my bags from the shelf of the dormitory closet where I'd placed them only six weeks before. As I packed, Orit's younger cousin Michal perched on the edge of my bed, brimming with advice and curiosity. "Don't forget about your classes," she said. "Don't forget to get *some* sleep. Don't forget to use birth control, Miss Swept-Off-Your-Feet."

While I hefted an armload of clothes from dresser to suitcase, Michal weighed a pair of my socks in one hand. "So how do you know this thing is right, with Gil?"

"I just know." I smiled at Michal, but my answer was directed at Orit, who was working at her desk across the room, ignoring my activities.

"Don't forget to visit us." In Michal's thin voice was an apology for Orit's refusal to participate in my excitement. "It won't be as much fun without you."

I pointed to the socks, which she dropped into my suitcase. "I'll come visit." My words were loud in the small room. "Don't worry, I'll be here so often you'll be sick of me."

Orit paged through her textbook.

I zipped the suitcase shut, my throat tight—whether with a plea or a rebuke, I didn't know. Ever since I'd told her of my plan to move in with Gil, Orit had been distant. But I had hoped that now that Gil had signed a lease on our apartment, she might be pleased for me.

Instead, she was making no effort to hide her boycott of my happiness. Perhaps Gil was right—Orit was jealous of what he and I shared. After all, Orit had broken up with her boyfriend only a month before my arrival. Now, as she sat at her desk, her slim neck supported by one hand, she seemed nothing but lonely.

Relieved at the notion that she might be simply hurt rather than annoyed with me, I concentrated on feeling sorry for her.

The truth was, I was eager to get away. During the past weeks I had stopped bringing Gil to the dormitory except when it was unavoidable. As soon as he entered the building, he was restless to leave. We would sit in the cramped bedroom Orit and I shared, Orit speaking and Gil answering in monosyllables. Under her eyes I was aware of every motion of Gil's body—the way he tapped his foot on the floor, the way he slouched in the hard plastic chair. As the silences lengthened, I noticed the defensive set of Orit's chin. Nervously I would offer Gil tea or coffee. I knew my fussing didn't escape her attention, but I couldn't help it. I would ask Gil about his work, trying to draw him out. In my mind I urged him, *Show yourself.*

But Gil's expressive hands, which mesmerized me when he read aloud from his favorite books or told wickedly funny stories about art classes at Bezalel, would lie on the armrests. He was bored with Orit's chatter and made no effort to hide it. As for Orit, she would give him a look whose meaning I knew far too well from all those times Ina and I had rolled our eyes at a particularly smug classmate at Purchase: *intellectual snob.*

When Gil would at last stand and announce that we had to leave for our movie, I felt both glad and resentful. Too uncomfortable to look at Orit, I would make excuses not to join her later for coffee at the student center.

"Why don't you give Magen a chance?" Orit said to me out of the blue one afternoon. We had washed our laundry in the bathroom sink; now we were hanging it on the line outside our window. "He's been asking me about you since the party. Maybe a few of us can go to the beach this Saturday and he can come."

"I can't go to the beach this Saturday. I'm going to Gil's."

Orit snapped a blouse in the air. A shower of droplets flecked the sidewalk below. We watched the dark spots on the sidewalk lighten, then disappear. "Be careful," she told me. "What I mean, Maya, is I don't care for guys who come across so surly. Plus, Yossi says Gil was discharged from the army. Of course there are reasons for discharge that aren't bad, but it's a little strange that no one seems to know why he didn't complete his service."

Slowly I formed a sentence: "But why would I go out with Magen if I'm in love with Gil?"

"Do you know why Gil got discharged?" Orit insisted.

I felt the rebellion taking shape on my face. "You think my boyfriend is some kind of criminal?" I asked in English.

Now Orit blushed. "No, Maya," she answered in Hebrew. "Look, all I'm saying is I get a bad feeling from him. That's all."

I held out a pile of water-darkened clothing, a grudging offering. "He draws, you know," I told her in Hebrew. Orit took a pair of pants from the top. She said nothing.

"Did you know that he draws?"

Orit shook her head. Leaning out the window with a clothespin in her mouth, she flapped the pants in the air.

"He doesn't just work at the gallery, Orit." I steadied her by the belt loop of her jeans. "He's an artist. You didn't know he draws?"

Orit pinned the pants to the line and ducked back into the room. "I told you a hundred times, I hardly know him at all. I've just seen him around campus now and then."

"Well, he draws."

Orit appeared to be holding back some stinging comment.

"And paints. The other day when I was at his apartment, he showed me some of his work. He explained every single piece, every single one. I'd never heard anyone talk about art that way before. Like it was so important. And then he pulled out a sketch pad, and he made a few strokes with his charcoal."

I tried to catch Orit's eye, but she was busy with another piece of laundry. "He showed it to me," I went on. "And it was me he'd drawn. A picture of me dancing. And it was . . . I looked, I don't know, *whole*. There I was, right on the paper, just like that."

But it was coming out all wrong. How to explain to Orit what I had seen that day? I had already thought that I might be falling in love, but nothing could have made me love him more than what he showed me in that crowded French Hill apartment, with fragments of charcoal littering the floor beside his drawing table, and sketch pads stacked in every available space, even the narrow hallway to the bathroom. On the wall over the mini-refrigerator, in the apartment's one amply lit spot where the light poured in through a window, were two pictures: a Chagall print with bold colors sweeping over the silhouette of a woman's face, and a charcoal sketch of a handsome young woman seated beside a window. The woman in the sketch had straight, thick hair that draped her shoulders like a shawl. Her eyes were dark, and she was looking hopefully at something in the distance.

"It's my mother when she was a girl," Gil said. "I drew it from an old photograph."

I looked at the two pictures and I understood why he had hung them side by side. The young woman in Gil's drawing was as intent and as beautiful as the woman in Chagall's, but there was something else that connected the drawings. The rushing colors in the Chagall, the impression that any second the painting might careen into another world of floating figures and prancing cows with umbrellas, was matched by a fierce energy in Gil's drawing. The clock behind Gil's mother was upside down; on the table beside her, a saucer sat atop a cup.

"The man was a genius," Gil said. He indicated the Chagall print. "He understood the world he lived in better than any realist. He showed the truth behind the façades."

I waited for Gil to say more, but he was studying the print. It occurred to me that I'd seen such passion for work in only one other person—my mother.

I was tired from the day's classes, and I took a nap on Gil's bed. An hour later I woke and, calling his name, went to find him. The air of the apartment was close, the windows were darkening. In the dim light I could see Gil hunched over his drawing board, deepening the lines of a sketch of a wadi. I moved closer and, when he didn't turn to greet me, lowered myself onto a chair behind him. Soon my shoulders were cramped from leaning forward, my eyes teared from straining. At last he put aside the drawing and lit a small shaded lamp. Still facing away from me, he opened his sketch pad to a fresh page. His arm moved down and up, he tilted his head to watch the lines emerge under his hand, and I spiraled before him on the page. I was turning on one leg, my head tucked. My arms wrapped my waist, and a few strands had escaped my ponytail. The speed of my turn was dizzying. If I just set down my other foot, I understood, I would shake loose of the ground.

I was embarrassed by what he'd drawn, and riveted. The figure on Gil's page was intent, lonely—even, it seemed to me, prayerful. Longing for flight, almost touching it instant by instant. Was this how he saw me, this whirling, hopeful figure? He'd looked past the person brooding on the bench at those Purchase parties, alone and unapproachable. He'd seen who I wanted to be.

Staring at his drawing, I wanted nothing more than to be that unashamed dancer. I wanted to dare more—push off from my other foot, break free at last.

Gil set down his charcoal. Then he stood and turned to me. I stood, too.

"I've never let anyone watch while I worked," he said. A warmth charged the air between us. He reached out to touch my chin.

I opened my mouth and told him I loved him.

Orit was seated on the windowsill, her arms crossed. Beyond her, the laundry flapped in the breeze. Her voice was flat. "Has he seen you dance? Did he ask you to show him?"

"He said he could see it in his head."

"Tell him he's missing the real thing." Orit's vehemence surprised me. "Tell him you're a damn good dancer."

"His drawing was incredible, Orit." The words shot out of me. At last I understood what must be bothering my roommate: Gil was stealing her new American possession.

As though reading my mind, Orit went on. "Maya, I just think you might be rushing things. You're new to this country, you hardly know anyone, and now you're spending all your time with Gil. Why don't you spend a little more time here? *I'll* show you Israel. I'll get a field trip together, we'll camp out in Timna, we'll go north. We can have a lot of fun."

I spoke deliberately, like a native addressing a newcomer to the language. "I'm sure Gil can get a few days off from work. Then we can all go."

A student passing beneath our window broke stride as droplets rained down on his head. He glanced at the cloudless sky, then at us, and waved before moving on across the courtyard.

Orit straightened. "Yeah, sure." She turned her attention to securing the last of the laundry with the remaining clothespins.

Panic rose in my chest. Gil and Orit were all I had in this country, other than my schoolbooks and the telephone number of some unknown relatives. "Orit." I caught her elbow. "Haven't you ever met someone and just known that this was it, this was the person you'd been waiting for?"

Orit looked at me. "No," she said. "No, Maya. Because I don't wait for someone. I live my life."

I hefted my suitcase with difficulty, and tugged a lock of Michal's hair. "I'll see you in class. I'll see you all the time."

"Maya?" Gil's voice sounded from the hall.

"You'd better. No cutting class just because you're in love." As Michal released me from a quick hug, Gil walked, grinning, into the room. He kissed me on the mouth, then straightened his glasses and took my suitcase with exaggerated effort. "What, that's all you packed?" he groaned.

"Hi," Michal said, and Gil nodded in response. Orit was silent.

"So where are you taking our Maya?" Michal asked.

"To Emek Refaim, near Gonen."

"Which part?"

"Off Rahel Imeinu. Down the hill from the new development."

Michal's eyes went wide. "But isn't that the black part of the neighborhood?"

Gil cocked his head and said nothing.

Orit was still sitting, but with one hand planted on her desk as if she might, at any second, push herself to her feet. "Why would you want to move there?" she asked Gil.

Confused, I looked from Orit to Gil.

"Yes, our apartment *is* on a black street, and so what?" Gil squeezed my shoulder, then let out a short laugh. "You think we can't handle it?"

"But why would you want to live right in the middle of those people?" Michal asked. "It's—"

"Just because you don't know how to deal with them doesn't mean we don't."

Orit was shaking her head.

I stood immobile, a silent barricade between combatants. There was something I was supposed to do now. This was the point at which my mother would have taken a deep breath, made a withering speech about racism, and walked out in protest. Organized the university and led a march to the maligned neighborhood, making up rhyming chants all the while. I pictured the concrete façade of the center she'd founded in Brooklyn, in the neighborhood where her increasingly few white friends told her she was crazy to live. I recalled the rousing lecture she'd delivered to a white taxi driver who locked his doors before driving her through East New York, and I knew what she would think of me now for the way I hesitated, wordless, as the conversation sped past.

"But why do you want to live there? And with Maya?" Michal set her hands on her hips. "You want to listen to blacks shouting at you every sabbath when you go to drive your car? Every time Maya wears a skirt that comes above her ankles, you want a rabbi in her face like some avenging angel?"

My face flamed as I realized my misunderstanding.

"I'm just saying," Michal continued, "that I don't want Maya to have to put up with too much trouble for being a secular young woman living in a black-hat religious area. Living with a man she's not married to, on top of it. You know what those religious can be like. Running to the yeshiva, saying they're better than the rest of us. Taking government money, and most of them don't even serve in the army." Michal faltered as she spoke the last words. She exchanged glances with Orit.

"Maya and I can take care of ourselves." Gil's voice was cutting; he enunciated each word. "And as far as the army is concerned, don't imagine I don't know what you think of me. You needn't bother spelling it out. Just keep the macho patriotism to yourselves, my friends. Because you haven't a fucking clue."

And Gil was gone from the room and descending the stairs.

I looked at my friends of the past weeks. I was met with blank faces, averted gazes. Then, as if washing her hands of Gil, of this entire conversation, and of her American roommate, Orit turned back to her desk.

Gil's footsteps were growing fainter. Stumbling, I followed him. In the stairwell, I tried to recall what I knew about the apartment. Gil had clipped the advertisement, gone to the place, and signed the lease all on the previous afternoon, while I scribbled notes furiously in a history lecture. "The landlord was visiting from Haifa," he explained when I called him from the cafeteria pay phone in the evening. "If I hadn't signed today, we might have lost it. And I'm sure you're going to love it, no point in waiting." I pressed the receiver to my ear, trying to forget the noise behind me. Gil sounded happier than I'd ever heard him. The reserve he showed everyone, I'd begun to understand, was only a veneer; there were days, lately, when I could glimpse beneath.

"What's it like?" I asked.

"It's a surprise."

Now I reached the bottom of the stairs. When I emerged, blinking, into the courtyard, Orit was watching me from the window. Dark curls rained down around her eyes. Her face was tight and I could see the effort that went into her smile. "Hey," she called. "Enjoy the new place." Then she waved, and before I could wave in return she was gone.

"Thanks," I called to the empty window. I imagined leaving Gil waiting in the car and running upstairs to talk things over with Orit one more time. Would she even want to? Or was she happier, after these weeks of tension, to be rid of me?

From the street came the honk of a horn. I left the courtyard and made for Gil's car. As I climbed in, something about his expression struck me. The smile on his pale, thin face reminded me of a child exhausted by tears, beaming through the traces of his misery. His smile, I thought, was heartbreaking.

For just a moment, I wondered how well Gil and I knew each other. Our conversations had a rhythm I loved—I spent afternoons layering story upon story, and Gil assessed each situation or character with a terse response: Ina, he declared, was the all-American girl he'd seen in a thousand Hollywood movies. My dance director was indeed too rigid. My chemistry professor was just a poor sod doing his job, I really should have paid more attention. Gil's sarcasm or appreciation spurred me to bring yet more of my life in America before him, and I did so in a sometimes flummoxed Hebrew that made him, then me, weak with laughter.

There were hours, too, entire evenings, when I sat in his apartment doing my course work and watching him draw. Sometimes he would turn and explain a point of technique to me, and the flood of historical references amazed me. We didn't visit with other people; it didn't seem to occur to him to do so, and I didn't mind. I could never tell quite why he liked being with me so much, and I wasn't confident I'd win if I had to compete for his attention. One afternoon, after we'd been for a long walk, he pulled me into the shower with him. As we washed the dust from each other's hair, I heard him inhale sharply. I looked up and found him crying. Water beat against his shoulders, tears rolled down his face. I craned my neck and squinted into the spray. Then he reached for me and hugged me so hard it hurt. He was sobbing. I called his name, but he seemed not to hear. "It's all right," I wanted to say, but the water was pouring into my face and I couldn't breathe. I fought to support his weight as he slumped; I tried to hold his shuddering body as hard as he held me, tried to duck my chin to find air. But I couldn't. I would never have guessed how heavy he was. Spots of black mingled with the glint of the water; the drops descended in slow motion. His arms were tight around my ribs. I could barely stand. Watching the drops and feeling my chest fight to expand, I thought: These arms could hold me forever. When at last he released me, I gasped for breath. But I said nothing; the emotion trembling on his face was more important than any rebuke. "I love you," he told me, and I could see he was shocked by the simple miracle of it. My chest aching, I stood naked before him, awed by the power of his feeling. What could I possibly do to deserve this much love? And what did it mean that my love was so muted compared with his? We left the shower, Gil leaning on my shoulder. I guided him over the sill and gently toweled first his body, then mine. His trust made me feel honored, and frightened. More than anything, I wanted to be worthy of the peaceful expression he wore.

The afternoon was hot, and the breeze that bent some nearby cypress trees offered little relief. While he waited for an opportunity to pull into the street, Gil turned on the radio and began singing along. I grinned; he was terrifically out of tune. He drummed rhythm on the steering wheel and, seeing my expression, grinned back and sang louder. Halfway through the song, his palm made accidental contact with the horn, and the loud bleat made us both jump. Briefly Gil lost the song's rhythm. Then, his face lit with mischief, he resumed his drumbeat, this time hitting the horn instead of the steering wheel in a salute that turned heads on both sides of the street. I joined in, beating time on the windshield and on the dashboard and on his body. I was, I knew, bright red with laughter; I wouldn't look out the window for fear of seeing someone I knew, and I hoped every single passerby was watching.

When the song was over, Gil gave a last, patterned honk, the kind

I'd learned Israelis considered friendly. "*Nu,* we're gone already, Orit," he addressed the silent dormitory building. "Go back to your pointless gossip." He smiled at me. "At least in our new neighborhood you won't have to worry about those busybodies anymore." He released the brake, and we swerved into the street.

I watched the dormitory disappear as we rounded the corner. I told myself that whatever part of whatever neighborhood we were going to, whatever it was that had just passed between Gil and Orit and Michal in the dorm, everything would be fine.

From the university we drove downhill through residential neighborhoods, past low trees and two-story buildings, parks and playgrounds. When I'd first arrived in Jerusalem, gray downpours chilled the university lecture halls and slicked the stone pathways of the city. Now it was April, and the sun had dried the ground. As we descended the hill, the domes of the mosques glinted against a pale cloudless sky.

A left turn set us onto a main thoroughfare, where crowds of pedestrians signaled our closeness to the open-air market. Gil wove through the traffic, now and then executing a tight turn around a slower-moving car. I watched two middle-aged women hail each other and move on together down the sidewalk, their string bags bulging with vegetables and bread. An old man, struggling up the steps of a crowded bus, accepted the assistance of a woman soldier.

I reached over and smoothed the fine red hair that hung over Gil's forehead, then brushed his gaunt cheek with my fingertips.

"It's perfect," he said. "The apartment. And it's a classic Jerusalem neighborhood, not one of those ugly modern spots. You're going to make us both crazy, you'll be thanking me so much."

I squeezed his hand until he pulled it free to steer. I tried to picture narrow streets, stone archways, dark-red flowers edging the tops of courtyard walls. A spotless apartment, with quiet streaming in through the shutters at midday.

"The apartment is in a religious area?" I asked.

Gil glanced at me. "Yes."

"Do you think we'll have trouble?" I ventured. "I mean, I have no problem with it or anything. But I've heard stories, about very religious people in black-hat neighborhoods who shout at women wearing jeans. Or even throw rocks at them. Things like that."

Gil raised his eyebrows in annoyance. "First of all, this isn't some closed-off religious neighborhood like Mea Shearim—there are some secular people on our block too. Secondly, your friends who tell you stories are paranoid." He shook his head. "They have that word in America, yes? *Pa-ra-noi-ot?*"

We had reached the *midrehov*. Here, at the heart of the modern city, the streets were wide and lined with windows displaying fabrics, sports clothes, trays of pizza sprinkled with hyssop. In doorless shops, standing men ladled spicy paste onto paper-wrapped falafel. We passed the glittering front of the Mashbir, its escalator rising endlessly beyond the glassed-in entryway. As we waited at a light, American tourists stepped from an air-conditioned bus with the name of a Jewish organization on its side. While a knot of girls from the bus eyed two soldiers strolling past, the tour chaperones placed coins into the browned palms of beggars. "We Are One," the tourists' blue T-shirts proclaimed.

I looked away from the tourists, hoping Gil hadn't noticed them. "The soft ones," Gil liked to call Americans. "You can tell by their faces." I was an exception, he'd said. My hand rose to my cheek, checking for some feature that might give me away.

The neighborhood was well into the valley, far below the light-green arcade of Liberty Bell Park. Gil turned down a wide side street, where shops gave way to quiet homes, then to square buildings with low walls around them and names across the doorways: Tent of Solomon, Tent of Moses, Sanctuary of Aaron. In front of one building, two boys in white shirts and dark pants were sliding down a railing, heavy skullcaps all but overwhelming their curly blond sidelocks. Next to another, marked Tent of Sarah, girls stood talking in a tight circle. As we passed I saw that their hair was cut in straight bangs, and all wore dresses that covered them from neck to wrists to dark-stockinged ankles.

Gil turned off the main street and onto a narrow alley. Lining the pavement on one side was a waist-high stone wall, purple flowers growing in its crevices. Between the buildings I saw gardens and low trees. "Almost there." Gil winked at me.

He turned yet another corner and immediately hit the brakes. This street was a weave of black against a background of blue sky and tawny stone. Dozens of bearded men in black hats and long black coats crisscrossed the pavement. Sidelocks hanging under broad-brimmed hats, dull white fringes swinging from beneath their coats, the men conferred in small groups, now and then lifting their pale faces to glance warily at the sun. From windows and doorsteps kerchiefed women called out, and children mingled everywhere. The crowd of dark figures was dizzying to watch.

Gil inched the car forward, and people moved aside with the merest stirrings of curiosity. I tugged the short sleeves of my blouse down toward my bare elbows.

"Look at this!" Gil pointed. The crowd had begun stringing yellow placards from balconies and hammering them to telephone poles. I watched a middle-aged man in a misshapen hat fix one to the top of his car. "Prepare for the Coming of the Messiah," the signs instructed. The street was beginning to look like a parade ground, lined with the single slogan repeated over and over, and peopled by a remarkably drab crowd eager to welcome some foreign dignitary or hometown hero. The sharp sound of hammers made me want to roll up the window of the car.

An ancient, white-bearded man stood in the center of the street, talking with a young man hanging a sign from a narrow pole. Gil slowed the car to a stop and, when neither man moved, tapped his horn in quick rhythm. The old man turned his head and peered through the windshield at us. Then, motioning to his companion, he moved unhurriedly off the street.

Gil pulled to the curb. "This is it," he said.

Three boys turned at the sound of the car doors opening. As I stepped out, one of them spat onto the pavement.

"Gil?" I clutched at my elbows. Gil glared at the boys and settled an arm around my shoulders. "They'll just have to get used to a woman in short sleeves," he said, loud. The boys had already turned their backs.

"What are they all doing out on the street?" I whispered. "Do you think this is normal?"

Gil pulled me closer. "Don't worry so much. Nobody was out on the street when I was here before. Maybe their rebbe declared this was a particularly good week for the Messiah to come, so they're having a sign-hanging party. Either that or they all just turned out to welcome us." He kissed the top of my head ostentatiously. I kept my gaze on the ground, afraid to look up and see my new neighbors staring.

We followed a narrow path through an overgrown garden to the entrance of a modest three-story building. As we climbed the airy stairwell, the sound of our footsteps echoed up past quiet apartments.

When we reached the third-floor landing, Gil pulled a key from his pocket and opened a red-painted door.

"They've just put another coat of white on the roof," he said, "so it shouldn't get too hot during the afternoons. And I already checked that the water heater works." The apartment was large and breezy, with a wide living room and bedroom and a narrow kitchen. A half-circle balcony cropped out from the living room; Gil had known at one glance that it would be just right for his work. "Look how much sun this place gets," he said, and even with the shutters closed I could see: light shone in through the slits, the apartment would glow with the shutters open.

I walked the length of the kitchen. From outside the narrow window I could hear hammers pounding and men shouting instructions. When I turned, I saw Gil waiting. His hands were clasped in front of him, and he was watching me so closely that I felt myself blush.

I smiled at him. "I love it," I said.

"I knew you would." His face softened in relief.

Yet again I asked myself what he saw in me.

By early evening the hammering had stopped, and as we unloaded the car I noticed that a few of the passersby wore secular dress. "See?" Gil said. "These buildings have a few nonreligious people." When our work was done we sat on the balcony with the doors to the living room open behind us, glasses of lukewarm tap water by our feet. The street was still.

"I love you," I said.

"Prepare for the Coming of the Messiah," the signs declared in fading light. Gil kissed me, then rested his cheek against the top of my head. With the dusk, the street took on a blue tint, which faded as the moon rose and the breeze from the west began to sweep the clouds across the sky.

3

A gathering of shadows, a swelling of sounds. In this building in this building on the third and highest floor. In this building on this street after all these days and years, something new.

An American, smiling so nicely at everyone, *the postman tells me. He, foolish man, is pleased.* The new tenant is who I'm talking about, *he explains before disappearing down the path. For he, like the rest of them, believes I am simpleminded.*

An American, smelling like soap and apple juice and new leather sandals. Did he think I had not noticed? Leaving her shampoo air behind in this echoing stairwell.

Back in my apartment I fling my hands in disdain. My neck protesting, I admonish the ceiling. After so many years I see you will betray me in your love for the new. *This ceiling which is now a floor for American feet to march or dance upon as they please. I examine the chipping paint for proof of infidelity. I have no use for Americans, I announce. But the speechless paint disbelieves me.*

I turn from the ceiling in disgust. My neck sings relief and spots sway weary before my eyes. Later when I cannot help myself I listen for foreign footsteps on the stair.

❦

April 21, 1993

Dear Maya,

Thank you for writing to me about Gil. He does sound like a thoughtful person, and talented in his work.

FYI: you've misspelled Fanya's last name. It's not Goodman like mine, but rather Gutman. I'm afraid my parents were responsible for the Americanization, much as they liked to claim they resisted assimilation in all its forms. Or so they were fond of insisting, when they were angry with me for marrying a non-Jew. I suppose they might have been satisfied, had they lived to see the divorce and my return to their family name.

Fanya's spelling is, I suppose, the original, though the relationship between our American branch of the family and the Dutch branch Fanya married into is distant. In any event, she's certainly been in no rush to make any change in her name.

Writing this letter from my office on this rainy Saturday makes me whimsical—I'm recalling a story Tami once told me, when I asked her about Fanya's choice not to make their name more Israeli. (You have to ask Tami to get her to say anything, or at least that's the way she was in her twenties, when I met her.) Apparently, name-changing was still common when Tami was a child. This was less than two decades after the Holocaust, and in the midst of all the fervor of the young state. Tami's grade-school teachers erased and rewrote their roll books whenever a student stood and announced a new family name: Negbi from Nussberg, Shlomi from Slomowicz, etc. There were Tami's classmates, casting off a shackled Europe they'd never seen in exchange for a wonderful new conspiracy of Hebrew words.

Words that sound like sunlight—that's what I've always thought about the Hebrew language.

Tami was in the first grade, and came home from school one afternoon and asked her mother, "When are we going to stop being Gutmans?" According to Tami, this was the only time she drew enough of her mother's wrath to get slapped. Fanya told her, "I was born a European and I'll die one." And wouldn't speak to her the rest of that day.

I trust your classes are progressing well and you're not putting any less energy into them now that you're living with Gil. I know you'll resent my saying this, Maya, but I think you need to be careful not to let your sense of focus slide. A word to the wise.

Your Mother

P.S. Keep trying that number. No one talks on the telephone all the time.

Her letter is folded in neat thirds on my knees. I resist the temptation to reread it. I sit on one of Gil's metal chairs, my bare feet brushing the dusty tile of the balcony.

Writing to my mother from the dormitory was hard enough. But at least there, Orit's impatience prompted me to finish my letters quickly. Twice a week I would sit for a few minutes at my desk and pen a few sentences about my classes; I might even share some carefully edited details of university social life. While Orit protested, I hovered over the final sentences. Then I sealed the envelope, and mailed it on our way to meet her friends.

Here in Emek Refaim, with my morning classes behind me and Gil at the gallery, there is no one waiting for me to finish. As the neighborhood drowses I sit beneath the heavy afternoon sun and compose paragraph after paragraph—only to crumple the translucent pages and begin again. My knapsack and sandals ready beside my chair, I write and rewrite, and put off leaving the apartment hour by hour. My planned afternoon exploration of Bakka side streets, the search for the local bakery reputed to sell the neighborhood's best *borekas* . . . these small excursions, which seemed attainable only this morning, recede. *This is what I saw this morning at Mount Scopus,* I tell my mother. *This is what I heard on the street.* I imagine her reading my observations, then setting the letter aside, unimpressed.

Today I have promised myself that I won't waste yet another afternoon. I will write only one draft of my letter. I will be as decisive and resolute as she. Then on to exploring in Jerusalem, and an early start on my studying before Gil's return.

The two words I have written make a bold imprint on my airmail pad; I dashed them off recklessly, half an hour ago. *Dear Mom.* The letters grab the eye like a banner headline. I have looked at them in the bright sunlight until it's no longer the dark ink I see, but rather the fine troughs the pen has made on the delicate paper.

Sentences form and scatter in my mind. I press my bare toes together, then stare at them as if they were alien creatures. Baby aliens squirming in a nest. (What would they eat?) I dust off my feet and rise and pace; sit again to chew on my pen. The sun reaches past me through the double doors, stretching my shadow at a precarious angle along the bare floor of the living room. I gather and sort phrases. I concentrate. I reject subjects as too dull, search my memory for interesting places I've seen. In my imagination I send spies to explore other neighborhoods, encounter Israelis, and converse deeply; I record their reports with care. I choose sentences as if they were peaches in a market bin, turning each to look for the hidden flaw.

Dear Mom.

Once again I picture her narrow olive-skinned face, thin shoulders in a thin sweater. The green eyes set in deep hollows, passing over each line I write with a judgment that I know to be swift and irreversible. I think to myself: Two years of hardly speaking. I don't let myself breathe until the sunburst of anger is past.

April 23, 1993

Dear Mom,

The apartment is sunny during the day, just as Gil said it would be. From the balcony you can see a patchy land of rooftops mined with antennas and solar panels and the just-visible tops of water tanks, which look like small white mosques peering over the walls. On one roof nearby, there is a blue plastic chair on which a middle-aged man balances the television set he carries up with him every evening at the news hour, and an identical chair on which he sits to watch it. As the light fades you can see the screen flickering, and the man sitting motionless listening to something you can't hear.

Emek Refaim, by the way, means Valley of Ghosts. But Gil says the only ghost around here is our downstairs neighbor. He says she's the evil guardian spirit of the stairwell. Or at least the second-floor landing. She must sit in the entryway of her apartment all day long, because every time Gil or I go up or down the stairs she's there, holding the door open a crack to watch us. There's just enough time to catch a glimpse of her hunched there on a stool in the dark, with her bedroom slippers on the floor below her. Then, the second we turn to face her or say hello, she shuts the door. I've gotten used to it by now, the door clicking shut every time I pass.

Gil says maybe she isn't a ghost after all. He says maybe she works for the Mossad. Peering into everyone's business, overseeing the goings-on in our (hardly crime-breeding) stairwell. Keeping a keen eye out for the country's future.

My professors remain interesting. Here is some of what I studied this week: it started with a reading about pre-Zionist European Jewry. . . .

It is late when I finish the letter. The Arab rug peddler has begun his passage through the neighborhood, and from the balcony I watch his slow progress along the sidewalk, rolled carpets balanced over his shoulder.

I tried to reach the Shachars and also Fanya Gutman in Tel Aviv, I add as a postscript. *But their lines have been busy.* It's a small lie, and can't do any harm. Besides, I'm going to call soon. Tomorrow. It's just that I've been preoccupied with other things, like the new apartment.

Woozy from the heat, I rise, slide my feet into my sandals, and make my way out of the apartment. The neighborhood is sun-baked and quiet. My feet slap steadily along the concrete. I mail my letter, sliding it carefully into the box's narrow bomb-proof slot. "Are all girls so pretty in America?" asks the man at the bakery as he counts my change. The light against the pavement turns golden; returning commuters pick through the bins of fresh vegetables. I wait endlessly on line. As I head for home, I can no longer pretend the day has any life left to it. Even my neighborhood stirs with the shuddering exhalation of buses, carrying weary men and women home from work. Tomorrow, I resolve, I will explore Jerusalem—right after that phone call to my relatives. Tomorrow I will begin my old exercise routine. I'll lose five pounds, get in dancing shape again. Temples throbbing, I bang my closed fists against my thighs. Who in the world, I ask myself, spends an entire afternoon writing a letter to her *mother?*

Back in the apartment, I put away groceries. The long minutes of sunset are lost to minor adjustments: the clothesline, the few items on the kitchen counters, my hair. Anchored at last by Gil's steps in the stairwell, I listen gratefully to the news of his day.

∽∾

Today is a still and warm day and right for this mission I have chosen. Today no one will discover us, of this I am certain. Here in the dark apartment I prepare myself hastily; straighten my kerchief, pinch color into my cheeks. My lips trembling in a smile, I cry out for Halina. "We will go to the forest today," I whisper to her. "And I will help you study. Mother and Father will not know."

And it is not long before Halina appears before me, her cheeks bright too, as if she has pinched them as well. Or perhaps, I fear, from a sudden illness?

I ignore her affliction, I pretend she is flushed only with excitement and I tell her I am excited also. I show her the papers rolled in my apron. And the forest path melts before us as we walk side by side. My sister and I. "Tell me, Shifra," she wants to know. "Do you remember Mother?" "Of course I remember Mother. Mother is still alive," I insist. Halina shakes her head politely, as if correcting the mispronunciation of a name. She walks on. Her dress is hazy with forest light, in her eyes I see the reflection of lines and letters, the equations and periodic table she commits to memory when she knows no one is looking. And now we sit in the deep shade of pine trees, here we will hide as long as there is light to study by. The sun above is gentle and warms Halina's bare downy arms, the dirt beneath our shoes is soft. Reading question after question, checking Halina's answers until the symbols are a glorious blur in my shaking hands, I am careful to pucker my lips hard. Sucking in my cheeks I hide the wrinkles; I wish to appear yet as a girl, so Halina will not be shamed. That I have grown old, and left my elder sister trapped here, eager and seventeen.

But Halina is weary of her drills, today she makes deep trenches of dirt beneath the heels of her shoes. Suspiciously she watches me watch her feet. Their motion halts; the charts in my hand crumble to dust.

"You are old," she says to me, looking on my ugliness.

I show her my palms, their dry cracks and creases. All that is mine, I offer to her. "I have a new neighbor," I tell her.

She is unmoved. Blinks her annoyance; I must get on with my point.

"An American."

Halina tilts her head, she is listening for Father's summons through the darkening sky. I see her lip quiver.

"I hate her," I tell Halina, to assure her I am not so easily duped as others. "She smells of sweet things and she knows nothing. And she is hideous to look at, so hideous the sight of her would make you weep." Halina knows this last is a lie, but she smiles, grateful. Together we laugh. We laugh until I cry, and for a moment she falls silent, disapproving. Soon we are walking home from the forest and after a time she begins to talk to me merrily of Lilka Rotstein. Lilka is consumed with jealousy, Halina tells me, because Lilka's beau fancies Halina. "And I couldn't care a bit about boyfriends," Halina repeats. "I'm going to the University no matter who tries to stop me."

Halina squints at me through the dusk. Now in the growing shadows I read her fear, which she hopes to conceal from me with this brave talk. She knows, then, that I have grown old and abandoned her. "Shifra?" she

asks me. I bow my head in apology for this stiffened clumsy body I can-
not shed. She stops mid-step on the path, the forest falls away and we
stand in my apartment.

"Don't trouble with a foolish American girl," Halina advises me. She
gestures with her arched eyebrows, her gentle clear eyes, at my ceiling.
I know she is right, still I cannot help but plead for her understanding.

"There is an American," I whisper to Halina before she leaves me in
my silent apartment, "on my head."

∽∞∽

Today the street below our balcony is dull in comparison to the sur-
rounding neighborhoods. Everywhere else, blue-and-white flags wave
in preparation for tomorrow evening's Independence Day celebrations.
Everywhere else, the streets vibrate with shouts as Israelis hang blue-
and-white banners from walls and rooftops. Vendors sell cans of Silly
String and offer demonstrations: "The plastic hammer squeaks when
you bonk someone over the head with it. Like this, see?" The city's secular Jewish neighborhoods are poised for celebration, but restrained as
well; tonight begins Memorial Day, twenty-four hours of mourning.
Not like our Memorial Day, I will write to my mother. *No picnics.* There
will be exhibits, speeches, and periodic sirens, signaling the entire country to stand at attention for a moment's silence. Buses will stop in the
streets, I've been told; business will stop in the middle of transactions,
radio stations go silent. And then, at nightfall, Independence Day will
begin. *Picnics galore,* I will explain in my letter. *Mourning turned to fireworks.*

But this street anticipates nothing; signs hang motionless under the
sun. My religious neighbors seem to be the only people in the city
without interest in the coming festivities.

"The religious and the Palestinians," Michal corrected me this afternoon. I see Michal two days a week, after history class. She makes her
way quickly across the room and the instant she reaches me explains
why she didn't sit with me: she didn't see me when she came in. Her
laughter is keyed to a high pitch. She praises my bravery; after all, it's not
every American who would sit in an all-Hebrew lecture with Israelis,
not to mention take notes in Hebrew. Even if I did study the language
for months before I got to Israel, she's still impressed.

Across the rows of seats, Orit waves and keeps her distance.

Today, in answer to my question, Michal explained that the most extreme of the ultra-Orthodox think that the true state of Israel will exist only when the Messiah comes. There will be omens, of course, signals from on high to let them know the end of this world is near. Then the Savior will show up on a white donkey, blowing the shofar. This to be followed by the rising of the dead and such. *Then,* Michal assured me, the ultra-Orthodox will have their Independence Day party.

"So why do they accept government benefits, if they think this state is a counterfeit? Don't they accept stipends for yeshivas, things like that?"

"Most of them do." Michal glanced over her shoulder toward where Orit was waiting for her. "Which is why I can't stand them. But some of them live like everyone else, do their part, even serve in the army. Those are the ones who really use modern Hebrew—the others just speak Yiddish among themselves and save Hebrew for religious study. Can't profane our holy tongue with everyday speech, you know." Michal made a dramatic face, sticking out her own holy tongue in defiance. "Still, no matter what side of statehood they fall on, they all vote. You can be sure of that. Can't count on them to serve in the army, but they'll swing the government to the right every time. Nobody gets out the vote like the religious."

The longer I kept Michal busy, it seemed to me, the more likely it was that Orit would relent and come by to fetch her cousin. And maybe, this time, skip the politeness that was all she'd offered me since I left the dorm. Maybe, this time, talk to me. "So how come there aren't any of them here?" I asked. I pretended I had only now noticed that the university was populated almost entirely by secular students. Here and there in the crowd, a knitted *kippah* or a long skirt announced a modern Orthodox student. But there wasn't a black hat in sight. I indicated the throng of classmates in jeans or shorts or the occasional miniskirt. Platform shoes seemed to be making a comeback; I caught myself wincing. *The shallowest of American culture*: I recalled my mother's words with irritation.

"They have their own schools. We're far too sinful for them." Michal flipped the hem of her jeans skirt and flashed one bare knee. "Ooh, sinful me. Listen, I've got to run." She hugged me, and promised we'd get together soon.

Yellow: the color of bright ballpark mustard. The color of boring signs in a boring neighborhood that can't even celebrate independence when everyone else is gearing up for a party. If Orit is hosting a get-together, she hasn't invited me. And Gil will have to work a special exhibit at the gallery. So I've been thinking I might take the bus into town by myself, just to watch the crowds. But Gil says it's mobbed and there's never room to dance anyway. He says everyone packs together in the streets and the kids go mad with that Silly String. The festivities, he tells me, will be almost as bad as the memorial ceremonies. Which he never attends. He won't tell me why. I'm free to go on my own if I like.

But I'm embarrassed to go alone. I don't want to peer in on other people's grief, like just another American tourist in this country where so many people have lost a friend or relative.

Dear Mom. Dear Hope. Greetings and salutations. Darling Mother. Mom?

How can I tell her I'm sitting sun-drunk on a balcony while the rest of the city is involved in Profound Events?

Yellow: a stubborn color. Are there any other yellow foods? Grapefruit. Lemons. Bananas.

Cheez Whiz.

Maybe instead of writing to my mother, I'll write to Ina. I'll tell her I'm thinking of her, even though it's been weeks since she's heard from me. I'll tell her about Gil's drawing of me. And about the way his mouth drops open when he concentrates on his work. I don't think he knows how goofy he looks, and I won't tell him—he might get self-conscious. I don't want to change a thing about him. *I'm the luckiest gal in the Middle East,* I'll write. But then, Ina has never had much patience for the serious type. *Hey.* I hear her laughter clear as a bell. *If that's what makes you happy . . .*

Better to tell her about Gil's eyes—the way that light-gray gaze searches me, never resting, scanning my face at every moment to be sure I'm with him. Sometimes at night when he's up with his insomnia, I wake to find him watching my expression in the dark. As though he's waiting to see what I dream.

It's warm on this balcony, and the birds come and go. I know I ought to call my relatives. I imagine them as a perfectly tuned chorus, chastising me in unison for not calling earlier. I ought to stand up, go to the telephone, and get it over with.

Yellow: it's got to be the world's most irritating color.

———

The sound of Gil's key in the door springs me from my chair. While he sorts the mail, I bring him a glass of water.

"Thanks again," I say. "For coming home early to help. Next month I'll know how to do this by myself."

He jangles the keys in his open palm.

"Hard day?" I ask.

He takes the stairs two at a time, and I follow, past the soft click of the door—that woman spying on us again. As we leave our street and enter the wider avenues, I struggle to keep pace. I don't know whether it's the errand that makes Gil impatient, or something I've done. In an effort to slow him, I ask questions. Did he play in this part of Jerusalem as a child? Has he tried the pizza place on the main street yet? Can we invite some friends over for dinner soon? Gil's responses are terse. When, suddenly, he turns his own questions on me, I first believe he is only mocking my talkativeness. But his curiosity seems real, and so, after an uncertain start, I answer the best I can. What was my favorite course in American university? Why didn't I study art? Did I know any artists there?

"What is it you write about to your mother all the time?"

"Nothing. I mean, everything. Israel, what I'm learning in classes." I smile slyly. "You. Good things about you."

"And what does she write to you?"

My face goes leaden. "Politics. Morality. The decline of Western civilization. That's the kind of stuff my mother talks about for fun."

But Gil isn't dissuaded. "You say her work is against poverty?"

"Against poverty, racism, all of it. Everyone else in the country has forgotten about the sixties except her. Or rather, they've remembered the sex but forgotten the politics. My mother, on the other hand, was always too busy with the politics to even notice anything else." Even as I speak, my own disloyalty opens a pit in my stomach. Didn't I promise myself that now that I was here in Israel my attitude would be different? "She's a hero to a lot of people," I amend.

Gil receives my answers with no judgment, only a ceaseless stream of questions. What are the issues my mother works on? Why does she think she can make changes? What, exactly, are the conditions of the poor? And how can the American government talk about equal opportunity across class and race, if it doesn't even provide classrooms for inner-city children?

I'm startled by his knowledge; I don't know how to respond.

He reads statistics, he explains impatiently. It's all there in the newspapers, if you want to open your eyes to it.

As we pass the construction site and turn up a hill, I tell Gil about the poverty and the crime in East New York, where my mother moved several years ago to be closer to her work. He looks stricken. How can such conditions be allowed to exist in America? I am unprepared for the intensity of his curiosity and the completeness of his outrage; I even notice a slight quiver of his lip as I describe my mother's neighborhood. I notice, too, how he reins his anger in, as if to step over some invisible line of restraint would be to tempt disaster.

And then he is finished. I wait for further questions, but it seems he's learned all he needs on the subject. We walk on in silence.

"Your mother is an admirable person," Gil says at length. "Even though the two of you fight. Some people just make it hard to love them."

It's all I can do not to stop in my tracks and stare at him. My friends in college always commiserated when I complained about my dour mother. They groaned about their own demanding parents and passed another beer. No one—not Ina, not anyone—understood why these reassurances didn't cheer me, why I partied and ignored my schoolwork like everyone else but still tore up each semester's mediocre grade report in fury, imagining my mother reading the page along with me, imagining her unsurprised reaction.

But Gil sees what I've always known: My mother isn't like other people. She cares about more important things, has higher standards. All my life I've hated her and hated myself and despaired of earning her affection.

And as if my thoughts were spread before him, Gil addresses the question forming in my mind. "Do you know why I love you?" he asks.

After a moment I remember to shake my head.

"You're eager. Maybe a little like your mother. You care about things, even things that don't make sense. Like this country. You believe in people." After another half-block he pronounces two more words; it seems to me that they are not a compliment, but an accusation. "You're hopeful."

"Naive?" I tease. I wait for him to deny the insult, turn it into praise.

"Yes," he says.

We pass the bakery and the *shwarma* stand and emerge into the foot traffic of the main street.

Inside the bank, we join a meandering line of customers, plump grandmothers and bored-looking teenagers inching forward. The bank may have reopened for its afternoon session, but it seems the employees have not quite awakened from their midday naps. Gil appears to have no more need for conversation, and I stifle my own impulses to speak. After forty minutes we reach the front of the line, and Gil tells a clerk we've come to pay our rent into our landlord's account. We are told to wait.

Ten minutes pass.

A series of bank tellers, somehow all on break at the same time, promise their imminent return. "I'm already back," one insists. "I'll be back in just a second." Finally a black-haired teller settles behind the desk and speaks to us in a voice about as subtle as the cleavage revealed by her V-neck blouse. "Address?" she belts.

Gil watches her. Softly he recites our address.

Annoyed, the teller rakes her eyebrows with polished fingernails. "What?"

Gil repeats the information, even more softly. She watches him. Only when he's finished does she lick the tip of a pencil and record.

"Telephone?" I wonder whether she did her army service as a drill sergeant.

"Six three nine . . ." Gil whispers.

The teller glares, then rises and, without explanation, wanders off into a back room. After several minutes, another teller appears in her place. "Do you have a name?" she asks wearily.

"Yes," Gil replies. "My parents were very thorough."

I guffaw—a loud, embarrassing sound in the sleepy bank. Gil regards me as if I've contracted an exotic disease. Turning to the new teller, he indicates me with a mild wave. "Must be an American thing."

The bank teller is blushing. Later, as we fill out the deposit form, I notice that she flirts with Gil. He ignores her attentions.

Out on the sidewalk, Gil shakes his head in satisfaction. "Never let somebody in authority bully you," he says. "I never do."

It's only three-thirty, and at my urging Gil agrees to accompany me to a destination on my untouched Jerusalem sightseeing list. We take the number 18 bus, and from the stop where we descend it is only a short walk up the sloping drive to the Yad Vashem Holocaust memorial. The long line surprises Gil, who hasn't been here since his annual trips as a schoolboy.

"Let's just come back another day," he says as we survey the tourists and the teachers shepherding children across the plaza.

"I don't mind waiting."

"There'll be other times." He starts down the hill. I hesitate, then follow.

"I'll come next week." I say it aloud so he can witness this promise to myself. My mother told me to come here as soon as I got a chance; she said I'd never conceive of humanity the same way. I'll be back, I tell myself. In the meantime, I brush the dust from the Yad Vashem brochure I find on the sidewalk beside the bus stop. I fold it and tuck it into my pocket.

That evening in our apartment I imitate Gil's unruffled demeanor, the momentary confusion of the bank teller. Gil chuckles as I strike her pose, recite her lines and then—assuming my best poker face—his. "My parents were very thorough," I intone. Later, after dinner, as I try to focus on a textbook, I am overtaken once more by laughter. Gil looks up from the sofa, where he lies with arms folded behind his head. "Enough with the bank joke already," he says.

Now it's my turn to blush. We watch the television news together, my shame deepening until Gil rests a hand on my knee. He kisses me on the neck, and I know my foolishness is forgiven.

As the announcer gesticulates in front of maps of the Middle East, I think once more of the bank teller. I fight to subdue my giggling.

In the morning, on my way to Mount Scopus, I slip my letter into the mailbox. It's only a small lie. I'll go to Yad Vashem next week.

4

There is an American, on my head. An American upstairs. She eats, sits, sleeps on my head. All evening I hear her bare American feet on my ceiling. There is music that she plays, too, with endless quick beats: an American noise.

Today the sky is pearl blue, a branch ticks against a balcony rail. The hammering begins anew, falters, stops. Quiet settles. The signs are complete at last, the blacks satisfied. Now they wait for redemption. Certain of themselves, they gather their strength. Prepare. In this silent building, I point my chin to the ceiling and instruct the American in her lessons.

Today I will tell her a story.

Once upon a time there was a river. The river flowed beside several farms and also beside a feather factory and a bank, several stores, also a forest. All of these things were very beautiful. Being American, you wouldn't understand. There were two girls who walked beside the river's shores. One was lovely and the other very ugly. These two girls were, although you would not have guessed it, two princesses who never had any troubles. None. Until one day they were trapped by a magical spell. Only the fierce angels who lived in the clouds could set them free. After a long time they did. The girls lived happily ever after.

The silence applauds me and I blush in gratitude; today, I decide, I will tell the American more.

When first I came to this city, the blacks thought I was one of them. They thought I believed in their shabbes, their candles, their egg yolks, their redemption. They thought they could invite me, feed me, knock on my door. Until they knew to leave me alone.

They are wrong about their egg yolks, the blacks. They are wrong about their shabbes and candles and wrong about their redemption. But they know, at least. How a city echoes the words of ghosts.

"Mushrooms," one of them says to me. It is a young boy, this one, with a dark-blue cap, and he says, "Mushrooms," and is gone. So I follow him, from my chair in the dark of my bedroom I follow him back into the forest and my feet sink in soft ground. The air by the river smells of damp, the hilltop and barn disappear as we pass under the trees. Calls of peddlers in the newly cobbled square reach us, then fade. "Our little town is becoming quite sophisticated," they cry, "after all we are not so very far from Warsaw." The boy, this boy what is his name? He swings his basket ahead of me. Mushrooms. I can feel them in my hands, damp and rubbery as I drop to my knees in the soft earth.

This one's name was Feliks, perhaps. Perhaps he wore a short brown coat, perhaps he had a sister named Lilka.

But I cannot ask him, because he is gone. I sit on the chair, waiting. And it is not long. Now Lilka, and she in a red dress. After Halina she is the prettiest girl in school, her hair is blond and her nose turns up like an aristocrat's. "You've gathered hardly any," she says to me. "Mushrooms, they're everywhere, are you blind?" Her basket is full, full to breaking, so full I would cool my cheeks with them, but Lilka would scorn my rough manners. "And how is your blessed sister?" she mocks. Her basket swings, back and forth. "And sainted father? Tell me, is your mother still after you to chase the Horvitzes' son? Doesn't she know he'll never love you?" The basket swings. "You and your sister. One a homely freak, the other a bookworm who thinks her fancy ideas about University make her better than the rest of us." Lilka laughs. Her laughter rises in a plume above the trees and floats over the hill.

My back aches from kneeling on the floor. Lilka is seventeen, I am fourteen and too thin. It is true then that the Horvitz boy will never care for me. Mother will be angry with me, she will shame me before him. My hands fly to my head I will fix my hair like Lilka's, I will smooth it back and wear a red dress and the Horvitz boy will lift his eyes from his father's account books and see. But my hand trembles over cloth. Gently I feel my head and understand that it is covered. My throat burns now before this one remembrance, out of the many: how we learned modesty. I recall the girl wrapping a first kerchief around my head, the rough brown cloth scavenged for such purposes. I feel her draw it tight then tighter. The finality of each motion, cloth singing against cloth. In those days in the American displaced-persons camp, before they released us into the world, the other girls learned well to conceal the lost. The girl's breath was steady in my ear, the cloth tight, tighter, her hands hurried and decisive. The hard knot made my forehead ache, but I did not loosen it. Round knob, signpost between my eyes. My head, a drum, echoed the slightest memory.

But it is all a misunderstanding; perhaps if I unwrap this kerchief, then Lilka will see. I did not mean to offend, it is not my fault that Lilka's boyfriend said he would forget her, forget her and every other girl, if Halina would only look his way. Perhaps Lilka will see it is not my fault her beau loves my sister. Perhaps she will lend me a dress, use her quick fingers to lace my hair. Perhaps then the Horvitz boy will lift his eyes. And Mother will not be displeased with me, after all.

My hands flutter over the cloth. If only I can will these stiff hands to loosen this kerchief. I will free the rough bush of hair beneath, Lilka will weave it soft again as a girl's.

It is the sound of the American's footsteps overhead that stills my hands. I start from the floor, but my knees buckle and I sag; I fall across the wooden chair. It is late, the light from the cracks in the shutters has weakened. I do not remember the passage of all this time. Years upon years, hours.

I pull myself up against the window. Through the narrow slits, rows of placards proclaim their single message. The signs are complete, the blacks satisfied. They wait.

I lift my eyes to the ceiling; I blink, once and then again, in gratitude for this first glimmer of understanding. Perhaps the blacks are right, in their own way. Perhaps they are right, after all. Perhaps the time is nearing.

Later I listen to the American push back her chair on the balcony above. I hear her walk to the doorway, into the stairwell. I close my eyes and see her descend; open them and peer through one slit in the shutter, then another. I watch her pass through the garden. Slender muscled calves, honey hair. Pixie face, turned to the street as she walks.

I am patient.

At last she returns, small fists clenched above grocery bags. Her steps rise, slow and gentle blows: up the stairs, past my apartment, into her own.

Outside, the sun stretches and melts into dusk. The signs sway. Above, the American is at her perch.

Night comes. I sit stunned by my new suspicion.
In this hushed apartment, as breathless as the blacks, I wait.

ೞ

May 10, 1993

Dear Maya,

Re your last letter, in which you wrote at length about your visit to Yad Vashem. After I put it down I continued thinking for some time of your description of that statue of the Biblical Rachel—the matriarch crying and crying for her children until there were no more tears to cry, and so she wept only stones. That image of the rocks piled up at her feet stayed with me for quite a while. Needless to say, I was impressed by your perceptive descriptions. Your letter was so full of information and anecdotes, I felt as if I were reading a guidebook.

By the way, I mean that as a compliment. People tell me often enough that I can be abrasive. People are too sensitive. All the same, perhaps I ought to be more careful that what I say isn't misunderstood. I do try, you know.

Reading those passages, I thought about how our Jewish nation is now filled with children throwing stones. Must suffering breed more suffering, catastrophe breed catastrophe? The ugliness of our desperation for security. As you know, I once was so dedicated to the idea of Israel that I almost moved there. These days I find it impossible to stand behind much of what goes on, although—unlike many of my colleagues—I do understand how matters reached their current state. Most people on the American Left are all too ready to paint Israel as just another unrepentant oppressor. I can't tell you how many times I've given a piece of my mind at a meeting, usually just after someone has used the word "Nazis" to describe Israeli policymakers.

In any event, I've chosen to make my contribution outside of Israel—here in the warzones of Brooklyn, New York.

I'm very pleased with all you're experiencing. Do tell me what you see of the Intifada, and of the women's rights movement. Tell me about the landscape and the mood of the country. Tell me everything.

It's good to be able to talk to you about the things I think about.

All those years, Maya. You know, it hasn't been easy. Sometimes I wondered whether I'd ever have a daughter again.

> With affection,
> Your Mother

P.S. By the way, Emek Refaim doesn't really mean Valley of Ghosts. I looked it up. Refaim does mean ghosts in modern Hebrew, so that's probably how it's translated by most people, but there's an older root to this particular Refaim. It's the name of an ancient race of giants that used to populate the area, according to myth. Thought you might like to know the proper translation.

"So if the black-hats are running their own campaign for the End of Days, how come we have to hear this Messiah stuff in lecture, too? It's enough already." Michal's grumbling merges with a yawn.

Now that summer is almost here, it's hard not to get drowsy in class. Gil's insomnia has been worse lately, and although I tell him I don't mind when he keeps the radio on low to help him sleep, the truth is that I wake at the top of every hour to the barely audible beeps that announce the news report. I keep myself alert through my afternoon classes by chewing on my pen whenever I'm not writing. Luckily, that's rare. It doesn't matter whether what the professor says is relevant or not; I copy it down, every lecture, every phrase I can.

Today I'm torn. Our history lecturer, en route to tackling the birth of Zionism, has chosen to detour through medieval Jewish history. Speaking with his usual intensity, he's assembling an array of double-dealing European princes and false messiahs for our consideration. It's new material, and the Hebrew is rapid as ever. If I want to understand anything I need to give it my full attention. But Michal, seated beside me for the first time in weeks, gossips incessantly. Orit is absent, gone north on a long weekend, and Michal seems intent on proving her friendship with chatter.

"What's in the messianic age for us?" she whispers. "Do you think my hair will stop frizzing?"

Definitely not, I tell her. The redemption of the world is one thing, but for smooth hair she needs to use product.

"So the dead may rise, but I'll still be Jewish and so will my hair." She twirls the smooth wave of my ponytail. "How come you got so lucky?"

"A gift from my non-Jewish father."

Michal pulls back her hand. "Wow. I didn't know that."

I shrug. "I hardly know him. He left when I was ten."

While Michal searches for a response, I turn my eyes back to the lectern.

In the warm hall, with its rows of squeaking chairs, the professor's speech seems to accelerate. His Hebrew blurs, so that I can't understand a third of what he says. I guess at phrases and dates, transliterate unfamiliar words into the margins of my notebook for later examination. The other students slump across armrests, blinking their protest at the harsh fluorescent lights. I take notes furiously, pretending not to notice the student who snickers at my concentration. The professor goes on about medieval society, about persecution, about the plague and Europe and families who kept a packed suitcase by the door, to be ready in case the Messiah came in the middle of the night.

"What product?" Michal whispers.

In the evenings, Gil returns late from the art gallery. He kicks off his sandals, pours himself a glass of water, and sits at his drawing table. I have to be quiet while he's working, because the slightest sound makes his back stiffen with reproof. I sit cross-legged on the sofa, puzzling over my history assignment with a dictionary propped against my ankles. From time to time I look up to see a child in a Jerusalem alley, the face of a middle-aged man, the huddled form of a woman, flying out from under Gil's hands like newly minted souls. These are just sketches, Gil has told me, warm-ups for what he wants to do next. He considers the lines emerging beneath his charcoal. I imagine his evaluating gaze as a keen and bright light.

Some nights Gil can't stop talking about his boss, Roni, and the artists who frequent the gallery. The owner of the gallery is impressed with Gil. He's already talking about giving him a promotion, even though Gil has worked there only two months. And in the fall, a co-worker recently confided, Gil might even have a chance to exhibit his own work.

With each passing week, Gil becomes more intent on this possibility. Every night he works later at the gallery. By now I know not to expect him until well after dark. Sometimes we sit on the balcony after his return, Gil pondering aloud his ideas for a show. Old work, or something new? A scattering of themes, or a single motif? Over and over, he holds a notion up to scrutiny, explains its pros and cons, then rejects it. He doesn't want to do just any collection of drawings. He wants to mount an exhibit that will demonstrate just how much he can do.

This evening I've bought shnitzel and vegetables for our dinner. The packages wait in the refrigerator. I know that Gil doesn't need me to delay my own meal for him, but I avoid the kitchen all the same, ignoring the growling of my stomach in the hope that he's on his way home. I consider calling him at work, but don't. Last week when I called, Gil was short with me on the telephone. And when he returned to the apartment he was tight-lipped with anger; I could only sit on the sofa and nurse my own stunned misery. I'd embarrassed him in front of Roni, he informed me. There he was, in the middle of an important conversation about his exhibit, and someone had to come get him because his girlfriend was on the telephone. "Just don't try to control my life," he told me. "We'll be fine if you can remember that one thing."

Sitting on the balcony, I watch the sky dim, darken, and turn a deep cobalt. I wait for the breezes to begin trailing luminous Mediterranean clouds across this quivering Jerusalem sky.

As I wait, a sound declares itself: the low rhythm of feet stamping. Hundreds of feet, muffled by the stone walls of one of the yeshivas across the street. I realize now that this sound has been growing for some time. There is music, too, though faint, and scattered voices singing along.

When the music grows suddenly louder, I guess that someone has opened a door to let in the cooling wind. I am surprised to recognize the melody. For some reason I'm convinced it's a wedding song. Although I think there must be women present at the gathering, it's only the men I hear; I picture them singing together, dancing with their black hats and flying sidelocks.

I find myself humming bits of melody under my breath.

It was my mother who sang this song to me. I recall a hand, thin but firm, stroking my forehead; a patch of warmth where she sat on my bed as I drifted to sleep. I must have been still young enough to pretend I needed this sendoff at night. But old enough to watch for the signs of her sickness. In the dark, I measured the sharpness of her profile. She'd learned these songs back in the days before she almost got on that ship to Haifa, she told me; she pronounced the words like a mystery we

would puzzle out together. Her wavering whisper was soft and beautiful, different from the efficient daytime voice that instructed me not to
slouch, not to be shy with strangers. I longed to turn on a light and see
her, confirm that this sharer of nighttime secrets was indeed my mother;
that she was, for these few minutes, all mine; that she was indeed well
again, as the doctors had promised. Instead, I pedaled my feet beneath
the covers, as close as I could to the warmth of her. And when I thought
she was distracted, I slipped a hand into hers. "I would have gone," she
told me then. "I was ready to start my whole life over in Israel. Ready
to work on a kibbutz, or wherever help was most needed. I wanted a
grand adventure, an adventure with purpose." She fell silent. I listened
to her breathing. "But I got involved with the movement here in America. And met your father. And once you were born and I'd started the
Center, I knew this was home for good. I almost never think about that
old plan anymore. But back then, it was the world to me."

She sang until she thought I'd fallen asleep. I lay with my eyes shut,
committing every phrase to memory, adding each melody, each new bit
of information, to my trove. Long after my mother had left the room,
I recited the litany in a whisper—every item a talisman to ward off a return of her illness. My father, passing down the hall, was a momentary
silhouette in the doorway, his footsteps stiff and hesitant as they receded.

That was when I was just a child, and still my mother's confidante.
Before the divorce, before I became the daughter who hardly cared
about anything—who cared only about twirling her days away in the
dance studio, and failed even at that.

The men across the street sing on in a noisy chorus. If they were to
hear my voice from the balcony, would they call it an omen, call me an
evil spirit, and a curse on the wedding? As I imagine them dancing in
a huddle, I am convinced that they never feel alone, or sit for hours
watching the clouds pass overhead on the way to a forbidden country.
Waiting for someone to come.

I stand at the balcony rail. My voice is soft, a tuneless whisper.

It is nearly eight o'clock when Gil arrives, tired and preoccupied.
After we've eaten dinner, he immediately sits down to work. He works
without interruption for almost an hour before he calls to me.

I rise, stretch, and stand before him; he pulls me nearer.

I stand inside the V of his open knees and look down into his pale, drawn face. He reaches around me, then clasps his hands behind my back and rocks me slightly, side to side.

There is a sorrow on his face that I don't recognize, and I hunt for a way to unloose his smile. I spin in his embrace, a pirouette ending in a flourish, and as my arms descend he catches my hands in his.

"I want to show people something with my art." His serious expression doesn't waver. "I want to make people *see*. Like Chagall did in his day. I want to show our world, our problems."

"You will." I giggle. I try to spin again, but he holds me still with his knees.

"You're the one I want by my side when I do it."

I balance my palms on his. My fingertips reach only the second knuckle of his callused hands. The apartment is quiet. "Why me?" I attempt a joke. "I'm naive."

He squeezes my hands, hard. "You'll understand. You'll understand what I'm doing and why. What it all means."

Looking into his eyes, I feel at one instant more loved and more unsure of myself than ever in my life. I bite my lip to keep from blurting, *What* am I going to understand? And how do you know I will, what if I don't?

Instead, I move behind Gil and examine the drawing before him. Centered on the page is a soldier in uniform—a tall and angular man in his forties with a bright questioning gaze, his jaw shadowed with stubble. The man looks like he's about to speak. One shoulder strains forward, and he gazes out from the paper as if offering a strong and warm embrace. Something about him is familiar. In one hand he holds a small leather pouch.

With a brief nod, Gil acknowledges the man on the page. "My father. The day before he died."

I set my hands on the yoke of Gil's broad shoulders—so broad they're almost an unfair burden on his light, tapered frame. "Nineteen seventy-three?" I ask. Only once, the first week I met him, has Gil mentioned his father's death in the Yom Kippur War.

The man in the drawing wears unlaced boots. Gil indicates the rumpled shirt half tucked into the man's pants. "He was called up during the surprise attack. He didn't even have time to find the belt for the uniform."

Gil's father is so real I feel shy in his presence. "What's he holding?" I ask.

"Those are his field glasses. A birthday gift, from my mother. They were in his satchel when he died."

Gil lifts his pencil, hesitates. Then, in one tight motion, he draws a halo around his father's head. Leaning back so that his head rests heavily between my breasts, he regards his handiwork. "After he died, I would listen to my mother talk about him. It didn't take long for her to dream up a different man from the one she talked about while he was alive. 'My husband was a hero,' she said at the shiva. As if she'd loved him."

"You don't think she loved him?"

"My mother?" His laughter rings against the walls. "My mother, the war widow." He reaches for his glass of water and lifts it in salute to the drawing. "Let's toast to the grief of the war widow," he says. But he doesn't drink. He sets the glass down and, so suddenly that I start backward, tears the page from the drawing table and sends it skittering, crumpled, across the floor.

Gil sits rigid in his seat, and I know not to speak. I move to retrieve the drawing.

"Don't," Gil says. The word is an exhalation of sadness.

I wait. After a few minutes I call his name, but he doesn't respond.

I leave him sitting there, and although I lie awake in our bedroom well past the hour when he usually stops working, he doesn't come to bed. I drift off at last to the sound of pencil scratching against paper.

Later, Gil is beside me. He reaches for me, and I wrap myself around him. When he kisses me, he's so tender I lie motionless with amazement. "I'm sorry about your father," I say.

He's silent for a long while, and I don't know whether he's asleep. When at last he speaks, his voice cracks with exhaustion. "No one understands," he says. "The fucking army didn't understand."

I keep my breath as soft as possible.

"This country hurts my heart," he says.

After a few minutes, I can tell he's fallen into a deep sleep.

I lie beside him and remember how he held me when he first told me he loved me. I wonder when he will tell me he loves me again, and then am ashamed of myself for the thought.

5

I hate the American. With her flat footsteps tromping up the stairs. Her music playing, her chair creaking. Her lazy footsteps sliding down.

Making noises that drive my hands to my ears, making dust that hurts my eyes, making the milk go sour in my refrigerator.

I know about Americans. Big, slow faces that look like they never expected to see you. Like they never expected it, any of it, like they think wrong things happen only to wrong people. Americans wear clothing that smells of toothpaste and glittering stores. Opening their mouths so big when they talk, too, a person could walk in and out of the mouth of an American while he talks and he wouldn't know.

Every morning they leave together, the Israeli for work because he carries no bag, the American for school because she does. A heavy bag. For eternity their apartment is silent. In the afternoon, when heat has settled deep into concrete crevices, she returns.

The American gets mail. I see these things. I see everything. The letters wait in the box with a bent nail for a latch, and when the American finds them her step on the stairs is slow, slower, stopping completely. She stands on the landing in front of my door, she reads and cannot even wait to climb up to her own apartment. I can watch her through the peephole for a long time, then.

They are not married. On nights when they make sex they are almost as loud as the cats wailing outside, but there is no ring on her finger. And when I climb, so silent no one could ever imagine my presence, then I see two different names on the door. There are other ways to tell also, even were I not clever I would know she is not married, for there is a missing look in her eyes. Married girls are angels, Mother would chide Halina whenever she turned down a suitor. They are happy, so happy. Never sad.

And she, she chatters happiness but she is sad. A sad American. Americans have no reason to be sad.

This night she cooks their dinner and I smell bland, American smells. Smells that come with gravy and heavy sauces, ketchup and round puffy rolls like the food the soldiers fed us, after.

In my dreams the blacks dance before me. A celebration, *their eyes shine. The men's peyes sail with joy, the women's skirts balloon with wind.* There will be three signs, *they sing in their wordless melodies.* Three signs to announce the coming of our redeemer. *Their harmonies ring in my head, I wake into this dark echoing bedroom.*

∞

The sound of the telephone mystifies me. Who would call at two in the afternoon? The country is on siesta, everyone is asleep.

I reach the phone on the fourth ring. *"Shalom?"* I remember to say.

"Maya!"

"Yes?"

"And why haven't we heard from you?"

It seems I ought to know who this is, but my mind offers nothing. Girlish laughter breaks the silence on the line. "Your mother writes that you've been trying to get in touch. I said to myself, Perhaps our American relative needs some help navigating the telephone system in this godawful country."

Relieved, I cradle the receiver on my shoulder and ask, "Is this Tami Shachar?"

There is more pleased laughter, and I realize my mistake. This woman is much older than Tami would be, though her voice is so clear she first sounded younger. "This is Fanya Gutman. Tami is my daughter. I'm calling from Tel Aviv. Your mother writes that you've been in Jerusalem some time now, poor thing."

I'm not sure how to take this. "Yes," I reply with caution. "It's been wonderful."

I might as well have admitted a fondness for the gulag. I'm immediately reminded of the provincialism of Jerusalem and the relative advantages of Tel Aviv, with its international character, although of course the deficiencies of life in the Middle East cannot be understated. "And what's a city without a river," Fanya concludes with a sigh, before launching into her questions. What am I studying, what do I think of Israeli students, what do I hear from my mother?

"I'll be in Jerusalem again the weekend after next," she tells me

when I've satisfied her curiosity. "Call Tami's house before Friday. We'll
go to the museum. We'll have a picnic. For heaven's sake, we can go to
the ballet, your mother says you dance. We'll get acquainted."

Before I know it, I'm off the telephone. My head is humming with
the whirlwind conversation, and I start to laugh. That wasn't so hard
after all, was it?

It's late afternoon when the mail carrier's tread tamps the dust of the
garden path. By now I've learned to identify this sound among the others of the neighborhood: the bustle of the yeshivas letting out for dinner, the cries of the Arab rug peddler wandering the streets. I've learned,
too, to recognize the vibrating emptiness of the air in the instant before
the Friday-evening siren begins, warning the faithful that the sabbath is
approaching. This is the same siren, I've been told, that warned of
incoming missiles during the Gulf War. It rises and falls in a different
pattern so people know not to be alarmed, but it's the identical sky-
flooding blast. I've grown to expect the rush of activity that follows, as
children are called home to dress before candle-lighting and a flurry of
prayer ascends from the synagogue. For my part, I contribute the quiet
slap of my flat sandals on the stairs. I know to listen for the soft click of
a door shutting on the second-floor landing, and the low whine of its
reopening once I've passed.

When I reach the bottom of the stairs, I swivel the nail and pry the
small wooden door forward. Lately I've been rewarded with a thin envelope from Brooklyn every few days: a featherweight white rectangle
with blue and red stripes around its edges, containing a single delicate
page. This afternoon I'm not disappointed. On my way up the stairs I
tear the flap open with a clumsy finger, and my steps slow as I unfold
the letter.

By the time I reach the third floor, I have read the letter twice. In
the apartment I read it once more, then lay it on the bed.

The narrow drawer of my nightstand is crammed with paper and
sticks at first when I try to open it. With some difficulty, I remove a
handful of identical white envelopes. I open each and unfold its contents on the thin bedspread. From the drawer I also take several crumpled sheets of airmail paper—abandoned drafts of letters to my mother.
I sit in the middle of a field of pages. Since I moved here, I notice, my
letters to my mother have grown more frequent, one or even two full
pages every few days.

May 20, 1993

Dear Mom,

You ask me more and more questions about Israel. It will take me a while to answer.

You wanted to know what people talk about in the streets here. At the pizza counter the server cuts a slice, at the supermarket the clerk rubs her sore shoulders, and under their breath they say, "Oy oy oy." When I first got here, I thought they were saying, "Why why why."

It's a good question, don't you think? Everything in this country is upside down. For example, the black-hat ultra-Orthodox Jews are the "blacks," and the secular Jews have a pretty big bone to pick with them. There you are in Brooklyn, doing race-relations work ... here, some days I get confused and can't even keep track of who is cursing whom, which comments about blacks should make me angry and which aren't supposed to alarm me at all.

My classes on Israeli history are the most interesting. This week we're looking at the early state period and next week we're going to discuss the Eichmann trial. I'm learning a lot more about the situation here, of course (that's what they call it, the whole mess of war and peace and terror tied up in one bundle: "the situation"). And I'm seeing the sights. I'll write to you about all the places I've visited. But just now I have to run, so that will have to wait until another letter.

June 6, 1993

Dear Mom,

Here are some of the more interesting things I've seen this week. After class on Monday I visited a friend's house in the Armenian quarter. There is a potter there, he makes the most beautiful vases.

June 12, 1993

Dear Mom,

Thank you for your letters. It's really good to hear from you so often.

I've told you about Yad Vashem and the Israel Museum. But I don't think I've told you yet about the trip I took to the north last weekend. I was traveling with a group of students from the university, and we had a great time. The area near the Lebanese border was really beautiful. Here is what we saw.

June 21, 1993

Dear Mom,

Recently I've spent more time with my friends at the university. I learn a lot from them about the political picture here. But rather than telling you about that right now, I'll write to you about the Galilee, which is where Gil and I spent the weekend.

I sift the letters, twisting to view several pages beside my hip or a short note at my knee. I scan this crazy quilt of my own and my mother's greetings, and I imagine all the envelopes slipped into the yawning mouth of a mailbox in Brooklyn or the meager slot on my Jerusalem street corner. I imagine them flown across the surface of the planet—sheets of tissue-thin paper connecting two people so far apart that one's morning is the other's night.

In the back of my closet is a pile of travel brochures containing descriptions of all the places an adventurous tourist should visit. The brochures are well written, even anecdotal. I stack them out of sight, guiltily, after I send each letter. I've used them only a few times. When I really needed to.

As I read my mother's precise handwriting, I try hard to imagine each sentence spoken in her voice, without a hint of condemnation.

June 16, 1993

Dear Maya,

Thank you for asking about the children's summer activities. Yes, this time of year is a challenge. It's all we can do to keep the kids safe from the usual troubles, not to mention the fruits of their own boredom while school is out. An eight-year-old's curiosity can land him in the middle of a shoot-out. The parents are constantly afraid. I would be too, only it's my job not to be. So—at least during work hours—I'm not.

Fortunately, I work long hours. And living here at the Center, I don't have much time to reflect on any of it.

Except perhaps now, when I write these letters.

Everything here is fine. There is some interest in a new program. . . .

June 18, 1993

Dear Maya,

This week, a new development. Some tensions have come up in the neighborhood, two of the volunteers are refusing to work together in the Center. Faye is doing most of the mediation—she has more patience for these personal disputes than I, and I'm happy to turn that work over to her. I've decided to promote her to Assistant Director.

Also there's the usual tension between some of the African-American groups here and the Hasidic Jews (whom you would call "blacks"? an ironic coincidence) a few streets over. I'm organizing a community dialogue to see what can be done, though I'm not optimistic about the prospects for a quick fix. . . .

June 24, 1993

Dear Maya,

How full of life your letters are. I carry them with me to reread when I have a quiet minute. . . .

June 29, 1993

Dear Maya,

It's been so long, hasn't it, since you and I could talk.

You have regards, by the way, from Faye and the volunteers here.

I enclose some forms for you for the next school year at Purchase. I trust you've picked out your courses for the fall?

As you know, I never thought much of the sixties idea of being friends with your children. I always hoped, though, that we might someday be close. Strange how you're so much nearer to me now, halfway around the world. It's a surprise to hear from you so often. A pleasant surprise.

What happened, Maya, that we couldn't get along all those years?

Your Mother

I stare at this last one for a few minutes. Then I pick up today's letter, the longest of all.

June 30, 1993

Dear Maya,

I've been thinking all day of your doings in Israel. I'm impressed with your interest in your classes, with the thought and energy you put into traveling, and most of all with your devotion to learning more about the troubled country in which you're living.

I'll admit something to you. I've sometimes wondered whether my work at the Center drove you in the opposite direction. Away from activism, study, anything that required responsibility.

Please don't misunderstand me. I'm not trying to criticize you, only to understand. That's all I've ever tried to do.

Even when we lived in White Plains, the house was filled with leaflets and the ringing of the phone. Perhaps that was difficult for you. I suppose the house was a branch office of the Center.

Be that as it may, that's my life—an extension of my work. As you know, I would have moved to the Center far sooner, because living here simplifies many things. But I decided not to transfer you to a new school system. You were having difficulty enough concentrating on classes as it was.

What I'm saying is that perhaps our house wasn't easy to grow up in, after your father left. At any rate, it's good to see you now taking an interest in something outside yourself.

Things here are all right. We've had some trouble getting building inspections for the new day-care location. But Faye and I put up enough of a fight last week that the bureaucrats in their wisdom came through for us at last.

I'm proud of all you're doing in Israel.

Your Mother

At last I rise. I put away the old letters, and fold today's into the pocket of my shorts. I go to the balcony. The street is hot and quiet. A single black-coated student stands beside a low metal gate under the shade of an olive tree, and one kerchiefed woman gazes from a window at the pavement below. Both are motionless. A child standing at a balcony railing retreats when she sees me looking at her—I might report to her parents that she's cheating on her nap hour.

I reenter the apartment and put my sandals on. There are a few cucumbers on the kitchen shelf; I rinse them and put them in a plastic bag, sprinkle salt over the dark, ridged skins, and leave the apartment, swinging the bag as I walk.

Once on the street, I throw back my shoulders. I flex my writing hand, the dimpled and ink-stained fingers dotted here and there with new freckles. All morning at Mount Scopus I covered pages with a blanket of script; now I shake out my hand and regard it with satisfaction.

A ten-minute walk along increasingly busy streets takes me out of the valley, and in another ten minutes I've climbed the hill to the Armon HaNatsiv Promenade. The shallow stone steps are edged with modest flowers. I slip down this stairway and into the broad terraced park. Before and below me, Jerusalem is laid out like a treasure: the Old City sitting like a cap atop its hill, the domes of the two mosques glinting from within the snaking line of Herod's city wall. Only a few modern highrises intrude on the horizon, and their height seems nothing but presumptuous. I smile at the thought of these upstart towers pitting their own modernity against the rest of the city; it's a losing battle if ever there was one. The very rocks under Jerusalem must resist modernity. I imagine skyscrapers crumbling to dust, parking garages tumbling under their own weight, for the crime of daring to assert too bold a presence in the city.

Of course I know that the timeless look of the city is less magical than that. Orit told me the first invasions of the Jerusalem skyline caused such outrage that all further construction of that scale was barred for years. And of course, the city's sunset blush is carefully guarded; the only legal building material is the pale pink-gold stone quarried from these hills.

I trace the arc of the city down the sharp curve into the Silwan Valley. For several minutes I look at the Arab villages' clustered buildings, the windowpanes that catch the sun. Beyond the last houses the land stretches on, a low brown hum against the sky. Lighter rock turns darker, then slopes toward the desert. In the distance I can make out the mountains of Jordan.

City of Gold, city of copper and light. I try to shrug the words away. But the litany of tourist-brochure phrases won't leave me. *Thought by many to be the most beautiful city on earth. Here three of the world's major religions coexist in—*

These words aren't my own. Nothing I've shown my mother has been my own.

A few schoolchildren drag their knapsacks along the stone pathways or swing them widely at each other's knees, their feet almost leaving the ground with the effort. Except for these children and one elderly man making his way slowly down a short passage of steps, the park is deserted. No one is watching; I stretch my hand toward the open skyline of Jerusalem. I cup a palm along the edge of the desert as it sweeps out into the distance.

I'm proud of all you're doing in Israel.

Have I fooled my mother so easily, then? After all these years?

But that seems about as likely as the moon rising out of my ear. I may be the dancer, but my mother is the one who understands motion. She assesses people without hesitation—this one is an aid, this one an obstacle. She sees through them and doesn't balk at letting them know it. The line of her jaw demands respect.

I've never been anything but my blond-haired father's child, afraid of the ticking of branches against the windowpane at night. Afraid of the junkies my mother counsels, jealous of the battle she loves more than anything. And ashamed of my jealousy.

When the junior high school nurse recommended movement classes to improve my posture, she had no inkling of the gift she was giving. But I reached for it with both hands. Those were the dead-still years after my father left, the house silent as a deserted schoolroom in the wake of my mother's work day. Into that silence, the disapproving skid of the nurse's ruler down my spine brought music. Music, and a whirl of color, and a wash of light reflected in studio mirrors. Gauzy fabric that swirled around my legs, rhythms firm enough to bear me through junior high and into high school. Within a year I'd been placed with the advanced students. I signed up for extra classes, and on weekends I worked double waitressing shifts to pay the extra fees my mother would never have approved of.

In the beginning, the high school students left me out of their conversations because of my age. But they watched me with respect all the same. The studio was bright and golden, sneakers squeaking in the entryway as arrivals shed their street clothes and stripped down to leotards and tights. I would already be spinning beside the mirror, light as air, light as nothing. Over and over, my ponytail whipped my face. I pivoted, I turned, I was dizzy with flashing reflections. I had spent yet another evening in my bedroom, ignoring my mother's tread in the hall, later listening through the wall while she argued a child's case over the telephone with a court probation officer. Sleep, hard-earned, had been punctuated by her brief curse as she set down the receiver. The next afternoon I endured the drone of my final class, until the ringing of the bell released me to make my way down the crowded hall. Returning classmates' greetings with a smile or nod, I hurried to the bus stop, afraid someone would tangle me in conversation and I would miss the 3:05. I boarded the bus, reached the building just as Ms. Stuart dismissed her early class. If she spoke to me, I answered her questions shyly, and she soon went down the hall to smoke her cigarette.

In those few minutes before the other students arrived, the studio was mine. I whirled on bent knee, my head back. The walls, the mirrors, the ceiling, were a cape wrapping endlessly around my shoulders, a blur of liquid color: my world melted down.

Only after Ms. Stuart called the class to order, after dozens of patient stretches and knee-cracking pliés, did the world stop turning around me. Together we moved through each exercise at a deliberate pace, and I mutely followed instructions. Two hours later I emerged into the flat afternoon light. Pinned, once again, by gravity, I walked along dull, solid streets.

My teacher's gift of a studio key cut the last tether holding me to restless school days and evenings of thin resentment at my mother's kitchen table. No one, not even Ms. Stuart, knew how many hours I spent in the studio. I skipped classes, I even passed up friends' parties, and was surprised at how relieved I was not to have to pretend to like the music they liked, or search my mind for a comeback to some junior-varsity outfielder's flirtation. After a few weeks, my absence stopped attracting notice. Broadcasting their private jokes down bustling school hallways, my classmates assumed I was someone else's best friend.

My days began and ended at the corner of Elm and Concord streets, third floor. Lights on bright, or the studio darkened; the thump of my footfalls the only sound in the echoing room, my body at its limits and aching. Sometimes I waited while the night janitor cleaned, then I stood before the mirror and practiced his motions from memory: the sweep of the arm bearing a cleaning rag, the slow drag and swirl of his body over the mop. I learned to be an old man, I learned to throw my whole weight into each step like a toddler. I repeated each week's lessons until I could see my own flying image with my eyes shut. I switched on a tape player and ran and leapt until my sweat spattered the floor with the shape of my movements. I danced until every step punished, and at last I held myself up against the barre, the world slipping past me gray and grainy.

Evenings, my mother was tired from her work in the city. She spoke her disapproval evenly. I could be doing my schoolwork instead of just frittering away my time with my friends, couldn't I? And who was that boy who kept calling every night and never so much as left a message? If she was going to keep making such a long commute to the city every day so I could stay in my high school, the least I could do was be responsible. She never liked the suburbs anyway, it was what my father wanted. So many years after he was gone, why did I think we were staying here, if not for me?

I never bothered to explain that I didn't know who the caller was, either, that I wasn't spending my time with my jock friends anymore. What was the difference between one world she disdained and another? After an evening when I reached for a third helping of pasta and saw her take note of my appetite, I started buying hot dogs on my way home from the studio. I could eat one full meal on the street and a second with her, and she wouldn't know the difference—my dancing, I decided, was none of her business. And if she noticed my hair, wet from its dousing in the studio sink, she said nothing. She left Wellesley applications for me on the breakfast table; school, apparently, was the only pursuit worth discussing. "If you want to change the world," she advised one morning, before swinging the door shut behind her, "get a degree from the best. Then when you pound on the palace door they have to take you seriously."

She wasn't alone in calling me irresponsible. Outside the studio I daydreamed; in class I avoided speaking, and the school counselors scolded me at every end-of-semester conference. But I had no intention of pounding on anyone's palace door. I was going to dance. After a September master class, the choreographer's assistant had taken Ms.

Stuart aside to tell her I had promise. Now Ms. Stuart was urging me to audition for a new Manhattan troupe. Of course, my body wasn't quite right—too compact for ballet, too short for easy elegance, so small the driver's ed instructor wouldn't pull away from the curb until I showed proof of age. Ms. Stuart and I both knew I wasn't the most natural dancer. My body refused some movements, and every day I worked to force it further. I had talent, but I'd never pick things up as easily as some. Still, Ms. S said she'd never seen anyone work so hard. In a modern troupe, she said, there might well be a place for me. Just be careful of my ankles—all those little injuries were warning signals.

"Look at the world around you." My mother hit her morning newspaper with the back of one hand, a lecture to start my day. "The least you can do is appreciate what you have, and try a little bit in school." My plan was New York, a spot in a troupe, my own apartment. And only at that point, only after everything was in place, would I break the news to my mother: I wasn't going to college.

And then, one Saturday near midnight, my ankle turned, and snapped as simply as a frozen branch.

I called the ambulance from the studio pay phone. Then I waited on the floor of the dark cavernous room, one calf propped on the opposite knee as the dispatcher had suggested. Slowly I rocked myself. I recited what I could of every poem I'd ever memorized in school. How was it I recalled so little? The faint light from the hallway phone booth glinted on the mirror and streaked my vision with long twinkling lines. In the silent studio, my mother's clipped words of that morning came upon me unexpectedly. "I can't say I understand why you pay so little attention to school, Maya. Maybe you just don't care what you're going to do with your life?" I would have stood, run, swept tight turns, anything to escape those words. But when I tried to rise, the pain that shot up my leg brought me, trembling, to the floor. Cautiously I touched my ankle and felt it hot and swollen, overflowing the bottom of my leggings.

I told my mother I'd caught my foot stepping across a gutter outside a friend's house. After the cast came off, the pain wasn't bad; it was the weakness of my ankle that brought tears when I navigated the high school stairwells, holding to the railing while the between-class rush clamored past.

Months later, Ms. Stuart sent a message through a classmate. Would I return my studio key, seeing how I wasn't using it anymore? I imagined she was relieved not to have to talk to me in person. After a call to me that first week, in which she praised me for braving the ambulance and hospital by myself, she hadn't phoned again. I understood and I wasn't even angry. My potential gone, I'd become irrelevant. The day scheduled for my Manhattan audition passed without incident. I sat in chemistry class and stared out the window, and returned my exam paper without a single mark.

By that time my mother and I weren't speaking. Our fight about college was weeks old.

"I'm not interested in a degree"—I'd faced her across the hallway—"because I don't care about changing the system, and I'm not going to pound on anyone's door. They can keep their shitty door."

My mother eyed me, her crossed arms and slim figure imperturbable. I shook with rage.

"At least I'm going to have a life," I said.

"What's that supposed to mean?"

"It means you never did anything but work. So Dad had to leave you. Anyone in his right mind would have left, because you aren't even a real person someone can have a relationship with. You're the *director.*" I put all the sneer I could into the word.

"At least I believe in trying to do something in this world." She tilted her head, evaluating me. "What do you believe in?"

"I don't believe in you." I felt the words tear out of me. "I never have."

For an instant her eyes wavered. I stood tense, my ankle throbbing, confused by her hesitation. It couldn't be that I'd hurt her. How could I hurt her if she didn't respect me? "Maybe you're a redeeming angel at the Center," I heard myself continue. "But in the rest of the world you're just some lady who works all the time to hide the fact that she doesn't even know how to talk to people."

"Fine," she said.

"I mean, it's not like you have any friends."

"Fine," she said. And then again, "Fine."

She disappeared into her bedroom, shutting the door without a sound.

My anger spent, I leaned against the wall, gratified and frightened by my own words.

After that, we didn't fight. We didn't talk unless absolutely necessary. She kept longer hours at the Center, I spent my evenings on the telephone. Since the injury, I'd gained the ten pounds and the curves my dancing had staved off, and I had even begun to go out with the guys in the varsity jackets when they called. Although I still skipped meetings with my guidance counselor, I cut fewer classes—I didn't want to miss the chance to see my friends. The month after I would have auditioned for the dance troupe, I filled out applications to the handful of colleges whose brochures I had received in the mail.

When I told my mother I'd decided on Purchase, she rested her morning coffee on the table. She looked over the top of her newspaper. I could read nothing in her expression. "How much does it cost per semester?" she asked, and I told her. "I can give you a third of that per year," she said. "The rest is up to you."

She was glad to be getting rid of me, I knew.

That August, before I went away, I found out she had known all along. She was busy showing the house, making preparations to move to a tiny apartment above the offices of the Center in Brooklyn. I was packing up my room when I realized I'd never retrieved my dance tapes from the studio. At my scribbled request, Ms. Stuart mailed back the cassettes, along with a Post-it note that said only: "All the best of luck—Ms. S." Enclosed in the envelope were my old audition application forms, as well as a letter, dated the previous year: "Dear Ms. Stuart, It has come to my attention that Maya is spending her time at the dance studio. I understand, of course, that she is in good hands with you. However, should there be any emergency or need to contact me for any reason whatsoever, you may reach me at the above number during work hours and at home after seven in the evening. I thank you. Best, Hope Goodman."

There was no further note of explanation from Ms. Stuart. I wondered whether she had simply included the letter for thoroughness, hoping through this final mailing to rid herself of all remaining traces of a student who had sorely disappointed.

So my mother had known all along. Not even the gold-lit studio was mine. I couldn't fool her, I couldn't claim a corner of the world free from her judgment. And I couldn't even make sense of her behavior. If she knew I was dancing all that time, why didn't she try to stop me? Why write to my teacher as if she accepted my choice—as if she didn't think I should be studying or marching, anything but dancing away every free hour?

All I understood was that my world had been deflated once more. There was nowhere I could hide from her, not while I lived at home. I counted the days until I could leave.

College was all I had hoped it would be. Other than brief telephone calls and the occasional mailed news clipping, my mother stayed in her world and left me to mine. I moved almost everything I owned to Purchase; my mother's new apartment had little room for storage. And I went to visit her for only a handful of vacations. I used schoolwork as my excuse—a lie I knew my mother wouldn't challenge. I found summer jobs in Purchase, and went home with local friends for long weekends. My mother never complained. "Your choices are your own," she said.

Between classes and dormitory life and the dance troupe, I had more friends than ever before. Chief among them was Ina, who shared my crushes on three different guys, and who knew to leave me alone after rehearsal when I cursed as I fumbled with the bottle of pain reliever and barked at her rather than allow the tears into my voice. "Okay, so you're just a recreational dancer now," she would say to me later. "No shame there."

Each fall my mother arrived for Parents' Day, sat through the obligatory programs, and shook hands with my friends and their families. As the morning wore on I answered her questions more tersely than I intended, and when I responded to her curiosity about my classes with open irritation she didn't persist. By the time it occurred to me to ask, as a peace offering, about the Center, she had already glanced at her watch. She never stayed past lunch.

Thanksgiving Day of my junior year, I arrived in New York City early in the afternoon. The first cabdriver I hailed at Grand Central refused to go to the part of Brooklyn where my mother lived. The second noted the address with a grim expression, then punched his fare button and sped from the curb without a word.

I was prepared for the sharp shifts between neighborhoods, but they happened even more decisively than I had recalled. As soon as we turned a corner a few minutes past the bridge, the white people were gone. Signs in English and Spanish advertised lottery tickets and Caribbean groceries. A few markets that hadn't yet closed for the holiday spilled elderly women onto the streets and absorbed a few others; every customer was black or Latina.

Then suddenly, as we turned another corner, all the people were gone. Block after block of burnt-out or simply abandoned buildings lined glass-littered streets. We wove along pavement gouged with potholes, intruded on by gutted cars and corroded dumpsters. The driver checked the deserted street through his rearview mirror and drove faster. A few figures huddled in a park; a darkened sign advertised a check-cashing center. The driver shut the windows, sealing us inside the cab with the dull static of the radio news. Then barbed-wire-topped walls and heavy metal grates indicated that we'd reached populated buildings again. We passed church after church, low brick buildings hemmed in by high fences and identifiable only by signs announcing their heavenly mission. We passed the school most of the children at the Center's programs attended, one wall of its basketball court spray-painted with the street names of dead children. "That's the local roll call," my mother once told me. "The wall gets more crowded every year." I knew from years of overhearing her telephone conversations that many of them died not from gunshots, as outsiders so often assumed, nor from AIDS or even asthma, but in fires or accidents. The buildings we drove past were traps loaded with lead paint, unsafe elevators, unbarred windows, trash heaps, and always, rats.

Slowing in front of my mother's building, the cabdriver glared at me in the rearview mirror. "This entire neighborhood ought to be condemned," he said.

"It has been." Without meaning to, I'd parroted my mother's favorite comeback. I paid him without another word. He weighed my tip unappreciatively in his palm, then drove off.

The green letters on the sign above me read "Center for Community Renewal, est. 1972. Together We Rise." I rang the buzzer and glanced up and down the littered street. When the door unlocked I pushed against it; it hit the inside wall of the entryway hard. The sound echoed in the darkened honeycomb of rooms.

The guests crowding in the narrow kitchen of my mother's second-floor apartment were mostly strangers to me. Other than my mother's assistant Faye and her husband, there were a young black couple, an older woman with a Jamaican accent, and a red-haired white woman near my age. Faye's two children played on the floor with a boy I didn't recognize.

My mother kissed me on the cheek, murmured a greeting, and turned away so fast I hardly had time to answer. Then Faye, whom I'd met only twice before, greeted me with an unexpected hug. When she released me, my mother was already sitting at the table and indicating that I should take the empty seat beside the couple—as far away from her, I noticed, as possible.

I sat and took small helpings, cursing silently when my knee hit a leg of the table and the jolt rattled dishes. As usual in my mother's presence, my body felt as clumsy as if I'd tripped in the middle of a dance and fallen to the floor. I didn't speak.

At the table, the usual conversation.

"But if we push the community initiatives first, the jobs program may suffer." Faye was shaking her head at my mother, and soon they were embroiled in a debate about strategy and timing. The couple chimed in now and then, as did Faye's husband; the Jamaican woman, who stared moodily at the barred window, and the red-haired woman, who looked stunned to be at this gathering, were both silent. The red-haired woman was sharp-jawed and pretty, and her slow gaze, which landed on me several times, didn't seem to be taking anything in. I guessed that she was a newcomer to the Center, one who had ended up in the battered women's shelter at last and was being enrolled in a job training or educational program. I stopped meeting her vacant eyes; we would both be more comfortable.

I rearranged the food on my plate and passed dishes on whenever they came to me. I focused on my diet; in a few weeks I would have to dance in the winter show, in a skintight costume.

As the conversation continued, it seemed to me that my mother's interest was waning. Her braid had come undone, and as she listened she raked her fingers distractedly through her fine brown hair. Then she rebraided it down the back of her neck, and clipped it with a sky-colored barrette. The navy dress she was wearing hung loose on her shoulders.

"You look great, Mom," I offered across the table, after a long pause in the conversation. "You've lost weight, haven't you?" I meant it as a compliment. On the train from Purchase I had promised myself: This time I would try to get along with her.

No one spoke. And then my mother laughed so brightly that, sitting at this table full of strangers, children giggling on the floor behind me, I felt something turn into place. It was a window, or a door, swinging firmly shut, closing out the light for good with the breath-catching length of that laugh, its high, unaccustomed pitch.

I waited through dessert and coffee, through the couple's repeated refusals of second helpings of pie, the Jamaican woman's refusal to indulge in a first, the red-haired woman's silent acceptance of whatever was put in front of her. The children were summoned to the table and my mother gave a long speech about how glad we all were to welcome Yvette to the Center; the red-haired woman blushed.

At one point, the Jamaican woman looked up at me, and I thought I saw something pass across her face. An instant later, her expression was once again blank. But for some reason I felt sure that she also saw what was happening. My mother, not usually one for pleasantries, was delaying her guests; she was hoping I'd tire and excuse myself before the two of us were left alone.

After the guests were gone, my mother denied it for more than an hour. The apartment was quiet, the dishes stood drying in the drain. Still I persisted. At last she said that she hadn't wanted me to know the cancer had come back. "You're happy at school," she informed me, and I understood that the grim smile that twisted her face was meant to let me off the hook. I thought of the time, after my first semester of college, when she said she was impressed that I had made decent grades and hadn't dropped any classes. She didn't have to say anything more—the compliment said quite enough. I knew I had finally stopped being a disappointment to her, because she no longer expected anything from me.

Now her smile accused me of more than any words could. What would have been the point in letting me know the cancer was back? I'd hardly proven myself the type who could be leaned on.

Our fight that night felt preordained, each question and retort inevitable, as though we were playing out scripted parts.

"Why didn't you tell me?" I asked for the dozenth time.

"It seems to me, Maya, that a person needs to figure out how to take care of herself before she takes care of anyone else. And you've got plenty to sort out in your own life."

I threw my hands up in anger, which prompted her into another prim lecture. "This is exactly the kind of thing I'm talking about. Immaturity. You've always wasted your energy on distractions—"

"Distractions?"

"You've got enough to worry about with your schoolwork and choosing a direction for yourself. When you get your life in order, then you can worry about other people's troubles."

"Don't you trust me?"

"Trust you to do what? What could you do? Personally administer chemotherapy?"

"Don't be ridiculous. I can help."

"I don't need help. I'm going to be fine."

In the end she was too tired to continue, and I trailed her to her bedroom. There, some magic possessed me. Without pause for thought, I approached her, and she, caught off guard, allowed it.

She cried as I loosened the laces of her shoes and slipped them off her feet. "I'm perfectly all right," she said. "I'm just upset." Her dark eyes were ringed with fatigue. "You tire me out."

Kneeling before her, I rolled the knee-high stockings off her calves and held one of her feet in my hands. The rough skin was cool against my palms. Her eyes followed my motions. In my outstretched hands her foot looked like a child's, narrow and helpless. I stared at the contrast between the pallor of my skin, the olive cast of hers. With her dark hair and my pale coloring, my mother and I had never looked anything alike. When, as a child, I became separated from her in a crowded place, I would be shocked, then injured, by strangers' inability to recognize us as mother and daughter. Walking down the street with her afterward, I would imagine a narrow golden thread connecting us; I wondered whether, if I turned my head fast enough, I might one day catch a glimpse of it.

"I'm not an invalid." She kicked my hands away. "Leave me alone."

"I'm not going to leave you alone." I wagged my head angrily to mask my own confusion. "I'm going to help you into bed so you can rest." But the spell was broken. As I locked eyes with her, I was struck only by the differences between us. On this night, in my mother's small bedroom, we might as well have been strangers.

"Since when do you care about my life?" she asked, and there was no bitterness in her voice, only a matter-of-fact exhaustion that made my hands tremble as I turned off the lamp beside her bed.

From the street one story below my mother's window came the sound of a bottle smashing.

"Go to sleep," she said.

The spare room where I stayed that night was full of unfamiliar sounds. The sheets whispered with my every motion, the bed frame creaked when I knelt to look down on the glittering pavement. I watched long angular shadows loom and sway on the street well before their owners appeared and passed along the block. From several blocks away sirens wailed, and fell silent. Twice there were loud bangs that could have been doors slamming, and once someone shouted a woman's name and there was laughter. At each noise I started, then sat alert with the covers drawn to my chest.

In a room above mine, in the part of the building not owned by the Center, a radio played. All night, music and Christian sermons continued, soft but insistent as the snores from the radio's owner. I strained to make out the words, telling me when danger was near, when salvation was due, how hard was the struggle of those who worked toward that day.

At six o'clock, when my mother came into the kitchen, I had her coffee waiting on the table. I put the sugar bowl in front of her as she sat down.

She looked at it, then at me, with annoyance. "This doesn't change anything, Maya," she said.

"It changes everything."

"No." She shook her head fiercely. "You listen to me. You listen to me good just this once. This changes nothing."

I didn't answer.

"You and I have our differences. But even if you'd known earlier, you still couldn't have done a thing to help. So don't tire us both out with torturing yourself for not guessing sooner. And don't trouble me by deciding all of a sudden to be involved in my life, simply because I've got a struggle ahead. I've beaten this before and I'll beat it again. You just take care of yourself, and I'll take care of myself."

She gripped the sugar bowl in both hands. "Do you understand me?"

My cheeks burned with shame. Even my guilt was dismissed in advance, my worry preempted. There was nothing I could say. I sat across the table from her, a hundred miles away.

"Does Dad know?" I asked.

"Why on earth would he need to know? That was another age, Maya. We don't speak anymore, I don't even know his address. Listen, I don't need his help or anyone's. I'll be fine."

She sipped her coffee. Sitting back in her jeans and pressed navy blouse, a small red ribbon pinned to her lapel, she waited for my reply.

My voice was clotted with anger. "I heard you."

She arched her eyebrows: a single gesture binding our agreement.

After she went downstairs, I sat at the kitchen table for a long while.

A shawl of sunburn is draped around my bare shoulders. The reddened skin is hot when I press my cheek to it, and the bag of cucumbers resting against my leg is fogged.

I unfold my mother's letter one last time and reread in disbelief.

I've fooled her.

Once I'd signed up for a semester in Israel, I waited for my mother's scorn. I knew she would accuse me of turning over this new leaf all for her sake. She would label my sudden interest in the local synagogue's Hebrew classes just a sorry attempt to please her, she would scoff at the nights I stayed home from parties so I could pore over vocabulary lists. I could almost hear her telling me not to bother. Anticipating her disdain, I vented my fury in front of my dorm room mirror. *Can't you believe just for once that I'm capable of doing something for reasons of my own? Maybe I've always wanted to go to Israel. Maybe I did actually listen in Hebrew school, maybe I'm curious about what I hear on the news. Maybe I want to go.*

Why, I asked the mirror, *does everything have to be about you?*

Privately I didn't search my reasons. I filled out the forms, I sweated over my Hebrew homework, and I got busy making what Ina—miffed when the extra shifts I took at Sly's Pizzeria to save for my travels left little time for her—mocked as the World's Most Compulsive Packing List.

My mother never challenged me. She said only that she was pleased at this "new sense of purpose" in my life. Boiling with unused replies, I could only accept her praise with a tight nod.

I stand at the top of the Promenade, munching on a cucumber. My mother was right on at least one point, I think. I turn down the hill toward home. A new country *is* a new start. Here I am in Israel, doing the very thing she always wanted to do. And letter by laborious letter, I'm giving it all to her. For once, I'm proud of myself. It's a strange, giddy feeling.

From now on, I promise myself, I will travel. I will visit my mother's relatives, ask them questions, learn the country by heart. I'll capture the feeling the bright winding streets of Jerusalem give me, but not in the words of some anonymous brochure writer. I vow to see Israel through my own eyes, make true the lies I've told in my letters and redeem them a thousandfold. I'll be the American who sees it all, who isn't just a tourist but instead takes the time to understand.

And then I won't even need to lie in my letters anymore. Why did I ever think I needed to lie?

∞ **6** ∞

It is early in the evening when one of the blacks comes to my door, a young man. I have heard him climbing the steps, knocking on door after door. Speaking to the boy downstairs, to the woman next door, to the neighbor across the landing. I watch him coming.

He has scarcely touched his knuckles to my door when I have opened it, opened it only a crack. He peers in at me sitting on my stool beside the door and when he sees me watching he smiles. He has a pale face. He is asking for alms for students. For poor brides, to help them buy wedding dresses, he tells me.

I scowl at him. Does he not see I have more important matters at hand? Does he not see I must be vigilant and not distracted? For the American has returned to her perch once again, she has climbed the steps and I must listen with all my strength.

He waits for my answer, this boy of swirling sidelocks. He thinks I am one of them, one of the blacks, with my head tied in a kerchief as their women do to hide their hair. But modesty is not my purpose. "I don't believe in you," I say to him. I spit at his feet. The gob lands on the tiles between us. He is astonished, then frightened. His eyes wobble with his fear. He stares at me through the opening in the door, then tries to see beyond me into the dark of my apartment.

"You must go up," I tell him. "You must climb the stairs. Don't you know there is an American upstairs?" He does not move. "Americans have money," I persuade him. I close the door further, so that he must lean forward to see my face through the narrow opening. "Go to the American," I whisper to him. "Americans are salvation, Americans are death. Go."

He leaves me, he climbs and his ankles have already vanished from view when I call to him. "The messiah is coming."

"Yes," he answers. "We must be ready."

≫≪

July 10, 1993

Dear Mom,

How are you? Classes are fine. The new apartment is terrific. You don't need to worry, I have plenty of friends here. Things with Gil are terrific.

Gil and I continue to speak only Hebrew at home. Gil does know some English, of course. He even reads books in English. But we both think it's better this way.

I lift my pen to evaluate the words on the page. I'm keeping the promise I made on the Promenade. I'm writing the truth, with no embellishments.

Yesterday when I came into the apartment, the heat pressing on the roof overhead, Gil was home. Beside the door were his sandals, and I heard the rustle of his newspaper from the kitchen. As I kicked off my sandals on top of his, I glanced into the living room and saw a rectangular shape above the window. Before I could stop myself I blurted in English, "What the hell is that?"

"Hebrew," Gil called from the kitchen.

I went to the doorway. Gil was sitting at the table, sections of newspaper discarded by his feet. "The gallery closed early today," he explained, and turned a page.

Gesturing in the direction of the living room, I asked again, in Hebrew. This time my voice was thin and uncertain. "What is that? Over the window in the living room."

"What does it look like?"

I crossed the narrow hallway and took a few steps into the living room.

A shadowed yellow sign, with a red sunrise and black lettering, rested atop the window frame. Its message was angled toward the sofa and chairs below.

Gil's words curled and teased from the kitchen. "I thought it was what we needed to round out our decor."

"Gil?" I was having trouble finding the words I wanted in Hebrew. "Why did you bring one of their signs in here?"

"Because it's funny. Don't you think so? Besides, shouldn't we have a sign to welcome the Messiah, too? Just in case he decides to show."

I paused only long enough to read the lettering on the sign once more; then I heard myself speaking English. "Don't you care whether it bothers me, whether *I* want one of their signs in here? I can't even walk down the street in shorts without getting nasty looks from those people."

"Sorry?" He laughed. "What was that? I didn't quite catch it."

In the living room, the breeze carried the sun-filled curtains toward me, and away. "Fine. Hebrew." I took a careful breath and tried to remember what I'd wanted to say. "But Gil," I said at last in Hebrew. " 'Prepare for the coming of the Messiah.' Doesn't it—I don't know—annoy you?"

When he didn't answer, I went to the kitchen door. Gil had pushed back his chair. He sat with both feet planted on the floor, as if poised to spring, yet he seemed absorbed in the newsprint that partly shielded his face. "I like it, Maya. 'Prepare for the coming of the Messiah.' Why not? Besides"—he regarded me over the top of the newspaper, and there was something dangerous in his expression—"I live here. I can hang a sign on the wall if I like."

That was yesterday. This afternoon Gil is at the gallery, and I'm home alone as usual, on the balcony.

My Hebrew is really improving. I add the next true sentence to my letter.

But how to explain that it makes me uneasy, this living with Gil in a language that still sounds to me at times like a low blur? How to explain that I don't trust my ears to tell me what he says, and don't trust myself to say exactly what I mean. "Gil's my hero," I kidded once in front of a co-worker of his we met on the street, after explaining how I made Gil change the apartment's light bulbs because, even standing on a chair, I was too short to reach the fixtures. That evening, Gil looked stonily past me until I was sure my very existence irked him. I had to beg him to tell me what was wrong.

"Did you want to make me look like a fool, Maya? You're doing a pretty terrific job."

The next day I looked up what I'd said in the dictionary; I even repeated my words to Michal after class. "I don't see anything wrong with that," she told me. "Are you sure he wasn't overreacting to something?"

"I don't know. I think I must have made some mistake."

"Have other boyfriends been so picky about everything you say?"

"It's not like I've had so many boyfriends. I mean, not any *real* boyfriends, you know?"

She gathered her books and turned for the door. "It sounds to me like his mistake, not yours."

It's the language, Mom, I want to write. *I don't know how to live in it.*

But my mother's new trust in me is a fragile thing. So for now, I'll skip that part. I'll move on to another subject. I *am* keeping my promise, I assure myself—I'm writing the truth. Only, not too much truth. A little at a time.

The sun is hot on the back of my neck, and the yellow signs dangling over the street reflect the glare; it's impossible to look at them. I write a stream of words.

The old woman downstairs is still a mystery. I think she's lonely, or confused. In any case, she's certainly not eager for company. So many times I've thought I was finally going to get a good look at her, but no luck yet.

There is a knock on the door. I drop pen and pad, and run barefoot through the living room and into the entryway.

"Who is it?" I ask in English, without thinking. There is no answer. "Who's there?" I say in Hebrew.

A man's voice answers me in Yiddish.

The building is so quiet it seems to me that the owner of this voice and I must be the only two people here. "I'm sorry," I say in Hebrew. "I don't understand. Who is it?"

There is a pause. "A poor Jew," the man answers in heavy Hebrew.

Standing on tiptoe, I look through the peephole. Less than a foot from me on the other side of the door stands a black, pale-faced and skinny. He speaks in a rapid, rasping voice. "Can you open the door?"

My heart jumps in my chest. I try to calm its pounding with reasonable words. "What is it you want?"

Once again he enunciates: "It's a poor Jew."

The statement sounds ritualistic—a password to which I am supposed to know the response. My visitor stands expectant in the dark-rimmed circle of the peephole, his face widened by the curving glass so that his features jut out at me. My view of him trembles and bobbles; I steady my balance against the door.

"A poor Jew," he elaborates, "waiting for the Messiah. Can you open the door?"

Despite the alarming distortion of his face, he looks timid, and I realize that he is my age or even younger. It occurs to me that he's probably being set up for marriage. I picture a matchmaker knocking on door after door throughout the land, searching high and low for a girl with goggle eyes and a bulging forehead.

He clears his throat, and I can see that he's puzzled. Then he begins speaking to the closed door of my apartment, as though willing to pretend for the moment that I've opened it and invited him in.

"I am collecting money," he says. "For poor Jewish brides and students. For the community."

I know that my American instinct not to open the door to a stranger is out of place here in this sleepy Jerusalem valley. I know that he couldn't harm me; his wrists are as thin as mine. In his ill-fitting black outfit, he looks like a crow. He looks like a college student who's raided the costume collection of a museum. He looks Amish, with exuberant sideburns. What am I afraid of? Some secret incantation known only to the ultra-religious, some deadly curse?

I don't open the door. "Sorry," I say. "I can't."

"You don't have any money?" he asks, peevish now.

"I'm sorry," I tell him.

"You can't open the door to hear the request of a poor Jew?" He speaks deliberately, and all at once he seems far older than I, and invested after all with authority. Disapproval furrows his bulbous forehead. I half expect a bolt of lightning. "Of a *poor* Jew. Waiting for the Messiah. That he should only come soon."

I say nothing. I breathe quietly and wait for him to think I've gone away from the door.

At last, after what seems an eternity, he turns and starts down the stairs. He sets a bony hand on the railing, then pauses to look at the closed door. "Wretched person," he mutters.

I back away from the door. My head is light, and a tight circle around my eye aches where I pressed against the peephole. My vision swims, as if I've been crying.

∞

Wretched person, he called her. Wretched American, wretched girl, wretched brown-haired American girl, he called her. And tonight I dream of Americans, tens of Americans, brown-haired and black-haired, yellow-haired too. They are all talking at once, and they speak words that I do not understand but that always mean the same thing: Prepare. Shifra, they call, and I wonder how they know my name.

When I wake my covers are wet with sweat and chafe my ankles and wrists. I sit on the edge of my bed. There is a wailing of cats from outside and a refrigerator hum from the kitchen. I am breathing like a heaving thing, like a train engine.

My room is small and close, and now it is inhabited by Americans. Americans flitting beneath the sofa across the dark floor, Americans slipping in and out of the slats of the shutters. They murmur, talking to one another, to me. Shifra. It is nearly dawn when they leave me, and I sit in my apartment alone.

After camp, after the years when I knew only how to be looked at by no one, it was the Americans who looked at me. The Americans looked at me and saw I was a dry, brittle thing, they looked at me and knew I was a burnt remnant, a shard. And then, after they liberated the camp.

After they liberated the camp, then.

A wailing of cats in this Jerusalem morning, a refrigerator hum, a bee buzzing in my brain.

And when they took us to the refugee center. "We'll make you whole

again," the yellow-haired soldier said, and repeated it to the line stream-
ing past him. "We'll make you whole." I heard him telling it to the pro-
cession coming through the gates until he was hoarse.

Only the Americans can make things whole. Only the Americans
can bring redemption.

Oh the blacks think they know. Prepare, the blacks say. Prepare. I scoff
at them, they that bounce back and forth with their black hats and their
prayers for their messiah. They that pray for their white-donkeyed sal-
vation that must come here to Jerusalem and trumpet a turd on the streets.
Signs, they say there are. Signs of the coming. I scoff at their signs.

I have seen signs, heard them. On my own. I have heard the wind
blowing the sound of rain in the palm tree. I have heard the sighing and
soughing of an American in the breeze.

Above me, the American creeps mildly about her tasks. With a crum-
pling of paper she rumples my thoughts. With the whisk of a broom she
sweeps cobwebs from my mind. She delays, tests my patience.

She has tricked the blacks, she has tricked them all only she cannot
hide her secret from me. The blacks think the salvation will be a red ris-
ing sun but they are merely fools, for the sun will not bring the answer.
The sun brings stabbing pains in the head, only. Nothing more. For the
salvation they must listen. Listen for the sound of rain to free us from
this burning life. For the sound of foreign footsteps, in the stairwell.

Descending, rising.

I listen to the American and I ready myself. Soon, soon, she will give
a first sign and I will know for certain what I suspect. She has come for
me. For all of us, she has come.

I wait for the one who will make things whole.

꒰ꪮ꒱

When I emerge from class, Michal is sitting on a windowsill in the hallway. Her hair is tousled and she wears sweatpants. She waves me over.

"Slept late again?" I ask.

She nods and raises a hand to shade her face from the noon sun
flooding the glass. "Can I copy your notes?"

I don't bother to keep the irritation out of my voice. "This was an
important review session."

"I'll bet it was." She smiles blandly. "I was out late last night with
Yoram."

"So I guess you and Orit both need my notes?" Orit has missed so many Sunday classes that I would rib her for taking American week-ends, giving herself two days off instead of the Israeli one and a half. I would rib her, that is, if she and I were still friends.

"No." Michal yawns. "Just me. Orit never studies. I don't know how she manages, but she always does fine."

I shrug: It makes no difference to me whether Orit wants my help.

We walk past the cafeteria and out the swinging doors toward the rock garden at the center of a stone-paved plaza. "I thought you didn't think Yoram was anything special," I say as I set my backpack on a bench.

Michal takes her lunch out of her bag. "He's cute. And he likes to dance with me."

"Anything else?"

She pauses, considering. "Hell no. But we're having fun." She chuckles, but I don't join in. I'm thinking about the way Gil held me when he came home yesterday afternoon.

Just because I missed you, he said. *Isn't that ridiculous? I'm an idiot. Just because I missed you so much, I came home from work early. You scare me, Maya.* Why did I scare him, I needed to know. *Because I can be more open with you than with anyone else I've ever met, that's why. Because you're misguided enough to love me.* As I groped for a reply, I blushed hard. All my years of dancing, I realized, hadn't prepared me for the weight of one admiring gaze. *Whoo whoo!* I mimicked his Israeli accent. He stared at me. Uneasy with his silence, I tried again. *Whoo whoo,* I sang out. *Is that scary enough?*

We poured our laughter into each other's eyes.

"I guess I just don't see the point," I argue aloud to Michal, who has eaten half of her sandwich and is eyeing the other half.

"Don't see the point in what?"

"In going out with someone if, you know, you're not all-the-way about him." I pull my lunch out of my backpack.

Michal is looking at me. She drops the remainder of her sandwich into its bag.

I busy myself with my lunch, wishing I hadn't spoken. When I raise my head Michal is still watching me. "The difference between me and *romantics* like you"—she doles out the words as if laying bricks—"is that I don't look for some guy to be my whole world. Or try to be some guy's, for that matter. Orit was right."

"What's that supposed to mean?"

Michal smirks, but her eyes water. She speaks rapidly, as if afraid of her own spite. " 'Oh, Gil will tell me what to do.' 'Gil is always right.' 'Gil knows best.' 'No one else can understand Gil like I do.' "

"You don't know what you're talking about." My voice is hollow.

"Maybe I'm just sick of this high-and-mighty shit, that's all."

My sandwich tastes like dust. I force myself to chew.

There is a commotion across the plaza; a lecture has let out and dozens of students exit the buildings. "Who for soccer?" one student is calling. A group detaches and moves down the broad steps; high over-head, a ball spins against the pale blue of the sky.

Michal blows her nose into her napkin, then winks at me. "Hey," she says.

I say nothing.

"Hey," she repeats, and I know that this is her apology. I watch my hands fold my lunch bag into neat squares, smaller and smaller. "How about those lecture notes?" she says.

I give her my notebook without a word.

While she copies, I think about the question I was going to ask but now won't. I wanted to know whether it's very unusual in Israel for someone to have no dealings with his family. Every Israeli I've met spends Friday nights with grandparents, Saturdays at the beach with cousins. But Gil has told me he never sees any of his father's family. And last night, when he hung up the phone after only a few terse responses, it occurred to me that he never goes to see his mother, although she lives in Jerusalem.

"That was your mother, wasn't it?" I asked him.

"Unfortunately," was his reply. She had called a few times since we'd moved to the apartment, Gil told me when I pressed him. His face tightened as he spoke of her. She was always calling him, but he didn't see the use in talking anymore. All she wanted to do was hassle him. He was sick of her distorted stories and half-truths, sick of her accusations every time he did something that reminded her of his father. And he'd told her so. Any contact they'd had since then had been from her side.

"When did you stop calling her?"

"February."

"Just-before-we-met February?"

Gil's mouth clamped shut. Right away I regretted pushing. Shouldn't I understand this kind of family quarrel, after all?

When Michal has finished copying, she runs the tip of her pen slowly up and down the wire of her spiral notebook. "Orit misses you, you know?"

"Yeah." The whisper is not what I intended. "Will you tell her hello for me?"

Later, when I sleep, I dream of rain. I am in a house with paper-thin walls, and outside the grass is thick and cool. A soft rain is falling, sweeping closer every minute. At last it blows sideways against the walls. My head resounds with its patter.

I wake feeling light and expectant, as if a gentle hand has passed once over my forehead and I am awaiting its return. The clock reads two thirty-five a.m. Beside me, Gil breathes evenly. I lie without moving. I imagine that I am in my old house, in White Plains. My parents are both here, my mother is well, she tells me something I cannot quite hear.

The sound of sweeping rain has not disappeared along with my dream, although now that I'm awake it's quieter, and more tentative. Moving with care so I won't disturb Gil, I kneel on the mattress and look through the window. Outside, the heavy sheath of the palm tree rustles again. The dead layered fronds, hanging like a beard below the new growth, lift, sway, and shimmer with each sustained breeze. Here, so far beneath the clouds passing across the Jerusalem night, the wind dips down to touch every building and treetop and stone. The fronds rustle once more: a silvery hush just beyond my window, like a promise being spoken.

∞

Night tests my watchfulness, but I am strong and do not sleep. These stones and I remain awake beneath the high moon. I must forget the weariness in my own bones and learn stony patience. At last the sky pales, this neighborhood wakes. Daylight taunts my burning eyes.

She is afraid of me, the American is, you can see it in how she looks at me. As if I am the animal behind bars, and she, she the foot soldier come with gun to stare before setting such trapped things free. Today when she tromps up from the garden I am in the stairwell. My key falling through my fingers so I have to bend and bend again to pick it up, her feet stamping closer. The key at last in the lock, but she arrives before I can turn it.

I flatten myself against the wall as she passes so I won't touch her, and she pauses to gawk. If she's searching for a number on my arm she's a clumsy monster, all of them clumsy monsters, doesn't she know not every camp tattooed. But being American she has no intelligence, despite so much intelligence.

She opens her mouth and speaks a strange Hebrew. "Good afternoon," she says.

I close my eyes. Press against the wall. If I am very quiet, she will soon not be able to see me. I will become a shard, I shall fall away like a dried-out husk. Americans cannot see what is silent. Soon I will vanish and then she will vanish as well, to her American tasks.

It is working. I hear her turn away, I hear the pat of one hand on the rail. But there is no sound of shoes on stairs.

"Are you all right?" From only a few paces away, she addresses me.

My eyes closed, the voice scalds my brain. I feel that I have shaken my head. I open my eyes and she is still there, her face a pale floating thing. Only this time it is shimmering, merging with other faces, and I cannot understand why this American is wearing the mouth of Feliks, the eyes of Halina. Laughing eyes, mouth. The hair, the hair Lilka. The eyes, mouth, Karol? I do not know what to do with her face, it swings and sways before me. I stare at it, I strain to read its message, the message I have awaited. I draw ragged breath, I attend with all my strength.

But now it is only the girl again, the American, the soldier with gun, the girl with flat footsteps and no knowing about things that everyone knows, numbers and burning and waiting for rain.

The key turns in my hand, turns in the lock, and I fall through a doorway into stifling dark. I shut the door behind me, and years pass before I hear the American walk away.

∽

Gil steps into the apartment, drops his bag to the floor, and stands without a word. Gradually his gaze passes down the hallway and falls on me, sitting on the living room sofa.

"I don't want to talk about it," he says.

The soup I heated for our dinner waits cold in the darkened kitchen; it's been more than two hours since I turned off the flame. I am holding a book whose first page I've read half a dozen times.

"Bad day, huh?"

"Bad day?" Gil's speech is so clipped I have trouble understanding him. "A very bad day, you might say."

A breeze ripples the lace curtain that divides the living room from the balcony. I watch the moths clinging to the outside of the curtain, drawn from the dark street to our lamplight. I wait for him to speak again.

"It's not that I'm complaining," he continues in the same curiously tight voice. "It's only that Roni is trying to back out on his promise to give me a show. It's only, Maya, that I ask for a fair shot in life. And no one wants to give it to me."

He moves into the living room and sits on the other end of the sofa, just out of my reach. He doesn't speak. I shift closer to him and touch his shoulder, and he flinches.

My voice is reasoned and gentle. "Honey," I begin.

"No English," he mutters, and buries his hands deep in his hair. Staring at the square of tile between his feet, he curses with quiet ferocity. "The bastard. The damn bastard. He thinks the world should fall at his feet just because he was a pilot. Says he was looking up my records and wants to know why I didn't discuss my Profile 21 discharge when he hired me." Gil stands and begins to pace. His Hebrew thickens, accelerates. "Says he'll have to *think* about whether I should be representing the gallery. And am I certain I can manage the strain of preparing an exhibit?" He moves with his hands clasped viselike, across his forehead. *"Son of a whore."*

I watch him pass from the center of the living room to the verge of the balcony, then retrace his steps.

"What's a Profile 21?"

"A Profile 21?" He spins on his heel and regards me for an instant, then resumes his progress across the floor. "A Profile 21 means you couldn't hack it. A Profile 21 means even if you tell the truth, no one needs to listen anymore. A Profile 21, Maya"—he slows, and his next words are a cruel jeer—"means nobody loves you."

He stands in the center of the living room, absolutely still. His eyes are closed. He lowers his hands.

I walk to his side. Words of consolation and curiosity offer themselves simultaneously in my mind. I place a light hand on his shoulder.

He jerks away from me and then the back of his hand smashes into my cheek. The floor tears out from under my feet and I fall against the drawing table behind me, first with my shoulders, hard, and then with my head. My weight knocks the table off balance. I grab for it clumsily, as if I might save it from toppling.

It hits the floor with a slam. Gil's sketches are scattered across the tiles. I lie on the floor, too, a burning sensation on my face.

The room is quiet. Close to my shoulder is a drawing of two boys dancing. Their faces are hidden, but their ink sidelocks swing with the motion of their dance.

I lift my head and look at Gil. He is facing away from me. With a few long, angry steps he reaches the entryway. He hesitates at the door; then he unlocks it and is gone. The door stands open behind him.

Carefully I rise and walk to the entryway. I close the door and lock it. Then I unlock it, remembering that Gil might not have his key.

I sit back down on the floor with the sketches around me. I do not disturb anything, to the right or to the left. Watching the moths flutter and land on the curtain, I sift Hebrew words. The right combination, I am certain, will explain this.

What I want to say is, *I didn't mean to make you.* What I want to say is, *You shouldn't have.*

What I want to say groups and scatters around me. I know that something very important must be remembered, but I cannot think what it is. I listen for his footsteps, and the possibility that he might not return makes my heart knock in my chest.

In Purchase in December, Ina said that the director was counting on me for solos; he couldn't understand why I'd suddenly stopped coming to rehearsal. Ina knew I was busy with my preparations to go abroad, but didn't I miss hanging out with the troupe? Didn't I miss hanging out with *her?* Besides, the dance director said he'd take me back. "And girl," Ina said, "even if you'll never have a dance career with that ankle, you'll sure look sweet on that stage. I'll try not to be jealous."

My face throbs with heat, but I don't move to get ice.

Today's date is July thirteenth. The Purchase semester is long over, and I realize I don't know what the troupe has planned for the fall. I've lost touch with everyone from school. I will write to Ina and ask. I will call Ina and ask. I will call her and say, Please let the director know I'm coming back to dance. I will tell her, I miss you, too.

I gather myself, checking my body for damage.

It occurs to me that I may have done something wrong. That I must have. There's no other explanation.

Then it occurs to me that my mother, who fights to protect people who are victims and can't help themselves, would be ashamed of me lying here on this floor, doing nothing to help myself.

So I rise. I cross to the bathroom and I lean over the sink and douse my face with cold water. I straighten, and pat my skin dry with a towel. Then I aim a gaze at myself in the mirror. I take my makeup bag from the cabinet.

Years of performing have left me with enough makeup and enough know-how to hide any imperfection, at least until a show is over and the audience gone. Standing before the mirror, I choose to leave the mark on my cheek untouched. I erase the lines of fear around my eyes, disguise my pallor with blush. As I evaluate my reflection, I experience a sense of control I haven't felt since those lonely, punishing hours so long ago in the studio. I am an old man, I am a janitor, I am a dancer, I am whatever I decide to be. I am all right. I know I must have made a mistake, which Gil will explain just as soon as he explains his own mistake. Because I'm sure of one thing—it was a mistake. If Gil loves me, he can't mean to hurt me. That wouldn't be love. I don't think that would be love.

So what I need to figure out is only one thing: Has he stopped loving me?

When I've finished, I put away my makeup and return to the living room. I wait. I am patient and calm. If only Gil will come. Soon. If only he will step into the stairwell, climb to our apartment, bearing his affection in outstretched hands.

It's more than an hour later when the front door opens. I've dozed on the couch, my fingers laced into each other so tightly that for a moment I can't unlock them.

He is crying. I stand and, as he stares at me, I wait. His eyes linger a long while over the mark on my cheek. Then he stumbles toward me. He embraces me until my neck aches. "I love you," he says, and I am crying hot tears although I don't know why. *Then tell me you never meant to do it,* I want to say. *I'll believe you.*

He lets go of me, pulling back to look once more. There are shadows under his eyes and he blinks in the light, but he's smiling at me as though he knows some wonderful secret. He takes my hand and leads me around the apartment, turning out all the lights until every room is dark. When he pulls me toward the bedroom, he is tender. He kisses my shoulders, my neck, my ears, and the sound of his kisses shuts out every-thing else. Seating me on the bed, he kneels to undress me. With each piece of clothing he looks up, and his expression asks, *And this? And this?* and each time I nod faintly, watching him work. He undresses himself in silence.

I can see his eyes shining in the darkness as if he never wants to stop looking, looking and looking at me, as if he is scarcely restraining tears of joy. He is sorry, he does not have to say so because it is in every touch. *Tell me you never meant to do it,* I want to whisper, but he doesn't read my mind. He loves me, this he tells me once more. And the gentleness in his fingertips promises everything. He loves me, I explain to myself; he didn't mean to hurt me.

When he moves on top of me there is no sound other than his breathing and the hush of his skin sliding against mine, and when he comes to rest he is a pulse beating inside me, the heartbeat of a small frightened animal.

☙

It took me too long, too long to see. But now I understand, and happi-ness fills my heart and makes each heavy task lighter.

I have read the first sign.

All week long they told me. Prepare. *Flitting through the shutters of this apartment that I have closed against the sunlight.* Prepare. *Feliks Lilka, Halina. Prepare, they urged me. But I, I did not know. I did not see. I followed them about the room, I bumped my shoulder on furniture and scraped my knee on the floor, but they would not tell me where to look. For her signs.*

And then, a night of swift breezes and cats wailing and American fighting upstairs. One crash and one set of footsteps down the stairwell, these things made two; the sound of one sink running made three. Later, the stifling of an American sob made four, five, six. My hands filled to brimming with this new information. Why should an American girl cry like that?

Through long darkness I waited. At last, the quiet of his return, si-lence above like the sealing of a pact.

And in the middle of the night I woke to the sound of the palm tree whispering my name in the courtyard, and understood at last: The fight was a sign.

Yes. The fight was the first sign, brought to show me the American is the one. The American, at last, will reveal herself.

For so long I have waited. My eyes have grown dry with the stacking of days.

Above me the American moves in her appointed place. She knows I have seen her, now she awaits my devotion. Out of such darkness I lift my gaze to the ceiling, whence will come my aid at last.

And now it is plain what is necessary.

In the dim room I rise and grope my way to the closet. Tears of joy blur my vision. Somewhere, here. Leather shell creaking open, cloth lining the inside, shredded. A case. Given, so long ago, by American relief workers.

I kneel and open the case on the floor, and the air that rises to meet me weeps rust and disinfectant. I close my eyes against the smell, I gasp for air. Nothing must stop me.

I begin to pack. First a dress, then a pair of shoes. I fold and place each thing; I must not waste. I will be worthy. I will be patient, and good.

I listen for the scuffling of the American's feet, I listen to her soft music in the apartment above, and as I pack I ready myself for each further sign that will come. Each further sign to bring the day when the American will sweep aside all that has passed, right tumbled years and redeem every hour. Even the blacks will rejoice, on that day when they see why she has come among us.

Sitting at last next to the door with my case beside me, I listen for the signs that will bring me closer each day.

Part Three

When I dial the number of my relatives at last, the reprimands are immediate and unabashed. The man who identifies himself as Nachum Shachar berates me cheerfully over the telephone. "So many months here and you couldn't find time to call? What, not a minute? Not two minutes?" My protests are brushed aside at once—he appears to find his own complaint far more entertaining. "What, no five minutes to call family? All right, so never mind. You'll come tonight." I take down the address and directions.

"They're good people, my mother says," I tell Gil once more as he pulls up beside the building on Wolfson Street. "Some kind of distant cousins. Are you sure you don't want to come in and meet them?"

"Not a chance, thank you." He taps the steering wheel impatiently, then smiles and pulls me to him by the waist. His kiss is airy and gentle. "I've got to work tonight." And I know he will, the bare bulb above his drawing table burning until well after every other apartment in the building is dark. His boss at the gallery has decided to give him the exhibit, after all. Talent, Roni says, is what's most important, and he doesn't need to know anything beyond that. "So the subject is closed," Gil reported in such firm tones that I decided to postpone asking my own questions for the moment. I'd find out what a Profile 21 was in some other way, then I'd broach the subject with Gil.

Since Roni changed his mind, Gil has been working with double his previous intensity. He's kept his moodiness in check around me, and were it not for the soft curses I sometimes hear as I pass the living room, I wouldn't guess at the tension behind his fierce concentration. One day when I woke there were flowers beside my pillow, and every afternoon this week he called from the gallery. I could hear the telephone ringing from the bottom of the stairwell, then cutting off as I climbed, only to start again a few minutes later, when I had unlocked the door and stood breathless in the dim entryway. "I just wanted to see if you'd gotten in from classes," he would say. "And tell you I miss you." Every evening he sat opposite me at the dinner table and asked after the details of my day, patient and careful not to miss a thing.

In the car, Gil's touch is a bright and perfect light. I delay pulling away from his kiss, in the hope that he'll change his mind about coming into the Shachars' apartment. I want to bring him into the building with me, up to where my faceless relatives wait. I'll meet these strangers armed with good news; we'll sit in their living room, sip orange soda, and marvel together over every proof of how loving Gil is.

"Are you sure you won't come?" I ask.

At the door, Tami Shachar accepts the flowers I give her. She seems mildly puzzled. "You didn't have to do that," she tells me.

She is a plain-faced woman, with short light-brown hair tucked behind her ears, and an unnerving air of preoccupation. She smiles briefly as she thanks me. "Welcome." She turns to rummage in a cabinet for a vase.

"We're thrilled to meet you, at long last." The woman who introduces herself as Fanya takes me by the arm and steers me down a narrow hallway into the living room. There, a man I assume to be Nachum Shachar shakes my hand and settles back into a worn armchair. I sit in the chair that Fanya indicates. There is a short silence. Then Fanya, all satisfaction and charm, smooths our way into conversation. In pleased tones and with little assistance, she carries on a discussion of which distant relative I most resemble, which one had honey-colored hair like mine or those same blue eyes and heart-shaped face. I'm very Dutch-looking, Fanya announces. Surely people have told me? Blushing under the attention, I respond to each question. I watch Fanya perched on the edge of the sofa, her legs crossed elegantly at the ankles, and I'm struck by the sharp contrast between this woman and her daughter.

The Shachars' apartment is small and tidy, with a sense of barely restrained clutter. The furniture is simple. Slightly blurry framed posters line the walls, showing wadis carved through pale stone, a view of the

Galilee from the shore. Nachum, seated across from me and listening to his mother-in-law with amusement, is just as I pictured him from his voice on the telephone: wide-faced and stocky, with a heavily stubbled jaw and an easy smile. And playing quietly under a side table is a girl whose name I don't catch. Every now and again she peeks out at me from a house of pillows and cardboard dividers that she builds and re-builds under the awning of the tablecloth.

Now the girl crawls out from under the table and pads over to the sofa in stretched-out pink socks. She taps my wrist, lisping something I have to lean forward to hear. She is eight years old, she informs me, and is going to show me her dolls.

After a few more digressions concerning a great-uncle's famous green eyes and a recollection of my mother's dark hair, Fanya sighs. She pats her hands contentedly on her knees—a sign, I assume, that she is finished with her subject.

Nachum turns to me. "Where's your boyfriend?"

"He had to work tonight. He was sorry he couldn't come, he said to say hello."

"Work, at night?"

"He's very busy," I explain.

"Better he should relax here with us."

"You know, your mother writes to us every few months. She has for years." Fanya speaks as though granting a favor with each statement. "She's an unusual person, yes?"

Passing in and out of the living room, distractedly offering me more Coca-Cola or nuts, Tami says almost nothing as the conversation pro-ceeds. Nachum is telling a story about the workers in his shop, and al-though I don't follow all the details, I see that he's a good storyteller, his laughter ringing out easily as he gestures and pauses and begins anew. All I need to do is nod, and I'm grateful.

Dinner is overcooked vegetables and soggy couscous.

"Thank you, it's very good," I tell Tami, who from the look of it doesn't believe the lie and doesn't care enough to be hurt.

The girl, whose name is Ariela, eats dutifully, one forkful after an-other. Nachum—intrepidly, it seems to me—asks for seconds.

"I'm sorry that you won't get to meet Dov tonight," Fanya says, lay-ing aside her fork. "He arrives only tomorrow. Dov is a fine boy. You'll have to meet him. And he has friends, your age. Good-looking boys."

"Fanya," Nachum says. "Maya has a boyfriend already."

"So what's wrong with a girl having more than one boyfriend?"

"Not me," I assure her solemnly.

Fanya rolls her eyes. "So *serious,* all of you young people."

We sit at the table in silence after we've finished eating. The noise from the street sounds very far away. After a while Fanya excuses herself. Then, at some wordless cue from Tami, Nachum stands and leads me to the living room. I hear the banging of pots from the kitchen.

Nachum is talking about the day's headlines, which apparently had something to do with peace talks. I sip at the coffee I've carried with me from the kitchen; it's black and bitter.

"Peace. If they can make peace here"—he stretches his legs in front of his chair, props one foot atop the other—"they can do anything. If it works, they should go fix up Ireland. Africa, too."

Last night, when I paused over a letter to my mother and asked Gil about the talks under way in Washington, his sarcastic reply surprised me; now I recall a pained expression on his face as well, softening the sharpness of his response. Here in the Shachars' apartment, I repeat Gil's words to see how they sound in my mouth. I say to Nachum, "But how can they expect to make peace if Israelis can't even agree among themselves what they want?"

"Ah." Nachum claps his hands together and squeezes them tight, obviously relishing the opportunity for argument. "Well. I'm not left and I'm not right, understand. I'm not dove or hawk. I'm not anything but a man who runs an electronics shop and knows how to watch out for bad customers and dishonest dealers." His mouth twists wryly. "So I'm not an easy one to convince. Everyone will have to prove they can behave and make peace before *I'll* believe."

Ariela has chosen this moment to climb onto Nachum's knees. Giggling, she lays a plastic doll on his head, then retreats to the sofa to observe. Nachum continues to speak, holding his head at a slight angle so the doll will not fall. "But if we can do it . . . If we can do it, we can do it. What I mean to say is, we *will* do it. If the leaders agree, then the hard-liners and black-hats will make way. They'll have to. And whatever terrorism problems or repercussions come, we'll hold our course."

Tami, circling the living room, hands me a plate of cookies. I balance it on one knee; my coffee cup and saucer rest unsteadily on the other. My first attempt to take a bite of a cookie is short-lived—the plate teeters, and I lower my hand. I glance around for a table, but none is within reach.

I realize that Nachum is awaiting my reply. "Maybe that's right." I stall.

His cocked head is still, giving the impression that he is attending to my every word. I search for something intelligent to say. Frozen in my own precarious pose, I think how ridiculous the two of us must look. "What if Arab terrorism is too strong and moderates are too weak?" I ask. "Or what about the Jewish side? What if the leaders make an agreement, but some Israelis just don't want to give up land for peace?"

Nachum makes a tsking sound, shakes his head slightly. The doll shifts. But somehow it doesn't fall. "People are better than that."

I don't know what to say. I stare at the doll, its coarse blond mane flopped in a synthetic puff over Nachum's thinning hair. "My boyfriend thinks maybe they're not," I blurt. "He says there's no peaceful solution."

Nachum's stiff posture makes me wonder whether I've offended him. "Is that so?" he says, his expression thoughtful. Ariela's doll slides to one side. Just as it's about to drop, Nachum reaches up almost lovingly to catch it.

The soft patter of feet reminds me that Ariela has been watching us. She runs to her father's side as he straightens, then bears the doll safely back to the sofa. Nachum shrugs. "If I believed even half of what's said about us in the American press, I might be inclined to agree with your boyfriend."

I redden at the accusation.

"So why do Americans want to judge us for our problems?" Nachum warms to his new subject. "You also have terrible problems and people warring in your own country. I see it in your movies all the time. Cities, black people and white people fighting."

"But that's different. First of all, black people are American and have the same rights as white people. Plus you have to consider—"

"What about your riots? Last spring. *Los Angeles.*" He pronounces the name with such obvious pleasure, I wonder if it's the sum of his knowledge of English. "This isn't what people do when they think they have rights."

"But that wasn't like—"

"Tell me, do you live in a black people's neighborhood or a white people's neighborhood in America?"

"It's not that simple."

"Look, you criticize us for our situation. Because, for example, we seal off territories after terror attacks. But you seal your neighborhoods too, when you're afraid—all right, so maybe you don't do it with soldiers and barricades, but still, there must be a reason black people don't like to go to white people's neighborhoods in America. Here we suspect strangers in our neighborhood because they're Arab, there you do because they're black. In America, white people put black people in jail all the time. I saw this on the television—black people in jail."

"But it's not that simple. It's—"

"Also, there was a program on militias," Nachum continues meditatively. "This is another thing I don't understand about America. How can you like Hitler after you defeated him?"

I struggle to keep track of the objections and counterobjections competing in my head. "Things are better now in America than they used to be," I begin. "I'm not saying we have it right. But at least we're trying."

Nachum raises one eyebrow in silence.

"Some people are," I say.

"Maybe so. But what I'm getting at is, change isn't easy. Do you go every morning to the other parts of your city and stand on the street shaking hands with people who maybe hate you? It takes more than a few people trying. We haven't figured it out yet, neither have you." He winks at me, then adds generously, "But I believe if it works hard, America can fix itself."

I stare, ashamed that I don't know how to answer him.

I'm relieved to hear Fanya's laughter from behind me. "Let the girl alone. You forget she's not one of you news-crazy Israelis."

"Well, all right." Nachum is smiling. "But of course we're news-crazy. We live in a country with some difficulties."

"Life isn't so easy in America." My face is still hot.

"Ach, you have no idea what living in difficulty is." Nachum shakes a hand at me pleasantly.

"Don't you know how to treat a guest, Nachum?" Fanya scolds. "She's not her mother, her mind isn't filled with these political matters."

"All right," Nachum concedes. "Maybe so."

I'm startled by the crashing of my cookie plate to the floor. The plastic plate bounces, cookies scatter beneath my chair. I wave off all offers of help and clean the mess myself, then escape to the kitchen to dispose of the crumbs. When I return, I don't take my seat again but rather kneel beside Ariela, who is playing with three battered dolls beneath the table. She makes space for me on the carpet as if she'd been expecting me, and presents the dolls in a dumb show: one blond, one brunette, one with a mangy scalp sprouting pink hair. Her silent acceptance of my company is a relief, and I compliment each doll with enthusiasm. Ariela smiles but doesn't reply. If I hadn't heard her speak earlier, I might wonder whether she had a voice at all.

Tami is seated on the sofa; standing behind her, Fanya brushes invisible lint from her skirt. I notice only now that Fanya has fixed her hair and is freshly made up.

"The rest of you can sit around chattering politics all evening if you like," Fanya announces. "I'm going to walk the galleries in Yemin Moshe."

"So late?" Nachum teases, and I see that Tami has a tight look on her face.

"Yes, so late."

"And who is the lucky man this evening, Fanya?" Nachum persists.

Fanya dimples and lets a girlish giggle escape. "Really, Nachum. When I visit Jerusalem I like to go out and see friends. I don't know why you assume there's a gentleman involved. Although there happens to be, this evening. Rafael Berenbaum. He's a friend of the Lebensohns'."

Fanya puts on a pale-blue cardigan, one sleeve at a time. She buttons it carefully and smooths her hair. "Maya, I thought perhaps you'd join us? Breathe a little night air, see what's to be seen?"

I consider the lateness of the hour, wonder whether Fanya will feel the need to inform her friends of other ways in which I'm not like my mother, and can't escape the conclusion that I'd rather spend the remainder of the evening under a table with Ariela. "Do you think I might join you some other time?"

Fanya's soft smile is a promise.

Nachum has hoisted Ariela to his knee and she is whispering excitedly, her hand cupped to his ear. When she has finished, he nods and rests a broad hand on top of her head.

"Why don't you stay the night, Maya," he says. "You've made a friend here."

The invitation catches me off guard, and I smile wholeheartedly for the first time in the evening. "Thank you. But really, I wouldn't want to make trouble."

There is a clucking of tongues from all around; even Ariela has piped up.

"Trouble, what kind of idea is that?" Nachum says. "That's the American in you talking, so formal about everything. Trouble, nonsense. Stay. Stay, you can sleep in Dov's room."

"No, really . . ." I want to show them why I have to get back to my apartment. But I can't think how to explain that I don't want to miss out on the wonder of Gil's tenderness, proving daily that everything is really all right. I can't think how to explain, either, that Gil needs me; that lately when I've been gone too long he seems to crumple. I return to the apartment to find him despondent at his drawing table, speechless with a sorrow that he can't explain and that only my presence seems to relieve.

Ariela is watching me from Nachum's lap. She slides to the carpet and crosses to her mother.

Tami bends stiffly to Ariela's hurried whispers. "No, Maya can't stay in your room with you. She'll stay in Dov's. You can play with her all you want before you go to bed." Tami turns toward me. "That is, if she stays. Maybe she'd rather go home."

"It's not that I want to go," I say. "Not that at all. It's just that Gil doesn't think I'm staying, so—"

Nachum responds with satisfaction. "So if that's all, then you just call your Gil and tell him you'll stay here for the night, and that's the end of it." He opens his palms in an expansive gesture, and I can see why Tami must have fallen in love with him. His eyelids crinkle at the corners and his smile has time in it to spare—it's a broad and leisurely grin that says, Now that wasn't so hard, was it? "It's not every day we have a cousin from America come play with Ariela."

I turn to Fanya for help, but she is gazing at me benignly, as if I am a character onstage who may or may not amuse. "All right," I hear myself say. "I'll have to call and see, maybe. Maybe I'll see if Gil . . ."

Tami points to the telephone.

I cross to the table and lift the receiver. My relatives are standing in a tight band behind me, and the warmth of their united concern undoes in an instant my resolve to leave.

When Gil answers I speak to him in English, but they listen un-abashedly all the same, and I wonder whether they understand.

"Honey?"

"What?" His voice is hoarse, his English tentative. I've woken him from a nap.

"Who's she talking to?" Ariela asks in Hebrew.

"Her beau," Fanya whispers.

"I'm going to be staying here tonight," I tell Gil. The English words feel feathery and buoyant in my mouth.

"I fell asleep," he says. "What time is it?"

"Nine o'clock."

"You're still at the Shachars'?"

"Yes." I want to linger over his English, unsteady and miraculous. It occurs to me that I can unsay what I've said, make my polite excuses to the Shachars and rush home to be with him.

But Gil is speaking again, this time in Hebrew. "Never mind. Never mind, I've got to make some coffee and get back to work. I'll talk to you tomorrow, okay?"

For a few seconds, neither of us speaks. "I love you," I say in Hebrew.

From behind me there is embarrassed shifting. "Give the girl some privacy," Fanya intones.

Gil's voice is faint but clear on the other end of the line. "I love you more. I'll see you in the morning."

Night settles into the apartment with the sound of soft church bells in the distance. Ariela leads me to her bedroom. She chatters to herself, holding dolls and stuffed animals by the legs, laying some down and picking others up and playing out conversations between them. Occasionally she places a plastic figure into my hands with great care. Lying on the floor with her chin to the tile, she addresses me without lifting her eyes from the figures in her hands. "Your mother is sick," she tells me, her fingertips tracing ghostly patterns around her dolls' feet. "Why don't you come live with us?"

"I can visit from where I live," I assure her, but she doesn't pay me any attention. Instead she begins a story, a long and convoluted fairy tale of young girls and an enchanted forest, a precious secret and a magic spell. The three dolls she had earlier seem to play the central roles, the shabby pink-haired one breaking character now and then to explain events for my benefit.

When Tami calls for her to wash for bed, Ariela lets the dolls drop abruptly. Her face has become sharp and careful. Without a word to me, she stands and steps into the hall. Soon Tami's voice rises in exhaustion against a low whine from the girl.

"No, Ariela," Tami is saying. "Tonight you need to try to be a big girl."

After a moment's hesitation, I step out of Ariela's room. Tami nods at me distractedly. She is standing at the far end of the hallway, her back to the bathroom door. I hear Ariela calling from inside.

"Are you there?" The girl's voice quakes with terror.

"I'm here," Tami answers.

There is a pause. Then a scramble as the door opens and Ariela, her eyes big, stands grasping the door handle. "I want it open, I want the door open," she begs.

Tami shakes her head. "We're going to keep it closed this time."

"Open." The girl's face knots. I cringe against now inevitable tears.

"In." Tami directs Ariela back into the bathroom. "Until you finish washing." She closes the door behind her. Then she turns to me, and smiles unconvincingly. "It's good that you came to visit us," she says.

"Thank you for having me."

Tami nods. "I met your mother years ago. She was your age then, more or less." She looks me over, as though startled by her own observation. "Why hasn't she ever come back to Israel?"

"She's wanted to. But her work takes all her time. And money has been tight."

"But you're here."

I feel my cheeks flood with color, although I couldn't say whether it's me or my mother being accused. "I worked and saved money," I explain quickly. "My mother helped, too. She'd been saving money for a trip herself. She was going to come, this summer."

"But then her cancer came back?" Tami says flatly.

"She's feeling much better now."

From behind the closed door comes a faint quaver. "Are you there?"

"Yes, I'm here. You know I'm here. Can't you hear me talking to your cousin Maya?"

"Ima, keep the door open."

"We have a guest here, Ariela."

I find myself wondering what Nachum ever saw in Tami. "It's okay," I say. "Really."

"It's just since the last war." Tami indicates the closed bathroom door with a backhanded gesture. "She doesn't like being shut in."

"It's okay," I say again. "I don't mind if she keeps the door open."

Tami seems not to have heard me.

"Actually, my mother will probably visit Israel next year," I tell her. But my words are made senseless by a whimpering from the bathroom. Ariela is at the door, and then she is somehow out the door and in the hallway, her shorts around her knees and her face streaked with tears.

Anger flashes across Tami's face, and she turns away from the girl. "It's impossible to do anything with her."

"I don't mind, really, she can—"

"She has to learn," Tami says matter-of-factly, and I think she's going to shove Ariela back into the bathroom right away. But I see that she allows her to cling to her knee for a moment in silence before steering her back inside. Ariela goes quietly now, and Tami shuts the door behind her softly.

"Earlier you were explaining your plans . . ." Tami begins, but she seems uneasy.

"I'm going to spend the summer traveling around the country, and then I'm going to enroll for fall courses here. At first I was just going to come to Israel for one semester, but I've changed my plans. I want to study more, see things." I'm echoing what I wrote in a letter to my mother today, and the sound of my own resolve pleases me.

"I'm right here waiting for you," Tami says to the door behind her. Her words sound awkward, and apologetic. She turns back to me. "That's very interesting. What you just said, about your plans."

Ariela is knocking at the door to be let out. She stands in the doorway, sniffling. Although she can't speak, it's clear that she's proud.

"See, it wasn't so bad," Tami says quickly, and steps away from the door, but not before Ariela has reached for her mother's hand. Taken by surprise, Tami pulls away for an instant before catching herself and allowing the girl to slip a hand into hers.

"Go get changed for bed," Tami says after a minute. She seems bewildered. We watch Ariela shuffle to her room.

Something in what I've just seen roots me where I stand; I feel an urgent need to explain it to Tami, although I can't think how. "She really loves you," I say at last.

Tami stares at me, and the expression on her face is almost hopeful. It's the first time that I've seen her animated, and it makes me wonder whether this unfriendly cousin of my mother's doesn't have some soft spot, after all.

Then Tami is shaking her head. "She loves me because I'm her mother." In her voice is a tide of bitterness. Still, her expression retains some eagerness, and when she enters Ariela's room she touches the girl on the forehead, gingerly, as if unaccustomed to the gesture.

When, at last, Ariela goes to sleep, it is only because I have agreed to sit with her. Her bed is low and narrow, and a nightlight sheds a watery glow on a fan-shaped section of floor. Ariela speaks in a whisper, picking up and dropping the dolls that are too many for her hands as she glides them across the bedcovers. She knows each by feel, gauges its shape and heft in the dark. I want to reach out myself and take her hand as she lies in bed, assure her that everything is going to be all right. But I sit with my arms to my sides. "Why don't you come live with us," she says to me as she twines her fingers in a doll's stiff hair. She coos and sighs the dolls to sleep.

※

He is thin. Alone, he climbs these stairs with sketchbook open. Past my apartment door. A shirt hangs loose from his wide shoulders, veins offer themselves on his arms. And in his unknowing hands, secrets of old and young.

Drawings, he carries. Charcoal outlines, figures that blur one into the next. The face of a yeshiva student, filling the paper. Drawings, more drawings, he turns page upon page. There is no need for me to shut the door as he passes, so close I could touch a shoulder. This redheaded adam's-apple boyfriend does not look at me, and when he does he will not see. He knows how not to notice what does not interest him and so I can look until I am sated.

Black by black, haunted face by haunted face. I see he draws this neighborhood. Pale boys and gaunt elders, charcoal-black eyes. Charcoal eyes, smoke-lit faces, figures dissolve to ash at the edge of his page. He does not understand, still he draws and will not rest.

After he has passed I whisper into my dark room what I know.

They died in a flurry of words, the blacks. Praying to their east, their precious east, praying to the east side of the camp at sunset sunrise: to smokestacks. Whispering psalms while they worked sorting machine parts and golden jewelry, children's clothing. They never fit on this earth. Even among us they did not belong. In uniforms, even, heads shaved and no kerchiefs on the women, you could see which were the ones.

Mother always told me. The blacks are different. They're not like you and me. Primitive people. Simple like children and dangerous. People keeping once upon a time, yes, a packed suitcase beside the door, in case in the middle of the night the messiah. And the family would be ready. People who refused to belong, could not belong like everyone else. Could not see, they were a public spectacle earning the rest of us the revulsion of passersby. Mother hated the blacks, she said.

No one could touch the blacks. No one. Not even then, not even in camp. Wearing their sorrow like a shield, saying their mourning prayers before we even had a chance to die. Holding the world at bay with their precious faith. One could not touch them, one cannot touch them, even this very moment they escape understanding, their swirling gestures fade to dusk on the margins of a page.

And this redheaded boy. Trying to fix them with his charcoal as if he could capture what no one can. Above my head, he jingles keys. A door opens and shuts, he treads the length of the apartment, drops kitchen things and curses. He is a knotted branch, a broken child. When the American returns he will rain his own devotion on her pale American skin, he will punish her love of him. Again there will be cries and silence, she will stumble before his small fury.

Such fury as cannot frighten me.

How they died like faithful servants, humming the story of their own sorrow. A line of them. A breeze, the shine of leaves rippling on trees past the fences. The sky clear blue high over camp. And one, waiting at the end of the line for death, looking back at me and saying, nothing.

I could not turn my eyes from his.

Mother, you were gone already, you could not have seen the slow-burning cinder of his gaze.

Evening passes. I sit beside the door until long after dark. My back is stiff, my knees bruise against the suitcase beside the stool. I am awaiting American footsteps. For now that she has revealed her secret, I will

*unravel my own for her sake. I will prepare for the day of her triumph,
every story I will lay at her feet.*

*When I slide down to the floor it is night. I am faint from hunger.
Oh Lilka. How you would have cried.*

∞

Tami is waiting for me when I step, blinking, into the hallway. "I've set
up Dov's room for you," she says.

I go to the door Tami indicates. Inside are a single bed, a small desk,
a wall hung with magazine clippings that I cannot make out in the dim
light from the hall. The room feels shadowy and cavernous until Tami
reaches behind me to flip a switch. Jolted into light, the room is stark,
its four walls confining.

She indicates the towels and T-shirt folded at the foot of the made-
up bed. "If there's anything else you need, let me know."

"Thank you." I stand in the center of her son's room and wait for her
to go. Still she lingers in the doorway, until I'm convinced there's something she'd like to ask me.

"Good night," she says, finally.

As soon as she's gone, I close the door. Then I turn off the lights. I
like the room better this way. In the dark the space expands once more,
and as I undress, each shadow gradually transforms itself into an identifiable object.

The T-shirt is a soft, worn cotton and must belong to Tami. I pull it
over my head, noticing how the fabric has stretched to the shape of a
body different from mine. Crawling between the sheets, I dip my feet
to the cool perimeter of the bed and realize that this is the first night
I've slept alone in months. Gil, I imagine, is still working. He'll work
until he's so tired he thinks he can defeat his insomnia. If this is a good
night he'll fall asleep quickly, his breath slow and even.

I think I can picture your apartment almost perfectly now, my mother
wrote in her last letter. *It sounds beautiful.*

With one fingertip I trace a circle on my cheek. I press lightly here
and there, confirming what I know—it isn't tender any longer. Although the mark has almost disappeared, I've been careful to apply
makeup several times each day. Recalling Fanya's scrutiny of my features,
I'm grateful for my vigilance. I complete my exploration of the curve

of my cheekbone and find nothing amiss. The smoothness of the healed skin is comforting, yet it makes me uneasy as well.

The air is still, and a mosquito whines nearby, dipping closer every few minutes. One window, across the room, is partially open. A strip of tape, I now notice, hangs from its frame; I imagine someone starting to peel it away but becoming absentminded. The other window is sealed on all sides. The tape glints in the moonlight, and I sit up to look. This was the Shachars' "Saddam-proof" room, Fanya explained to me, where the family slept during the SCUD attacks two winters ago. I examine the shadowed furniture with renewed interest. It occurs to me to wonder why Nachum and Tami haven't bothered to unseal the windows. Although I know Gil would laugh at me for this foolishness, I tell myself: It's as if someone still lives here, secretive and quiet, awaiting the next war.

Or maybe, like people back home who leave Christmas lights up until spring, the Shachars just stopped noticing the tape on the windows. I'm ashamed at this thought, and recall what Nachum said about Americans and our easy lives.

Back in Purchase, I watched the escalation of the crisis on television, each broadcast heralded by the station's bold Persian Gulf logo and musical motif. The war we watched from my dormitory lounge was ungainly, a rough and poorly timed pageant of gas masks, missiles, an Israeli spokesman with his head held high. And then stretches of empty sky as the camera wavered and dipped, and the American newscaster, nervous as a schoolboy on his rooftop halfway around the world, speculated to fill airtime until the next missile.

Over the telephone, my mother's voice was tense with worry. "I want to be there," she said. "I want to be with the family there."

It was my first year of college, and although I'd been watching the broadcasts with an oddly personal dread, I found myself impatient with my mother's praise of brave Israel and all its hardships. In just one phone call, her dedication to Israel undermined any connection I might feel— as though she and I were rivals staking out loyalties, and first dibs trumped all. "What would you accomplish by running off to Israel?" I challenged her. "It's not like you could win the war for them."

During the silence that followed, I realized that I sounded jealous.

"You don't understand the way I feel about these things," she said.

"You're just like your father, you know." I held the receiver loosely, recognizing it for the foreign object it was; why didn't I just put it down, instead of holding it to my ear as my mother continued? Anger hollowed my head and filled it with static. "That's just fine. I don't ask you to understand, Maya. Only don't pretend you do if you don't."

Watching the war at parties, at late-night pizza study sessions, and even at dinner when the resident advisor wheeled a television set into the cafeteria, I grew irritated at the newscaster's uneasy repetitions and the camera operator's unsteady hand. Under that explosion-lit sky were relatives I'd never met, places my mother had tried to tell me about. I saw a report showing sealed rooms and children with gas masks, and the pride I felt was shot through with resentment at those curving streets and drowsy children for being a part of the world my mother knew I wasn't cut out for. "It's crazy to live like that," someone said. Silently I agreed.

Around that time, during one of our brief twice-monthly conversations, my father asked as usual after my mother. Someone had sent him a clipping of a newspaper article about her work. The writer had made the usual big deal over her name, titling the article "Hope for the Hopeless." My mother had made some good points in the interview, my father conceded. And, he said, he was fond of the part where she called the city planners Neanderthals.

"Yeah," I agreed. "But after that article came out, she decided no more interviews. She says it changes nothing, and wastes her time. Apparently, everyone applauded her when it was printed, and no one donated money."

"That's a shame." He fell uncharacteristically silent, lost in thought. Then he asked, "How's she managing with the war on?"

"You know, Dad." My laughter hit a higher pitch than usual. "She wants to be over there."

The background ringing of his office phones seemed to rouse him. "That's crazy," he declared. "She wants to go visit a war? Does she think it's a party? War is hell."

"She says she can't stand watching on television and not being able to do anything. She wants to be there. She says the only reason she doesn't just go and buy a ticket is that there's some new program she's got to hold together this month at the Center."

"The woman has been through advanced cancer, for God's sake.

You would think she'd had enough chemicals in her life. What's she going to do, go over and get gassed to show solidarity for some country where she's never even paid taxes?"

Once again I was guilty accomplice in the petty mockery that kept me from feeling close to my father, or accepting more than a handful of his invitations to visit in San Diego. There, beside the swimming pool his new wife and sons enjoyed, my father recalled his days in the movement as a youthful enthusiasm properly deployed, and properly left behind. He wasn't the turncoat my mother thought, and I'd told her so time and again. He'd just become more . . . regular. Still, I kept a distance that appeared to puzzle him. The two of us couldn't talk for long without alighting sarcastically on the subject of Hope in a way that left me feeling ashamed: perhaps her criticisms of both of us were right, after all.

I knew my mother was only half right when she said my father had no stomach for hardship. My father could be as tough as she, when he wanted. The problem was simply that it exhausted him.

When I was seven years old, my mother was too tired to do laundry, too tired to eat—too tired to speak to me right now, my father said. Every third week the chemotherapy gripped her body and she retreated to the sickroom; I was instructed to go outside and find some friends to play with. But I exited the front door only to pacify my father. Minutes later I crept through the house, going as near as I could to my mother's room before my father reprimanded me.

Once, when my father was downstairs doing laundry, I stood in the doorway of her room. Her face was gaunt and shadowed. Her nightgown was askew and I could see the shiny pink seam of her mastectomy. Her lids were lowered, and I thought she must be sleeping.

Then she saw me. In her haste to cover herself, she knocked over a bedside lamp. It fell with a crash. She gazed at me. She stared at my face, my thin arms and legs, my pigtails, and her eyes drank me in until I was certain that, at any second, she would ask me to come to her.

"Go, Maya," she said.

I went. Downstairs in the laundry room, my father's long, controlled exhalation masked the approach of my footsteps. I watched him hunch his wide shoulders over the sink, wringing my mother's kerchiefs with his fingertips as if afraid of the fabric's touch. When he was finished, he reached down to clear the drain of clumps of my mother's hair. I teetered between retreating to the front yard and stepping forward to

offer some kind of comfort I couldn't fathom. Time after time, I simply stood and watched.

When the doctor declared the chemotherapy a success, I was eight
years old. "Remission" was a magical word: my father pronounced it like
the sudden sweep of a breeze, my mother like the rain breaking through
a stifling afternoon. In school, my teacher granted it to me like a prize,
like "gold star" or "milk monitor" or "A-plus-plus." And then no one
pronounced it anymore. No one needed to. The word had spread like
a firework, branched and hung for a moment overhead, and was gone.
My father leaned against the refrigerator and cried.

It was when "remission" was no longer a magical word, when it had
fallen to the earth in ashy traces and was forgotten, that my mother went
back to her work at the Center. My father, home so often during the
worst weeks of her treatment, disappeared once more into what my
mother called "your father's commute suit." Now when I let myself into
the house after school there was no one in the sickroom to greet me,
only the sound of curtains blowing against wallpaper. I stopped my
nightly bargaining with a god I believed in only murkily, although for
weeks I continued to keep each solemn promise: homework in exchange for remission, chores in exchange for remission, pretending I
wasn't hungry when my mother offered dessert. Eventually these
promises faded. In their place, I practiced memory. In the Hebrew after-
school program that my mother insisted I attend twice a week, we
spent that spring learning about the Holocaust. The teacher sang songs
of mourning, recited stories meant to keep the lost ones alive. And she
taught us that remembering was what would keep this thing from happening again. *Never again* and *never forget;* we could keep disaster from
recurring if only we were watchful.

Every night I whispered into the expectant darkness the story of my
mother's cancer, so it could not return. The luminous numbers of the
bedside clock flipped with a barely audible pat—every minute, every ten
minutes, every half-hour. I followed the ritual each night for months
after she was well.

Everything my mother had always wanted to do she now embraced.
A history class, extra volunteer work in Queens, a course to refresh her
memory of Hebrew. No longer careful with her energy, she flung it like
a net to the far corners of her world. She renewed her work at the Center, loosing her growing staff on the city's worst illnesses as though to

confirm that she herself no longer needed saving. She left the house early every morning, and continued making telephone calls hours after her return from the city every afternoon. The house buzzed with activity and smelled of carry-out Chinese food; brisk steps sounded in the entryway. My father spent his evenings playing basketball with the neighborhood fathers. As for me, I chafed at my mother's busyness during the daylight, and after dark I was absentminded. Drifting to sleep, too old now for my mother's bedtime singing, I would start guiltily and swear to be vigilant. I'd begin the whispered litany, and fall asleep before I was through.

I outgrew my mother's taste in clothing, packed my own lunch for school. I learned how to join in on the other girls' scorn for the enthusiasms of the Hebrew school teacher, and then how to cut class altogether. And I told my first lie: Yes, I'd been there, but nothing had happened worth telling. Now when my mother taught me words from the Hebrew poems she'd translated painstakingly on the subway, I forgot to listen. And on the single occasion when, coming down the hallway, she whispered a secret message to me in Hebrew, I was too embarrassed to admit I hadn't learned the words.

Months passed. My father argued that he wanted a romantic dinner once in a blue moon, he didn't see why my mother had to run off to work every hour of day and night. "How did you get to be a stranger?" my mother accused. I watched my father go from the kitchen into the hallway, rubbing with one hand at a tightness in his shoulders. It was a summer of heat waves and a daily paper route; with my new bicycle I ranged beyond our street and discovered the boys on adjacent blocks. I'd lost patience for stories about a ship almost taken to Haifa in '58; over and again I promised my mother that I'd get around to writing to my Israeli cousin Dov, so we could be pen pals as she wanted. *Next week, maybe.* I stopped promising, started rolling my eyes instead. My father threw out his back. Classes, like everything else my mother said she loved, fell prey to her schedule; her Hebrew died on the vine. She called attention, then, to each of my father's failings, and my father's accusation—*humorless*—rang in every room of the house.

It was August, and the newspaper lay unopened on the kitchen table. "I have enough of my hair back now, don't you think?" My mother, reattempting a wispy braid, stood in front of the mirror. She smiled, tightly, at my reflection. She'd stopped wearing her kerchief the week before, just after my father said he was leaving for good. I watched her fit a cloth pad into the left cup of her brassiere. She turned away from the mirror and hurriedly fastened the clasp across her back. "Your father called to see how you are. He'll call again in a few days, when he's found a place to live."

My father moved to Manhattan that year, to California four years later. My mother and I stayed in White Plains. Our usual movements, now echoing in the too big house, seemed fierce and unfamiliar, and quickly undid whatever it was that had made us try to understand each other. "Thanks for driving him away," I muttered when I thought she was just beyond earshot. At every crossroads in school I picked the simpler path, at every choice I made it easier for her to give up on me. I quit Hebrew school without warning one afternoon in the seventh grade, after a guest rabbi lectured on the idea of the chosen people. *Why are we chosen? Because God wants us to repair the world. What are we chosen for? To suffer.* One of my friends said she was sick of all the precious gloom, she didn't see why we needed to suffer, too, just because some rabbi couldn't keep his lectures short. We spent our final hour of class chewing pickles in Mama Lily's Diner and vowing never to set foot in Hebrew school again. "Let our people go," my friend snickered when another gleeful classmate joined us.

Somewhere on the rim of the valley, a bus brakes. From down the hall I hear Ariela shifting in bed.

Dear Maya, my mother wrote only last week, *I still don't know why you hesitated all that time to tell me you wanted to go to Israel. I would have found a way to help you go years earlier, if you'd only let me know.*

Suddenly my body feels clumsy, my chest weighted. Struggling to breathe in the close air of this room, I kneel on the bed, my panic growing with every second. If only I'd been more careful. I should never have strayed so far, resisted her so childishly.

Gradually, my breathing slows. I press my hands to my temples. She's fine, her letters say. She's going to be fine.

I know, of course, that being vigilant could never possibly have kept the cancer away. Still, recalling the magic of my childhood promises, I can't help but wonder what I could have sacrificed, what penance I could have observed, that would have banished the sickness for good. I promise myself that I'll double my vocabulary lists, make up word-remembering rhymes. *Refuah, refed, refaim,* I'll continue memorizing sections from the Hebrew dictionary. I'll visit the places she'd want to see, retrieve more of the missing pieces of her puzzle.

Outside, the leaves make only a dry rustle. The moon lights the floor beneath the windows, casting long shadows across the room. It lights, too, that peculiar half-hole in the wall over the desk, where the plaster is smashed. I listen for a while to the sounds of this building, voices winding faintly up the stairs, the long creak of a shutter. A radio plays in another apartment, music mixed with news spoken in a man's low voice.

I can almost hear the breathing of the people in the apartments all around me. I sit motionless, hardly breathing myself. And I think: Perhaps it isn't so wrong, living here in this room, with flashes lighting the sky overhead and sirens banding together across the sky. I picture a wide-open, enchanted night, the city's low buildings spellbound. The missiles are things of strange and stately beauty, rolling and rushing smoothly through a dark sky, giving off pieces of themselves to the night. I can see it all through the window, from where I sit in this room. A patch of fire, sinking, lights a ragged trail, and the missiles, pinned against the sky for an instant like rare night moths caught by the flash of a camera, are frozen mid-flight, preserved in black and white and shadow against any future that might deny them. The explosions, when they come, are silent too. Countermissiles hurl themselves unseen from the ground and shower the earth with debris, while families crouch face to face below.

The picture mesmerizes me, and it is some time before I realize I've left out all the sound. Blaring sirens and whistling air, and ragged breath in the crowded darkness of this room. I realize, too, that no missiles actually fell here in Jerusalem; the long nights of fear brought only the news of more distant explosions, in Tel Aviv and Haifa and elsewhere. And I know, above all, that what I've thought is terrible. That there could never be anything beautiful about living under such a sky, such a night.

Yet something about the picture holds me; I have a feeling of being so close to a simple truth that I can almost see its shape in the moonlight. As if here in this room we are larger than life—we are more than anyone outside could ever know, more than even we could have expected. As if there is nothing more real than this room, this night. As if this sealed room is the most beautiful place in the world.

I fall asleep thinking of Gil, and his voice rises and falls in my mind like a fitful wind. Tomorrow we will be together again. We will share news of our day, we will sit on our balcony in the evening and laugh quietly and watch the clouds pass across the sky. I am certain that if I am careful, we can be happy.

✍ 8 ✍

The American is gone.

Left as the sun was beginning its descent and did not return even for the awakening of the streetlamps, and still she is not back. No American footsteps above, overhead no American sounds. Without the American, the night catches its breath. Without her the pulse of the street falters.

Across a bed cold slanting bars of moonlight. Quiet footsteps, a tap runs and shuts. Night, and I cross-legged on taut covers. Night, and I trembling stillness. Night, I run palms across a blanket worn to gauze.

I must not close my eyes this night for fear I will miss her return.

For without Americans, there is nothing. Without them there is no time, without them the world cannot renew, without them there is only death. Americans promise future.

Long ago the American's boyfriend drove her away in his car. Long ago the American's boyfriend returned alone, turned page after page seeking comfort. Long ago, evening quieted the street, even the blacks settled in silence. And still the American did not return, my heart wept bitter tears. Into the darkness I stretch my arms: Why have you forsaken me?

And after the war, they said to me, Forget the past. They said, Put it behind you. At the bus station, at the seashore, I tried to tell what needed telling. No one would hear. Don't think about such things, they counseled. This is a new country, a bright country, it will banish our nightmares. See how they wither under this sun. Only Feliks came to hear me, and he would not stay to hear all. He too succumbed, he fell in love with the healthy and the new. So long ago, the world wound itself around others' hands and left me barren.

But the Americans will not forsake us. The Americans will come to start a world again. To right things, to make sense out of all. It has been promised. It was promised, in Dachau.

Rumors came of American armies, there came life to my sister Halina's eyes. No word was spoken but a current stirred in her. Then I recognized my sister. In this typhus skeleton was again Halina, eyes the light-streaked brown of chestnuts. All around us hearts beat once more, now in these skeletons lived a future, coming closer with every American step. Without a word, without a glance to me or a look to the sky for airplanes, Halina prayed somewhere inside herself for Americans. I knew it in the lowering of her eyelids. Americans to end this death that has always been and will always be and can never end. Americans to bring a future. Americans to make time that has twined upon itself unravel, and begin again.

Bars of light on the bed, silence from this Jerusalem street. For so many days the American has lived above me and now, now just as I begin to understand, just as I see that I must prepare for her with all my strength, now that I see it is me she has come for, me she will save, now she has gone.

Her boyfriend paces upstairs, until sleep overtakes him and he is silent.

And when dawn grays this room and dissolves these cold bars, I wrap my arms around shivering knees and listen. Morning footsteps winding in the stairwell, how this building echoes without an American. How stones tumble slowly to earth, how weeds crumble to dust, abandoned.

The last of night fades, now I hear the voices from bunks all around me, we are four to a plank and blanketed in stink. Doubt flows from their open mouths, they tell me the American has left and will not return. She has left you, they say, she is gone. She has left you with nothing to eat, nothing to drink but this moment, stink fills our nostrils with shit.

I stand to my feet in this dim apartment, my hands grope after such voices. No, I sing to them, my throat tears in anguish. You cannot take her from me, she whom I have just found. She will return. The American will come for me. I believe.

I believe with perfect faith.

And when she comes she will bring the redemption. When she comes, I sing to the voices, she will vanquish memory, free us from this past.

It is daylight when the voices fall silent. I sit by the door. My body is a withered arbor, splintering with exhaustion. Once more I reach to assure myself of this suitcase, packed with everything I will need. I am ready for my redemption. Now I wait.

The American will come. The American will come, even if she tarries.

Day is here, soon the street will be full of blacks. Upstairs the American's boyfriend turns on his heel. We wait, he and I.

For our American.

In my dream I am onstage, alone. It is the spring recital at school in Purchase, and from nowhere comes a fast, tinkling piano melody, played only for me. Seeing no one else onstage, I step toward the audience; I mean to see what holds them there so expectant in the dark. But the music grabs me and I can't help dancing, and when I whirl hard to the floor my hair brushes the stage. The auditorium fills with the flutter of translucent pages, and I hear, amid this strange applause, the sound of my mother's two hands celebrating at long last. Raising myself, bruised, from the stage, I turn to her with anger burning in my eyes. But the stage lights blaze in her face, and she cannot see me at all.

I wake with a start. It is warm here, and very bright. The taped windows of this room seem to vibrate with heat, and the morning sun reaching through one dusty pane paints a sharp white rectangle on the center of the floor, where my sandals are tumbled toe to toe. Lazily I raise my head.

In the doorway stands a soldier. He is watching me, one hand braced against the top of the door frame, one resting on the hinged stock of the machine gun slung on a strap across his chest.

I sit, pull at my T-shirt, tuck my hair behind my ears, and stammer like an intruder caught spying. "I'm your cousin," the apology comes out in halting Hebrew. "Maya."

He is tall and squarely built; his hair is close-cropped, and a red beret is tucked into an open trouser pocket of his khaki uniform. His face is suntanned, and his forehead and the corners of his dark eyes are marked with deep creases; it strikes me that he's been squinting against a cloudless sky for so long that his face bears not only the sun's engraving, but the proof of his resistance to it.

A silence grows in the space between us. I think of a dozen things to say. But there's something about him I don't want to disturb, a tension animating his lean frame. When at last he speaks, I understand that he does so only because he has chosen to—that had he not chosen to speak, the silence would have gone on and on.

"Dov," he says.

As I wait for him to say more, the shadow of a branch sweeps the sun-flooded windowpane, and the room appears to swing in the breeze. The trick of the light makes my cousin's face waver between boyhood and manhood. I see that he is my age, or younger: twenty-one, or twenty.

His eyes flicker to the window, as if he's noticed something, too.

"Sorry to take your room," I tell him. "I can be out in just a minute."

He makes a slight motion with his hand—that won't be necessary. Rocking forward in the doorway once more, he reaches up to tag the ceiling.

It's clear to me that he has no use for an American cousin.

"Didn't mean to wake you," he says. Then he's gone.

I dress hastily. When I step into the kitchen I see everyone is awake. They're seated around the table, a tousled and intent circle. Tami pours coffee with fierce concentration. Only Nachum looks up when I enter, and he invites me to the table with a smile. Ariela is seated on the yoke of his shoulders, her knees loose around his neck. Fighting to keep her eyes open, she droops on top of his head like a nightcap in an old children's storybook.

"Dov was just telling us about the training he's conducting," Nachum informs me, "for the new soldiers. He's commanding a unit of paratroopers, he's got some boys right out of high school."

"Let's get that right," Dov interjects. "I'm commanding a unit of paratrooping *hopefuls*. They've got a long way to go before they'll measure up." There is an economy to all my cousin's movements; his mouth opens no more than necessary when he speaks. Now, however, he lets out a proud laugh. "They're not so bad, though. Give me a few months, they'll be the best."

Nachum is grinning. "I'm not surprised," he says. On his shoulders Ariela blinks herself awake and taps his forehead to be lowered.

Dov cuts himself a thick slice of bread and bites into it as if he hadn't eaten in weeks.

On the wall above the kitchen table is a clock whose hands are stuck at the hour of three twenty-five. A layer of dust coats its glass face; I wonder how long it's been broken.

Fanya scolds Dov through a pretty smile. "Just don't let it go to your head," she counsels. "Pretend you don't know you're a hero, that's my advice. The girls will fall over each other to get to you." Fanya summons Ariela to a stool by her knees. "Or have you already stopped noticing all the girls except one, Dov? What's going on with that Rina, from your high school class?"

Tami passes me sugar and milk without a word. No one has so much as glanced at her since I entered the room. Like me, she seems a stranger, detached from the warmth of this gathering and easily forgotten.

Fanya reaches for her handbag, undoes the clasp with meticulously painted fingernails, and pulls out a comb. She parts Ariela's fine hair and smooths it straight to either side. "Look at your brother," she says. "He's blushing."

Dov turns away. I see that his ears are a deep red.

While Fanya combs her own hair, Ariela leans over to me and whispers, "Dov has a girlfriend." Her face is soft from sleep and washed of the fear of the previous night. "And do you know what?" Her breath is warm in my ear. I shake my head and she continues. "Do you know what? His soldiers are so tired at the end of a day, they want to sleep for a million years." Ariela giggles, pleased.

Still flushed from his grandmother's teasing, Dov looks around the kitchen. His eyes light, unexpectedly, on me. "How long will you be in Israel?" he asks.

"Maya came to Jerusalem for a semester." Tami speaks up abruptly. "She's staying the summer."

"I'm staying for more than one semester," I correct her. "I'm enrolling for the fall, too."

Dov looks me over as sternly as he would one of his recruits. "Don't just stay in classes the whole time, you won't see the real Israel."

"Maya has a boyfriend." Tami chimes in once again. She's looking at something in a cabinet and doesn't turn when she speaks. "He'll take her around."

Sipping my coffee, I deliberate, then make the confession to Tami's back. "Actually, Gil is working very hard. He has a new job. So I haven't yet traveled quite as much as I'd like. Maybe you can suggest places I should visit?"

"You ought to see everything." Fanya snaps the comb back into her handbag and appraises me. For a moment I think she's going to retrieve the comb and fix my hair, too. "So long as you're already in this country, you may as well travel Israel top to bottom. There's not as much to see as in some other places, but there are things. I'll take you to concerts, and you must also visit the countryside. If you can't stand the driving here, then find some nice American tour group and go along in their bus."

"Why?" The single word sounds harsh in the small kitchen. Dov faces his grandmother. It's obvious he's still defensive from her earlier teasing. "So she can be one of those Americans who go to every tourist spot and think they know something about Israel?"

"Dov, don't be rude." Fanya dismisses him with a lift of her chin.

"But it's true. You know what the tour buses are like." Dov's voice is bitter. "Haven't you seen the newspapers? Everyone taking opinion polls in America about how to make peace—what, American Jews who have gone on maybe one bus tour know a damn thing about what it means to live here?"

"Don't be rude," Fanya repeats. She is not smiling now. "And watch your language around your sister." She turns and addresses me energetically. "But now you see, it's perfect that Dov has such strong feelings about this matter." Fanya's enthusiasm requires a response, and I bob my head at her as she connects me and my cousin with a wave. "Dov, you show Maya everything. That way she'll see whatever it is you think necessary. You can begin today—a person shouldn't waste a single day when she could be out exploring."

Nachum lays a hand lightly on Dov's shoulder. "Everything?" he says. "Fanya, Dov has to get back to his base tomorrow morning."

"So he can start showing Maya around now, and show her more when he's home next."

"I'm sure Dov has a lot to do while he's home." I say. "Really, it's fine. And anyway, I have some travel plans of my own."

"Nonsense. He'd love to show you around. Wouldn't you, Dov?" Fanya insists with a lilt that could be described only as fetching. I try to picture the beauty she must have been forty years ago. Even now, she has an undeniable grace. She's swept away her grandson's challenge without a ripple on her smooth forehead.

Dov stares into the bottom of his coffee cup, then looks up at me. His face is expressionless. "Sure, why not," he says.

I look away from him, embarrassed. "I'm sorry," I say. "I can't, today. I'd better go. I promised Gil I wouldn't be late."

"Next time, then," Fanya declares.

"Next time."

Dov nods his good-bye.

When I open the door to the apartment, Gil is standing just inside. "I heard you coming." It's obvious he hasn't slept. "Come into the living room, I've got to show you something."

"What is it?" I'm still holding the door open, as if I might retreat— down the stairs and out into the sunshine, perhaps as far as the Shachars' crowded kitchen. "Shouldn't you be at work?"

"Work?" Gil's wan face stretches in a grin. Puzzled, I shrink back as he comes near, but he doesn't seem to notice. He kisses me on the mouth. "I *am* working. Forget the gallery. I called in sick."

The living room is a dizzying corridor of paper and wind. Gil leads me by the hand. He has run a string the length of the room, from door to balcony and back two times over, and clipped to it his sketches of the yeshiva students. I had no idea he'd done so many—sheet after sheet, men's and boys' faces defined in spare charcoal lines. Somewhere in the night he must have used the final sheet of his sketchpad; the last few figures tremble on the onion-skin translucence of my airmail paper.

Gil is standing in the center of the room watching me. Beneath his smile, I'm amazed to notice, he's nervous. He waits for my response.

I scan the drawings.

"This is just the beginning, of course," he says.

He's searching for a sign of my appreciation, and for some reason I move even more slowly along the rows of drawings. Gil follows me.

"Don't you see?" he says. "I've found it. The subject for my exhibit."

I turn to look at him. "The blacks?"

Gil indicates a drawing of a boy; all that can be seen is a black skullcap and the soft outline of the boy's cheek. "There's something about them I don't understand," Gil says. "It's like this." He is reaching for words and looks to me for help, but I have nothing to offer. "They see something no one else sees. No matter what, they just keep hoping for their deliverance. Or whatever it is that they hope for, who knows exactly what. They've got their heads full of hundreds of years of tradition and their eyes on some world-to-come the rest of us can't comprehend—they hardly even notice today. Everything around them shows that they shouldn't believe, but they do. It makes no sense, still they do." Gil stands beside me as I look at a sketch of a bearded middle-aged man. "Everyone is cynical, except for them."

His eyes ask my approval.

I say nothing. I'm thinking about the blacks and their singing and their traditions. Now I'm ashamed of myself for not admitting the yeshiva student who came to our door, and glad I never mentioned him to Gil, who can see things in our religious neighbors that I can't.

His fingers, reaching to touch one sheet after another, are gentle, and his words are soft as he tells me, "I wish I could be like them."

I think: I could love him forever.

It's only the faces of the black-hatted men that keep me from pouring out my affection to Gil. The haunted and expectant expression of an elderly man, captured in a series of layered drawings, glowers at me. Avoiding the old man's gaze, I ask, "This is the project you're going to exhibit?"

"Yes. This is the project I've been waiting for." His mood is turning sharp.

"Gil." I cup his cheeks with my two palms. "You're going to do an incredible job."

A smile blooms on his face. He hugs me hard.

"When is the exhibit?" I ask into his chest.

"Roni says he can give me a spot at the end of the summer, between two big shows. He said if I can be ready by then, he can bring in some critics. He thinks it will be a big opportunity even if it's just a short exhibit. I told him of course I can be ready. It's going to take a lot out of me, Maya, but I know I can do the work in time."

"What exactly are you planning?"

Gil hesitates. Then he winks. "It's a surprise."

The afternoon passes to the sound of Gil working in the living room. In the kitchen I make my way through the Hebrew newspaper, dictionary open on the table before me. When I bring Gil cold melon for a snack, his eyes brim unmistakably with gratitude; I'm ashamed at the smallness of my gift. "Just don't go leaving me again for this family of yours," he jokes. "A few moments last night, I thought you might run off and never return." His lips, when he brushes them against mine, are chapped, and his eyes are shadowed.

Just before dinner there is a long period of quiet. In the living room, Gil's charcoal is motionless. When I call him to the kitchen, he is moody, and only shrugs when I ask how the work is going. "Your project is going to be incredible," I say, but this time he doesn't seem moved by my approval. Still, over shnitzel and salad he seems to recover and asks for the details of my visit. I describe Fanya, Tami, and Nachum, then Dov and Ariela. "The girl is eight," I tell him. "And the boy, he's near my age."

"Ah." Gil munches a piece of cucumber. "And what does he do in our nation's blessed army?"

"Paratrooping."

"Lucky fellow, to be in a select unit," Gil mocks. "Best at all the war games." He leans back in his chair, balancing on two legs. "So, Maya, do you want to know more about how the army gets the best and the brightest?"

I wait for him to continue.

"When I took the psycho-technic exams for army placement," he instructs me, "my teachers couldn't understand the results. I was first in all my classes, so why on earth didn't I end up in a prestigious unit?" Gil gasps in pretend astonishment. " 'Shocking! And such a pity.' "

He lowers the front legs of his chair until they reach the tile with a quiet tap. "I threw the damn tests, Maya. Sat in the room and whistled tunes until the monitors came in to tell me time's up. I wasn't going to give an ounce of my energy to that crap. All those boys like your cousin are being taken for a ride."

After dinner, we walk through our neighborhood and up beyond the valley, turning unfamiliar corners until well past dusk. The cool night air is so refreshing I'd be glad to keep walking. But Gil is restless to get back to the apartment. We return to the silent valley under thundering stars.

In the living room, where I carelessly opened a window to air the apartment while we were out, the afternoon's sketches are scattered on the floor. One by one, Gil picks them up. The slide of each page against tile is a cry of dust and despair. The snap of Gil's voice is terrifyingly precise, like water splashed on simmering oil.

∞

And the American has returned, I knew she would not forsake me. So long I have waited. Now I nod to the blacks' signs as I pass. I am preparing. Each day I rehearse all I will explain to her; I wander in a haze of hours, years flit like shadows. At last she will come for me, my joy will know no bound. Already we are almost together. I pace my apartment and her footsteps caress the ceiling above me. The sound of her thin voice halts my progress across the floor, and I: I stand rigid with expectation.

∞ 9 *∞*

July 18, 1993

Dear Maya,

Here we're sweltering in the humidity. It's a struggle just to breathe, the kids want to go to the pool every day and I don't have the heart to insist on anything else. I'd send them to a movie—at least there would be air-conditioning—but of course we can't spare the money.

I deeply appreciated your description of the waterfalls in the north. It sounds so beautiful, what with all those flowers in the middle of that rugged landscape. Your letters add color to my days that, I'll admit, is much needed.

The only view available through my barred window is of wreckage. I don't mean just physical decay, but lives gone to ruin, and a few sparks of optimism that don't live long. Most of them get snuffed no matter what anyone does.

And would you believe, a politics addict like me has finally stopped reading the newspaper? At first it was because of spotty delivery—par for the course in this neighborhood. Then it was my own exhaustion. I'm tired of reading about wrongheaded policies, pronouncements that don't go anywhere. All those political analysts who have never set foot in a neighborhood like this speculating on why children end up in jail. It's not only ignorance, it's willful ignorance, and that's a crime.

I don't mean to lecture. I suspect you've always hated it when I do. But this blank paper seems to invite me to relieve my mind.

People wonder why I've marooned myself here. Most of my old friends have given up on all the causes they used to work for. Sometimes I think America has become a country of amnesiacs. Maybe it always has been—maybe I deluded myself in thinking it could ever be different.

But whether it's out of forgetfulness or simply distaste or shame, my old friends don't call me anymore. Frankly, I don't call them either. A few still do anti-poverty work—they commute from the suburbs, where they live with nicely salaried spouses. If I run into them, they ask me, "Hope, why don't you get out and live a little? What are you doing at your job twenty-four seven, don't you know it's not healthy?" They look at me with pity for being a woman alone. They think I've lost it, because I'm still here, in the kind of neighborhood everyone who has a choice leaves. But this is where I belong.

Some mornings I look out on these barren streets, and I cry. That's something people here will never know. My job is to show optimism. If people coming for job-skills training or AIDS-bereavement counseling knew that the director sits upstairs weeping like an idiot, that would slam a door in their faces. They don't have time for my weakness. And neither do I. I've been here long enough now to see the campaign promises come and go. I've watched the neighborhood sink, and I should know that tears help nothing.

It's the children's lives that break my heart. Roaches, rats, asthma. Schools with so many kids dying, they reserve a Grieving Room for classmates. Streets so dangerous that children are kept indoors after school—they're kept in lockdown, Maya, children already in lockdown as soon as they can walk. It's perfect training for doing time at Rikers Island, don't you think? Try to get the politicians to understand that.

So I cry. It's my secret, and now yours.

Your Mother

The rhythms of this neighborhood have become as familiar as my own pulse. In the afternoon, the cry of the rug peddler alternates with the calls of other Arab men selling knickknacks in the streets. *"Alte zachen,"* these vendors shout. Gil explained to me that this is Yiddish for "old junk." He told me that's how Israelis refer to the vendors—"Call over the *alte zachen*."

At every hint of wind these rooms shuffle like a restless river of paper. Sometimes I can't tell whether it's the whisper of the palm tree outside that I hear, or the breeze passing through the drawings Gil has hung from walls, clotheslines, shelves. Now there is hardly any time, day or night, when the apartment is silent.

The other day Gil brought home three flat parcels and a small box, and stood smiling at me as I guessed: cloth, books, old maps? He had me check the parcels for airholes; he swore the box moved if you left it on a table; he said I should be careful not to go near it at night. "Don't you like surprises, Maya? So why not let my new materials be a surprise?" Finally he took me in his arms. "Look," he said, "you're the most important person to me. I want to watch your face when you see the whole thing. I want to show it to you when it's complete, not before."

Gil has asked me to leave the living room to him during his work hours, and he's become meticulous in his cleaning, so other than the sketches hanging on the lines there's no trace of his work when he's through—only a lingering scent I don't recognize, a musky and ancient smell. I know by the tension in his back when he climbs into bed each night that he is unsure of himself. I massage the knots slowly, waiting for the few morsels he'll let slip: trouble getting used to a different kind of surface, something about the thickness of ink. I keep my guesses to myself, and after a few days the excitement of the game grows in me and the faces of the blacks in the living room become almost friendly, partners in a conspiracy.

When Gil can't sleep, he reads in bed half the night—books of art theory and history, and newspaper after newspaper. The light penetrates my fluttering lids, the pages scrape against the sheets.

Some mornings the pillowcase beside me is smudged with newsprint. I blink in the sunlight and curl beside the empty spot where Gil was, concentrating as if my prayers could be heard along with the blacks': Let his work be well received, let him be pleased. Let his anger stay away and leave behind the loving, arrogant man I adore.

Two weeks after the end of exams, I receive my grades. As soon as I see them, I'm impatient to write to my mother. But no matter how many times I try that afternoon, I can't find a way of reporting my 90s and 95s that doesn't seem to beg for approval. Irked by the nakedness of my hunger, I tear the pages to pieces. Then, on a new sheet of airmail paper, I write that I'm pleased with the results, that I think she would be, too.

Gil's new materials are proving difficult; he paces the apartment with rings under his eyes. I watch the tightening of his jaw from day to day, and try to banish my fear. The least noise sets him on edge. Once, as I struggle with the rusty shutters in the bedroom, I hear his chair scrape on the living room floor. He comes in and strides toward me, arm raised. Just before reaching me, he stops. I stand against the window. We look at each other. He lowers his arm without a word, and shuts his eyes. Then he returns to the living room, slamming the door behind him.

The next afternoon I accidentally drop a pot in the sink. I cringe at the clatter, and whirl to find Gil behind me, laughing. Laughing, that's all, with nothing else behind it. My own laughter leaves me weak.

I dream that he is in danger. I wander the city searching for him, I dodge through courtyards and twist through empty marketplaces. I know I'm the only one who can help him, but I'm lost in a snarl of unfamiliar alleys. My steps slow until I rest under an archway, and in my fatigue I struggle against the temptation to become part of the architecture winding around me, a stone fence or column, unable to move. I feel him growing farther away, and I know he's anxious for me to find him before it's too late.

Waking to the momentary silence of the radio newscaster drawing breath, I know that my attraction to Gil is gravitational.

August 1, 1993

Dear Maya,

Isn't it funny how our letters cross in the mail. I hardly ask a question before I find your answer in my box. . . .

August 12, 1993

Dear Maya,

I'll make another confession. During those difficult years with you, I often wished I had a friend I could consult. But you know how it is with me. Faye and I discuss work mostly, and since the divorce I've gone it alone.

I know that often the things I say come out all wrong. I don't mean to hurt anyone. There are times when I offend people and I can't understand why. Faye has always said I'm too brusque with the volunteers. I suppose I'm just that busy, I don't have time to worry whether I've ruffled someone's feathers. Is that too much to ask, that people take care of themselves?

What I'm trying to say is, maybe I was too hard on you.

Sometimes I wondered whether you would ever forgive me for the divorce. I wondered whether you and I could ever get along. You were so wrapped up in your own concerns. Understanding you was hard for me. When I was in college, I was so different from you.

But there's no need to dwell on the past. Everything here is fine. I think of you often.

And it makes me happy to feel like I'm seeing Israel again, after so many years. You're my eyes and ears there. And more. As I told Dr. Green, it's not the treatment that's helped so much. It's the news from my daughter living in Israel. It's knowing she's thriving there.

I sound like a fool, don't I?

Your Foolish Mother

The murmur of shifting pages fills my nights; the tide of Gil's anger breaks against the tumbled wall of my body. A shove, a single slap; an apology.

When I open the shutters to morning, the light that flashes off the white sheets in the living room is blinding.

This Friday I will go on a picnic with the Shachars. But in my letters to my mother it will be my third or fourth visit with them, not merely my second. I won't mention that the Shachars invite me out at least once a week, and that I've declined every invitation; instead I'll enlarge every story Nachum tells, send brightened reports of each conversation.

If I could write the truth, I would tell her that I didn't accept Michal's invitation to go with her friends to the north because I'm afraid to leave Gil overnight. I didn't accept the invitation, though I knew it would be Michal's last, because I don't want to miss a day's happiness. Because I don't want Gil to forget me while I'm gone. Because I don't want to return to find him sad.

Because I don't want him to hit me.

I came to this country to learn. I came in order to see everything, to do it all right. Only I didn't expect life here would be so hard to understand. I didn't expect that the fear of getting things wrong would paralyze me. I want to ask my mother: Would it be better to be one of the tourists my cousin scorns, to travel the country with experience fed to me over a tour-bus microphone? I want to write: I don't know why it's so hard to leave this apartment.

Here America seems so far away, is what I write instead. *It's difficult to explain what Israel is like, entirely.*

Gil works at the gallery only mornings now, and spends his entire afternoons at the drawing table. The heat is more intense every day, and Gil's eyes water with headaches that a cool washcloth can't cure. Sometimes he abandons his work before sunset. He's too tired to move, he says, too tired to eat dinner. We sit on the balcony, shielding ourselves from the last of the sun's rays, hopeful for the first evening breeze. Now and then the breezes don't come; we sit suspended in a still pool of air. I find myself chastising Gil over nothing—a chair left askew, a book laid carelessly across the top of a bookcase, plant leaves crushed by the closing of a shutter. Before I know it, accusations fly reckless from my mouth. I have become the protector of small things; Gil disturbs their order and, thinking of the chaos that spreads under his hands, I am choked with fury. Hateful words rip out of me, some bring him to tears. Selfish, I call him. These damn drawings, why should anyone want to look at pictures of people who won't even meet their eyes.

And then I am apologizing to him, apologizing desperately. When at last he forgives me, I know that he would forgive me anything. No one else would ever love me enough to forgive me this.

Summer parches our throats, shunts our lives into narrow channels of words so that a missing beat between question and response can signal the beginning of a struggle that will leave me staring off the balcony that night, listening for hours to the steady sound of my own breath. In the morning I stand dumb and exhausted before the empty hours ahead.

Sacher Park is a wide bowl of scrubby grass bordered by trees. Several boys run across the uneven field, kicking a soccer ball.

"Sure you don't want?" Nachum Shachar offers the container of green olives again, then sets it on the blanket and pops one into his mouth.

Fanya's voice warbles on from chorus to verse. "We were beginning to think we'd never see you again, Maya. I told Nachum, Maya must have enough friends and admirers to keep her busy. Either that, or that boyfriend of hers keeps her locked up."

How quickly words flicker through the air, and pass.

"But at least you've come to our picnic. Dov will be here soon, too. He called and said he's letting his boys go early this weekend, they've worked hard and need a rest."

We've eaten our first round of lunch. Tami stands to take Ariela on a walk, and I watch the two of them make their way across the field. Ariela seems to be telling a story, her small fists shape grand circles in the air. I can't tell whether Tami is listening.

The two of them are halfway across the park when Dov appears. The steep slope from Ruppin Street sets him jogging, and he passes us with a wave. In seconds he's across the field and scooping up Ariela, spinning her in the air and setting her, giggling and shrieking, back on her feet. The soccer players hail Dov by name and race to him, then cluster around him with shy delight as if he's their local hero.

The shade in this breezeless afternoon could lull a person to sleep.

Fanya's speech is a seamless fabric of sound. It's rare that she looks at me, and when she does I'm nodding agreement. So I'm surprised when she turns abruptly silent and faces me directly.

"Tell us about this boyfriend."

Words come thick and slow. "What about him?"

" 'What about him,' she asks." Fanya is shaking her head. "Start with everything."

"He draws."

"This we knew."

Behind Fanya, Nachum chuckles appreciatively.

"He's very tall." My words come from a distance; it's an effort to speak in this afternoon heat. "He has red hair. He reads a lot. He used to be an art student, then he left his program."

"What did he do in the army?" Nachum asks.

"Tanks," I fabricate on the spot. "He has a gallery showing in just a couple of weeks," I add. "He's working, that's why he's not here today."

Dov settles on the blanket beside Nachum and begins investigating the plastic containers.

"Now, tell us why you liked him when you met him," Fanya prompts.

"Don't feel you have to answer all her questions, Maya." Nachum leans back on one elbow and dips a pita into hummus. "What do they say in America—'You have a right to remain silent.'" He wags the pita at me before taking a bite. "Now please tell me, so how come if this right is so precious to Americans they don't use it more often?" Nachum winks and holds the container of hummus out to Dov. *"Oprah Vin-free,"* he pronounces, satisfied. "I read about this in the newspaper. The things people confess on television, I couldn't believe."

Fanya smacks Nachum lightly on the shoulder with a plastic lid. "Don't interrupt. Maya hasn't told us anything yet."

I feel the hostility in my voice even before I speak. "I love him," I say, and look away. I wish I were somewhere else. I wish I were resting in my dim whispering apartment.

"Love?" Fanya seems startled. "What's your hurry?"

In vain I try not to sound peevish. "It's true."

"Love"—Fanya considers each word—"is a very serious thing." Now she smiles. "It's different from just having a boyfriend, you know. Tell me, how did you decide all of a sudden it's love?"

I'm not in the mood for Fanya's joking. I say nothing.

"But I'm asking you seriously, how do you decide?" Fanya is looking into my face with a concentration I don't understand. My throat is too tight to permit a response, so I pretend absorption in the hummus Nachum has passed me.

Fanya waits a long while for my reply. "Just remember," she counsels at last, "don't commit yourself. Remember, one day at a time. Keep him on his toes. And always be sure he knows to treat you like a queen."

Beside me, Nachum is stretched out on the blanket. In the hope of diverting Fanya's attention, I turn and address him as cheerfully as I can. "How did you and Tami meet?"

Nachum stifles a yawn as he speaks. "In the army. We were on the same base."

"Tss." Fanya presses her hands to her knees and stands. "This story I know already." Shading her eyes, she looks toward Tami and Ariela on the far side of the park. I watch her step onto the field, gesturing to the soc-

cer players to tame their wild game while she crosses. They obey. Once on the other side of the field, Fanya joins Tami and Ariela. The three of them walk together until they disappear down a tree-shaded path.

"We met on the base," Nachum begins, and the corners of his eyes crinkle with pleasure; it's the expression I've come to think of as his storytelling look. "Tami said we'd known each other in high school. I didn't remember her at all. Still, I noticed her in the army. She was very"—he searches for the proper word—"quiet."

Dov sighs. The air escapes him like a leak from a bicycle valve, slow and hardly audible. He lies on his back, and while his father speaks he keeps his eyes closed, so that I can't tell whether he is napping or simply doesn't want any part of our conversation.

"But not just quiet, something more. Everyone else would be joking, and she would be looking out the window. *Thinking.* She was always thinking." Nachum reaches to pick a blade of grass. His glance at me is almost bashful. "Sometimes it took a lot of work, you see. She would be so serious. But I could make her laugh." He squares the grass between his thumbs and raises his cupped hands to his mouth. But then, instead of whistling, he lowers them. "That's why I married her," he says.

Dov's eyes open in astonishment.

For an instant Nachum's face falters. He looks tired. Then his mischievous smile returns; he lifts the grass stem to his mouth, and blows.

Dov is staring at his father; I have only a second to notice this before he sees me watching him and shuts his eyes once more. His face hardens in resentment. By witnessing his surprise, I understand, I've violated his privacy. I want to pacify him, but can't think of any way to apologize for learning something about his father just as he learned it for the first time.

Dov lies so still I might almost believe he's asleep.

The only way I can think of to break the silence that has fallen upon us is to mimic Nachum with a grass stem, and he gives energetic instructions while I blow hopelessly through my hands. After a few minutes Dov sits up, and soon he and Nachum are deep in speculation about the rumored retirement of a Maccabi–Tel Aviv forward. I puff into my hands, dizzy and relieved.

"So what's the weekend plan, Dov?" Nachum says. "Are you and Rina going to the beach?"

Dov looks cornered.

Nachum nods cautiously; this is a cue he's been waiting for. "You two had your same fight again?"

It seems to me that Dov's complaint is a request for guidance. "*I* don't have that fight. She does."

"Well, she's a smart girl, maybe. Maybe she's right to want you to consider university instead of life with the army." Nachum toys with an empty cup. "You have a good head. Maybe you *ought* to consider that engineering program."

Dov's eyes tighten, registering his father's betrayal.

The sound of Fanya's greeting from close by sets us all into energetic replies. She walks briskly up the incline, apparently oblivious to Tami and Ariela behind her.

While Dov moves to make room for his grandmother, I'm aware of Nachum trying to catch Tami's attention. Tami, her head averted, is busy pouring Ariela's juice.

Nachum wants to tell you, a vindictive part of me is tempted to announce, *that he tried to talk to Dov about something but he's not sure it worked.* How, I wonder, would *they* feel being put on the spot?

Fanya settles onto the blanket. "Did you ask her, Dov?" she says.

Dov does not answer her but turns to me instead, his face impassive. "Some friends and I are planning a camping trip in the desert in a couple of weeks. Do you and your boyfriend want to join us?"

Fanya sets a hand on my shoulder. "You will," she says. "Won't you?"

"Sure," I tell my cousin. "Thanks."

It is late afternoon when we leave Sacher Park, and I walk along roads filled with soldiers my age toting bags of laundry, hitching rides from the bus stop for the last leg of their journey home for the weekend. As I pass them, I wonder whether any of the more exhausted-looking ones are Dov's charges. I spend several blocks pitying the soldiers unfortunate enough to be under his surly command.

When I turn the corner onto my street I see an old woman moving slowly along the sidewalk. It is the woman from the apartment below mine. I've never before had more than a glimpse of her, and now I quicken my steps and approach her with mounting curiosity.

She wears a faded brown cotton skirt and a beige sweater, and her head is wrapped in a dark kerchief so that she looks like one of the ultra-Orthodox women. But there's something different about her—perhaps the way she carries herself, walking intently, her eyes on the path directly ahead of her, as if each step brings her closer to some thirsted-after relief. She is so slight it appears a puff of air could send her stumbling.

A yeshiva student tags along beside her, gesturing emphatically. Under one arm he holds a yellow sign.

The woman stops walking. For a moment she examines the boy. Then she shakes her head. As I near them, I hear her speak in an accented Hebrew. "I don't need a sign," she is saying.

"For your home," the boy says. He is respectful but insistent; she must hang this sign from her balcony.

"I don't need," she tells him.

I am almost even with them now, on the opposite side of the street. I trail my fingers along a low stone wall, pretending to be lost in thought.

The yeshiva student has begun speaking again, but the woman is not listening. She has seen me and now she stares.

She has a flat face, sallow cheeks, plaintive impoverished features. But it's her eyes that nearly stop me: watery and intense, a pale blue that cuts through everything. Her expression is suffused in wonder, as if she has just received an unexpected blessing. She turns her back on the boy beside her and, keeping her gaze on me as I walk, performs a strange and elaborate nod, almost a bow. Then she reaches out a hand, palm up, as in supplication or praise. Still facing me, she speaks to the black-hatted student behind her. "I don't need your sign. I have already."

My steps have faltered. I want to stand and speak to this woman, but I don't know what to say.

"You have a sign already?" The student circles her in an attempt to regain her attention.

She says nothing, only watches me as I idle past. I crane my neck over my shoulder to watch her as well. Our gazes are locked. For a second I feel dizzy. Instinctively, as though I were navigating the edge of a chasm rather than an ordinary stretch of pavement, I check my balance against the stone wall.

I wrench my eyes away.

"So why didn't you just tell me you had a sign already," the yeshiva student is saying. "Just be certain to hang it where people can see it."

I turn down the path toward my building, and I can hear the woman's soft footsteps behind me. When I slow, she slows; when I stop, she pauses, diffident.

"Let me know if you need help hanging it," the student calls out behind us. "Soon every home will have one, God willing." I don't turn back, and I can tell without looking that she doesn't, either.

At the bottom of the stairwell I face her.

She steps sideways off the path. Half hidden in bushes, she waits.

"I'm your neighbor," I say. "Maya."

She says nothing.

"I live upstairs."

She is shy now, like a schoolgirl, a hand raised uncertainly to her mouth. She steps back farther into the bushes.

She is waiting for me to go.

"Come visit anytime." My words sound idiotic and I see her flinch. I start up the stairs. Twice I hesitate, and twice footsteps stop abruptly behind me. When I have passed the second-floor landing I hear the sound of a key in a lock behind me, then a soft click.

∽

The American: her presence ignites memory. I wander in a haze of days, years flit like shadows.

There will be a war, *the man behind the post office counter repeats as he counts out my pension.* Do you understand, a war.

Yes, I tell this man. I know what is war.

Listen to me, old woman, *the man insists. His voice follows me to the door, his voice pleads as I stand in the doorway facing the street.* I'm not talking about whatever part of Europe you hail from, I'm talking about Israel. A war in this city, an invisible war, coming from the sky. There is a dictator, and missiles, a war coming to your building. A war in your bedroom, do you understand, please you must get a gas mask. Tape to seal a room, baking soda in case of chemicals. Don't you have anyone to stay with, a grandmother shouldn't spend a war alone.

Live a war, alone, they are coming from the sky. Do not be frightened. This door sealed there will be gas.

Saddam Hussein, do you understand? *the man calls to me.* The Persian Gulf. *I turn to see him. There are veins bulging on his neck, they* www automation.org

are purple and I wonder has anyone told him this. No, *the man pauses, red in his face.* No one has. *A woman laughing behind me. The man shakes his head, slowly.* Someone make sure this lady gets a gas mask, he says, *and I turn back to the street.*

That week, a city full of masks, people disguised with war. They carry it in cases on the street, at the sound of sirens they will strap war to the faces of their children. Women walk by with rolls of tape, they are preparing a chamber for their families.

One of the blacks stops me on the street, talks excitedly leaning close. Do you hear? The Rebbe has declared it, we won't need masks after all. The Messiah is coming, the next world is approaching. Don't let these city officials frighten you. We lift our eyes to the hills whence cometh our—

In this city sealing its windows, the blacks fling open sashes, they brim with assuredness.

But in the evening as the street grows dark, I see a kerchiefed woman crouched on her balcony with radio to her ear; across the street children open their windows and peer up curious. Night settles. In my Jerusalem bed I lie and dream of Warsaw rain. I dream wet cobblestone and bubbling gutters, suddenly I wake rooted with sound. At first it seems a shofar, we are gathered here to repent our sins, the cantor's assistant in the Great Synagogue is calling us all to Yom Kippur judgment. Even Mother bows her head before the rabbi, For our sins are grievous, *she chants.* O Lord how we stand before you humble. How our wickednesses have multiplied our wrongdoings grown bold.

Still the sound blasts on, even the young cantor with his puffed straining cheeks cannot charge us with our transgressions for so long.

I step out of bed, go to the window. Across the street the blacks stumble onto their balconies to look as well, then duck inside to their psalms and do not appear again. Another siren joins the first, together they wail to the city gathered below. In an apartment nearby, a woman screaming then sobbing. Let me put a mask on the baby. Let me do it just tonight, God will understand. *Her words are smothered in sound, the sirens layer one upon the other, the cry of Jerusalem sealing itself in airless chambers.*

On the street, nothing moves.

O Lord how we stand before You.

Barefoot I run to the balcony, I fling open the shutters. They are heavy and the motion wrenches my shoulders, there is horrible pain but I do not stop. I push open the windows, rush breathless to the door and down this stairwell. Outside I stand in nightdress without jacket or hat. The streets are deafening, they are empty of people, they are empty of cars, this night trembles with sound.

Shadows quiver and rear across alleys, bits of fire drop slowly through sky. The city is struck dumb. And still the sound, deafening. The sound that might make a girl hold her head and weep. My heart eases in its pounding, I walk now slowly. Down the path I pass. Through the park, these soothing streets. There is no one, no one, and I nod my understanding. Tonight the city is my home. A ragged white light shoots across the sky. It sails triumphant and I raise my arms to it, I embrace the sky as it fills and drains of light. I lift my eyes to the heavens whence cometh my voice, with my eyes I follow the path this falling star has seared across the night and I sing back to the sirens, I sing loud and rhythmic and fierce and my song charges the heavens to atonement.

∞

Hours after my return from the Shachars' picnic, my stomach is knotted with hunger. Gil and I have planned to cook an early dinner, but he is out somewhere on an errand. To pass the time, I read yesterday's paper. When I can no longer concentrate, I hit on the idea of hanging a plant in the living room.

I remember that Gil keeps some nails on the top shelf of his closet, so I drag a chair from the kitchen and swing his closet door wide. As I grope above my head along the dusty shelf, my hand closes on a hard leather pouch.

I step down from the chair, and sit on the bed. In my hands are the binoculars that belonged to Gil's father. With great care I remove them from the pouch.

They are worn, the black plastic deeply scratched. There is a dry smell of long disuse. I examine the small round eyepieces, the smooth dark lenses. Then I slip the cracked leather strap over my head. I sit holding my neck straight against the drag of the binoculars. Resting against my breastbone, they seem unnaturally heavy, and dangerous—unapologetic reminders of war. Witness, I recall, to the making of a widow. I picture a soldier Gil's age, looking out on a threatening world through these glasses. On his face the hard plastic cylinders are a mask of battle: formidable protectors, shielding his wondering eyes. The soldier rises, peers through his glasses at the horizon. He sees a world of swirling dust, enemy tanks.

When Gil enters the apartment, I don't try to hide the binoculars. I look at him, then at my knees, knobby and naked.

Gil stands in the bedroom without speaking. Then he lifts the binoculars from around my neck and sits beside me. He turns them over once in his thick-jointed hands, then cradles them to his stomach. After a while, I notice that he's crying.

With a hoarse laugh, he wipes his cheek on one shoulder. He looks at the stain on his T-shirt. "Well, my mother always said I was a very sensitive boy."

He drums his fingers on the binoculars. Then, without warning, he is all bright-eyed sarcasm. " 'Gil always saw things other boys didn't see,' " he simpers. " 'Things hurt him. He used to come to me and say, Why? And I would have no answer. Sweet boy.' " The words are a curse in Gil's mouth. " 'He and I were so close, then.' "

"Maya," Gil addresses me urgently in his normal voice. "Someday when we have children, that woman is not to come near them."

I start at the ease with which he says it: *When we have children*. Not knowing how to react, I keep my face blank. Can you say that again, I want to ask.

"My father," he says, "always thought that she was waiting for the opportunity to betray him."

I tell myself to focus on what he's saying. My face is flushed from excitement, and nervousness. "You think your mother was unfaithful to him?"

"Who knows what that woman did or didn't do?" Gil fingers one worn eyepiece, then the other. "But you know what I do remember? It was about five years after he died, I was eight years old. And it was the evening of Memorial Day, the scouts were putting on their ceremony to commemorate the people from the neighborhood who'd been killed. All the kids were participating, they were going to read the names of the fallen soldiers who'd grown up in their scout troop. We had to get there early to sit on the benches reserved for bereaved families. Tsipi, our neighbor, was going to drive us. But when she arrived, my mother didn't come downstairs. Tsipi led me up to her room, calling out all the while for my mother. When she didn't answer we went into her room. There she was, sitting on the edge of the bed that she and my father had shared. She was dressed in the same dark dress she always wore to the ceremony, makeup and hair in place. But she was just staring into the dresser mirror and didn't turn around when we came in."

Gil lays the binoculars on the bed and looks at them. After a pause he continues quietly. " 'Aren't you coming?' Tsipi asked her. And my mother said, 'Did you know, Tsipi, his dying was the best thing that ever happened to me?' "

Gil looks exhausted. He reaches for my face, and he speaks to me as if I am the dearest thing in his life. "Tsipi rushed me out of the room. She took me down to the kitchen and she told me, 'Your mother meant nothing of what she said. Do you understand? Nothing. Your mother is just feeling sick today, so she says crazy things that aren't true. I'm going upstairs now to talk to your mother until she feels better.' Then Tsipi, Tsipi who waddled like a hippopotamus when she walked—my father used to call her Tsipi the house-on-legs—turned to go back upstairs. But my mother was already on her way down, one hand on the railing, cool and composed. She walked to the bottom of the stairs, she said to Tsipi, 'Let's go.' Then she took my hand and led me to the car. And we drove to the ceremony and walked through the crowd, everyone was so respectful, and we ducked under the string and went to sit on the front bench. And I watched her play widow for everyone who cared to look."

His eyes fix on the window beyond me, reaching for daylight. He chuckles.

"Wouldn't you guess it, when the results came back from the psycho-technics, the teachers said, Look what a bright young man, he panicked on the exam and now he'll have to put up with a terrible army placement, they'll put him in the green army when he ought to be in the gray.

"*Idiots.* I threw the exam because I didn't care to jump through hoops for the army that answered my mother's prayers. Do you think I cared what they thought of me? So place me with the dregs, I'll spend my three years laughing at you all."

Gil sits in silence, his face shuttered with thought. Then he rises, slips the binoculars into their pouch, and returns them to their place.

He kneels on the floor so that he is not above me or below me, but looks directly into my eyes as he makes his confession. "I know I'm difficult. Sometimes things feel very"—he hesitates—"not in control." He shakes his head gravely. "It will get better, I promise."

The next afternoon I take the last of the laundry from the sink and carry it dripping through the living room, careful to dodge between drawings as I pass. Gil has gone to the gallery. The air is unusually still, even the sketches hang motionless. On the balcony the sun burns my bare arms as I pin T-shirts and jeans to the line.

Under the glare, I am too tired for pretense. Today, I freely admit, will hold no adventures. I will not explore new neighborhoods, I will not spend the afternoon touring educational museum exhibits or quaint ethnic neighborhoods. I will write a letter full of lies, and steal phrases from travel brochures to prove them.

Since yesterday I have been thinking about the woman downstairs. I don't know why, but the more I recall her standing rapt and speechless on the street, the more convinced I am that there was something she wanted to say.

The street is quiet. There is no one in sight.

Last in the laundry pile are two rags that Gil uses for cleaning charcoal dust from his work area: stained and misshapen things. I pin one to the line, and weigh the other in my hand.

When the rag slips through my fingers I lean over the balcony rail to watch its path. Straight down it falls in this breezeless air, then catches with a soft huff on the empty clothesline of the woman downstairs, and bobs there satisfyingly.

I slide my sandals onto my feet. I step through the living room, past rows of mute disapproving faces; I leave the apartment and go down the stairs to knock on her door.

The American's tears are diamonds, her laughter is gold and spills over and fills this apartment with light. She and her boyfriend tease in rising scales, love-sounds climb like questions until giggles burst to gales stealing their breath, and mine as well.

The sun is coming through the cracks in the shutters, stretching fingers into my room, a person must huddle to the corner to escape. Today is quiet, no motors churn the blacks' sabbath air. Outside, stone and sky. Cardboard signs fading in the sun.

On a day like today, the river running slow. And Father strolling in gray hat and coat, his black knobbed walking stick sinking in grass. Mother and Halina and I behind, on the shaded slope of the bank. We step through softness, now breeze dips sunlight in arcs to the ground. The river reflects flashes of sky, even through these closed eyelids such an afternoon steeps color into the mind, tea leaves curling fronds of red or brown in a steaming clay pot.

Breeze, like silk between the fingers.

I would tell Mother, The river is a patient mare pulling a cart toward sunset. I would ask her, Shall we go lay our hands on its skin and press until we are admitted, the riverwitch will nod at ripples but will not wake.

But Mother would scold, Dream too much listen too little, Shifra. Fool for fancy. It's good you're a girl, no boy like you could last an hour. The world tells bitter time to nitwits. When the day comes you'll have to marry before the family finds out you're simple. Come inside, sew with your sister Halina this afternoon, don't trouble her with your fairy tales.

Shifra, haunting daughter. Mother speaks low as she pours out dark tea in the parlor. Sometimes my own child's eyes frighten me when I've finished waiting on a customer in the shop and I turn to find she's watching me. Who can blame you, Hannah, Aunt Riva consoles. I'd be uneasy too. Such eyes the girl has. At least you have Halina. Halina will bring mazel. Once she gets over her school-craziness. All those boys after her and she doesn't even care. Won't look up from her books. Already near the end of gimnazjum, what will you do with her?

But Mother and Father don't know Halina's secret. Only I.

Halina brings a basket of long green peapods to the door, we crouch to shell them. She pulls a paper from under the basket, unfolds it into my hands and I am ready. "Test me." She is proud, she wipes golden hair from her forehead. "Quick, before Mother comes. See if I haven't memorized them all." It isn't sabbath that she fears, for Mother knows we break sabbath, she breaks as well and Father too, he carries on business from the back window of the shop and neighbors come and go in whispers as if quiet will keep them from being recognized. Mother sneers at the religious and makes Halina shut the electric lights only once each month for Grandmother's sabbath visits from Bialystok.

No, Halina's secret and mine is in these papers, these tables and charts. Letters and formulas. Halina studies, late at night. No one else knows she is learning chemicals, symbols and signs that she says are blocks to build a world she and I will escape to. Halina will pass the examinations, she will go to University despite Mother and Father. She has saved money, tutored after school, no one knows but me. She will be a chemist, when she scores higher than the boys on the examination Mother and Father will have to let her go. And I, I will join her as soon as she has earned her first salary.

You're not dull-witted, Halina tells me. They're wrong about you, I know that.

There is a knock at the door.

I stand ragged with alarm. Groping to the entryway I search for words, I cry out Yes, Mother?

"It's Maya," this voice speaks. "Your neighbor from upstairs."

I cannot remember any neighbor upstairs, in our house on the town's main road. The basket of emptied peapods sits now on the doorstep beside our muddied shoes; in the parlor, green curtains shut out sunlight. On the second floor, our bedrooms, and no one living above, I am sure of it.

"I live in the apartment upstairs," the voice insists. Someone is come from the roof, then, a dangerous thing. I slide away from the door.

There is another knock, louder. "It's Maya," the voice says in a light and timid Hebrew. "The American," it adds.

The American. An American. I know about Americans. My fingers trembling, I unlatch the door and open it the width of my shoulder. Peering into the stairwell I can see pale brown hair and a heart-shaped face. Her eyes are a clean strong blue, they are cat eyes, delicate hollows underneath. High round cheekbones. Her hair like honey in a knot, her legs strong and suntanned in short pants that stop at the knee. She is as beautiful as I have always wanted to be. She is, I see, almost as beautiful as Halina.

I press my head against the door. "What is it?" I ask her, humbly. My eyes are brimming.

She smiles at me, laughs. Embarrassed, the American is. "I'm so sorry to bother you, especially for something so . . ." She is searching for a word, she is bashful, and I help her by thinking of words myself: Feverish, salty. Matchbook hiccup kerchief bread.

"For something so idiotic." She smiles again, and I crack my lips in my own smile. I nod encouragement, my neck stiff. "I was putting out laundry on my balcony, and while I wasn't paying attention, the breeze came and blew a"—she pauses, and I think to her sparrow, balloon, flatulence, liberation, push-broom—"a rag off my clothesline, and dropped it right down onto yours."

She waits. I wait also, watching: the lacing of the American's lashes when she blinks, small knobs of lint on a shoulder of her cotton blouse.

"So my rag is on your clothesline. I was wondering if I could just get it," she says. "So it's not among your things."

I nod to her, once. She nods back to me, encouraging. I shut the door tenderly in her face.

The porch shutters scream with rust as I open them. I step, into sharp sudden day. The balcony sunlight pierces my eyes and I reel back, I fall to my knees and my forehead bows to dusty tile. A lizard streaks in front of me.

Hanging beside the rail is the cloth, a rough white square. I pick it from the line and rub it to my cheek. How warm it feels against the skin, it is an American touch and will comfort. But such whiteness in the sunlight looses Halina's voice in my head. "Shifra, be nice to Pan Gregorow, last time he complained to Mother that you wouldn't say a word to him, only stared. Behave yourself this time." Daydreaming girl, even Halina grows impatient. But I do not like my father's partner Pan Gregorow, who goads me for my silence and pinches above my knee when no one looks. I cling to the sash of Halina's dress; today I will be good, I will do everything as she does. Gently she unfastens my fingers. "It will be all right," she says. "Don't worry, I won't let him touch you."

Once there was a Yiddish theater performing in the square, Father said Shifra can mind the shop this afternoon, but I locked the store and stepped down cobbled streets toward the sound of the crowd. The play was ending. A man, his chest draped in cloth, knelt and exclaimed his love to a girl whose hands fluttered emotion. A woman with face painted white, black circles under her eyes, wandered blindly in a circle. I see before me a dybbuk, she sang out, I am haunted, then she fell to the pavement, only at the last flung out a hand so her head did not hit ground. She stood for bows, soon the crowd started to spread from the square into the streets. Father would be returning. I ran toward the shop, slapping shoes on cobblestones, but the neighbor children Lilka and Feliks had seen me, they ran to catch up. Help, it's a dybbuk, Lilka called and pointed. I faint! she shouted, and as I ran I turned to see Lilka fall giggling into her brother's arms.

I knew what Lilka and Feliks's parents said about my family, I heard them, afternoons on their balcony. "Feldstein drek. But what do you expect from such a family as tries to marry its sixteen-year-old daughter to a rich man almost three times her age? They say she put up so much fight even her wretched father couldn't bear it. That one, Halina, she's got promise. A strong-headed girl, to resist such a family. Some good may come of her."

"Unlikely," a soft titter. "She'll just marry the next rich one who's only twice her age. That family would do anything to advance themselves, she'll give in to them soon enough."

"You're dirty liars," I screamed up from my hiding place below the balcony. "Liars all of you and pigs."

Silence, then laughter fading as I ran.

There was more they did not know, if the truth had been seen they would have called the police to our house. They would lock away Father and even Mother, and it would be my fault. For only I held the secret, and the terror of speaking it aloud in sleep kept me staring awake *into blackness at night, reaching for Halina's hand across the narrow space between our beds. And even Halina I did not tell, although Halina knew everything, every fairy story I made up and every lie I told Mother to hide Halina's studies. Still I would not speak when Halina asked me why I did not sleep at night.*

Only I had seen Father beating the neighbor's son. Father told us later, The boy stole, such is what happens to children who steal. But Feliks Rotstein did not steal, *I was behind the flour barrel and I too saw what Feliks saw: Grandmother finishing her monthly Sunday inspection of the shop's goods and leaving through the glass door for her train to Bialystok. Father slipping Grandmother's envelope of bills into Mother's purse, instead of the register. Feliks bumped against a crate of candlesticks and Father heard the noise, he saw the fear arching across Feliks's forehead and he crossed the room in two steps, his palm raised high.*

Feliks told his parents he had been beaten by a Gentile boy whose face he couldn't recall, behind a building he couldn't point out even when driven in his father's car through the neighboring villages and into the countryside. The son of the head of the kehillah has been beaten, *word went out through the community. Orphans from the institution the Rotsteins sponsored, the poor elderly men Mrs. Rotstein sewed for with her own two hands: all wrote cards and sent handmade gifts. Talk of the wealthy Rotstein son's bruises spread for days in the courtyards, some eyebrows danced too over the simplemindedness of such a boy who couldn't even describe an attack.* My mother says this is what a family like ours gets for living in a backward village, *Lilka confided to the schoolroom, and abashed sympathy flowed all around her, children whispered on the way to their seats.*

Even Halina whispered. Halina, her skirts rolled shorter, laughing so often lately. I had seen her across the square with three girls from the gimnazjum, there they stood locked together by talk. All that spring these bright-faced girls visited Halina, included her in hikes with boys to the mountains, took her to swim in ponds with the Jewish Sports Club. And Halina laughing. Halina knowing things about cinema stars in pictures she had never seen. My sister has escaped the Feldstein curse, *I thought.* Soon she will shout names at me too, I will have no companion.

Halina humming, folding Father's shirts one by one.

"When will you tell Mother and Father?" I ask her.

"When classes at the University have already begun," she answers. She will live in Warsaw and become a professor, Halina repeats, and I will keep house across the street and write stories. I will look after her children if she has them. "You'll marry too," she tells me. "Don't you worry. Maybe I'll be looking after your children and I an old maid, who knows?" A skirt lifted, shaken, laid out for ironing. "I'll tell Mother and Father my plans when it's too late for anyone to stop me. I didn't work for so long just to let Mother and Father rule the rest of my life."

"Halina," I say. "Why did you never tell me they were going to make you marry Turkevich?"

Halina looks at me in alarm. Then averts her gaze, tosses her wavy hair.

It is true then, she has gone to her new friends and will forget me. She has poured out her secrets for them, my ears are stunned with silence. "Halina why did you never tell me? Why did you never tell me, what did you do to make Mother and Father listen to you?" My voice is breaking with my heart. I turn from Halina and weep to the parlor wall.

Halina kneels beside me, she calls my name then she takes me in her arms. With one palm she presses my head to her shoulder. Rocks me, and hope breathes into my spirit even as tears blur the parlor lamp. "You know I don't mean to keep anything from you. Just don't ask me that question, my Shifraleh, please? Any other question, but not that one. You know I can't lie to you, so please don't make me answer."

I pull away and wipe tears with the back of my hand. "Will you forget me for your new friends?"

Halina regards me sternly. Then she smiles. "What, the Kino girls?"

At the miracle of these words I look up. I have found Halina's copies of the cinema magazine in our bedroom, have pored over each for clues of how these new fairy tales enchant her.

"Oh, some of them are all right, a couple of the girls will be friends at the University perhaps. But what does that matter, Shifra? You're my everything."

I lace my fingers into the clean warmth of her hair. "You are mine."

In late summer came the letter from University, which Mother tore open in the entryway. For weeks then, Halina did not leave the house, Mother barred the door with extended arms. Grandmother was sum-

*moned from Bialystok, she slept in my room and snored in the bed along-
side mine. Day after day my sister was forbidden to me: Halina, accepted to University, curled pale in a sheet on the parlor sofa. She would
not speak to anyone and so I did not speak either, day after day I uttered
no word. Grandmother was the only one who noticed, after each night
of threats and promises to Halina she lifted her glass of bedtime
schnapps to me. "L'chaim," she said. "May birds fly from your mouth
when at last you open it." Although the weather was mild all week, the
Rotsteins took their tea indoors; Mother's and Father's shouts reigned on
the street. In the parlor Grandmother offered in a low voice dowry,
curses, bribes; tuition for a trade school—a nurse or seamstress in the
family, a compromise for all. At the end of six days Grandmother
boarded a train for Bialystok. "The girl is as stubborn as I," she told
Mother. "Let Hayyim bring his wrath of God on her, perhaps to that she
will listen."*

*Next week came Uncle Hayyim from Bialystok, sent by Grand-
mother with his black hat and peyes and his smell of unwashed laundry
to pray for Halina's benefit. O Lord let her not go to University, a girl
at University will never marry. Hayyim, with his limp—he reminded
Father the hour he arrived—from the Gentiles. From the pogrom Father
spent hunched behind a barrel of kosher wine, Father a boy hiding behind wine as dark as the blood flowing in village gutters that spring day.*

*Father would not let Uncle Hayyim inside the house. Your God-
soaked ways are the one thing worse than a girl at University, he
called from the parlor. So Hayyim stood on the street, aiming words at
the window a neighborhood boy said was Halina's.*

*The Rotsteins withdrew from their front parlor, their porcelain
teapots steamed behind shuttered panes.*

*No one knew when Hayyim slept or ate. Father said the momzer
could camp out in a sewer pipe for all he cared, even if he was his own
brother. And Halina should remember this because that was where she
would be sleeping if she did not forget this University madness. Halina,
dreaming in the parlor, how drained her face in the moonlight. How like
a crow Uncle Hayyim looked from above in his coat and black hat. At
dawn and dusk and through the night he stood on the cobblestone street
and chanted his psalms meant for Halina to the window over my bed.*

Give ear to my speech O Lord, consider my utterance.

All night, all through the night.

Have mercy on me Lord, heal me, I am weary with groaning, every night I drench my bed in tears. *My dreams twined with his words.* Away from me, all you evildoers, for the Lord heeds the sound of my weeping. All my enemies will be stricken with terror; they will turn back in an instant. I will praise the Lord for His righteousness, sing a hymn to the Lord Most High, for happy is the man who has not followed the counsel of the wicked. Like a tree planted beside streams of water he will flourish.

Threat and promise and comfort filled my nights, I woke in the mornings to the echo of Hayyim's exultation. I will bring before You copper and gold, cedar and sandalwood I lay at Your feet.

One morning I wrapped bread saved from breakfast in a paper and dropped it to the black figure below. Hayyim did not cease his prayer though he stared with longing. From the parlor I heard rushing footsteps. Mother raced to brush me aside and wave a bucket of water from my window, below us the front door flew open and Father emerged on the stoop, shouted My brother whom I do not call brother, this is not a house of mourning. Go pray for someone who needs psalms, take your cursed blessings and go!

Uncle Hayyim closed his prayer book and sighed a sigh of the ages. How his black shoulders sagged. From the parlor Mother's hoarse monologue stopped short as Halina erupted in sound. "Complain about me, Mother, but leave Shifra alone. She isn't dim-witted, curse this family! If she walks in a mist it's because she chooses to dull herself to your lies, and you like to think her dull so you can set her to work like a drone all day in the shop. But don't ever think she doesn't see and understand everything, and better than most."

From the stoop Father's shout, Good-bye and good riddance, Sir Hayyim of the Dark Ages!

"I'm going to the University," *Halina said in the parlor, and this time Mother said nothing.*

That evening Uncle Hayyim limped along the street toward the train station with battered suitcase in hand. He did not look up as Halina strode past on her way to the market, basket swinging against her skirt. When Halina had disappeared and Hayyim was far down the street, then Mother came behind me in the front parlor and clutched my shoulder. "What will you do when she leaves?" *Mother asked.* "She'll be in Warsaw, you know, she'll come home only for weekends. You'll need a *friend. Why don't you find someone from school or visit Lilka Rotstein next door, or join a club?" Bitterly Mother stared at my motionless form as I stood before the window, my fingertips resting on the window frame. "Of course you don't answer me. You never answer." Then she seized my hand and was crying into my open palm, kisses and hot tears. "You were always my most beloved child," she said, "can you believe me?"*

I made a party for Halina's farewell. Invited all her friends. They hardly knew me, but when I said I was Halina's sister they looked in my face, and when they asked what time was the party some of them smiled. The day of the party it hailed, the sky dark as if it would boil. Everyone said cancel, even Halina, but I laid the plates on the dining room table and set a flower on every napkin, one for each. Halina said she shouldn't bother, still she put on her best blue dress when I asked. She bound my wet hair in a braid and when it dried I loosed it so it shone in ripples and waves. Mother said it wasn't a decent way for a girl to wear her hair but I said to Mother, Mother I do not care. Mother touched her heart and said nothing.

And they came. One after the other they came. While I brought tea, Halina rose to greet each. Cakes with lemon, cakes with berries, crumbs to wipe on cloth napkins. Boys held chairs for girls, girls held their chins high with attention. So gentle, this sound of cups lifted and set. Then after tea we sat on the steps beneath the balcony, we sat all of us together with Feliks's mandolin and we sang songs of longing as ice danced solemn patterns on the roof. Ice sang songs of longing on the roof, I danced a solemn good-bye for my sister.

The pounding of hail on a shingled roof.

Knocking.

The American, knocking at the door. Knocking at the door, and I stuff the cloth square into the pocket of my housecoat, run from the porch into the dizzying dark of the apartment. A bed, a suitcase, a photograph, a soup tin, an American. There is an American at my door. Through the walls I shout at her, "Rude American!" I fling the door open. She stands on the landing, her face so eager it pains to look on it.

"Rude! American!" I shout at her. "Do you think you can just come here to this place and expect us all to fall to your feet with gratitude? Don't you know we had lives, we had whole lives without you?" I wad the fabric deeper into my pocket, I shoot out a fist and this American steps back, I see she can't understand that I have tried to hit her. She is

confused and I see I have spoken in Polish. Americans cannot hear Polish, I recall.

"What's wrong?" she asks, she reaches out a smooth American hand to touch me. "What's happened?"

Americans, *a woman screams, why have you come to save us now, you did not come before my Yakov was killed now let us die. Americans, pressing candy bars and cigarettes into her bony hands, desperate to be rid of such gifts.*

"Did you find it?" the American asks.

"No," I whisper in Hebrew. I move to shut the door between us, but she is standing in the way.

"Are you sure? I saw it right there from my balcony," she says in her feather-light, smoke-light Hebrew. "Maybe I can come in and have a look?" She smiles at me with a great and patient understanding, a smile for an animal one does not wish to frighten. "Perhaps," she says, "we can talk."

Halina, don't ever leave me again. Will you promise?

I am so very tired, now. "Go away," I say. "It's not there."

"Oh." The American looks at me. Then she nods, the vigorous nod they make when they are willing to be lied to. "It must have blown down to the ground, then. I'll go look. Sorry for bothering you." She backs away, a brief smile. She is gone.

I close the door with trembling hands that do not want to obey me. They want to fling the door wide, these hands. They want to follow the American to her apartment, flutter at her feet, pull on her sleeve.

I slide the latch. The apartment is quiet, as after some great intrusion.

The heat on the porch hits like a wall but I square my shoulders. I move on, stealthy, toward the railing. Peering over, I wait. Soon the American appears. The alley is full of garbage, plastic bottles and dented metal cans. She walks unsteadily along a sagging board laid across cinder blocks; she balances with hand against the side of the building. Once she looks up at my porch, but I have pressed myself to the drainpipe and she cannot see me. She trips over a can and says soft swears to herself in English. Before she turns to go she even looks under the board she stands on. She rakes the dirt beneath and lets bits of dried palm frond fall between her fingers.

That evening when I lie down to bed I cannot sleep. The cats have quieted for the night and by the garden path the palm tree beckons rain once again. With each rise of breeze my eyes fill with tears of gratitude.

The American startled me, she caught me by surprise and I was undeserving. I sent her away, I turned her back. But now I lie with new hope. I reach under my pillow. The cloth is thick and wrinkled, and when I touch it I think of soft waves of hair.

The American has left me this gift: a second sign.

Soon. Soon she will hear my story, she will vanquish the past. Soon, to this burning life the American will bring cool water.

And I have been unworthy but I will prove worthy. I have been ungrateful but now I will bring my offerings to her feet, my gold and copper, my sandalwood and cedar and wine. All that I have I will bring to her, three offerings in thanks for the three signs that will prophesy her glory.

And then, her light will shine.

Yes, Her light will shine.

In the morning I rise, and begin.

∞ 11 ∞

Dear Maya,

This is the way the fog sits in Brooklyn, before the daylight is sure of itself. . . .

Dear Maya,

This is the way the children drag stubs of chalk across cracked schoolyard pavement, scrape their knuckles bloody. . . .

So much needs describing—the latest program at the Center, the latest rally, the latest political outrage. My mother's handwriting is loose with hurry. Often there is nothing in my mailbox for days; then two or three envelopes arrive at once, reports from a distant battlefield.

The morning after I lose Gil's cloth, I find a small ragged bundle at the door.

"What's this junk?" His satchel over one shoulder, Gil steps, yawning, into the stairwell. He kicks at the tattered newspaper wrapping.

As I follow the motion of his foot with my eyes, I am positive that the bundle is from the woman downstairs. I respond with reflexes I didn't know I possessed. In an instant I'm in front of him. "Garbage," I say, and hug him so hard he laughs and loosens my arms.

Only after he leaves do I stoop to gather the parcel. It is misshapen, and has an unbalanced heft.

I set it on the living room sofa, then go to the kitchen. I drain my glass of grapefruit juice, wash it, and set it on the rack. As if some suspense is required, I forbid myself to rush a single motion. I'm strangely excited to see what is inside the newspaper—a welcome from someone in this neighborhood, at last? Perhaps, I tell myself, my spying neighbor has simply been shy about her accented Hebrew. She's wanted to befriend me all along, now she's chosen to make this first overture without words.

Finally I've waited long enough. I lock the front door like someone about to handle stolen merchandise, then take a knife from the kitchen drawer.

The paper, on closer inspection, is not only tattered but speckled with age. The twine is easy to cut. Inside the wrapping are several daisies, their crushed stems staining the newsprint a faint green. Shrouded in newspaper beside the flowers is a small tin. Faded Hebrew print on its label identifies it as Moshe's Asparagus Soup Wonder Mix. "Just add water," the label boasts. I examine the tin. It could be ten years old, even twenty. I pry the lid open: the contents are dry and hard as stone, a petrified block of dull green.

I turn the objects over, lift the bunched flowers in my fist and nudge the stems that droop almost double. I scratch the brick of soup powder with the nail of my little finger and taste the grains of powder. A sickeningly salty glob forms in my mouth and I rush to the toilet to spit.

The taste in my mouth is bitter; the woman downstairs has left me her garbage, a spiteful joke.

I don't know what I expected.

I walk, aimless, to the balcony, and squint against the brightness for several minutes before admitting to myself what it was I had hoped for. I wanted some gift to fulfill the promise of that arresting stare. Some powerful wisdom to break the tight rhythm of my days in this incomprehensible city.

Advice.

Weary, I make my way back to the sofa to dispose of the package. Out of curiosity I check the newspaper for a date. March 3, 1951. *Ha'Patp'tan—Your Hebrew-Language Weekly.* On one side of the paper, in dense columns, are listings, presumably of jobs or community events. I scan these columns without reading, then flip to the other side. Here I read an advertisement for truck parts and irrigation piping, and a headline: "Farmer breeds two-headed calf, Rabbis in tumult. 'Is it kosher?' asks religious court." I laugh despite myself. Even in 1951, I see, Israel had rags—gossip parading in the awkward triumphal Hebrew of the new state. "Ashkenazic agricultural leader walks out of Sephardic debate in protest," a sub-heading informs.

The noon heat is heavy on the rooftops. A car drives through the neighborhood, its loudspeaker blaring "Prepare." The word drains away down the street. The blacks have stepped up their campaign with the summer heat: perhaps their amplified words might coax redemption out of the midday sky arcing above like a shell of beaten copper.

I sit, fingering the newsprint. I recall the flat-planed face of my neighbor, and the peculiar gesture she made on the street. Then I imagine that instead of simply holding out a hand to me, she beckons me up the stairs to her dark apartment. I can almost see her thin sloping shoulders, the piercing eyes that blink at me in expectant silence.

I turn the newspaper over on my bare knees and read the first column of listings. The small, mottled print is difficult to decipher, but with patience I make my way through it. Manya Probman, of Lodz, arrived in Jaffa this month, seeks any family or friends. Itzik Simion, age twelve, of Krakow I. L. Peretz School, lost parents Rachmil and Klara in Birkenau, seeks sister Rosa, last known of in Warsaw. The listings go on and on, giving ages and nicknames, home villages and school graduation dates. At the top of each column the instructions are repeated: Those who find the name of a loved one can contact the Program for Family Reunification in Tel Aviv at the address listed here. In the help of God we will place our trust.

Near the bottom of one column, a single name is underlined in muddy pencil: Feliks Rotstein. Seeks sister Lilka, last known in Dachau, or any person with information on her whereabouts.

I stare at the newsprint, waiting for it to reveal more. It doesn't. In the quarter-hour that I sit on this balcony, the only revelation I'm privy to is that the sun can give me a ferocious headache. When at last I retreat to the living room, the sweat is rolling down my back.

Laughter from the outside. A key turns in the Shachars' apartment door, and Nachum and a slight dark-haired man all but fall into the entry. The smaller man says something indistinct, then the two double over, gleeful as children, hooting until they have to grip each other's wrists for support.

Seated across the table from me, Fanya eyes them with amusement. "And what have you two fools done now?"

Tami, who has said almost nothing in the ten minutes since I arrived, rises and takes down another two coffee cups from the cabinet.

Nachum is wagging his head at his companion; tears vanish in the stubble of his jaw. "Unbelievable. It was all I could do not to laugh aloud and give him away. Those poor Frenchmen, I've never had much sympathy for the French before, but now . . ."

Nachum's companion straightens and attempts a solemn look. "See here, Nachum. The non-Jews"—he drops a hand through the air, a dismissive gesture that proclaims his precise opinion of non-Jews—"either they want to kill us, or else they want to kiss our Jewish behinds. Look, the tourists can't get over their love affair with the Promised Land. 'Isn't it romantic, Jews living at last, despite all difficulties, in their own country.' They want to see some brave Jews firsthand, surviving by their wits. So Nachum, it's not so terrible. All we did was show some French tourists a little Jewish wit."

"Nachum!" Fanya's voice cuts through the men's talk; I see that her music students must not only admire her, but also fear her slightest reprimand. "Tell," she says.

Nachum turns to the kitchen table, where Tami, Fanya, and I sit, and his eyes shine with warmth. "Ach, Fanya, we've been bad at the shop today. Yoni worst of all, but Moti here and I, we weren't much better. We had more visitors from the university's beginner Hebrew-language course today, this time two Frenchmen. Came with their list of items to find and questions to ask storekeepers. Don't ask me how the teachers dream up these assignments, sending students who don't speak a word of Hebrew all around town. These two were straight out of a cartoon. Thick accents, one even had a big mustache. 'Good afternoon,' they said. Very polite. Yoni behind the register and Moti at the door of the back room, and I sitting on a rung of a stock ladder with my arms crossed like so, we all said, 'Good afternoon.' Good afternoon, good afternoon. Then the taller one opened his mouth and read off his sheet of paper, and you must believe me, he laid down each word like a trowelful of concrete. All the while the other one is smiling beside him and ready to copy down our answers on his homework paper. 'Where is the merchandise from?' the tall one asked.

"And Yoni blinked and answered them just as slowly. 'The merchandise is from my asshole.'

"The short one started thumbing through his dictionary. Shaking his head, conferring with the tall one. They had Yoni repeat it, too, and when they couldn't find the word, they looked at their sheet and moved on to the next question. 'Where is the transistor radio from?' the tall one asked. 'The transistor radio is from Moti's asshole,' Yoni said, and pointed to Moti. They looked at Moti, they smiled, they waited. Moti started choking, he went to the back of the shop, where he laughed so hard"— Nachum jabs his companion, who nods weakly—"you laughed so hard, Moti, I heard the tool rack rattling."

Tami pours two cups of coffee and nudges them to the center of the table. She reaches for the newspaper and rolls it, tight.

"The students, so polite, they went back to their vocabulary sheets and found a question that suited them better. 'How much costs the telephone answering machine?' they wanted to know.

" 'Aaaah.' Yoni lit up and held his arms out to them: now at last he understood. 'The telephone answering machine. The telephone answering machine is from both of your assholes and it costs fifty shekels.' 'That's very cheap,' the tall one said. He was quite enthusiastic, and made sure the other one wrote down the price correctly. I swear it, he beamed his gratitude at Yoni. Yoni said, 'Yes, considering where it comes from, it's a very good price.'

"And they thanked him and walked out." Nachum sighs, then turns a wondering expression to the ceiling. "God help me, I felt sorry for them and I followed them into the street, I told them give me their pencil and I will answer their questions. But they were very proud and said they did not want to cheat, they would do the whole assignment themselves. And then, God help them, they went next door to Yoel's shop."

"Yoel the Mohel!" Moti crows.

"Oy, Moti, watch your manners around the women." Nachum smacks the crown of Moti's head, then looks at me apologetically.

"A mohel is someone who performs circumcisions," Fanya explains for my benefit.

"We call the shopkeeper next door by that name because he's likely to . . ." Nachum pauses; I even think I see him blush. It appears he has a firm, if unusual, definition of the limits of crudeness. "If you don't watch Yoel carefully, he's likely to undercut . . . that is, to be so dishonest you feel you've been—"

"Nachum, we get the idea." Fanya turns to me, and her expression sweeps an invisible curtain between these juvenile men and us women. Then she smiles at Nachum and Moti, wrapping all of us in one mischievous conspiracy.

Moti, a brown-skinned man with jug ears, looks at Nachum with the undisguised admiration of a younger brother. He speaks, and as he does Nachum grants approval, looping an arm around his neck. The two of them are a picture of contentment. "You should have seen what happened when the Frenchmen got next door," Moti says. "We were watching from the stoop. Yoel thought they looked too old to be students. He thought they were government tax people sent to check his inventory, and he chased them from his shop with a broom. And you can believe me, what he shouted after them in the street made Yoni sound like a saint." As they hum with laughter, Nachum disengages his arm and cuffs Moti on the shoulder. "Ach," he sighs, drawing a cup to him and slurping from its rim.

"Ach," Moti agrees.

There is a strange noise from Tami, a pained release of air that might be a cough or the clearing of her throat. Pivoting to the kitchen table, she throws down her newspaper with such force that it bounces to the floor. Her face is clenched. "You could at least say thank you for the entire afternoon I spent picking up after everyone in this house." She spits the words at Nachum.

Moti looks at the floor; I concentrate on my folded hands. Out of the corner of my eye I see that Fanya maintains a clear and steady gaze at Tami, as if nothing out of the ordinary has happened.

Nachum speaks up. I've never heard such a cautious tone in his voice, yet clearly it is not new, he has recited this apology until it is a route he walks blindly, a path worn into stone. "But honey, I didn't mean to be rude. I haven't even looked around yet to notice." He swivels in his seat and sweeps the kitchen and living room with a glance. The rooms are bright with dust motes, clean, and—in spite of simple furniture and occasional wall hangings—barren. "It looks terrific in here," he says.

Tami lifts a hand in anguish, but her fury is already losing momentum and she roams among her own words as if lost. "Don't try to make up for it now. Don't bother pretending you care. You do what you like."

Nachum raises heavy lids to watch Tami. He has forgotten his friend and the doings at the shop; he is alert only to his wife, and he searches her expression as if he may yet find the thing that will please her. "Is there something I should do to help?"

"No. There's nothing." The words are a mumble. Tami's gaze wanders, homeless. "Do whatever suits you."

"If there's something I can do . . ." Nachum's voice trails off into silence.

Moti, his ears a hot red, wears the confused expression of an abandoned playmate. His eyes flicker across mine, I see he is looking for a neutral topic. His glance falls on the newspaper lying flat on the floor. "So they say there may be some chance of progress," Moti says. When no one responds, he reads aloud from the headline: " 'Talks focus on hopes for peace—work begun in Madrid is affirmed.' "

Tami opens the faucet and scrubs at a plate. Nachum twirls a spoon between his fingers and stares at nothing.

Moti leans forward. He seems to physically will the vigor into his voice. "What did you think of Madrid, Mrs. Gutman?"

"Madrid? Good heavens," Fanya says. But I see from the set of her chin that she will help Moti. "The food is good, I suppose. And of course they do have a reasonable art museum."

"I mean the peace conference."

Fanya twists her mouth into a pretty bow. "Like I said, Madrid. Food and art. If some Jews and Arabs want to go and have a peace negotiation there, I wish them well. They only shouldn't miss the Prado."

Nachum nudges the newspaper closer with his foot, and his face brightens. "Some progress would be nice, what do you say?"

Moti grins. "Progress would be nice."

"What do they say in America?" Nachum asks me.

"America is a great country," Moti breathes.

"They say there should be peace," I chime in usefully.

Nachum starts in his chair, a playful imitation of surprise. "What do you know? America is very smart, then. There should be peace. We can all agree to that."

Moti pulls away from the table. His expression takes on a dreamy solemnity; he speaks with his eyes half closed. "Peace. We need peace." He hesitates. "Only I worry. For my kids, if we bargain wrong. What if we agree to a peace and it turns out it's still not safe? Will there be more terror for the next generation, and worse?" He opens his eyes and looks self-consciously around the table, as though he does not recognize this meditative tone in his own voice. Hastily he reaches for the familiar; his speech accelerates, and his words are too loud for the small kitchen. "What I mean is, maybe we need to ask what kind of peace are we looking for. What I mean is, if we're not careful, if we're not very careful, we'll end up with a kind of peace . . . we'll have a peace from Arafat's asshole. Or worse, from Kahane's." In the quiet sunlight of the kitchen Moti guffaws; then his face registers alarm. "Beg pardon for my language." He waves uneasily in Tami's direction.

Tami stands rubbing her shoulders beside the sink.

Still chuckling, Moti shifts in his chair. Nachum pats his friend's forearm absently. "It's all right," he says. "It's all right."

Soon Nachum and Moti leave, and Fanya goes to pick up Ariela from her scout program. Tami sits at the table. I know it is time for me to leave. As Nachum was going out I heard him repeat that the apartment looked wonderful, and although Tami did not seem to hear him, he lingered a moment before following Moti into the stairwell. If I leave Tami alone in the apartment, perhaps Nachum will return and they will speak. But for some perverse reason I stay. I sit across from Tami and cradle my empty coffee cup in my hands. If I were the person I pretend to be in my letters, I tell myself, I wouldn't just sit here like an idiot. I would use every minute to learn.

I open my mouth with no idea what will come out. "Do soldiers like Dov get weekends off?" I ask.

Tami blinks. "It depends."

"And what if he chooses the army for his career? Will he have regular time off then?"

"It depends."

Wondering whether anything outside of her husband's failings will engage this woman's interest, I try another tack. "How long has Fanya taught singing?"

"Years."

"It's great that she does that."

Tami says nothing.

"I mean, I always used to wish my mother liked the arts. I danced, in high school. College, too." I examine the brown ring at the bottom of my coffee cup. "But doesn't Fanya live in Tel Aviv?"

Tami nods.

"Then why is she always in Jerusalem?"

"It's summer. The concert halls in Jerusalem are cooler."

"That's why?"

Tami shrugs.

"So—if you don't mind my asking—why does Fanya live in Israel?" As I speak, Tami looks at me warily. "She talks about Europe all the time. And it seems she's the first in line for every European cultural event that comes through Jerusalem. The way she talks, it almost sounds like she wants to be there, not here."

Tami picks something from under one fingernail.

I continue. "I know a lot of Jews stayed as far as possible from Europe after World War Two, but Fanya doesn't seem to be bothered by any of that. She doesn't seem to be bothered by . . . by trauma." As soon as I speak the word, I regret it. It sounds like something out of a television talk show, and not at all what I meant to say.

Tami is watching me. Her light-hazel eyes reveal nothing. "Fanya doesn't care about trauma," she tells me matter-of-factly. "It doesn't touch her, it never did."

I don't know what to say. I try a different topic. "What was your father like?"

"Quiet."

"Nothing like Fanya, then?"

Tami purses her lips.

"What did he do?"

"He was a businessman, but mostly he did relief work with the war refugees." Before I can ask anything further, Tami heads me off. "I barely remember him."

"That's too bad."

Tami seems poised to make a tart reply, but instead she turns on me with a question. "Do you and your mother get along?"

There is only the briefest pause before my answer. "Yes."

"Then why are you here while she's sick?"

"She's not sick. She's doing fine. It makes her happy that I'm here." I trace the chipped corner of the tabletop with my fingernail. "Her cancer came back last fall. But she's doing very well now. The doctors think she's going to be just fine." I force a laugh. "I guess she's just the opposite of Fanya. She wants to come back to visit Israel more than just about anything, she won't bother going to Europe even though it's cheaper."

"Then why doesn't she come, if she's feeling well?"

Now it's my turn to shrug. "Her work."

"Have you invited her?"

"I'm sure she'll let me know if she's free to visit. For now she just likes hearing about Israel through my letters. You know, I write about all the things going on here. All the issues."

Tami doesn't seem impressed. She looks away, bored. "You think I'm humorless," she says, "because I don't gush over Fanya."

It's a feeble answer, but it's out of my mouth and there's no taking it back. "I didn't say that."

"You're charmed by her, like the rest of them," Tami says flatly. "You think you'd be thrilled with Fanya if you were in my shoes. But you don't ask your own mother to come visit you."

"It's not that I'm not inviting her. She can't come because of her work."

Tami rises to return the milk to the refrigerator.

I feel my pulse pounding in my temples. Before I can stop myself I am talking at her back. "At least I try."

"*Try?*" And for the first time I know that I have Tami's complete attention, for she nearly chokes on the word. "What kind of trying do you want from me?"

The words come haltingly, but Tami's bluntness creates an opening into which I can say anything. So I say what I have no business saying. "Maybe you ought to give Fanya a chance. Or Nachum. He wanted to make it up to you before, he just didn't know how."

Tami opens the refrigerator door. She sets the milk on the shelf and closes the door firmly. Then she says more than I have ever heard her say at a stretch. "What's the point?" The desolation in her voice is so complete that I find myself trying to shut out her words. "After the miscarriages after Dov, do you think *Fanya* tried? She sailed in from Tel Aviv for an afternoon each time, she said, 'You'll be all right, Tami. You always could take care of yourself.' Checked her purse for bus fare to Tel Aviv, patted me on the shoulder, and walked out the door." Tami draws a deep breath, then releases it. She eyes me with what might be satisfaction. " 'Give Fanya a chance'? I don't believe in new beginnings. Look around you. People get stuck and they stay stuck."

We're both silent. Then Tami looks down to the floor and points a sandaled foot at the newspaper. "Everyone talking about new beginnings, and do you know what? I don't believe any of it is going to happen."

I stare at the headlines, the worn sandal straps, Tami's narrow toes. "Maybe you and Fanya can change things between you. These things aren't impossible." I grope for words. "My mother believes in new beginnings. She works at a place where she has to." I've already said too much; Tami's gaze drifts to the window. But whatever she may think of me, I want her to understand at least this one thing. "She's the strongest person I know."

Tami says nothing, and I realize that the conversation is over. As I get up to leave, I know that there will be no hard feelings. Tami has spoken her mind and I've spoken mine. She won't waste her energy bearing a grudge, and I take peculiar solace in her indifference.

"Dov sent a message," Tami says. "He wants to know are both you and your boyfriend coming to the desert."

I lift my coffee cup, but instead of taking it to the sink I stand motionless. "He really wants me to come?"

Tami's answer is brutally faint. "Didn't he say he wants you to come."

"Why?" The question is a demand for honesty. And I know that Tami, of all people, will not disappoint me.

She meets my eyes, an artless woman caught in a thin band of sunlight in this Jerusalem kitchen. "I don't try to guess why he wants anything, anymore."

ᔕᔓᔕ

No, Lilka. No, it cannot be so. But Lilka says yes. Shakes her curls. Look, there. Look. She stands in her school uniform and stretches a pointing hand. Look, America is burning.

No, you have misunderstood, I tell Lilka. That cannot be. American footsteps caused the fire in camp but then Americans came to stop it. Americans bring salvation, how can America burn? Lilka insists, but I stop my ears and will not hear her. You are wrong, I whisper, it cannot be.

"It can be," Karol says. My apartment is gone, Lilka has vanished, I search for her in vain. Now I stand in woods by the river and I smell the machine oil that streaks his trousers. I turn to Karol, I reach to brush his rolled woolen sleeves. "It can be," he repeats, and his thick hands are helpless with gentleness. I watch the horizon of cloth stretch across the width of his shoulders. "Why do you say it's impossible," he chides, "for a non-Jew to love a Jew? I know it is possible. So answer me only this. Is it possible, is it possible that a Jew loves a non-Jew?" His voice teases, but in his face a sudden stillness. "Little girl, is it possible she loves him already?"

It was after the party, hail melting in gutters, street punctuated with white pockmarks, that he first stood before me. My head ringing with change: morning fading to afternoon, the guests one by one departing, and then Halina calling her final good-byes. Halina holding steady a brave smile, helped onto a train by a uniformed porter who swung her suitcase wide. Exhaustion drew my shoulders to earth. It was the last of the trash from the party that I carried now on my hip, down the alley and he stood waiting. Easily he lifted the heavy wooden lid from the garbage bin. Fair-haired goy, Gentile boy, I dropped my eyes and did not look. How Halina would have smiled at the size of his boots but she was gone, I was alone now, I could not show her this Gentile stranger. I waited for him to step aside. And then, he spoke my name. How could I not look? Up and up into a face the heavens made for receiving their rain, a blond brow to furrow at faraway thunder. Cheeks flushed at their crests like hilltops crowned with buds, blue eyes that would lift in steady gratitude. And the curious smile as he held high the lid, one corner of his mouth rising in greeting, the other tucked down in humor. "I know you," he said.

His name Karol, and he asked only to walk me to the river and back.

Our feet made faint prints in packed earth, hail melted quiet rings into the darkening soil. As the path curved back toward town he slowed, he said You are the girl who makes up stories. You walk by the river, you step under the trees and dream fairy tales, then you tell them to your sister. But perhaps, he said, perhaps since your sister is gone you will be silent. His solitary voice seeded the twilight, I stood still to listen. Perhaps, he said, I might someday hear one of your stories.

A week after I meet him I have shuttered the Gentile in memory, he is a tale untold and so the world shines autumn yellow and does not believe in him. During my afternoon walks I too cannot recall the sound of his voice, the span of his boots on cobblestone. I work in the shop, I lie awake in a deserted room. I notice one evening that I too have grown invisible, without Halina I am a story unspoken and no one sees.

Then a Sunday afternoon and his shirt smelling stale and dangerous, the smell of incense swooning from the dark stone doorways of churches. Yet he, wearing danger in the fibers of his clothing, stands patient awaiting my greeting. How long he must have walked from their village's church, flecks of mud on his Sunday trousers. Hat in chafed hands. I lift my head to him in recognition. May I walk with you? he asks. We cross narrow streets and leave sunlight behind as we step into woods: a Gentile boy and I, two passing cloud-shadows no one sees. I've watched you for a long time, he says. Only a few moments, he says, and then I will turn and begin my walk back to the village. Let me tell you a story now, I will tell you about my father's farm. And perhaps someday you will tell me a story in exchange.

Halina, I breathe when she comes for her first holiday. Halina I must tell you. Words cluster and beat inside me, how shall I utter a thing no one will want to hear?

Halina watches my struggle for words, then as if she tears her own heart she speaks. I know, she says, her slim arms loose and helpless at her sides. I know, you have met with a Gentile boy. Shifraleh, do you love him? My sister's breath sings ragged, my sister's lovely hands lift and drop, repentant. If Mother and Father should find out, she says.

Karol, touching my chin until I look up into still blue eyes still blue heavens. I will wait for you again next week, he says. I will stand beneath the bridge until you come and we can walk, will you walk with me once more?

Karol is like rain, I tell Halina. He comes to meet me in hush and

*whisper. When he is gone there is peace, and a stirring of things begin-
ning fresh. He is the stranger who teaches, the Gentile who listens. Karol
shows me the newspaper that he reads, dark print curled in his hands.
He works all day on the farm but at night he reads about what he has
seen while bringing the harvest into Warsaw. He studies machines,
Halina, he will bring machines to the farm so that his family will not
have to work so terribly hard. He will show his family they do not have
to be afraid of new things, and when he does then we will share a life.*

*Halina, rosy with University, has grown pale, she has fallen into a
well of silence. From deep she looks at me, her eyes are moons reflect-
ing the uncertain glimmer of my words. Shifra remember what this
would mean, she begins. A Gentile, a Catholic. Remember what they did
to Uncle Hayyim.*

*But now Halina stops, she is heavy with words unspoken. She bows
her head. I want only your happiness, she says. And I see now. You are
so happy when you tell of him, I know your voice Shifra and I hear him
living there. Is it, perhaps? Is it perhaps possible? She reaches for my
shoulder, she is a blind girl groping for a handhold. She is my fearless
sister whom they cannot stop from dreaming of charts and tables, her
throat is bare in the new fashion she has brought from University. A soft
white cotton—Father has forbidden it and I have seen Mother take the
blouse from Halina's suitcase in secret and iron it with admiration.*

Shifra, she says. If you truly want to be with him, then I will help you.

Yes, I say, Halina. Yes I love.

*Oh but Lilka takes my arm and Halina is gone. The forest fades as
well, Karol drops his hand, he is helpless clay. America is burning, Lilka
says to me in the harsh yellow light of my apartment. Karol, I cry out
his name. I listen for his receding steps on the damp dirt path. But it is
only Lilka again now, Lilka as she was in camp before the bullets took
her, now she quivers with fear in the stale air of my apartment. America is burning, she insists. Hunger has stretched her face until it is taut
with surprise, her eyes watch from deep in their hollows as if she is an
old woman and not a girl. I know she would laugh if I set a mirror before her. But there are tears in her eyes, I do not dare. Someone must put
out the American fire, she mouths.*

*Lilka, you are wrong. Don't you remember, I charge her. Don't you
remember. The Americans are not burning. The Americans come to put
out the flame.*

In camp those who would have cried out the rumor like gulls instead opened their mouths and summoned unknown strength to whisper. Americans. The Americans are coming. Guards' faces drew tight with fear. The Americans, thousands of Americans, closer with every step every second every beating of this stone this heart.

There was a fire. Lilka, the Americans did not start it, can you understand? The camp guards, the camp guards fearful of the blank palms of their own hands, doused the records house in gasoline. They stood singly, they watched the evidence of their victory swallowed in layers of fire. Women on work detail beside the building were painted with flames, how they pivoted with fantastic strength as they burned, some leapt out of the building's flames and some in, it was impossible to tell which leapt from and which into fire.

I was across the barren square when the flames shot to open blue sky. Women danced in fire and I ran toward the flames. I ran, I danced, I would have plunged into flames with the writhing women. I will dive into the embrace of flame I will rest in the peace of death. But an arm wrapped my chest, wrenched me back. "Americans," this skeleton clutching me hissed. "The Americans will come. They are coming to save us. If you believe, if you last a few days longer, the Americans will come."

Americans, bringers of antiseptic and water. Americans, round faces contorted from a stench I no longer smelled, one poured a full can of shining water over his own head, a can of water wasted into hard earth only to rid him of our touch. "We will make you well," a freckled American soldier said. "We will make you whole again, we will make—"

"Drink," said his companion. "Slowly. A little soup at a time."

Lilka, do you understand now, the Americans did not make the fire. It came because they came, but they were not to blame. The Americans promised to free us from past, they promised us a future.

Lilka reaches out as if to touch my face. I must be patient with her. The questions we never asked each other, now she wishes to ask. The things we did not say, circles of regret. She is sorry she has waited so long to speak. How could you keep such a secret as a non-Jew without anyone knowing, she asks now. Shifra. How did you speak to him? Could you really have loved him?

Let me tell you his stories, Lilka, I begin. I will tell you his stories and mine, I will explain all. About Karol, about your brother Feliks and his poor memory for the face of a Gentile boy who beat him at the side of a road he could not describe. And more, Lilka. At last you will hear every secret, for now I will hold nothing back from you.

But Lilka is no longer listening. America is burning, she whispers. Helpless, she raises a hand and points. At the television. Here, in my apartment. And I look to the television at last, and it is true what Lilka says. America, burning. We watch together in silence, her fingertips caressing the loose buttons of my sleeve. The Israeli announcer announces and he says that it is a city of angels, Los Angeles of America, he says, consequences of last year's riots are still apparent in— Community rebuilding efforts have done little to change the— Now he gives way to an American announcer and there are subtitles but I do not read, I watch only the lips of the American announcer that waver in the heat of a city of flame behind him. On the television, black forms twist against streets of fire. An American future burning. These blacks are not like ours, they have grown tired of waiting for their redemption, now they dance before an orange-lit sky. Leaping against fire, leaping out of and into fire as we did.

The picture switches to the agricultural report and I turn from the television.

And I say to Lilka, No. I will not allow you to utter such things. America cannot be on fire. America is the future, how can it be burnt by past? Americans know how to press cigarettes and chocolate into trembling hands, how to turn blowing of flames into the sound of pouring water. In America, ice cream comes from a machine when you press a lever, boys drive cars without roofs in America, and no one weeps. It is the promising land, America. Our future has been promised.

Above, a wind rustles the American's apartment. Night and day I have waited for Her, I will not allow doubt to enter my heart now. Americans will bend the sky and come down, I chant as Lilka leaves me. Touch the mountains and they will smoke. O Americans, You will not ignore us forever. You will not hide Your faces always. Restore the luster to our eyes, lest we sleep the sleep of death; lest our enemies say, We have overcome them.

But I trust in Your faithfulness, my heart will exult in Your deliverance.

I will sing to my American, for She will be good to me.

Uttering my devotions with all my strength, I leave my apartment and climb the stairs.

∽∾

It takes Gil several days to notice the missing cloth, but when he does he knows immediately that I am responsible. "How am I supposed to get work done in this apartment?" His eyes are dark with fatigue, his throat is corded with tension. When he rocks forward in the entryway and seizes my wrist, a stranger might think he was merely reaching out for balance. "How am I supposed to get work done, Maya, if my supplies disappear?"

I do not hear the footsteps, exactly. But I feel them, coming closer as I stumble from Gil's blow. With every throb in my veins, every rush of air between Gil's quick-turning frame and mine, they near.

The door is not locked, not even properly shut; Gil was upon me the instant I entered the apartment. So it is easy for the woman from downstairs to open the door. Easy for her to stand in the entry while Gil goads me to produce the cloth. Only I, my cheek against the cool plaster of the wall, see her. Her features are as plain as I remember, she wears the same faded brown skirt and her kerchief is askew, revealing a spongy tangle of gray and blond. She looks at me and I at her. The apartment is dark and bright, sunlight sweeps Gil's tired face and leaves her figure in shadow.

Something about her stillness makes me hold myself motionless as well, as though Gil's swinging arm could not hurt me. Her eyes, glittering like sapphires, are trained on me. The hunger on her face is so intense I hardly notice when her lips begin moving. Like a person swept up in prayer, she sways.

It is the sound of her chanting that makes Gil pause, arm raised halfway above his head. He stares at me as though, for just an instant, he believes I am the source of this odd speech weaving between the two of us; as though, frozen mid-blow, he's glimpsed some life in me he cannot reach with his restless hands.

Then his gaze falters. "What the hell?"

I lay his voice gently aside. I strain, instead, to hear her words.

Her speech is a papery croon that begins in a Slavic-sounding language and shifts to Yiddish, then blends into Hebrew. And now, out of nowhere, come English phrases, nonsense mixed with the ancient Hebrew of psalms. I am transfixed. *I lift mine eyes whence will come my help I lift mine eyes. For lo my sight has grown dim but my help will come. New new all-new flavor, Cadillac convertible the wind in your hair my help will come feel like one hundred dollars. Drink Coca-Cola and smile. New shirt new shoes new fresh lemon scent whence cometh my help from the skies and smile.*

Gil lowers his arm.

She stops. She has not taken her eyes from me since she appeared; now she bends her neck and backs away stiffly, a petitioner departing a formal audience.

She is gone.

"What the hell," Gil breathes. His arms hang helpless at his sides; his hands, forgotten, remain curled in two fists that seem to belong to someone else.

I slip past him into the kitchen and take a tray of ice from the freezer.

"What's a black woman doing walking in on us in our own apartment?" Gil is still facing the door.

"She's not one of them."

"What?" He blinks, distracted.

"She's not one of the religious."

Gil turns at my words but there is only bewilderment in his voice. The danger of the afternoon has disappeared, for now. "She was chanting psalms and who knows what other babble," he corrects me.

"Still." In my single whispered word is an unexpected defiance.

He glances at me suspiciously. "Since when are you on such close terms with our downstairs neighbor?"

Just a bit more water for the blooming cactus, then. A twist to rotate it in the sun, a finger to test the dampness of the soil. "I'm not, it's only a guess."

"If she's not religious then why does she wear that kerchief?"

"Maybe just to cover her head."

"And why does she live in this neighborhood?"

"Why do *we* live in this neighborhood?" I'm breathless at my own boldness, but I don't back down; I act as if our neighbor is still standing in the doorway, protecting me with her strange performance.

The pale angles of Gil's face seem naked, vulnerable. "We live in this neighborhood," he tells me, "on a lark. I doubt that spook from downstairs would give the same explanation." He rubs his arm. "I'm inclined to go downstairs and tell her it's pretty damn rude to come bursting in on people." He doesn't move.

Later that afternoon, he will sigh. "Just too fucking weird," he'll say. "The black-hat men interest me but their women are just too fucking weird."

Dear Maya,
Did you ever wonder how . . .

Dear Mom,
I think it's because of the situation here that so many people . . .

Dear Maya,
I never appreciated before how much you're . . .

Dear Mom,
This week I went to the ruins of . . .

Dear Maya,
I'd like to tell you why I decided to . . .

Dear Mom,
Yes I know . . .

Fanya wafts into the entryway with a faint smell of lilacs. So few women wear perfume in this country the scent makes me light-headed. I have cleared Gil's drawings to one side for her visit; she looks at them curiously, but comments only on the prettiness of the lace curtain, the arrangement of furniture in the apartment. Her compliments fluster me but warm me as well.

At last Fanya perches on Gil's wooden stool. "Now tell me," she says. "Why don't you get out more often? You're a pretty girl, you're dazzling when you smile, and that mysterious boyfriend of yours should know you need to get out and be seen. Why don't you come to a concert with me tonight? And you'll join me for a walk first, won't you? It is simply a crime to stay inside on such a mild day. Who knows whether we'll get *hamsin* again tomorrow, and then no one will want to leave the house." So many people Fanya must introduce me to, the Grinbaums and the Hellermans and that Yosef Cohen, of course they're all elderly and I'll be bored, still it would do me good to see some culture, heaven knows culture is in rare enough supply. The concert will be piano duets, any skirt I have will be fine, I'll need a sweater of course for the evening chill. Her enthusiasm propels me to the bedroom. As I change my shorts for a skirt and search the dresser top for a hair clip, Fanya keeps up the conversation from her seat in the living room.

"When I was a girl in Amsterdam," she is saying, "my aunt Rivka had a shop that sold brassieres and ladies' undergarments. My girlfriend Klara and I used to pick out the finest finery and Rivka would make a gift of it, we only had to promise not to let our parents see. We'd wear that silk and lace under our regular clothing, we'd promenade all over Amsterdam and no one would know. But *we* knew. And it made us act bold as princesses. Sneaking into parties, milling with the crowd at the opera house simply because we felt we were the most elegant young ladies in the city. And everywhere we went, people believed we belonged, and made way for us without question. You are who you decide you are, and we were the toast of Amsterdam those nights. Now, that was a life. That was a city. Of course the boys never stopped following us, sometimes we'd make a game of eluding them. We'd step into a building and then from a window we'd watch the schoolmate who had been trailing us and make bets on how long he'd loiter on the street trying to run into us 'by accident.' " Fanya smiles softly. "Oh, but we were terrible."

My hair pinned in an approximation of a French twist, a white blouse tucked into my longest skirt, I step before Fanya and am relieved when she smiles her approval. I'm ready to leave now, yet Fanya makes no move to stand. "I never had trouble finding boyfriends," she reflects. "But Klara, she was always the prettiest of all." Fanya looks down at her folded hands, the mother-of-pearl-polished fingernails. When, after a moment, she looks back up, there is no wistfulness in her expression— only a cheer so vivid it puts me to shame.

I hear the key turn in the door and wish I'd hurried Fanya through her story. As Gil's footsteps sound in the entryway, I am aware of a small, dense pocketful of anger; I want him to leave us be.

"So finally I'll meet this mysterious fellow," Fanya says.

We hear Gil drop his satchel to the floor.

"Fanya Gutman," I explain, as he appears in the living room.

Fanya smiles and offers her hand.

"I've heard a lot about you." With a slight bow of his head, Gil takes her hand. Then he smiles at her, and I'm possessed by an absurd jealousy.

"And I you," Fanya says. "Maya speaks about you often, but she never said how charming you were."

"Maya speaks about me?" Gil asks. I could swear he's blushing. "Well, I'm sure not as often as I do about her."

And as if it were the most natural thing in the world to do, Gil rests a warm hand on my shoulder. He plants a kiss, then, on my forehead, a gentle kiss that cannot be anything but sincere. I accept it without moving. Confused, I allow Gil and Fanya's conversation to pass me by. Through a single gesture, my anger with Gil has been undercut. I think I must be crazy.

"Now tell me, Gil," Fanya is saying, "who is that woman peering like a criminal from behind her door? She nearly frightened the wits out of me on my way up the stairs."

"She's one of the black-hats," Gil says with a sour face, eliciting a titter from Fanya. I wonder if he is going to dare more. And he does. "We even caught her spying on us up here once. It was while we were having an argument." Gil makes the confession with an amused, apologetic expression; even the best of couples, after all, have arguments. "She was so curious about what goes on between a modern secular couple, she couldn't stay away."

After he's finished speaking, there is a short silence. As Gil's eyes linger on Fanya's, I am able to let go of my envy long enough to realize that he's not flirting with her. He is searching for absolution. If she allows his account of our argument to pass, there can be nothing wrong.

"What do you expect from the blacks?" A hint of bitterness tinges Fanya's laughter. "They can't get over their own solemn selves, of course they want to see a secular couple having a difficult day. Otherwise, can you imagine their resentment?"

"I don't think that woman is religious," I say, but my words are lost as Gil takes up the subject enthusiastically.

"But Fanya, don't you think there's more to them than that? Don't you think there's something remarkable about the black-hats? Who knows, maybe they're happier than the rest of us, because they're not worried about anything—they're just trying to stick to traditions, and be worthy of their deliverance."

"Remarkable?" And Fanya does something I have never seen her do while speaking to a man: she takes a step backward. "My dear boy," she says, and there is no trace of charm in her voice. "Anyone who can't let go of his dolorous history and enjoy a sunny day is as big a fool as ever lived. Good heavens." She laughs without mirth. "They could at least learn to dress for the weather."

Gil insists. "Still, don't you think they have something the rest of us lack, something maybe we need?"

Fanya's shoulders press back; her stance is almost militant. Although Gil towers over her, her posture is uncompromising; it invites no intimacy. Without her coquettish manner her features are suddenly dull and heavy; I see in them weariness, and a terrible fear of age. And something else—a blunt and frozen rage. "I don't need anything the blacks have," Fanya enunciates.

I couldn't say where it is that I walk in the hours after attending the concert with Fanya. The smell of simmering onions floats along the street, together with the sound of soft conversation and laughter from kitchen windows as families gather for a late dinner. Lamplight brims over sills, dresses the walls of buildings in gold and shadow. The uneven planes of stone look soft—individual as familiar faces, and susceptible to interpretation. Darkness, deepening, grants and snatches away: three whispering schoolgirls in shorts cross quickly through a park, loose sandals slapping the stone-paved path; then they are gone. I pass down the sidewalk, my own footsteps an apologetic murmur.

At Ticho House, it seemed everyone knew Fanya. Even the pianists, a father and son come from Russia only this year. After the concert they greeted Fanya with obvious pleasure, the father bowing ponderously at the waist, his bald head red from effort. They had played duets, two pairs of hands in unison, two minds in perfect and wordless agreement. I'd sat in the audience and imagined geese circling and skimming, landing together on a dark surface. Or, I'd asked myself, was it supposed to be swans? Geese weren't graceful enough for this picture, were they? I imagined geese braking wildly as they landed, their outstretched feet shooting jets of water at delicately indignant swans.

Listening to music in this safe and orderly gallery with its domed ceilings and rows of folding chairs, I realized how long it had been since I'd joked in the privacy of my mind. This recital was gentle, slow-tempoed; the notes spilled forward and then came the diminuendo, Europe nestled beneath pale-blue arches. I sat in an audience of men and women, few younger than forty and most wearing glasses. Fanya marked rhythm with her stockinged foot; she nudged her discarded shoes beneath her chair and ignored the woman fanning herself nois-ily with a program in the row behind us. The hardness I'd glimpsed in her earlier had been erased. Fanya's demeanor as she listened was of the most rapt delight.

During the reception, a gentleman Fanya introduced as Shmuel Roseman took my hand in both of his and shook it for a long while. He addressed Fanya in a lilting banter that could not mask the hope shining in his eyes. "Fanya, you're here in Jerusalem again and you haven't come to visit me? Not even one little outing to the jeweler's shop to say hello?"

"I scarcely arrived from Tel Aviv this minute," Fanya told him, and Shmuel blushed before asking if she would be so charitable as to ac-company a poor doddering gentleman on a picnic the next day. I watched Fanya drift between No and Weather Permitting and finally alight on Perhaps, promising to call him the next day at noon. At which Shmuel retreated, turning on me a beatific smile.

Afterward, Fanya and I walked together as far as Herzog Street. "Men," she sighed when we'd been walking for some time. "They won't take no for an answer. I'm sure you feel that way sometimes about Gil." On the quiet street, her laughter was a call to sisterhood—an invitation to join her in observing with pleased exasperation the follies and weak-nesses of men.

An invitation, I thought, to be normal.

I could have spoken at that moment, I could have told Fanya just one small thing about Gil. The way he sat over his work for hours at a stretch and did not hear me, even when I called his name. The way his shoulders tightened when he came home frustrated from the gallery. Fanya would have dismissed Gil in an instant, flicked his temper away with one toss of her head. *Out of the question, such behavior.*

I stood on the edge of Fanya's charmed circle, and its warmth made me shiver with envy. Then rebellion. She wouldn't understand. What-ever she guessed of the truth, she would be wrong. She would think Gil didn't love me, would think I was a fool to believe he did. But she couldn't see what I saw. Gil did love me. It was a different kind of love, only. A kind I hadn't seen before: stronger, harder to bear.

So I said nothing. I walked on, my hands clenched in obstinate loyalty.

Fanya's silence announced her disappointment as clearly as if she'd spoken it. My loyalty to a man, my refusal to share minor frustrations, hobbled me in her eyes. Bitterly, I wondered what she would think if she knew the truth.

At the intersection where our paths would diverge, Fanya faced me. "Something you should know," she said. "About your cousin Dov. He's behaving"—Fanya searched for the proper word—"regrettably. But it might help to know something, a thing that happened two years ago, in the summer. His best friend died. Dov has handled it terribly."

Standing opposite Fanya on the street corner, I tried to absorb what she was telling me. I tried to add it all up in my mind—Dov plus friend plus tragedy. But the sum was not forthcoming. Gradually the spectacle of my selfishness reared inside me. How small and bounded I had become. Tears started in my eyes, but they were tears for myself. In vain I tried to stamp down my self-pity and feel something for my hostile, bewildering cousin. To drown out my confusion, I spoke. "What happened?"

"His best friend, Rafi. Dehydrated in a *hamsin*. A training accident, Dov hasn't been the same since, and this time of year is the worst. Now he's making his decision about whether to stay in the army for his career. Of course he wants to do only the most dangerous assignments. He's worked up and arguing with everybody, no one can talk to him."

Somewhere, I knew, there existed another version of myself: a person who understood how to react to pain. Recalling how Fanya had blushed at the gentle flow of Mozart duets, I wondered whether she might, after all, help me find a way back to that other person. Silently I called to her for assistance.

Out loud I said, "I'm so sorry."

"Sorry?" Fanya's voice cut the night air. She waved a hand. "What's sorry? There's no sorry. There's only life before, and life after. Dov should know not to drag the living down with the dead. He's got to leave it behind."

"But his friend died. I'm sure he—"

"Rafi was a sweet boy," Fanya sighed. In the dark I could distinguish the outlines of her features, and her beautifully composed face offered no refuge. Without warning, Tami's hopeless tones echoed in my mind: a register of protests unspoken and emotions deadened. I imagined Tami as a child, frantic over some schoolyard slight, her mother's elegantly shawled shoulder turned in indifference. Now, under cover of dark, my tears flowed freely. I told myself they were for Tami.

Fanya checked the sleeves of her jacket, straightened each with a tug. "That's why Dov perhaps hasn't acted as nicely as he should. So now you understand not to take it personally." She spoke pleasantly, but the iron will behind her pretty words could not be mistaken. Nor could the charitable lie. "Dov thinks very highly of you, he told me so."

For a long time I walk the quiet streets. I wander in loops through the residential neighborhoods, turn corner after corner. When I make my way home, the night is blank with clouds. The buildings are emptied of light, their cooling stone walls yield no comfort.

The apartment is dark. I flip on the lights, first in the entryway, then in the living room. The clock on the wall reads two a.m. A stained feather quill lies below the empty drawing table, and several ink bottles have rolled into a corner. Propped against the stool are three cardboard tubes, which, I assume, hold Gil's new work. I look at them, but I don't go any nearer. The old paper sketches observe me from the clotheslines.

Holding my breath, I listen for movement. I hear nothing. I leave the living room and approach the open door of the unlit bedroom. When my eyes have adjusted I see that Gil is lying in the bed, watching me. He is swaddled in covers; only his head is visible. I stand with my hands resting lightly on either side of the door frame.

"I thought you weren't going to come home," he says at last.

I've never heard his voice so small.

I don't move. An unfamiliar thought sings in my head: *Run.*

"Maya?" he calls.

I step forward, for no reason other than that I am called.

"Maya," he mumbles.

I kneel beside the bed. I touch his lips, the damp streaks on his cheeks. Gently I cradle his neck and stroke his forehead, the soft roots of his hair. His hand reaches for mine and grips, so hard it stuns me. He waits.

"Don't ever think that," I tell him.

His hold on my hand is painful but the smell of him is sweet, he is a boy purified by soap and fear.

"Will you always come?" he asks.

His need exhausts me; to stand against it requires more energy than I can muster. So I open my mouth and speak. "I'll always come." Once I've begun, the words multiply with astonishing ease. "I tried to get home early, but Fanya wanted me to meet so many people I couldn't even get to a telephone. I was thinking of you the whole time."

Kneeling on the tile, I feel my heart pound with a new secret—I am lying to him.

And he believes me. Motionless beneath the sheet, he awaits reassurance. How weak he seems. How trusting and in need of protection. And clear as daylight, I see the flaw in myself, the knot of feelings his hands cannot penetrate—I don't need him as much as he needs me. I don't love him as much as he loves me.

Compassion rises wildly inside me at last so that I can barely speak; the pity I could not feel earlier for Dov now pours out, a desperate stream of fear for Gil. His vulnerability is everywhere I look, everywhere I touch. I caress his eyelids, his arms. The understanding that I could betray him fills me with panic, even as I experience an unexpected surge of power.

"Why do you believe in me?" he whispers, but I drown these words in affection. "You're moody," he says. "I don't understand you. You're so good to me and then you hurt me."

"Come, sleep," I say.

"I'll try," he tells me.

In the morning, I knew even before I look that there will be a bundle on my doorstep from the woman downstairs. I gather the loosely wrapped package into my arms and deposit it casually on a shelf. When Gil is gone I will pore over my neighbor's offering for hours—its faint smell of age, its black leatherette cover, its tiny print. I know that she has not read this book of psalms often, for although it is old the binding still crackles. Still, she has presented this gift for my eyes, and she means me to understand her message. I open the yellowed pages at random and read aloud. "Have mercy on me, O Lord, see my affliction at the hands of my foes, You who lift me from the gates of death." The words draw me in, lead me tantalizingly along a narrow trail of expectation, and tell me nothing. "So that in the gates of fair Zion I might tell all Your

praise, I might exult in Your deliverance." This time the wrapping is a
newspaper from the 1950s, a story about a kibbutz in the north closing
off its roads for fear of a repeat of the previous week's attack, which left
so many dead and so many wounded.

The woman downstairs is crazy. People who aren't crazy don't give
presents to strangers.

I write easily to my mother, sentences flow from my pen. These are
the things I have done, these are the places I have gone. I fold the sheaf
of pages into the envelope, I don't let myself pause. I have become a liar
and not even seen it happening. My words comfort Gil, they fly to
America and keep my mother well.

I set the addressed envelope on the kitchen table. I search for
stamps—in the bedroom, in the living room, in my pockets. I have
none. I sit at the table. My hands, unoccupied, trace the edges of the envelope. They look foreign: short stubby fingers, guilty of deceit. They
are trembling; I'm horrified by the shaking that passes from my hands
through the letter. I seize it and I rip and rip until this envelope of lies
is scattered on the table before me.

From amid the scraps I take the small black book. Once more I
open it, and with uneven breath I read.

O Lord, turn and rescue me. Deliver me as befits Your faithfulness.

Crazy. Completely crazy.

*I adore you O Lord, my strength, O Lord, my crag, my fortress, my rescuer,
my God, my rock in whom I seek refuge, my shield, my mighty champion, my
haven.*

It's clear there's something she wants from me.

As I read I walk to the living room, where I sit on the sofa. I close
the book and finger its binding. When I lift my eyes to the room around
me, Gil's sketches assail my vision.

Why would anyone believe I had something to give?

At last I see how fully my own lies have trapped me. I've worked
hard to win the warmth in my mother's letters—I've even enjoyed
shaping my own story for her benefit, feeling in control. But instead of
closeness, I've won isolation. Every hard-earned scrap of her respect
raises the stakes. I can't disappoint her now, I tell myself as I begin each
new letter. I can't, after all I've written to her, admit my own confusion.

Time after time I've searched my mother's replies for help. I've imagined I might find some piece of cryptic advice; tucked into the turn of

a phrase will be some instruction for how to understand this country, how to assure Gil's gentleness, how to endure. But my mother's letters contain no instruction, only testimony to her own endurance. And pride in me.

Tami can't help me. And I can't trust Fanya to understand. As for Orit and Michal, even if I knew how to contact them over summer vacation, their impatience would burst out before I'd spoken half a sentence. I started, once, to write a letter to Ina at her parents' address outside Purchase. But the words looked wrong on the page. No matter how I tried to tell the truth, I couldn't find a way to explain things properly. She wouldn't care how beautiful the sunsets are here, how the buildings catch the light and the people move more gracefully on the street because of it. How people look you in the eye when they pass, share their food at the bus stop, how the women hand their babies to strangers while they fumble in their purses for change, and know without exchanging a word that whatever they might think of each other, there is trust. They touch when they argue, here in Jerusalem; they touch when they joke, and when they embrace they clasp so tightly I'm convinced they'll never let go. I don't think they notice how their admonishing, imploring, sailing hands shape the air and the city and—I swear it—even the pink and gold sky above them.

Ina was hurt by the way I neglected her, studying and working extra waitressing shifts in the months before my departure. "I think I'm jealous of Israel," she told me once. I don't expect her to see what appeals to me about this beautiful, difficult country. "Just come home," she'd say. "Come back to where you belong."

There's no one I can talk to.

I sit on the sofa for a few more minutes. Distracted, I leaf through the book of psalms once more.

"Dov's trip is next week," I tell Gil at dinner that night.

"Dov who?"

"Dov Shachar, Dov my cousin. His camping trip to the south is next week."

"Maya, I've got the opening in a few days, I'm not thinking about taking a vacation right now."

"But you'll be done by next week, won't you? You'll open Friday, then the exhibit is up and you're free to travel."

Gil rubs his eyes hard and looks at the slowly heating coffeepot. "I *will* want to be away when those idiot critics come out with their opinions."

"Then why don't we go?"

His voice is packed with resentment. "I don't give a shit about camping or about your macho paratrooper cousin."

I ladle soup into a bowl and pass it to him.

"You know, not everyone in the army is a hero," Gil continues.

I wait.

"I mean your cousin and his macho friends, they're not all heroes just because they're in the IDF." Gil makes a gesture of annoyance, then draws the bowl to him. I see that he'll relent; we'll go to the desert with Dov.

And although I've never been enthusiastic about Dov's halfhearted offer, I'm suddenly eager to go. Next week Gil will be, at last, freed of his project. The old sketches rustling in the living room, the tubes of new work I'm forbidden to see, will be gone.

As will the moods that have ruled our lives. Gil has told me over and over that the exhibit is all he can think about for now. It's something he needs to do, there's something in this work that's important to him. When he's through, he told me one night, he will be changed.

He will be gentle, I tell myself.

Imagining our trip now, I can hardly contain my excitement. Dov's telephone call just before Gil reached home took me so by surprise that I even fancied I heard something warmer than indifference in my cousin's terse instructions. "Seven o'clock sharp on Sunday, don't forget your water bottles." Of course I don't really believe Dov wants us along. Thanks to Fanya's machinations, he'll despise me every kilometer of the way to the Arava and back. But the prospect of leaving this neighborhood—of actually taking one of the trips that I describe to my mother in my letters—seems to herald a new start. We'll go to the desert; everything will be different.

Gil lifts the spoon, watches thin green liquid trickle down to the bowl. "What's this?" he asks.

"Asparagus soup," I tell him, and as he eats I take the newspaper from him and read.

I shan't tell, Lilka repeats. You can't make me. Halina steps toward her, menace radiates from her like electricity but Lilka stares flatly and does not back away. Will you beat me, Lilka taunts, be a brute like the rest of your family? It won't make a difference. I won't tell you how I knew about Shifra and her filthy goy lover.

Vicious bitch, Halina breathes. You knew what would happen when you told our parents. But you went ahead and did it just out of spite.

It is the ghetto, we do not yet know that there is worse that can happen. Thinking we have come to the end of the world we are reckless. Even the husbandry of our strength falls in the face of our rashness. Halina, her features translucent with hunger, snatches at Lilka's blond curls and misses narrowly; Lilka bleats but glares back. Halina is changed. Her University manners have left her now, she no longer dreams at night. Halina is a wild cat loose in these stinking alleys, she is not sorry for the scratch she has left on Lilka's temple.

Lilka is laughing. With one hand she sweeps sky, rotting buildings, puddled pavement. What does it matter now? She is convulsed with laughter, she fights for breath. What does any of it matter?

Karol used to say I was a fountain filled with stories, more tales brimming every minute. Tell me, he asked, a story about a boy named Otto. "Once there was a poor boy," I began. "He lived in a village in the mountains but in his heart he pledged to marry a particular girl from the valley." Karol's touch like warm rain on the small of my back. One day, I told him, I would begin to speak every tale I knew and I would not stop. No one understood yet, but I would be a teller of stories, a weaver of lives. How far I would travel, from country to country, no border could stop me.

Now it is only summer; there is no war yet, no ghetto. We stand together in the woods, Karol and I. Halina, home from Warsaw for the weekend, has arranged it. We are mushroom-picking in the forest. Father and Mother suspect nothing, only ask Why must you girls go always to the forest, why so far? It is my favorite place, Halina says. Father smiles. He is pleased now when Halina is home, the results of the examinations arrived in the post and now he tells everyone that his daughter has been honored in Warsaw. A Feldstein, honored in Warsaw. Father hangs the report on the wall of the shop.

In the woods Halina sings. Melody upon melody, one lullaby blends to the next. As long as we hear her we are safe from intruders, and the sound of her voice warns us of her nearness so that, searching through forest to gather enough mushrooms for two, she will not come upon us embracing.

Karol speaks, the thrum of his rib cage against mine. "I won't let anything stand between us," he says. The ground is wet beneath my thin shoes, his heavy boots. I have risen on my toes to kiss him and he sets me gently back on my heels, he will not permit me to strain to reach him but rather stoops to my upturned face. His hands rest on my shoulders. "Shifra, little one. I've been preparing everything, in the fall it will all be ready. The priest has agreed to marry us." From the pocket of his shirt he pulls a letter. Stamped by the government, his army notice. We will marry the week before he must go, he will bring me to his family. They are ready to meet me, his mother has agreed at last and his father is preparing a house for us on the farm. And then it will be only a short time until his first leave.

When Halina calls out for me we walk hand in hand to meet her. Karol touches my cheek, stands back respectfully from Halina, with a soft thank you tips his hat. Halina nods, she looks away.

All summer we eat mushroom salad, mushroom sauce on potatoes, mushroom soup with dill. Pickled mushrooms fill jars lining kitchen shelves. Father says he will go mad from mushrooms but Halina smiles across the dinner table and asks Father does he mind so terribly, she loves wild mushrooms in the summertime. She will be very busy at University next year, but, she tells Father, there are many boys after her, boys from good families and soon she will pick one, she will bring him to Father for approval. The woody smell of mushrooms thickens the air and Father beams from beneath his mustache. I always said she'd come around, he tells Mother. Even with all her University nonsense.

How did you know about Shifra and Karol? Halina repeats. Above us ghetto walls crash together, obliterating sky. Lilka shrugs. Why didn't you talk to us first, Halina insists, instead of going to our parents?

Lilka turns to me now and I see that there is no fear left in her. The ghetto has blunted her prettiness, now she will scrap with us over bread but not over this quarrel from a world long past. Only this summer her boyfriend told her that he would leave her for Halina, yet here inside this barbed-wire city he has proposed marriage; they say Lilka accepted without a word. It will not be long before a shadow of starvation rings her eyes. *Even I am willing to let her go, release her from this alley we have backed her into like a cornered animal. But Halina's eyes blaze with fury. She has become a ragged thing, eyes bright with rage and dread.* Did you know, Shifra, the anti-Semites chased us down the street this week? *Even before the end of summer brought war, Halina's reports from Warsaw were grown angry, one breezy weekend I heard for the first time fear in my sister's voice.* Did you know, Shifra, they beat my friend Shmulik with their heavy canes, and when the test scores came back they knocked my books down the stairs, ripped my paper and called me yid because I had—*Halina's breath uneven, the trembling begins and will not stop*—because I had the highest score in the class.

Now in the ghetto Halina lifts her hand to slap and Lilka recoils. But Halina does not slap. She twists to one side, her cry is the end of hope and she walks slowly away down the alley. Lilka watches. She spits warily on the pavement.

After the war, when I found Feliks in Israel, he had to know everything about his sister. Feliks who had escaped the ghetto, who spent the war's remainder in the barn of a Gentile family. Of camps he knew only rumors. Telling him about Lilka, I became mute. Stories choked inside me, I could barely begin and so I spoke in half-sentences. Fragments, I showed him: symbols of elements too fiery to touch. The smell of Lilka's fear as train doors sealed shut, and such a terrible crush of bodies, one might not raise a head to ask a question.

Train doors opening to cold white daylight, blinding skies, blinding. We reached the concentration camp, guards and shouts and dogs. A uniformed man motioned Mother and Father to one side along with the Rotsteins. Here we are, Mother said. It can't be so bad now. She laid a hand on Mrs. Rotstein's shoulder, and Mrs. Rotstein made no motion to brush it away. Lilka and Halina and I stood on the other line, Halina and I straining to glimpse Mother and Father.

When Lilka spread her word about Karol it was only one week before the war, the radio counseled preparations day and night. The Germans might attack with gas, the announcer warned. Mother stocked our shop with gauze for face masks. Troops were gathered, I waited for news from Karol. But that afternoon Father was ready when I entered the shop. Without a word he began to beat me between cartons of gauze rolls stacked high as my shoulders. Mother watched for a time, then stood from her chair and rushed for Father's arm. "Stop hitting her!" Father sat wheezing in a corner while Mother screamed. "A Catholic pig, how could you? Don't you know they'd kill you for sport? Don't you know what those people are like, they eat swine." "Defile sabbath," Father chimed in. "Defile sabbath," Mother continued, "and what's more, they drink like horses at a trough." Father rose to his feet, his tread was full of menace. "You would love an uncircumcised animal? You are forbidden to leave this house. You are forbidden to meet him, I know you have plans but we will keep you here until you forget his name and he yours, we will keep you here until you forget your own name since you are so eager to bring shame upon it."

And then, at the door, Halina. Her jaw swollen, a purple egg of bruise on her forehead threatening to engulf one eye. "Halina?" Mother stepping forward, fingers extended. Halina brushed her away. "They said my sister was defiling the Polish population." Halina winced as she spoke. Her face contorted with pain, I would have rushed to her had Father not pinned my arm. "Catholic pigs," Father said softly. "Catholic pigs," Halina repeated as quietly, then her eyes burned into mine for a moment before she looked away. Running down her cheeks, two neverending ribbons of tears.

After the war, when I reached the new country Israel, they said to me. They said leave behind the past. They said, You're in the Jewish homeland now, a new life. Let us then look to our future.

Halina's tears, ribbons of living water until ghetto emptied her face of feeling and camp hollowed her body to a husk. Halina, receded into this unrecognizable frame.

My sister.

The Americans are coming, the stranger said as she held me back. How can you run toward this fire when the Americans are almost here. Every moment every second every beating of this heart. The Americans are coming to quench the fire.

Halina.

And now. Smoke. Rising to the ceiling, feathering to the walls, brushing these shuttered windows. Smoke, curling tendrils under my kerchief, and a rushing noise, flame singeing the air so I can barely breathe. Smoke billows in the dark hollows of this apartment, tumbles to such a blue sky.

My hands tremble so that I cannot clasp one to the other. Standing,
I know what I must do. I open the door of this dim choking apartment.
I make my way to the stair, sharp air pierces my lungs. One step, then
another. The echoing of unsteady footfalls, pain behind my eyes. At each
moment I might turn back. But it is too late, for I have knocked.

And the American opens the door. She is golden, smooth hair twisted
upward to the heavens, blue eyes soft open face. I whisper my plea. Fire,
I say. Can You smell it? Can You hear, this wind this fire? It is here, oh
here come quickly before they destroy what You have come to save, come
find us before we blow away on the wind of the flame.

Fire, I call out to Her, fire I dance, fire brims from my lips scorching,
blinding. It is a fire song that I chant to the American, swaying and
weaving before Her among these flames.

ာ

It happens so quickly I have no time to prepare. I've just put a teakettle on the stove when there is a shuffling of feet outside the apartment
door, and one soft knock.

The woman from downstairs wears an old brown sweater, elbows
nearly transparent. She has a kerchief wound around and around her
hair, the whole thing comically askew, as if she had wrapped a cabbage
rather than a head. When I swing the door wider she flinches, and I
think she is going to run away again, down the stairs and back to the
perch behind her door. But she clasps her hands at her waist and stands.

I take a deep breath. *"Shalom,"* I say.

Now she looks to the floor, bashful. Almost imperceptibly, she sways.

"Can I help you?" I ask.

There is a long pause. Then she speaks one word in a heavily accented Hebrew, and she speaks it quietly enough that a moment passes
before I understand that what she has said is *fire*. She looks at me helplessly; this single word has exhausted her.

"Oh God," I hear myself say in English. "Where?"

She doesn't answer. She waits, alert to my every response.

Beside the kitchen sink is the basin I have been using to wash lentils
for dinner. I dump the contents and send water splashing from the tap.
"I'm coming," I call, my voice quavering.

My neighbor stands at attention.

Fire, in this building. My mind races with possibilities: windows, doors, hoses. "I'm coming, I'm coming," I chant. The basin is only half full, but I take it from the faucet and brush firmly past her down the stairs, water sloshing my arms, my sandals slipping on tile.

The door to her apartment is open. In the entryway I nearly trip over a small suitcase standing on the floor, and as I regain balance my heart pounds. My shirt is stained with water. I hear the woman's footsteps behind me.

In the small, dim bedroom is a single bed, and a dresser with a dusty television on top. I turn on my heel and see a half-kitchen, a lone empty pot on the stove. I wheel again, breathing nothing but stale air. I set the basin roughly on the floor and brush past the woman once more; I run to the stairwell and in a panic I pull a breaker switch. The stairwell light is extinguished, the hum of appliances on the floor is stilled. Now even the low buzz of the stairway light is absent. I smell nothing. The woman and I stand together in the silenced apartment. Fear fills the darkness between us.

She waits.

Bewildered, I turn my back on her. I check the stove jets and the electrical outlets. I check the overhead light bulb, as if there might be some fire trapped inside waiting to burst out. "Is it something electric?" I ask, but she says nothing. "Something with your stove? Your refrigerator?"

She does not appear interested in my questions. She stares at me openly and without shame. Her expression is adoring, expectant.

And now I think maybe I smell smoke too.

We stand together in the bedroom, sniffing air like two animals mapping out danger. The apartment is stifling, I am aware of the sound of our breathing.

By the light leaking through the shutters I see that there are tears on her cheeks, breaking into rivulets as they cross the fine wrinkles of her face.

"Do you know where the fire was?" I enunciate as kindly as I can. "I don't see any fire. Do you know where it was?"

She opens her mouth, and her voice is dry with disuse. "Was a fire."

"Here?"

She nods.

The apartment is utterly, impossibly silent. I slide a sandaled foot on the tile, just to hear the sound. "It's over now," I say to her. "The fire is over."

She shakes her head, gently. "No."

"Maybe we ought to open a window." I start toward the far wall. "Let's get some air in here. Then we can find the problem."

She doesn't answer.

"Should I do that?" I ask with my hand on a window lever. "Open a window?"

She sits on her bed.

I force open first the window, then the shutter, and breathe deeply. The air from the street is like cool water after a long thirst, and I stand at the window for longer than I intend. On the bed the woman cowers from the light. Leaving the window ajar, I close the shutter so that only a few thin lines of sun enter.

"How about some coffee? I can make some coffee if you like."

She ignores me. Her kerchief twists pitifully on her head and her narrow shoulders are slumped as though she's in pain.

I search for words of comfort. "It's going to be all right, you know." I don't know what exactly I mean by this, but I speak on all the same. "It's all right," I reassure. "Everything is."

She looks up sharply.

Uneasy, I continue. "I want to thank you for your gifts. The psalms are very interesting." I open my hands to her. "You shouldn't worry about a false fire alarm, these things happen. It's better to be safe," I tell her, "than sorry."

Her arms are folded across her lap. Gently she hugs her elbows.

"You can come upstairs anytime. It's quiet in this building during the day. But I'm home, usually. I spend a lot of time at home. You can visit, if you like."

She is listening keenly, her head tilted to one side.

"My boyfriend hits me," I say.

She nods.

I step closer. "I don't know what to do."

Her face is bright with faraway thoughts.

"Can you help me?"

My words hang in the hushed bedroom.

She gazes past me toward the window. "I will tell," she pronounces. "Will tell you everything."

Her shoulders heave as she draws a breath.

"Will be no secret left unsaid." She lays out the words one by one, as if she has been preparing this speech and must not be misunderstood. "And when I tell, you will fix. You will make us whole." She stares into my eyes. Her shoulders slump with exhaustion. She says, simply, "Then we will be free."

She has spoken with such intensity that I find myself frightened, although I can't say of what.

The flutter of her eyelids tells me I am dismissed.

I hesitate. I want to ask what she means by all of this; I think she has pledged her help, but I'm not sure. Would it be rude to ask for an explanation?

She has tucked her chin into her shoulder like a bird preparing for sleep.

At length I rise to go. She invited me here, I remind myself. She came to get me. Surely there will be other invitations; surely this is only a beginning. I take the basin from the floor and start toward the stairwell.

But before I reach it she speaks once again, a slight forlorn figure in the airless apartment. "I have prepared. Have read your signs. I have waited, now you will make it right. Will you promise? Have you truly come for us?"

Stripes of sun float on the floor, a dizzying raft of light in the darkness. "I'll come visit," I promise.

On the way out of the apartment I flip the power switch back to its usual position. After a pause to sniff the air one final time, I climb the stairs to the third floor. When I have reached my apartment I look through the doorway cautiously, like a burglar crossing the threshold of a stranger's home. Whoever lives here has left the apartment in a hurry; the door is flung wide, and I can see straight through to the back windows and outside to the palm tree. Stepping in, I see a teakettle on the stove, spewing steam toward the ceiling with a sound that is at once comforting and dangerous.

Part Four

Now. How the days pass like clouds. Now that I know the American is here. Dawn after dawn whispers Her name, night upon night utters praise.

You are here.

You are with me.

For when I called out from my distress You came. You showed me Your steadfastness, Your basin of water: a third and final sign. You will lift me from the dust, from the trash heaps You will raise Your faithful.

American.

How long I have waited. But it has not been in vain.

Shuddering nights, days like thunder, I am ever mindful of Your presence. You are at my right hand, I shall not be shaken. I have lain counting my bones and I was despised, but now the mountains skip, seas rejoice, thirsting hills prepare for Your rain.

Now, O American. Now. You have come.

May the words of my mouth and the prayer of my heart be acceptable in Your eyes.

And I will tell You everything. How Feliks delicate Rotstein son became a ghetto smuggler, hollow-cheeked quick-eyed boy. Sunday he sneaked past the wall to bargain his mother's last dresses for food, Monday transport seized his family. He reached their room with arms full of withered potatoes there was no sound.

I will tell You. From the scroll of my days I will read.

How Grandmother stood over Uncle Hayyim when Germans came, Hayyim who could not keep his lips from quivering as he slumped on his packed suitcase. Germans pounding up the stairs, trembling grip of her hand on his shoulder. As soldiers reached the landing Grandmother called out in Yiddish, You know what the problem is with your people's Christ? He was a bastard baby, you hear me? A momzer. That's the whole trouble with you people. *Move, the German signaled, and Grandmother followed Hayyim dragging her suitcase behind, because her steps lagged the soldier stopped in his tracks, raised his gun to the center of her back.*

May the words of my mouth and the prayer of my heart. I will tell You, O American, and You will know. How Uncle Hayyim's lame legs danced before bullets. How armbands grew dear, we gazed with envy: linen for the rich and paper for the poor, how we learned to shield them from filth for a soiled band would earn a soldier's beating. How Karol searched deserted houses and damp forest for my family only to learn we had been taken, news of his devotion reached me in ghetto walls, days before news of his unit's execution.

Restore the luster to my eyes, O American. Lest I sleep the sleep of death.

Along the street in their shtiebls the blacks sing songs of memory. On my ceiling the American treads forgetfulness.

How long, how long, time spread out its hands and was stilled. Americans, we called Your name under our breath. How long, winter froze the mind, the air echoed with American bombs dropped on German war factories but You did not turn Your face upon us, You did not bomb train lines that brought prisoners and gas, O Americans when will You bend the sky and come down?

And then You came, thick cloud beneath Your feet. How we gazed mute at Your airplanes, Your bombs, Your stamping marching feet; Your candy bars sweet as death.

It is my final offering that I leave at Your doorstep, it is my greatest treasure and all that remains. I give it to You, my American. I bequeath to You all that is mine. I have waited so many days and now You, American, will understand. You will mend pain, send rain, You will make this rent world whole. Now at last You are with me, above me, in my hands my ears, the wind in my hair. At the blast of the ram's horn I will come to You, at the sound of the shofar I will tell You all.

I adore You O American, my strength, O American, my crag, my fortress, my rescuer, my matchstick my chocolate my rock in whom I

seek refuge, my shield, my Jesse Owens my Gone With the Wind my
mighty champion, my haven newspaper soup my new Coca-Cola, my re-
deemer.

I shall dwell in the house of the American all the days of my life.

∞

Sunday we leave for the desert.

The week has passed more quickly than I expected, each day a miracle. Last Sunday, Gil stayed home from the gallery to put the finishing
touches on his project. He worked all day and through the night, stopping to nap on the living room sofa when necessary. When, at dawn, he
joined me in bed for an hour's rest, I could see in the gray light that his
face was haggard with hope and worry. "Your feet are cold," I told him,
and as I tucked mine beneath his he murmured his thanks. On Monday he told the gallery manager he'd be out the rest of the week; I
brought his breakfast to the living room, set his plate on the sofa without a word. He didn't reprimand me for entering, didn't even look up
from his drawing table, but later he came to the kitchen and kissed my
forehead. "I think this is going to work," he said.

That afternoon, as I shopped for our supper, I decided to walk the
extra blocks to buy pastries for dessert. Gil's words resounded in my
head, and I sifted them for each possible meaning. I remembered things
he had promised to show me months before, the day trips and picnics
we had deferred for when his work schedule permitted. I remembered
private jokes from the spring, and the way he made me laugh.

My plan to approach the woman downstairs for her advice could
wait until the next day. I bought enough pastries for a family of ten.

Tuesday Gil was animated. For hours I listened to the uneven beat
of his footsteps as he traveled from one sketch to the next. I left the
apartment only to check the mailbox; when I found it empty, I returned to my station in the kitchen. Occasionally I heard Gil tear a sheet
of paper. When he opened the door to accept a glass of coffee, I
glimpsed dozens of drawings on a yellowed, uneven sort of paper, laid
out on every available spot of floor.

In the kitchen I opened my Israel guidebook to the map of the
Arava and traced our route into the desert with the white crescent of
my fingernail.

Wednesday Gil left the living room to check on me every few hours.

I made falafel and salad and fresh pitas for dinner; the timing of the dough's rising meant I couldn't visit the woman downstairs that afternoon. Which was just as well. I hadn't yet gotten around to deciding what to say to her. Instead I wrote to my mother about our vacation plans. *It's been a while since your last letter,* I added as a postscript. *I hope things at the Center aren't too hectic.*

All Thursday evening Gil's early sketches whispered from the clotheslines in the living room as he packed the finished pieces for transportation. When he came into the kitchen he looked as though he could barely contain his excitement. "I don't want you to see them until they're installed." He touched my cheek. "I want you to be surprised at the opening."

I followed him to the living room door and stood watching while, singing under his breath, he closed the last tube.

When he caught me staring, he raised his eyebrows quizzically.

"It's been so long since I've heard you sing," I explained, "I'd forgotten you can't carry a tune."

Softly Gil began to laugh. He rested the tube against the wall, then came and stood before me. "It's finished," he said. "It's really, really finished." I placed my hand against his chest and felt the rise and fall of his ribs. Looking up into his eyes, I was met by his steady gaze for the first time, it seemed, in months.

And now it's Friday morning. I didn't want to leave our bed. All night Gil cradled me, and as he slept I lay awake. I touched my fingertips to his temples, felt the hopeful flicker of his dreams.

I sit opposite him over the breakfast table. We are too far apart; I lace my legs with his under the table.

"Maya," he says solemnly, his words like jewels on a string. "Thank you for being with me while I did this. I couldn't have dreamed how hard it would be. On both of us. But it's over now." He doesn't try to hide the emotion on his face as he speaks. "I'm sorry," he tells me.

Then a grin, irrepressible, steals up on him. "Things are going to change."

We finish our breakfast in silence. The sky outside the kitchen window is hazy, and it's hot for so early in the morning, but I don't let these things bother me. Today is a fresh beginning. I won't remember what's past; I won't remember anything. I sit at the table and watch Gil rinse his dishes, then set them in the drain. He gathers his work from the living room and opens the front door.

"What's this?" Cardboard tubes tucked under one arm, he bends to lift a folded cloth from the threshold.

Dreamily I look at the rag in his hand. At first I don't recognize it. When I do, I have only one thought: I want her to go away.

Gil flips the cloth to the kitchen counter. "I must have dropped it. Would you mind putting that with my things?"

You see? I argue silently to the woman downstairs. *He doesn't remember that I lost it. He doesn't need to cling to wrongs that have passed. Why should I?*

Gil turns back to look at me. "Thank you," he says.

I follow him to the street and wait until the bus arrives. As he moves down the aisle with his arms full of tubes, I step onto the bus to pay his fare, and after the driver has accepted my coins I linger. I see passengers make way for Gil with curious glances. Gil is blessed, beautiful, shining amid this crowd. I thank the driver and step to the street, where I watch the bus power its way to the corner and disappear.

On the way back to the apartment I check the mailbox. I'm relieved to find the letter from my mother; it's been two weeks since her last, and my theory of a postal delay has rung false for days. Opening the envelope, I fight to calm the panic in my gut. Could someone have told her my letters are full of lies?

The apartment is starkly silent; I head for the living room. The floor is littered with scraps of torn drawings, and here and there a whole one that survived Gil's laughing run through the room. The string droops bare from wall to wall.

I make my way between the discarded portraits, as if treading on one might be sacrilegious, or at least bad luck. I reach the sofa and sit and unfold the letter. Before I read I breathe deeply, bracing myself for a blast of fury.

August 30, 1993

Dear Maya,

Your travels sound wonderful, as does your plan to stay for the fall semester. I'm so pleased you've been spending your time wisely and happily.

The children are making everyone crazy with their griping about the end of summer vacation, but the volunteers are holding their own. And it will be a relief to know that for at least a few hours a day some of the kids are in school and off the street. Meanwhile I'm planning to take the younger ones out of the city for a day in early fall. Faye and I are thinking of an excursion to Bear Mountain. Many of these kids have never even been out of Brooklyn.

I'm sending you a photograph of a recent outing to Coney Island. Here all is well.

With love,
Your Mother

Folded inside the letter is a photograph of a line of black and Latino children holding hands on a beach. They seem to be shouting something in unison. The sky behind them is blustery, and at one end of the line a dark-skinned woman looks to the clouds, as though doubtful the rain will hold off even for the length of the shutter's snap. Wind whips hair and clothing, raises the skeptical brows of the women struggling to keep this wavering line of children in order. The children are wild-mouthed and joyful, their clothing impossibly colorful against such an indifferent sky. My mother is not in the picture.

I look at the scene for several minutes. Stubbornly I wait for her to appear in it.

The sun has climbed higher; I wipe sweat from my forehead. Birds peck at the balcony tiles. I imagine Gil at the gallery, racing to install his exhibit before this afternoon's opening.

It is only when I feel I can put it off no longer that I rise and retrieve the folded cloth from the kitchen. I stand, holding it, in the front hall.

I don't want to know. Whatever it is she has in store for me this time, I don't want to know. The woman downstairs is replying to what I told her about Gil, but she's wrong. Gil's anger is past. The words I spoke in her stifling apartment now seem deceitful, as false as the smoke my crazy neighbor dreamed up. I picture her walking in on Gil and me mid-argument, and in my mind I slam the apartment door before she can reach us. The force of my gesture creates a wind that blows her away like so much dust; she disappears, and with her go that terrible chanting and the irritating clicking of her door. There is nothing but silence in the stairwell.

Inside the folds of the cloth I feel the cracked surface of a photograph.

I don't want to know.

I walk through the living room to the balcony. My approach startles the birds, and they beat upward in a flurry of small brown bodies.

It is an old black-and-white photograph, curled and stiff with age, and it fits naturally in my palm. The picture shows a covered porch crowded with people. It's a party, I assume—a birthday or homecoming. The group spills over the porch railings and threatens to wash onto the front steps. The people appear close to my age, and their expressions are unnervingly familiar. They look mischievous, bemused; one boy has been captured with his face contorted with laughter. I think of Orit and Michal and the others at Mount Scopus. But in this photograph the girls' hair is rolled and bobbed in shiny waves. Some wear hats, and their arms, in short-sleeved blouses, are white and soft. The boys wear dark pants and jackets; one of them pushes his spectacles higher with a finger.

At the center of the photograph is a young woman who appears to be the focus of this gathering. Friends sling arms around her, incline their heads, cluster near. She is beautiful, blond and square-jawed. She gazes levelly at the camera. To one side, apart from the main group and just barely included in the frame of the picture, stands a younger girl. Even in this small photo I can see that she has light eyes, and beneath them dark hollows. Unlike the older girls, this one has pale hair falling in wild wavelets. She looks haunted, with those eyes, and two figures in the shadows behind her seem to swear it true: a portly mustached man leaning on a cane, a thickset woman in dark buttoned dress, her weight angled toward the girl, ready to snatch her arm and pull her back. The girl herself looks insubstantial enough to float away.

Impatient, I shake out the cloth. There's nothing else in it. Just this single photograph.

Did she hear, did my neighbor hear the happiness in Gil's voice this morning, echoing down into her mean, dusty apartment? Did the message penetrate to her single room with its faded, gnarled possessions, chewed on like so many bones in a famine? Didn't she understand that the past is over, that a new future has begun?

The picture is streaked with age. As if the photographer had focused through a fine sheet of rain or snow.

I tuck the photograph roughly into the cloth. Then I stride across the living room, my feet trampling scraps of sketches, and stuff it behind a stack of my notebooks on the dusty bottom of a shelf. "I don't want to be reminded," I say aloud. "Do you hear me?" My words quake against the blank walls of the room. "I don't want to know. I don't want your damn reminders of what's already past."

⚬⚬⚬

Now. Even the stones of this city will tremble with the cry of Your shofar. You have bent the sky, You have come down in order to lift me from the dust. The wailing will reach across the heavens, shake the scorched air. How this city will quiver, called to its final reckoning.

I turn the knob. I open the door.

The stairwell towers above me, I wind up and up. I never saw before such light, such brightness as comes in from these windows. I never saw before: This passage is a chute whose narrow tip might release me to blue sky. My suitcase drags behind me, I am ready. Hope rails at my mind, stuns my ears; at last it is time. Every story I will tell.

I knock at Your door.

You open.

You are strong, Your arms will be fierce in their sheltering embrace. You are beauty, water-blue eyes, Your hands speak miracles.

American, I cry.

You regard me. You hesitate, am I worthy? Your mouth shapes words, You invite me in with a gesture. The king has lifted his scepter I am admitted.

You dwell in a house of breezes, fragments of souls scattered at Your feet.

You are waiting. Beholding Your visage I tremble, I must not fail. I open my mouth, with all my strength I praise You.

Only You can erase past and bring future, American. Only You can start time that has stopped.

Now I begin, and my soul goes out to You in words.

Floods, torrents of words. Crashing sounds, clanging vowels, the screech and silence of such tales. I show it to You: the clenching walls of ghetto, the beating of Karol's great heart when we stood together under branches and did not know this would be the last. The machines he dreamed of for his farms, drowned out by motors plowing lives, the locking of metal doors. The clatter of Uncle Hayyim's dancing feet on cobblestone, he held his arms high as if lifting a Torah to the skies. And Halina, finding tears in camp when we had no more tears. Yet she came to me and wept. Shifra how can you forgive me? I will tell you now the truth, I will tell you now what I did to keep Mother and Father from forcing me to marry Turkevich. *Halina's penitence streaming up from these barracks to vacant sky.*

The words tear at my throat as I force them forward, they wrack my body but I speak and speak and speak to You American. Everything, You must know. After the war, Feliks, grown tall and full of rage, repeating his questions for he believed repetition would bring sense. Were you with Lilka when she died, tell me. *Feliks, saved by a miracle woman leading children through ghetto sewers. Feliks, saved, with his arms full of withered potatoes; Feliks in Israel, grown tall with his rage, his shame, his gift of a photograph.* See there, *he paused in his torment of words to point.* See there at the center. Lilka with her arm around Halina.

How long the sound of my voice carves air. Only when I have told You all will You set the past to rest. How long I confess under Your roof, among Your fragments, before Your watching eyes. How long.

I am here, I say to You. I am here.

ﬡﬡ

Standing just inside the gallery door in black shirt and black pants, Gil looks even taller than his six feet. As he watches guests arrive off the street he shields his eyes against the glare. I can hear people in the main room behind him. I kiss Gil, and shake hands with a rail-thin man who introduces himself to me as Roni, then turns back toward Gil and regards him without speaking.

A twist of Roni's mouth releases cigarette smoke. "There'll be results from this," he says at last. He claps a hand to Gil's shoulder and raises a plastic cup of red wine. "You'll be getting invitations to show your work elsewhere, that's for certain."

And Gil, after a pause (*Forgive him*, I urge silently), nods his acknowledgment.

"It's quite shocking." The man who has just walked over to Gil wears a tie, and I guess him to be the gallery's owner. "What possessed you to choose the blacks? And where did you come up with the idea of drawing them on the very flesh, as it were?"

I wait for Gil to laugh at the owner's pretentiousness, but he is nodding, serious and intent. Standing beside Roni, I see Gil's dismissive acceptance of the owner's praise, followed by the smile he cannot stifle. Gil is explaining something about visiting an ultra-Orthodox scribe to learn a technique for using a quill pen. In the middle of Gil's discourse, the owner winks at me. "Stick with this one," he counsels. "He's a find."

Gil is wrapped up in his conversation; he doesn't seem to notice when I excuse myself. I walk alone to the gallery's main room. My feet, confined in the black pumps I haven't worn since leaving Purchase, tap across the smooth white floor. After a few seconds I summon the nerve to look.

From every point in the gallery, religious men and women and children watch me raise my head. I stand in the middle of a ring of solemn figures, drawn in simple dark lines like the ones in the apartment. Gil has positioned the drawings so that each face is just above eye level. With clamorous indifference, the blacks look over the heads of the gallery crowd. The men, with their expressions of anguished faith, of wariness or condemnation, wear hats and clutch books. Some have opened their mouths in fervent prayer, others nod consolation. Their eyes, burning and demanding, are suspended between dream and life. The women, their gazes averted, rest heavy hands on the heads of their children. Boys pull at wispy sidelocks or balance their weight on one foot; girls wear their hair cut in bangs across their foreheads, in imitation of the wigs or kerchiefs they will wear when married. But instead of being sketched with charcoal on paper, these faces are drawn in sharp ink lines on parchment.

I step closer to the drawing of a boy and see that Gil has done his portraits on the same stiff yellowed hide used for Torah scrolls. At the edges of the drawings are elaborately penned words, snippets of newspaper headlines copied out in the calligraphy of the scribes.

These figures have been living with me in my home, scenting the air with their parchment fingertips, their heavy ink brows. Now, gathered in one room, they are an army of the haunted. They stare past me, preoccupied with their own knowledge. *We are not free,* their expressions insist. *None of us. There is nothing in this world but suffering, there is nothing in the present that matters, there is only hope for the world to come.*

Something about one of the portraits along the wall is familiar, and as I near it I realize the face is that of a well-known Israeli politician recently under investigation for corruption. Turning to the nearby drawings, I recognize other faces amid the depictions of men and women from our street. Now two visitors in the gallery are laughing; one of them points at the portrait of a black-hatted man who resembles a conservative general I've seen in the news. Farther along, people are gathering around the drawing of a kerchiefed woman with the face of a left-wing government minister. There are nods of appreciation, stares of disapproval. Walking the wall slowly, I examine figure after figure until I come to a drawing of Yitzhak Rabin, uncomfortable in a black hat that fits poorly on his high forehead. At a neighborly distance, looking more at home in his own black hat and peyes and with the same faraway gaze as all the others, is Yasir Arafat.

"Can you imagine," a woman near me says, "the two of them standing next to each other?"

Her companion laughs. "Can you imagine the two shaking hands?"

Of all the subjects pictured, there is only one who regards the viewer head-on. I cross the floor to study this drawing, placed lower than the rest so that she alone addresses viewers directly.

It is the woman from downstairs. Gil has drawn her peculiar wasted face with perfect accuracy, he has not forgotten the raised hands and slightly open mouth. Her kerchief lopsided, she seems a comic figure. I stand before the portrait, uneasy—Gil has hung her on these walls for mockery.

But gradually, something else emerges from the drawing: her face is vivid with hope. In this drawing she, too, looks to her redemption like the rest of the blacks, only with an eagerness unlike any of the others'. She looks as if she's in love. I want to take Gil aside and tell him he's gotten her wrong.

I start as Gil catches me by the waist. "Say something. For heaven's sake, Maya. I've been following you for ten minutes already, you haven't done anything but stare."

Gil laughs, but he isn't smiling. Seeing how closely he watches my face, I wonder how he would draw me, which of these figures praying for salvation I would most resemble.

"It's brilliant," I tell him.

He frowns. Scrutinizes my face. Then he grins.

The gallery is filling with people; Gil takes my hand and coaxes me to the entrance to greet newcomers. "This is my beautiful girlfriend, Maya," he informs them. "You'd be best off talking to her, she's my better half." Soon it becomes a game between the two of us to see who can step forward first, meet the proffered handshake and introduce the other with grander flattery. And the guests play along, complimenting me on the show and congratulating Gil on finding me. Everyone is looking at Gil and at me; everyone is eager to talk to us. Even Roni comes by again to make conversation. "Damn heat wave," he says, wiping his forehead with a napkin. "I hear it's going to lift soon."

From the walls the blacks keep silent vigil.

"You've implicated the whole country, making us out to be like the blacks." I can't tell whether the man talking to Gil is praising him or has taken offense. "What, you think we're all just waiting for God to fix things for us? You think we're all so powerless?" He has taken offense. But Gil nods energetically—it's clear he's pleased. I assemble a plate of cheese and fruit for him, and pour myself a cup of white wine. "I wanted to do it on a single scroll, like a Torah," I hear Gil explaining to a young woman. "But I didn't have time to learn how to sew the parchment."

Nachum, shepherding Tami around the gallery, pauses beside me. "I've never been to an art show before," he confides. In his white shirt and dark pants, he looks as uncomfortable as a schoolboy on class-photo day. "Your boyfriend seems very nice," he tells me. Then, to Tami, he adds, "It's too bad your mother isn't reaching Jerusalem until evening. She'd be in her element here. She could explain things to us."

Tami says nothing. She is staring at the portraits.

Near Nachum is a young man who has been standing before a single drawing for minutes. The man is pale, with droopy eyelids and a bit of dark beard centered on his chin like a forgotten puff of shaving cream. Smoke trickles from a corner of his mouth as he squints at the portrait of an elderly man. Under one arm he holds a notepad.

"So why do you think he didn't draw any happy ones?" Nachum asks.

The man doesn't take his eyes off the drawing, only breathes at it, his lower lip pushed forward although he has run out of smoke to exhale.

"The religious know how to laugh like anybody else," Nachum informs him amiably.

The man is dressed in black jeans and a plain black vest over a white

T-shirt, making his ashy skin look even ashier. His face wears an expression of practiced torment. He turns to Nachum and speaks with intensity. "These portraits ask an interesting question, don't they?"

"What's that?"

The man taps the bare spot above his goatee. "Are the blacks signified, or are they sign?"

"Pardon?" Nachum leans forward.

"What I mean is, does it matter who they really are and what they want, or does it only matter what they seem to represent?"

Nachum wags his head in apology. "Once again?"

The man gestures impatiently at the drawing. "Does it really matter who the blacks are, or only what they symbolize?"

"I suppose that depends," Nachum says in slow and friendly tones. "If you're not one of them, then you can worry what do they symbolize. If you're one of them, then you're too busy worrying about your prayers and your children and maybe your political party and your mother's health to think about what you represent, aren't you?"

The man rolls his eyes and ejects an avalanche of words. "Yes, but of course that's beside the point, isn't it? What I mean is, what are they asking of the world? What do they *really* want? Where do they fit in our paradigm? What does their presence ask of *me*?"

Nachum blinks. "What do the blacks care about you? Other than they don't like you particularly, or me, either. Other than they don't want necessarily the same rules we want for this country. They care how you vote, all right, and whether you gun your motorcycle down their street on the sabbath. But I don't think they care what you think of them."

Sucking his teeth in irritation, the man drifts away. Nachum watches him go, with undisguised bewilderment. "Who is that guy?"

The faintness of Tami's voice might hold irony, or simply resentment of her husband. "He's an artist."

Nachum scratches his chin thoughtfully. "He's a blockhead." To me he says, "Tell your boyfriend next time he should draw one or two happy ones. To be fair."

Abruptly Tami addresses me. "Why are you all going to the desert in this *hamsin*? Shouldn't you wait?"

Her concern surprises me, and I answer, "They're predicting it's going to break soon."

Gil is beside me; he sets a hand on my shoulder. Nachum, Tami, the notepad man with his poetic pallor flee my mind. The paint-scented air of the gallery has released a lightness in Gil; he pivots me under his arm and leads me into the center of the gallery floor, where I spin and land on one knee to the scattered applause of guests. I can feel the flush of my cheeks, the wisps of hair hanging loose as I bow. "She's a dancer," Gil explains to several strangers beside him. He sounds proud. When he takes my arm and introduces the man with the notepad as the art critic from a Tel Aviv weekly, I smile so warmly that the man pinches the bridge of his narrow nose to hide his confusion.

The heat doesn't lift with the approach of evening, and when I return to the apartment I'm relieved to change my long skirt for shorts. I pack to the sound of the radio—hip-hop in French, Israeli songs with a fast, pattering beat, songs from last year's American top ten. The music reminds me of Purchase and makes me giddy. I swirl, brush my hands along the walls, dance from the bedroom to the living room and back. How could I have forgotten how this feels? A step, a turn, a bag for me and one for Gil. Boots for hiking, bathing suits for Eilat. I pack water bottles and hats, sweaters for evening. Sabbath candle-lighting is only a few minutes away, and I brace for the sound of the siren. The gallery will be closing, Gil will be going out to celebrate with Roni and the gallery owner. I told Gil to stay out as long as he liked, and to remember to enjoy himself extra for me; I'd prepare everything for Sunday, since we'd be leaving so early. I want us to have Saturday to relax, just the two of us.

The radio is now playing an old Billy Joel tune, and on the second verse the steady rhythm is joined by a knocking at the door. I zip the bags shut and go to the entryway.

She is, inexplicably, smiling. A pained, dreadful grin. I wish I hadn't answered the door. "What are you doing here?" is all I can think to say.

She carries a suitcase. Understanding washes over me slowly.

"You can't come," I stutter. "There's only space in my cousin's car for me and Gil and my cousin's girlfriend. I'm sorry, there's no room for you."

She says nothing.

"I'm sorry," I repeat. "You can't come with us."

She doesn't move. Behind me, the radio bubbles Cyndi Lauper.

I wave my arm in exasperation. And as if this were a signal, she steps forward, her kerchiefed head bobbing in gratitude. There is a faint smell to her, stale and sour.

In a burst of anger I run to the living room, snap off the radio. I turn back, only to see that she has followed me. I face her. "What do you want from me?"

She says nothing.

"Tell me, what?" My hands are wild in the air. I know I am over-reacting, but I can't help it. Fury crowds my vision. "Can't you just let me enjoy my life? Things are going well with Gil. He's not like what you saw."

Her silence is more than I can bear. At once all the joy I have felt in the last twenty-four hours drains out of me. I stand opposite her, desolate. And then the effort of standing is too great. I sink to the sofa.

She sits down beside me, companion in sorrow. As she perches her hands politely in her lap, I know only that I hate her.

"Leave me alone, damn you," I mutter.

The last of my words is obliterated by the sound of the sabbath siren, which charges the air in the apartment. I speak on through the sound but my voice is wiped clean of words. I believe I am telling her, *I don't want your cursed witnessing, your reminders of his rage,* I believe I am saying, *Take your godforsaken reminders and leave,* but I cannot hear my own voice. My heart pounds as if I've summoned this unanswerable wailing from somewhere in my own body. In the heat the siren reigns uncontested, commanding us motionless.

As the sound dies away I hear running on the street; the blacks are rushing to their homes, their synagogues, readying their children for candle-lighting.

In silence she searches my face. Then the air shifts between us—after this great storm, a first rustle of tenacious life. She speaks. In the wake of the siren's blast, her voice is small and still and barely disturbs the silence. I can't understand her words. I lean closer, until I feel her breath brushing my face.

The jumble of her speech is steady, it is almost song. I don't recognize the language she is speaking. Or perhaps it is several languages, the phrases splintering and dividing. Now and again a word emerges whole in English or Hebrew: *Forest, gate. Dybbuk, actors.* Her voice, quiet and reasoning, gains speed; soon it is a steady wind, tossing treetops. *Hailstorm, window, plowing season.* The garbled insistent chant breaks from her throat, words surge forward, fall away softly: *Beneath above, station. Thirsty.* She speaks on and on in this language that is no language, a tender wash of sound. She speaks as if each treasured word burns her, her lips are scorched, tongue cleaves to palate and still she continues. Her voice has grown no louder, yet it blots out all other sound. *Forest, hum, this life.* Words tumble upon one another and I can find no order in them. *Gate farmhouse their faces, saw. Window sticks please.* Her words blur like the prayers of the blacks, but these are like no prayers I have heard. They are a gale tearing at the roots of trees; my own throat aches with her effort.

Displaced Persons, she pronounces suddenly in English, in the middle of a ribbon of speech.

She is a survivor of the Holocaust. How could I not have seen? Slowly my fists, clenched all this time in anger, loosen.

Plank, bird, ship, she whispers.

She isn't going to cast a curse on my new happiness. She's just struggling to tell me a story.

I try to recall what I know about survivors; I recall slogans. *Never again, never forget.* When we'd finished studying the Holocaust in third grade, our teacher invited a survivor to our Hebrew school class. For once, we sat through the hour without fidgeting. The man talked about cattle cars and camps, showed photos of his lost wife and daughters. He showed us, too, the number tattooed on his forearm. Afterward, satisfied with our stunned expressions, the teacher coached us in the ways of memory. Our job was to help people remember after Mr. Cohen was gone. *Never forget. Mr. Cohen is a walking memory. You are his witnesses.*

This woman who has haunted the space under my footsteps, this woman I've longed for and scorned, is a walking memory. I have no idea what to do.

She isn't here to lecture me about Gil. I allow myself to concentrate momentarily on my relief. Beneath it, I sense, is an undertow of fear. She doesn't have any advice for me; she's just an ordinary person with a terrible past. If things go wrong again with Gil, she won't have any power to save me. If worse comes to worst—I allow the thought for only an instant—I'm completely alone. Looking at her as she speaks, I think: *I wanted you to be magical.*

But nothing will go wrong with Gil. I tell myself I'm simply relieved. Gradually I relax my hunched shoulders. I concentrate on her.

She is entranced by her own speech, an unbroken chain of sighs.

I sit opposite her a few minutes more before I realize what she is ask-ing of me. She doesn't want to ruin my life, she isn't here to accuse Gil or drag me away from him; she is asking only that I listen, and remem-ber what she tells me. She wants me to be her witness.

"I'm listening," I tell her, but she doesn't seem to hear. She talks on. I reach for her hand. "Tell me slowly so I can understand."

She doesn't alter her unintelligible speech in the slightest, and the re-spect with which she addresses me makes me panic. I think of my mother at the Center, the echo of the dark offices at night. The glitter of shattered glass on the street. I think of the letters she writes, sitting in her small upstairs room. Trusting me.

I touch my fingers to this woman's dry cheek. Then to her thin chapped lips. "Show me how to make your words," I urge.

Her lips move on as though she doesn't even feel my touch.

I take both of her hands in mine, and they are impossibly cold in the throbbing heat. Her eyes shine feverishly. I don't know how long we sit like this. Evening darkens to night, the black men pass slowly along the street on their way from synagogue, climb steps, and are greeted at sab-bath dinner tables. It isn't long before I hear singing. Still this woman speaks, and still I understand nothing.

"It helps to talk," I say to her. But my words are more question than statement.

"You must start it again," she says in Hebrew. "It must be healed. You must bring it."

It's no use. Even when I understand her speech it makes no sense to me.

Before me sits a life smashed, a cracked hull of a woman. A cracked hull of a girl, telling stories no one will understand. Her fervor rivets me. And I recognize now the waif from the picture—the girl who might float above her family like a figure in one of Chagall's paintings, sailing above the partygoers crowding on the porch. With horror I re-call my anger as I hid the photograph away.

At last she falls silent. The only intelligible word of her last sentence hangs in the air: *suitcase*. She has finished.

Outside, the night breeze ruffles the palm fronds, and this time it is not the sound of rain, but of weeping. It is a sound of words lost, worlds lost and never regained.

We sit together on the sofa, exhausted. Then a joy steals over her. I have never seen such serenity. Or rather, I've seen it only once—in the peculiar drawing Gil hung at eye level in the gallery.

"What is it?" I whisper.

She looks at me. "Now you will make it whole," she says.

"How?"

"Bring future," she explains.

Trite phrases run through my mind: *Time heals all. Sharing it with someone is good.* I dismiss them—TV talk shows won't help me. I dredge lessons learned in Hebrew school: *We will remember the six million, we will preserve the memories, in our hearts we keep them alive.* I shake my head with confusion. How pallid, how insulting these phrases seem. *Always remember, never forget,* the Hebrew school teachers urged us. I want to ask them, What can that possibly mean?

No one has ever looked at me with the sort of adoration that lights this woman's face.

"Maybe it helps to remember," I choke out.

She tilts her head, the single motion dismisses my words.

Or perhaps she'd rather forget?

She is intent on my every movement, my slightest shift in expression. I cross then uncross my ankles, and she makes a sound like the hesitant burbling of an old and long-unused fountain. When she repeats this strange sound, I record the crinkling of skin around her eyes and understand that this is laughter. Her expression is peace, her breath a rough murmur. I shift my weight on the sofa and she is instantly silent, rigid with attention. She nods encouragement, then casts her eyes down and smiles coyly at some secret joke.

Abandoning memories of Hebrew school, I try to recall something useful from the psychology course I slept through at Purchase. I scroll through my mother's soft Hebrew lullabies, but it seems to me that my neighbor is looking for some other kind of comfort.

I have no idea what to do for this woman.

"What's your name?" I ask her.

She looks up at me, and she speaks in Hebrew with perfect clarity. "I am here," she says. "I am here."

∽

At the sound of the ram's horn I cried out to You.
    At the blast of the siren I called Your name.

American.

I spin down the stairs, twirl to the floor. American.

Why have You not answered my cry?

You have forsaken me.

But You promised, the words came from American lips. We will make you whole, the soldier said. America will come and time will begin. Past will be erased, future will arrive.

You have not made me whole.

America America, always future, how can You reach out empty hands? You touch my words but do not heed them, touch my heart but refuse to heal.

And how could I have been unworthy? For I told You everything, as I promised. How Mother and Father arrived at the concentration camp, suitcases clutched tight. How they endured the three days with this warm blanket, this crumpled hat, this book of photographs held close in the crush of despairing bodies. They stepped off the train optimistic. Our lives have been a battle, Mother whispered in my ear. Also this we will weather. How transport workers dove onto the hurled suitcases, scattered clothing and paper on packed earth in the search for food or jewels, in the single minute before the soldiers approached Mother and Father stood side by side and Father took her hand.

American, why have You forsaken me? You have seen soldiers march the yet-standing from train to train, camp to factory to camp. You have seen Lilka running late across the courtyard, a guard no older than she indicating with his finger her end. American you have heard Halina's words, You have listened with me to her story. Before you knew Karol, *Halina clutched my shoulder in camp as she confessed,* he spoke to me. He came to me he said I know your people have reason to fear Catholics. But I want to talk to your sister Shifra, only to talk. A Gentile, tall as summer corn, addressing me in the open streets as if it were a regular thing that a Catholic speak with a Jewish girl about her sister. I have seen the two of you walking together by the river, he said. If you would, if it is all right, will you tell me about her?

I knew about Gentiles, Halina told me. I knew what the Catholics had done to Uncle Hayyim. I told this boy, Know that your love will bring ruin on my sister. Let her alone and your fancy will pass. He said quietly, No, this does not pass. He drew his breath, he said, Will you consider what I have asked? I told him, My sister Shifra's life is pained, if you court her they will beat her and make her life misery. He said, I understand. He said, I will stay away for now, only tell me about her. So I told him. I told him your riverwitch stories, Shifra I told him your fairy tales and I looked into the attention on his face and my heart grew soft toward him, I told him your very words. And he listened, he thanked me like a gentleman. I never knew a Gentile could tip his cap and speak gratitude. He agreed to come back in a year. Perhaps then? he said. It will not change, I told him. But he said All the same. I will not speak with her without your permission, he assured me. I understand it is important in your families. The Gentile bowed his head to me. I would ask your parents, he said, but I do not think they would be pleased. For the first time I laughed with him and he smiled, dimples in his broad Gentile face. In a year you will forget, I said to him, so I wish you farewell. No, he said, I will not forget.

Halina's shallow breath drawn with difficulty. I said to her, Halina, what is it that pains you so? I understand, you wanted to protect me from Karol. You did not know him at first, just as I did not. *Halina knocked my reaching hand aside, such strength in her bony wrists.* I thought I was doing the best thing for you, *she said. Bitterness twisted her mouth.* I thought, It will cause my sister only harm, this Gentile who does not understand our troubles or our ways. I thought, Perhaps in a year, perhaps I will send him to talk to her in a year when she is older, when Mother and Father cannot afflict her so. Then she can choose for herself.

But that year they brought Turkevich to the house and, Shifra, his tired eyes made my breath seize in my chest. Shifra, I could barely speak in his presence, so frightened was I by the mottled hands that lay still on his knees as he spoke, hands impatient for nothing, only wishing to make comfortable their owner's middle years. For weeks Mother coaxed and Father insisted, nights I cried my eyes to burning with my fist in my mouth so not to wake you, asleep at last despite your insomnia in the bed beside me. I told you nothing, Shifra, to tell would have split me in two and you as well. In the mornings my chores loomed impossible, more complicated than I could have imagined, and in the evening when there was no time left for my studies I did not care. I stood perfectly still over the soup pot full of sliced beets and onions, I drew breath and for a moment I could not remember what to do. Then I saw the pitcher of water in my own hand and I poured until the pot brimmed crimson. On the night table my books, my charts, notebooks' blank white pages lay open crying despair. Don't threaten to kill yourself, we know it's only your trickery, Father said. Mother held my shoulders then, and rocked me like a small child. She said to me, You'll grow accustomed to him, it won't be so very bad. Trust me, I know.

When Mother and Father rose from the parlor with their plans for the wedding I lifted my head from my hands and I said, Father there is a Gentile from the countryside who plans to marry Shifra and if you force me to marry Turkevich then I will not stop this Gentile from eloping with her.

That is a lie, Mother said. You will not fool us so easily. But I said, Mother if you force me to marry then you will see. I will kill myself and Shifra will disappear one night, you will have no daughter and no one in this cursed house to slave for you in the shop. Will you chase away every Gentile customer, will you follow Shifra through the streets? You cannot keep him from her. Only I know who the Gentile is and he obeys only me. Only I can keep him from talking to her.

And they believed, *Halina said.* They believed and they waved Turkevich away without so much as an apology. I heard later he was so shamed he did not leave his house for two weeks.

For another year I kept the Gentile from you, *Halina whispered to me.* I had never truly known a Catholic, only the marketplace vendors, and then the professors who paced behind University lecterns. But this one's laughter would not leave my mind. Still, when he came to me in the marketplace that winter I turned him away, I would not hear him.

And then that spring I watched you grow paler and thin, I watched you turn your head in pain when the gimnazjum girls came to get me. I saw you become wary of the neighborhood boys who taunted you for your quiet.

On a summer morning I dressed for an outing, I told Mother and Father I was going for a picnic. And you, Shifra, you wanted to join me but I lied and said I was going with my Sports Club friends and you could not come. How the tremor in your voice ripped at me. But I could not allow you to follow. All morning I walked toward the farms, I hitched rides from curious Gentiles who slowed their wagons to ask my destination. I knew only his first name, over and over I motioned high above my head with my hand: a fair-haired young man, so tall. At last in the hot sun of late afternoon a barefooted woman led me to a field where I recognized the Gentile. Standing on marshy ground in my long dress and thin shoes, I told him he had my permission to speak to you. I told him you would probably not care for him and I would give him no help in wooing you. But he might find you by the river or beside the house, and I would do nothing to interfere. The Gentile did not answer at first, then he thanked me and he planted his hoe into the dirt and he drove me back to town. We rode in silence, the horses nodding their heads over the uneven road and my feet throbbing as I sat stiff beside him. I signaled him to let me off beside the forest and as I walked into town I thought, Shifra will have the chance to love, and I prayed I was not bringing injury to your heart.

Halina's long finger poked at packed dirt. Her chalky skin was streaked with grime. At the corner of the building behind which we crouched, the dying stood wordless, awaiting their turn at the latrine. Some who could not wait stared straight ahead and grimaced only slightly as they soiled themselves, shame or disgust too far past to recall. Halina did not turn to watch them. She crouched on the dirt, her own scarecrow bones folded at sharp angles. Knees and elbows pointed helpless at sky, at earth. Halina, a bird whose wings could not carry the weight of her, but could only map out the universe endlessly: There above is flight; here below, clay. I was wrong about the Gentiles, *she said to me.* They are not all bad.

Sounds of the dying and the still-living reached us but we did not turn our gazes from each other. Halina's voice rough, carrying no compassion only merciless fact. If I had let him meet you when he first asked, you would be married. You would be hidden in a Gentile farmhouse, you would wear a cross on a string around your neck. You would live.

We will live, *I told Halina.*

No, *Halina said.* We will not.

Regret is too small a word, this is too small a world hemmed in by wire and barking guards, by their watchfulness, and ours. We lift our eyes. Halina, *I said,* the Americans will bend the sky and come for us. We will make a home together after the war, we will drink and eat and live. No, *she repeated.* There will be no after. There is no after, there is no tomorrow. There is only now, there is only now and now and now.

In white clouded sky, nothing. No streak, no motion, no buzz of airplanes.

I forgive you with all my heart, *I told Halina. My sister shook her head, she would not receive my words.* I could have saved you, *she said. Her own dark pupils empty of all emotion, her scalp riddled with louse bites between scant tufts of hair. Her collarbone was so sharp it caused me pain to look on it, and although surely it was impossible that our hearts beat any longer, still a pulse could be seen faintly threading between the knobs at the base of her neck.*

I thought I would do anything in my power for my beloved sister, *Halina spoke one final time.* But I failed.

American, You did not come then.

Suitcases flung open on earth. Halina's elbows folded like the wings of birds, as if a mere gift of feathers could yet free us.

American, there is none other than You. I have hoped for no other.

But You have not redeemed. For I have lain counting my bones before You and still the past burns. O American of hosts, You have not used Your might to bring future.

And who if not You will make this fiery life whole? Who if not You, my rock my redeemer? I lift my question to the heavens and You hearken but withhold Your answer.

I spin to the stairwell You clutch my hand. Stay, *You say.* Are you all right, *You ask,* do you want a glass of water? *You want to hold me You want to caress me American. But You have broken Your promise, You have not shown me Your steadfastness. What can Your water glass do now to quench this scorching air, I drop it to Your floor. I have waited so long for Your redemption and You deny it. I spin to earth I stumble down these stairs I am the chaff in the wind, only memory is solid and I blow like dust.*

O American, my American, why have You abandoned me?

You bent the sky and came down, but You have not filled the oceans. You heard my cry but You have not quenched this fire this breathless air. My redeemer my rock I have waited for You. My redeemer my rock You have forsaken me. You touch my lips and heal nothing.

The morning sun beats down on the roof of Dov's dusty white car. We speed along the highway into the desert, air whipping in the spaces between us and flinging my hair into my mouth. Since leaving Jerusalem we've traveled along a road that carves through a landscape of rocky hills. Dov drives in amiable silence, his girlfriend, Rina, slouched beside him with her bare feet propped on the dashboard and her fingers playing with the worn fringe of a hole in her jeans. "Like they wear them in the U.S.," she said grinning at me earlier, when my eyes fell on the patch of knee showing through each hole.

Gil and I sit in the backseat, our sandaled feet propped on our bags; the Subaru's trunk could not accommodate them on top of the sleeping bags and camping gear. Sleepily I take Gil's hand. It occurs to me that Fanya's early-morning parting words sum up how I feel this minute. She rode with Dov and Rina from Wolfson Street to see us off at my apartment, and to remind us what a wonderful time the four of us would have together. "It couldn't be more perfect," she declared.

"The hills in the Arava are going to put another year's worth of wear on the car." Rina shakes her head as she watches the Judean Desert spread around us. "Then it will be an invalid instead of just a senior citizen."

"No," Dov counters, "another year's wear and it will be a fossil." I glimpse my cousin in the rearview mirror, and it is easy to recognize Nachum's broad grin. The tension in Dov's face has eased; he looks almost lighthearted. He pats the steering wheel absently, perhaps to encourage his car or himself.

Laughing, Rina reaches over to pat the steering wheel too. She's modestly pretty, this girlfriend of Dov's, with striking green eyes. I know from a comment Dov made earlier that she did her army service in Intelligence. But when I ask her about it, she only makes a face and laughs yet again. "It was a job," she tells me. "It would be better if it were obsolete." At this, Dov groans. "Here goes the peacenik again," he says. She ignores him and continues. "I want all our army service to be obsolete, then we can be college students like you Americans, we can spend our time joining sports clubs and worrying about whether we've *found ourselves.*"

It would be easy to feel insulted by her words; instead I'm warmed by the familiarity. Rina confides eagerly about the American magazines she reads whenever she can get hold of them. If I disregard Dov's callused hand resting on the ragged knee of her jeans, I can even imagine we might be friends.

The sun lays claim to every inch of these hills, every speck of crawling or rushing life. Gil wipes his forehead and fingers the strap of the binoculars in his lap. Yesterday's rest has left him peaceful. The day, it turned out, was nothing like I'd planned. All afternoon the telephone rang; two well-wishers even stopped by and asked for him. I had to tell them he was asleep. I watched over Gil while he lay motionless. I stayed in bed with him until my restlessness was too much to bear. I reminded myself to be patient. The weeks of work were etched on his face; he woke only to ask the time and nod off again.

"The woman from downstairs came to visit," I told him later, after our dinner in a dark kitchen. Gil had finished his account of the previous evening's celebration, and of the hints dropped by the Tel Aviv critic of a positive review. As I followed him back to the bedroom, I felt almost shy. Gil: miraculously content, his hair mussed, his voice quiet and deep. Gil, who saw things other people did not; who had seen something in the woman downstairs that I had missed, even if he didn't understand that she wasn't religious. There was no end to learning about him. So many misunderstandings he and I had to make up for. I readied to trust him with the truth. "It's not the first time she and I have spoken," I said. I prepared the next question in my mind: *Do you know what it is she wants?*

Gil yawned and laughed at the same time, which made him laugh more. "Honey, I'm still exhausted. How about if you tell me tomorrow? Because I want to hear about the crazy woman, but I'm so tired I can't move. And your bionic cousin is picking us up at, what, seven in the morning?" He rummaged high in his closet and emerged with the leather-cased field glasses. "Can't go see the sights without these." He yawned again, and laid them reverently on top of his bag before kissing me on my forehead. "Thanks for packing."

The telephone rang; Gil picked up the receiver, listened, then put it down after the briefest of replies. With obvious pleasure, he announced, "Your cousin says he listened to the forecast and the *hamsin* is lifting. 'So we can leave in the morning as planned,' he says. Was he going to cancel if the *hamsin* didn't pass? *Sorry, it's too hot to go out and play.* Not quite tough enough, after all, is he? Good thing the weather is indulging him." With a snap of his wrist, Gil turned off the bedside light.

Now, as the narrow strip of road weaves deeper into the hills, Dov turns on the radio. Even with the *hamsin* fading, the heat feels unforgiving. I imagine walking along the roadside. The first moment under this searing desert sun would be a pleasure. The next would bring danger.

On the radio, a man recites news of a manhunt for a suspected terrorist; Rina tunes to a music station. I touch the binoculars on Gil's knees, and he nods permission without turning his eyes from the window. Facing forward in the car, I lift the binoculars to my eyes.

For an instant the world careens and wobbles in a glorious stream of brown and blue and golden light. Then, as I adjust the focus, I am assaulted by a brightly lit field rushing at me: earth and stone and skyline coming too fast, too close. I jump back involuntarily in my seat. The world has been corralled into the ruthless eye of a microscope, the smallest objects tilt at me with excruciating sharpness; it's as if the window of my mind has been forced open and the world come pouring in.

I lower the glasses and return them to Gil's knees without a word.

Rina sings along with an Israeli pop song on the radio; Dov hums to a phrase here and there. In the determinedly cheerful manner he's maintained since picking us up this morning, he asks a polite string of questions about my studies. I'm certain most of his interest stems from Fanya's coaching; I wonder whether any of it is genuine.

"I'm enrolled for the fall semester at the university," I explain to the back of his head.

"What about your university at home?" Rina asks.

"They'll give me credit." I move closer to Gil, and he wraps an arm around my shoulders. "Besides, maybe I'll stay in Israel and finish college here."

"But why would you do that?"

Gil rests his chin against my temple; I am drunk on his calm. When I answer Rina, my voice is firm. "I just want to. I want to be here."

"Wow," Rina sighs. "If I had a choice, I'd go to university in the States." She winks. "Football teams, you know. Parties and excitement. Here we all do army before university, so by the time we get to our studies we're too old to make like *Animal House.*"

"American universities aren't all *Animal House,*" I venture.

"So how long will your drawings be on display?" Dov cuts in, with a nod toward Gil.

"Two weeks," Gil replies. He regards Dov with what looks like a dull-edged suspicion. Since meeting my cousin this morning he has addressed him only to answer his brief questions with briefer answers.

"Are you pleased with the show?"

"Yes."

I think I catch Rina rolling her eyes at me in the rearview mirror, but I can't be sure. Then, with a burst of energy, she takes over management of the conversation. "Tell us about it," she says.

And after a few false starts, Gil is talking. He seems cajoled by Rina's lively questions, and his answers grow fuller and scattered with detail. When he explains stylistic influences and trends in Israeli art, it's clear he's decided to shine. Rina startles me with her knowledge of the art scene; she asks more, and Gil warms to her interest. He speaks of his idea for a new project, a large-scale installation involving the Orthodox. "It's going to take people by storm." His smile is full of mischief.

Dov says nothing, but he looks annoyed. I don't know whether he's irritated because of Gil's brashness or because he recognizes even fewer of Gil and Rina's art references than I do.

As Gil's monologue continues, I feel a mounting anxiety. I've thought of this first exhibit as a milestone where Gil can rest, not as an opportunity to rush on to a next step. Pretending absorption in the landscape outside the window, I wonder whether Rina and Dov can tell that I'm hearing these plans for the first time.

In the middle of a description of various types of parchment, Gil interrupts himself. "Why aren't we heading south?"

"I thought we'd stop at Wadi Qelt," Dov says. "It's just a short loop before we turn south, and Maya might be interested in seeing the flood marks." He speaks quickly and without affect; we are not to make much of this act of generosity. The detour, I know, is more of Fanya's work. I picture her strolling away down the sidewalk this morning, her yellow-and-green scarf fluttering behind her. She refused a lift back to Tami and Nachum's apartment; the distance home from Emek Refaim was just right for a morning walk, and until the *hamsin* was completely past she surely wouldn't be taking her exercise in the afternoons. "Remember to see everything," she told us, "and be careful of the sun. I'll be waiting out the heat wave indoors, listening to music. Maybe reading some poetry in the German."

Dov pulls off the highway onto a narrow road, and a few minutes later steers to one side and stops the car. I look out the windows to my right and see nothing of note on the rocky landscape. To my left I see a hill rising steeply against the morning sky. At the center of the hill's crest there appears to be a small break in the rock: a shallow furrow, nothing more.

We step out of the car, and as Gil and I stretch, Dov and Rina start up the pebbly incline. I scramble to join them. "What's the hurry?" I hear Gil say from behind me. I slow my steps, but he follows at a distance all the same.

I reach the top of the rise and stop short beside Dov and Rina. Only a few feet before us, the ground vanishes. What appeared from below to be a furrow in the rock is not a furrow at all, but a chasm dropping a hundred yards down. I stare into a deep channel cut in the layered stone, a highway through sun-baked rock. The broad reach of air separating the spot where we stand from the cliff opposite narrows far below us to a slender twisting rock bed. There is not a trace of water in the bottom of the channel, only a faint trail of vegetation where water has been and might once again be.

We walk the rim of the wadi. Dov and Rina step ahead, holding hands; Gil is not far behind me. I concentrate on keeping my footing, as if a sudden urge might overtake me and, before I had time to stop myself, I might step to the edge and slip silently down.

Dov indicates the striated rock and the sharply diving sides of the channel; he is explaining flash floods for my benefit. The winter rain that falls in Jerusalem, he says, travels in growing rivulets over saturated soil, gathers force for kilometers, then bursts through the desert to carve the

wadi deeper each year. He points out the smashed carcass of an auto-
mobile molded to a rock wall at the bottom of the ravine. "That's the
force of the water when it hits. About an hour after it rains in Jerusalem,
you'll see quite a spectacle here. That is, if you're fool enough to stand
above a flash flood. Not a cloud in the sky, and then there comes a river."

I stare at the twisted metal frame that was once a car, slammed far
below us in a blind embrace with rock.

"People die every year," Rina comments from behind Dov. "Hikers.
Kids. People who haven't listened to the flash-flood reports. In the
desert, the water can be as dangerous as the sun." She peers down into
the universe of air just beyond our feet. "Still, you should see this place
when it's in bloom. There's nothing like the desert after a flood."

Only a few steps farther up the path, Dov points out the round
black mouths of caves in the cliff opposite. "That's where monks and
other religious types used to go for isolation. You know, voices crying
in the wilderness . . . this was one of their spots."

Rina leans into Dov's sturdy body. "I couldn't last ten minutes in isolation like that."

I squint across at the caves, each seemingly inaccessible; only after a
moment do I make out the vague outline of a narrow track leading to
one. I try to imagine days of silence along this curving channel of rock.
Birds sweeping close then away, feverish hours blending into one another. And through it all, the slow shaping of prayer, psalmists and lu-
natics chanting their faith against the parched world beyond cave
entrances. I know from the "Interesting Facts" section of my guidebook
that ancient written Hebrew had no spaces between words, and I imagine phrase merging with phrase, sound upon sound upon sound, until
it is no longer possible to know where one word of prophecy ends and
the next begins.

I think of the woman from the apartment downstairs.

The strangeness of our parting returns to me now, and I puzzle over
it once again. I recall the luminous expression on her face as she waited
for me to respond, then its abrupt snuffing. She didn't say what was
wrong, she didn't respond to my hand on her shoulder; when I brought
her a glass of water she dropped it to the floor, she gripped my arm and
stared at me as water pooled around her shoes.

Who will put out this fire? she said. *Who if not you?*

Closing my eyes against the bright twisting layers of rock, I'm hit with a longing sharp as homesickness: I wish the woman from downstairs had come with us.

"I didn't say that!" Rina's footsteps crunch against stone as she brushes past me.

My eyes fly open.

"And if you want to believe it," she tells Dov with quiet intensity, as though Gil and I were not standing between them, "then stay in the damn army your whole life and see if I care. Drop me a letter someday and tell me how it went."

Dov stands watching a hawk sail high across the wadi. His jaw is clenched with unspoken retorts.

The four of us stand at the verge, forearms shading our eyes.

"It's getting hot," Gil says.

"Let's go," Dov agrees. "The more driving we do before noon, the better."

At the base of the hill, I settle into the sun-blasted air of the car's interior. I tell myself, without knowing whether I believe it, that if the woman from downstairs were here with us this morning she could interpret the seared wilderness, and my cousin's strained hospitality, and Gil's unreadable face, which fills me with hope and unease. I swear to myself that when I return to Jerusalem I will figure out what she wanted, and find a way to give it to her.

Consulting a map, Rina grimaces. She raises a water bottle to her mouth and takes a long drink. "Here comes the fun part of the drive."

∞

You have betrayed me.

Air pools stagnant in this hall. Every patch of darkness every shadow reveals its shape to me.

O American.

A whispering beats against my eardrums. Halina's voice is harsh, my hands grasp in vain for hers but touch only each other. So you see, she says, the American did not make us whole.

All night I sit straight-backed against this apartment wall, my suitcase beside my knees. Day rears across the sky, too quickly. I press my throbbing temples, I must think. No food or drink passes my lips, my heart beats with stubborn precision.

O my American. You did not soothe their pain. You did not comfort me. Your promises Your promises were lies.

You are quiet as these sabbath streets, other pilgrims climb to Your door but You turn them away in Your displeasure.

Answer me quickly, American; my spirit can endure no more.

At last sabbath fades, the blacks bid wistful farewell. An evening, a morning, a new day. Above me You stir. First a ringing to wakefulness, then a smell of coffee.

Suddenly You are before me. You walk burdened with the Israeli. Your head is sunk You watch Your sandaled feet on the stairs, You are careful of every step. You do not turn to see me crouched here in this doorway.

But I see what it is You carry. You hurry past me but You cannot hide from me the suitcase You bear.

So You would escape from me and leave me here in dust, my knees folded to sky. You would escape me like a new-hatched bird beyond a fence, flying to Your own redemption while the earth below You burns.

You leave this stairwell silent, voices call from the street below. Slamming of metal doors, quick steps. A car engine jumps, fades into the distance before I have risen to my feet.

You shall not abandon me. You shall not. O American, teach me to do Your will, for You are my only hope. I shall stand on these stiffened limbs, I shall follow You with all my heart with all my soul with all my means, for without You there is nothing.

Halina, I whisper to the pearl-lit dawn as I descend in the footsteps of the American. At each labored step my suitcase bruises my leg. We must believe.

And my faith is rewarded, for You will not forsake me after all. On the street it is easy to find the one You have left behind to guide me to You. Her arms swing with vigor, her mouth breathes melodies. I am Your ever-grateful servant I shall follow.

≪≫

Dov drives with his hands at the base of the steering wheel. His face is hardened in a squint.

I've never seen land like this. The hills rise on and on around us, a uniform brown save a sprinkling of tangled weeds. Most are striated by narrow tracks constructed by the Bedouin to ensure that not a drop of scant rainfall be wasted; the rocky domes spiral toward the sky. On one arid slope a Bedouin boy stands amid a weary-looking flock. Heads dipping rhythmically between their bony shoulders, the goats nod up the hill around him. The boy wears Western clothing and a tattered white headscarf; his face is hidden from us. When we've passed him he turns, and watches until we disappear beyond another crest.

My head vibrates with the brightness. I've forgotten my sunglasses and I close my eyes now and again for relief. All around the Subaru, rocky ground touches pale blue heaven, with no clouds to blur the harsh line of horizon. There is no more than a hint of green to ease the eye, or distract it from gazing toward limits. The vaulting sky lifts my gaze, the glaring sun casts it down, and still the hills continue. I rest my palm on the window frame, and jerk back from the glinting strip of metal.

The highway makes a last pass between multiplying domes and then, impatient with playing in the atrium of the wilderness, twists to one side and enters the hills. The engine labors as we begin a first sharp ascent; not until we've crested the second do I remember to exhale. The road twists and curves on itself as we climb the hills deeper into the Arava. At each hairpin turn, the veined and marbled desert spreads farther below us; only a flimsy guardrail and a scattering of pebbles mark the edge of the road.

Dov has long since dropped out of conversation, and he concentrates on the view through the windshield. As we approach each curve, Rina reaches over and honks the horn to warn any oncoming drivers. Dov consents without a word. The two of them gaze fiercely at the road, eyes half shut against the glare.

The questions I'd thought to ask Dov and Rina, the comments designed to show them I am not so sheltered as they think, now settle in a knot in my throat. *What do you think of Rabin? What of Peres? What in your estimation is the impact of ongoing conflict in the territories?*

The spiraling car points into the noon sky. I don't want Dov to be distracted, I don't want him to lift his eyes from the road for even an instant to mull over some quirk of my Hebrew accent. I sit back and try to focus on the view swinging in and out of sight before us.

At one curve my fears are realized—the Subaru's horn is answered by a deeper one from above. Dov pulls to the right and brings the car to a stop. We wait flush against the face cut into the hillside, my window inches from blond rock. Ahead of us looms a tourist bus, glittering blue and dust-coated. It swings out in an impossible arc sure to carry it off the narrow road and tumbling into the valleys and plains below. Through the tinted windows of the bus I see the shadows of silent Americans or Europeans, looking out at a landscape as foreign as the moon. Swinging back toward us, the bus passes so close that when Dov reaches out a hand and pats its metal flank, we seem to be traveling through a tunnel of rumbling shadow.

After the bus is gone, I stare onto empty road. I blink at a new world of bright and blessed silence.

Dov starts the car up the hill again.

With the field glasses to his eyes, Gil scans the desert spread like an ocean floor below us. "Not even a camel out there today," he remarks.

Dov's fingers tap the steering wheel. I see him brace for the next curve.

"You'd need to be a camel to go out at noon," I say. "Or else drive a tanker full of water."

Gil sucks his teeth as if displeased, but I see that he is flirting with me. "It's not such a big deal, Little Miss American. All you need is a water bottle and a good hat."

"Yeah, well. A big water bottle. And a huge hat."

Now Gil is grinning. "Little Miss American." He repeats the new nickname like a badge of honor. He winks at me. "What kind of imbecile would want to run around in the desert at midday, anyway."

Gently Rina places her hand on the back of Dov's neck. I recall now what Fanya said about Dov: a friend dead, of dehydration.

But Dov drives on as if he's heard nothing.

Gil leans back, pats my thigh. "The only ones fool enough to enjoy it are those macho special-unit trainees. They've got to prove they're as tough as the camels, and as dumb."

Even the forced smile fades from Rina's lips.

The heat of the day is gritty between my teeth. My head begins to hurt from the sun.

"How about lunch sometime soon?" Gil says. No one answers him.

"There are a lot of reasons to be in the desert." My words fall into the silent interior of the car. "Sometimes if you're in the desert there's nothing you can do, sometimes there just isn't enough water. Sometimes no matter how much you bring with you it's not enough." I know I sound idiotic but I can't stop.

Dov has shrugged free of Rina's hand. He edges forward in his seat, his weight hovers over the steering wheel.

"It's easy to get stuck without water," I conclude.

Rina is watching Dov.

Searching the bags by my feet for our lunches, I cast about for a way to return conversation to more neutral ground. I ask myself, What would my mother say to defuse this situation?

I straighten. "What do you two think of the reports of peace break-throughs in Oslo?"

Rina turns and stares at me in open incredulity.

Dov is driving faster. The next curve slings me against Gil's un-yielding shoulder.

Gil gives a short laugh. "Where did that come from?"

I think I'm going to cry. "I want to know what they think the future is going to be. I want to know if they think there's a way out of it all."

"A way out of it all?" Gil hoots. "What, you mean a way out of war?" His speech has turned caustic. "No one's going to find a way out of that one, honey. Not the right, not the left. No one's going to clear up this mess. Not in this world, anyway." He falls silent for a few seconds. Then, in a softer voice, he asks me, "Didn't you see my exhibit?"

I catch Rina looking at Gil in the rearview mirror, and the expression on her face is pure distaste.

"I'm just asking what they see in the future," I repeat dully.

Dov has twisted in his seat to face us.

Rina reaches for the steering wheel. "Dov, the road."

Dov is looking at Gil with a pure, unreasoning rage. I know immediately from the knocking of my heart that I've seen this expression before. Dov turns back to the windshield; his hands are trembling, as if he, too, is afraid of what might happen next. The car drifts wide on a curve, spitting sand over the side of the road.

"Give me the binoculars," he says lightly.

"What?" Gil's face is frozen in an incredulous grin. When Dov does not answer, Gil laughs hoarsely. "What, you're going to throw my binoc-ulars out the window because I said something you don't like about pol-itics?"

At first Dov offers no reply, and I think he is going to retreat to his earlier indifference. Then he speaks. "Give me the fucking binoculars."

"Why should I?"

Dov doesn't answer.

Gil looks at me. I look back at him. I have nothing to offer. We sit side by side on the narrow jolting seat.

Cradling the binoculars, Gil hesitates. Then, without a word, he holds them out to Dov.

Something about Dov's laughter makes me shrink back in my seat. He lifts the binoculars, and then he is holding them to his eyes with one hand and patting the shimmying steering wheel with the other as he would a restless animal. The car veers toward the rock face, toward the line at the center of the road, and back.

Rina swears and grabs at Dov, but he shakes her off with one swing of his arm. "Dov," she shouts. "Dov, are you crazy? Give me the binoculars."

The car jolts ahead, swerves toward the center of the road and then across, narrowly missing the pebbled edge before swinging back toward the center. Below us the hills turn slowly. Dov is driving with one palm flat against the wheel. He holds the binoculars to his eyes, his face is contorted with laughter. "I'm looking into the fucking future," he whoops. "I'm looking into the future to see what's ahead." There are tears running down his cheeks.

Gil and I are thrown against each other and against the metal frame of the Subaru, and as Dov drags the wheel to the left I see the desert floor spin below, a garden of rock and heat and sun. Gil is gripping my hand tightly; all I can think is that my fingers will break. Then we swing once more, and I am aware of boulders, heaving below like waves in an ocean. Stones dance in circles and spiral to the heavens like mountain goats; hills skip forward to greet us, we will meet them in midair, fly to their embrace and lift our faces to the sun as we fall. I am free, I think. I am falling, I will plunge to that burning valley. How easy it is, after so much struggle; we are like puppets, Gil and I, flung about this metal frame that strains toward the desert floor.

Only Rina is real. Rina, sitting in the front seat screaming Dov's name. In her face is an intensity of will; her green eyes shine with a single message I can barely fathom: *Stop*.

"It's the future, look at it, it's beautiful." Dov is yelling, his voice sings with sorrow. The car spins out in its widest arc, the gravel at the edge of the road rains up against the metal below my feet. The car tilts at the edge of the paved surface and I know that the wheels are about to go over; there is a look of great regret and understanding on Dov's face. Gil grips my hand between both of his.

Then we are slowing. We have slowed. We are nearly at a stop. Dov has dropped the binoculars. He is staring ahead, his shoulders slumped, every bit of strength drained from him. Rina's hand is on the steering wheel. Her eye on the road, she edges the tilting car back toward the pavement. "It's going to be okay now, Dov," she is saying. "It's going to be okay. Let's stop the car."

We come to a stop. There is absolute silence. Gil is paler than I have ever seen him. He stares straight ahead. Dov sits with his forehead to the wheel, caught in a dream. Sun beats on the metal, inches above our heads. If Dov were to open his door it would swing out over air. His foot would land, lightly, on a few inches of loose stone. Then nothing.

"Do you want me to drive?" Rina asks. "I'll drive."

Gradually, Dov seems to wake. "No." The single word is filled with awe. He lifts his head and looks past Rina, out the side window, at the road. "No," he repeats. "I'm all right." Then he's silent. His eyes beg Rina's forgiveness.

He steers the car gently back toward the center of the road and carefully pilots us up the hill.

Near the top I am able to slip my fingers out of Gil's hands. He does not look at me; he looks out the side window toward the safety of the rock face. His jaw is trembling. "Crazy fucker," he says to the window.

Dov does not seem to hear him, and soon the road levels out onto a ridge.

೧೧

The barred and locked skies declare it. These glaring streets mock my failure. I am lost.

I search the pavement for clues. I taste the wind and listen, caress the concrete of this sidewalk; every sense strains to find her. I must not lose the trail now.

I have followed her through the hilly byways of this city, she who will lead me to the American. I have followed dragging my suitcase as she passed through narrow alleys and dusty parks, she would have escaped

*me ducking through a building's cool lobby but I would not be escaped.
Between us I measured half a block so she might walk ahead and pretend not to notice me, for I understood she would not want to be seen
with a Feldstein in public, even after all that has passed. Such courtesy
I gave her freely. And she, she my friend come to my aid at last after all
our struggles, she wove through these rising falling neighborhoods as if
she did not know me. As if I have not spent my girlhood listening under
her parents' balcony to insults spoken plainly over tea, as if she did not
recognize me from the nights we have spoken until dawn in my apartment, the vigils we have kept together. The times I have held her hand
and she has wept without ceasing. Without a glance over her shoulder
she danced me through this sun-shocked Jerusalem toward the American, to make amends for the wrong she did me.*

I forgive you, Lilka.

*Past playgrounds and shop-lined streets and close-built houses I hur-
ried after her, until I reached this place, this broad roaring avenue.*

And now she is gone.

*I stand on the sidewalk, the weight of my suitcase burns my shoul-
der. Cars whip past or stand honking outside doorways, a thin-armed
boy hugging a soccer ball dashes across the pavement. My ears ring with
confusion.*

*She has disappeared into this tall square building, windows piled
high into dazzling brightness. Could this be where she means me to find
the American?*

*Squinting at hurtling cars, I consider the wind that sweeps behind
them.*

*O American watch over my path I will follow Your ways all the days
of my life.*

*I close my eyes and step into the street. When I open my eyes I am
on the other side, behind me cars drag gales.*

*The walkway to the building is short and lined with pale red flow-
ers. I pull the metal door and step into darkness.*

*And the trail awaits me. My eyes tear with gratitude. Lilka's perfume
leads me patiently through the foyer up echoing stairs, to this narrow entryway this glowing doorbell.*

*"Yes?" Lilka's voice sounds in Hebrew from behind the door, round
and pretty like years of practice.*

I wait in silence and it is only a moment before she opens the door.

She looks at me. Raises her eyebrows to inquire my purpose. As though she does not know already, as though she herself has not brought me to this place. Her wary eyes steal my breath, I had not remembered such endless blue. She stands before me, face round and flushed from our walk, a book in one hand. Her neck draped with a patterned scarf, yellow and green circling each other in spirals, yellow and green again and again and again.

"Lilka?" *I whisper.*

"I'm sorry," *she says,* "are you looking for someone?"

"Lilka."

She shakes her head, her smile is honeyed. "My name is Fanya," *she says.* "Fanya Gutman."

How her face has rounded and grown pink since camp, I would not recognize her if I did not know.

"What is it you need?" *she asks.*

Tones like jewels.

She looks at my face, my hanging arms, my skirt. Displeased, she considers the suitcase which I have set beside my feet. "I'm not interested in buying anything," *she says.*

There is a long silence. I understand that she wants me to speak the words.

"The American," *I say.*

"What American?" *She looks puzzled. Then knowledge slips into her eyes. Among others she will pretend she does not know what I have come for, but now that we are alone Lilka will claim me her own.*

"You want Maya," *she tells me in Hebrew. She turns an empty palm to me.* "Maya isn't here. She's gone away."

Lilka, your accent has grown unfamiliar through these long years. Lilka your Hebrew words are round as raindrops, but still if I strain I will hear traces of our Yiddish.

She leans forward, suspicious at my silence. "You are the woman from Maya's building, aren't you?" *She touches her fingertips gently together. Her delicate nostrils twitch.* "I don't know what you want," *she says.* "But I saw you following me on my walk."

In the squared corner of her jaw, a pulse.

"If there's nothing else you need, perhaps you'd like to move along on your business."

"I need the American." I speak to her in our Yiddish, soft syllables flooding the parched gate of my throat. "We need the American. Do you not remember we watched the skies for Her, now She has come at last. She is close by, together we will find."

She stares, I know she has understood me.

"Maya isn't here." She lifts her chin, her Hebrew words shut a door on my Yiddish; she is chastising a simple child. "The American has gone away."

My throat is clotted with speech, I draw breath with difficulty. "I am not dull-witted," I tell her.

"I don't know who you are or what you want," she says in Hebrew. "But I have business of my own to conduct, so I'll wish you a good day." She reaches for the door handle.

A door closing, my foot in its path.

"If you had only asked Halina," I say. "She would have told you I was not dull-witted. But it is too late."

Her blue eyes widen, she tries to push the door closed again but my foot, battered, blocks it.

"What is it you want?" This time fear is scratched onto the surface of her words.

I say nothing.

She clutches the door with both hands and now she has shed politeness. Her face is washed plain with dislike. "You're one of the ones from the concentration camps, aren't you?"

Lilka, I address her in my mind.

"I can always tell." She spits the words. "You wear the ugliness in your face."

Slow and quivering, I reach. She watches, then starts back as I am about to touch her cheek.

Panic dances in her eyes. "Get away from me."

When the German guard shot you Lilka, did you feel the pain?

"If you have anything to say to me, speak Hebrew. Speak Hebrew or German or Dutch or Polish." Her forehead a deepening pink. "I don't understand your Yiddish and I don't want to understand."

"I forgive you," I tell her in Yiddish.

"You what?" The words escape her in Yiddish, one pearl-tipped hand flies to her lips.

"Lilka," I open my palms to her to show her I am her friend. "I for-give you. You did not know Karol, you could not know his Gentile ways."

"My name isn't Lilka and I don't know what you're talking about." Her Hebrew pelts my ears. "What Gentile? And what Halina? I've never met you before."

She is not as I remember her, Lilka's face shifts and dances before me. But I am determined: she will know me and bring me to the American. "I forgive you," I soothe.

But she is not soothed. Her lashes beat against her cheeks. "I've done nothing wrong," she pleads.

"Help me find the American," I say. "All wrongs will be righted."

Her mouth works, she whispers. "Why won't you leave me alone? I don't know what you want from me."

"The American," I say. It is important. She must listen. "The Amer-ican," I explain.

"But she's gone. She's gone away."

How white her knuckles on the door handle.

"The American is gone," she repeats.

From the street, cries of rushing traffic. Behind this woman is an apartment full of silence. Curtains hang straight in still air.

"How old were you?" Her hands fly fierce with her speech. "When the war started."

The words escape me, puffs of wind. "I am fifteen."

Her voice is ragged with fury. "You know, I lived through the war too. Perhaps you're not aware of that. I was a young woman. I had a whole life there, in Amsterdam, nothing like your backwater Polish villages."

How the tendons stand out on her throat, I would reach out a hand to smooth them.

"I don't know what you people went through. In ghettos, in camps. And I don't want to know. Do you hear me? I don't want to know." She steadies herself against the door frame. Tucks a strand of hair. Straight-ens her scarf, and when she looks up a veil of boredom shrouds her eyes. "I don't know why I'm even bothering talking to you at all, I should call the police."

"Lilka," I call her quietly. "Be careful there is a guard beside the fence."

"Put it behind you. Don't think. Just don't think. Take a walk, get *some fresh air. Sing a pretty song, not one of those horrid dirges. Why do you have to be that way? People go on, don't they? Why can't you just shut it out?" How hard comes her breath, she stands rigid with her pride. "I never give anyone that power over my life. I never let anything or anyone touch me that way."*

The apartment behind her is bright with sun and motionless, empty as an abandoned shell.

"There is a guard he will shoot," I say.

She turns from me, her shoulders shuddering disgust; she wheels to address me again. "I lost my whole family. I left for my honeymoon, came to this noplace, and my family and my friends and my Amsterdam disappeared behind me. Do you have any idea what it was like to wait for the postman every day, looking for replies that never came? You think I don't know what loss is too? My best girlfriend—" She stops more words before they can escape.

"You're wrong," she informs. "I'll tell you this, you're wrong to hold on to it. What can it possibly accomplish? You're nothing but a walking spectacle."

A bus rumbles on the street, girls shout a song.

"Lilka," I breathe my sorrow.

Slowly she shakes her head. Slowly straightens her blouse, combs fingers through her hair. "Live for the moment," she says.

From somewhere in the building, a radio blatting music.

She is not Lilka, this woman who pats fury from her soft face. I have been mistaken. Lilka has not come for me. She is not my friend, she will not help me find the American, she has taken my sister on a Sports Club outing, the two of them will whisper secrets and forget me.

From the doorway a stranger regards me, she wants something I cannot recall what. Following her gaze I reach to my head.

A knot, stubborn between my fingers. The breaking of dried-out threads as the kerchief loosens.

She stares; her blue eyes narrow with her revulsion. "Did it grow back that way after camp?" she whispers at last. "Or did you do that to yourself?"

I drop my headkerchief to the floor before her feet.

"I forgive you," I tell her.

The stairs slap the bottoms of my shoes. In the darkness of the lobby I grope to the exit, from the stairwell behind me there is no sound.

Outside, dry air caresses my arms, sun strikes my bare head. Children, a bus, automobiles. Such confusion assembled on one street. My heart is bitter in my throat. Where are You, my American? I search for You but do not find. Even my fast companions have abandoned me, even Lilka, Halina falls mute and Feliks does not goad.

Here on this clamoring street, I hesitate. Sun presses curious in the tangle of my hair, strange silence echoes in my head. Now rises fear. I am alone. My feet point to the safe darkness of my apartment but I am stern with them, for there can be no returning. I have left that shuttered place behind I shall not return, until You have conquered past, and brought future.

I seek You in the edges of the morning. In the shadows that rim this narrow path I search. In this alley, this valley, this concrete walkway that leads me up and up and up.

∞ 14 ∞

It is almost dusk when we reach the campground. Dov has driven slowly, and Rina has insisted on breaks with such frequency that I feel sure we've explored every possible exit off the highway; we even dropped in on elderly relatives of Rina's in Yotvata, and sat sipping tea with her great-uncle while his wife shopped for a snack for us. Since midday we've ridden quietly, every question and answer accomplished with a minimum of words. Gil sits beside me and watches the desert pass. His hands lie open on his knees; the binoculars are balanced on his palms.

Although the desert rolls without break or marking as far as I can see, I know from my guidebooks how near we are to the southernmost tip of the country. Fifteen minutes' drive would bring us to Jordan, half an hour to Egypt. From that corner of the Sinai you can see the coast of Saudi Arabia, and a bad encounter with the currents of the Gulf of Aqaba could sweep a swimmer or rowboat north to King Hussein's palace in minutes.

The turnoff into the nature preserve is sudden—a quick fork to the right, with only a minimal sign marking the park's border. We make our way between the final hills, Dov steering the Subaru along a faint, dusty track.

A cooling wind comes through the open windows. In the fading light, goats cluster around caper bushes and olive trees. To one side rise sharp cliffs and caves, pillars of reddish rock. Salt bushes, their leaves a white-dusted green, dot a rocky hill ahead. Gently I rub the fine layer of salt left on my own cheek by the day's heat.

Dov turns between two lower hills and, the last of the setting sun glancing the windshield, we roll to a stop at a set of broad steps carved in the center of a flat valley. Dov shuts off the engine.

The four of us climb out and stand beside the car, taking our bearings in the open space. The pink-streaked sky is dimming, the sun has eased its way behind the hills. Dov and Rina shake out their limbs. Gil and I survey the hills around us; we stand with our hands on the roof of the Subaru.

The air here has an oddly familiar softness, a soothing quality I struggle to identify. Small birds streak past us. I move stiffly away from the car.

Then I see the water. Just beyond the steps, the birds dart across the surface of a stone-rimmed pool that stretches along the valley's pale floor. The water is clear and still, disturbed only by the birds' knifelike paths. We've arrived at a manmade oasis: a narrow valley of mercy in this endless desert. My eyes, burning from the day's relentless sun, rest on the water. My throat trembles; I'm grateful that I don't need to speak.

From across the valley, on the far side of the water, a glint of metal catches my attention. Two cars are parked at the base of a low hill, and figures are busy unloading bags from the trunks.

"Hey, morons!" Dov shouts, and in an instant he's down the stairs and on his way past the pool. Rina follows more slowly, rubbing her shoulders as she walks.

Leaving my backpack beside the car for the moment, I start toward the pool, each stair requiring two of my own steps. Even Gil's long strides can barely accommodate them. I imagine that we've stumbled into the front parlor of giants. We descend, carrying our small offerings of sleeping bags and dusty hats before us. Gil skirts the water and I follow. To one side of the pool is an open shelter: five or six beams of a roof laid across a free-standing frame. It's an odd structure that could provide only the suggestion of shade against the midday heat, and I wonder whether someone started to build something else but became distracted.

We set down our things at the edge of the shelter, and it's not long before Dov's friends join us. A stocky redheaded boy in glasses heaves a pile of half-empty water jugs to the ground, and two girls with linked arms enter the shelter, one of them carrying a beat-up guitar. Gear tumbles on the dirt, someone unloads firewood from the trunk of a car, introductions pass in a blur. There are a dozen or so of Dov's friends, suntanned and loose with their insults; I catch only that the girl with the guitar is either Hana or Hava, and that Yair is the freckled one whose grin faltered only when he was shaking hands with Gil, as if he'd been reminded of something unpleasant. I watch Gil for a reaction, but he doesn't seem to notice anything amiss.

Dov and the others set up camp so boisterously I might assume they hadn't seen each other in months. But I recall Rina telling me while we packed the car this morning that the group has camped here every few weeks since the beginning of high school. It was harder to coordinate while they were in the army, she explained; now that most of them have finished their service and are working or studying, it's easier. Those still in the army figure out when they can get a few days' leave, then the others arrange their schedules accordingly. Dov used to come here all the time, Rina said. It was his favorite spot. But he hasn't been in a few years.

As I watch the noisy gathering, I think, Dov used to come here with his friend who died. Is this his first time back since?

A few flashlights have been pulled out of packs, and light swings busily across the rocky ground. Around us, the park is silent. The sounds from under this shelter seem to be the only ones in the valley. Dov and his friends shout and toss gear and bags of food; above us the beams appear to rise higher and higher as they fade against the darkening sky.

"We need kindling for our fire." Rina touches my shoulder. I hadn't realized I'd drifted, but now I see I'm standing at the edge of the shelter, the pool a few yards behind me. "Come on," Rina says. "Let's go."

It's a peace offering, and I accept it without a word. Beside a pile of backpacks we meet up with Dov, and the three of us set out.

I can make out the shapes of the hills around us only vaguely. But Dov and Rina know where to go, and I follow them around the perimeter of the pool. Dov's flashlight reflects in the eyes of two jackals pacing the far end of the water; he turns it off, and we move ahead as though there were no need for us to see. My feet scatter pebbles and slip along rocks, but there's something surprisingly easy about walking blind in the evening breeze. We feel our way along the trail.

Rina and Dov have chosen a path that rises into a fold between hills, and as soon as the first brambles brush my sandaled feet I understand why. Occasional low bushes promise fallen twigs; here and there Dov stoops to collect a stick from the underbrush.

"It's a beautiful night," Rina says.

"The most beautiful," I answer quickly, and I hear Rina's smile. For an instant I direct my thoughts to Gil. I picture him seated beneath the shelter, someone offering him food or asking his help with a small task. *Please,* I urge him.

We pause at a patch of bushes and Dov scans with his flashlight for twigs. While he fills his arms with larger branches, Rina and I gather what we can from the bracken.

"What will you do when you're finished with college?" Rina asks.

"Me?" The question catches me off guard. I open my mouth to tell her I don't know. Then, instead, I seize upon an answer that has never before crossed my mind. "I want to do what my mother does in America, only here. I want to start a center to solve problems between groups."

The notion must seem as ridiculous to them as it does to me. I have no training, I have no skills, I know almost nothing of the problems of this country I've lived in for half a year. But suddenly I'm decided. I'll get skills. I'll make a life here, make a difference. So what if my only experience with the issues is in my letters to my mother? If Gil can make a fresh start, so can I.

Rina sounds interested. "Problems between which groups? Mizrahi and Ashkenazi? Arabs and Jews?"

"I haven't quite decided," I admit.

Rina rolls a bundle of twigs between her palms, then nods approval. "Me, I want to be a schoolteacher. I want to work with children."

Together Rina and I snap twigs under the beam of Dov's flashlight. Wordlessly she directs me away from a thornbush. The events of the day have left us not adversaries after all, but friends. It makes me bold; I open my mouth, and as I address Dov directly for the first time since he almost drove us off the road, I let a sliver of anger slip into my voice. "What do you think *you'll* do next?" I ask.

Before he can respond, Rina speaks wearily. "He'll do more army. Dov is going to be a career officer."

Standing so close to him, I can hear the slow release of his breath. Instantly my anger transforms into fear.

Dov takes Rina's twigs and bunches them with his own. He snaps some to a more manageable size. "It's not that I like war, Rina. Why do you always have to make it sound that way? It's not that I like war. It's just that war is a fact."

She bends to pick up another twig.

"Rina." He speaks her name softly, a request.

"You have more talent than anyone I know," she says, straightening, "and you're going to put it into fighting."

"Defense." Dov scans the ground with his flashlight again.

"I know we need defense. I know we need the best defense. And I know you can be the best. But can't someone else do it?"

Dov's silence is filled with reproach.

"I know. That's how you think." Rina offers the single twig to Dov like an apology. "And that's probably why I love you. But I can't help how I feel."

Taking the twig, Dov turns off his flashlight. He starts down the path, but after a few steps he wheels to address me. "When I was eight years old," he says, as if picking up the thread of a long-standing argument between us, "I saw the funeral procession of my neighbor's older brother."

I stand on the path, uncertain whether to respond with sympathy or to remain silent. I have no idea why Dov should want to explain himself to me.

"He was a soldier and he was killed in a terrorist attack on his base. And I watched out the window and saw my neighbor's mother, the same mother who fed us poppy seed cake and juice after school, flailing at her husband. Trying to beat him, trying to punish her husband with her fingernails and fists, for giving her a son who would die in war.

"My father saw me watching and he said to me, 'Be a good soldier when it's your turn. Don't be afraid and don't let the nonsense get to you. Just keep your sense of humor and go where they tell you to go, and you'll be all right.'" Dov speaks with great precision. "'Keep your sense of humor,' "he repeats. His free hand lifts helplessly in the air, and drops.

"So I go. They tell me to go, and I go. They tell me what they need from my unit, and I find a way to make it happen and keep my soldiers safe." Dov continues to face me as he speaks. "Is there anything so terrible about that?"

Rina answers from behind me. Her words are heavy with regret. "I know you're doing the best you can. You always do. It's just that a lot of people who mean well end up doing things they would never have imagined doing. Like all those poor guys serving in the territories, who spend their time enforcing curfews on children." She hesitates. "Remember what Rafi used to say?"

"Don't talk about Rafi," he says. "Please."

"I'm sorry," Rina says, and I know that she is.

When she turns down the hill, I follow. Dov falls in behind me.

"A center to solve problems between groups?" My cousin's footsteps shadow mine. "You Americans." He chuckles, but his laughter is thick.

I make my way along the trail, my eyes on Rina's dim figure descending the hill ahead of me.

"You always want to fix everything," Dov continues. "Like other countries' damn business. Well, maybe not everything can be fixed by some pretty conversations between diplomats. Maybe war is war and there's no way out for us. Maybe your boyfriend is right on just that one point."

I hunt for something agreeable to say. It's not that I want Dov's approval—I've given up on that. It's simply that I don't want to be the focus of his attention.

But Rina is listening, and her presence shames me into going through the motions of argument. "What if the country gave the peace process a try?" I say to him.

It is the prompt Dov has been waiting for, and he lashes back bitterly. "What do you know about our lives here, our decisions? You Americans come here with something to work out. Some high moral position. You come here and judge us for a few weeks or months, then you go back to your comfortable houses and forget all about the problems."

I want to quote my mother to show him he's wrong. But my mind is blank.

Dov snorts his laughter. "Americans don't bother to learn, they just like to be photographed saving everyone. Maybe there's no way out of our situation. Did you ever consider that? Sometimes you try and try and there's nothing you can do because this is just the world we're given."

We've reached the bottom of the valley.

"You don't have any idea what you're talking about," he says.

A few more steps would carry us to the rim of the pool; voices come filtered over the water. Rina stops in her tracks and turns on Dov. "So I suppose that makes us bigger than everyone else," she accuses. "I suppose we're better, nobler people because we have hardship? And no one else can *possibly* understand us, because war brings out the best in us."

"I didn't say that."

"Didn't you?"

Dov stares at the dry branches in his arms. Then he turns to me. "You," he says hoarsely. "You walk in and out of this country. I live here."

My voice rises. "All I'm saying is maybe there's another way."

The harshness in Dov's words is out of proportion to anything I might have said. "You want us to take risks? People die as it is, but more people will die if we take a risk that goes bad. So if you want to try another way, be prepared to lose someone. Be prepared to lose some- one you love."

I make no answer.

Dov shakes his head in disgust. "You have no idea what that means."

I listen to Dov's footsteps fade along the rocky edge of the pool. A minute later he reappears, a sturdy figure in the gathering beneath the shelter.

"I'm sorry," is all Rina says. Then she too is gone.

Across the water, flashlight beams flit conversationally. A peal of laughter draws me closer. I wander to the stone steps, where I can watch the group from a distance. Someone has laid a metal drum across a pile of rocks and propped a blowtorch beneath it. Two girls bend over the torch, then one spits chewing gum into her palm and uses it to patch the torch's fuel hose. I see Dov, standing shadowed behind them like some ancient warrior, pouring oil from a jug into the drum. After a mo- ment's conference among the assembled figures, the blowtorch blooms with a popping sound—a blue flower clasps the bottom of the drum. A low picnic table beneath the shelter has become a chopping board, someone ferries ingredients from table to cooking drum. Scattered about the stone rim of the pool, others sit in twos and threes.

On the steps I find my backpack and pull my sweater over my head, grateful for the scratchy wool on my bare arms. I take a clear ribbed bottle from the pack as well, still half full. The water is warm, and tastes of plastic. Across the pool a jackal paces and stands, perhaps hoping for scraps from dinner. Its pale-brown body flickers in the reflection of the blowtorch across the water. I lower the bottle to my hip. As I watch the jackal turn and disappear, the wind, rising from beyond the valley, vibrates a low note across the top of the bottle.

It is the sweetest, most comforting sound I can recall. I stand perfectly still, afraid to move and lose this low-voiced blessing. As I focus on the bottle humming in my hand, I fight a sense of foreboding. What if Dov is right? What if he and his willfully miserable mother are both right, about fresh starts?

As the wind fades, I watch the others. They cluster around the blowtorch and dip ladles into the drum. I try to pick out Gil, but I can't; Dov and Rina, too, are anonymous among the milling figures.

The beams of the shelter, lofty and invisible at dusk, have reappeared: blank timbers against the brightening stars. The girl with the guitar plays something unfamiliar, and a few others sing along. They gather on the stones along the water's edge, plates in hand.

The wind has died; my hands are emptied of sound and my vision shimmers with tears. Looking over the friends seated on the rock sill, I know that they love each other fiercely. For a long while I watch them, huddled beneath this shelter that provides no shelter. It occurs to me to wonder whether a whole community with its members' arms wound tight around one another can still be lonely.

I wish I were bigger. I wish I were big as a giant, big enough to protect them.

When I join them, they make a place for me on the rocks and offer steaming coffee without a word. The girl with the guitar starts singing once more, and raggedly the others join in. Israeli pop and Hebrew folksongs and the Beatles. Someone makes a request for "I Want to Hold Your Hand" and she obliges with enthusiasm. I stifle a groan at their English. "I want to fold your hand," some of them are singing.

Only after the final chorus do I think to look for Gil. At first I don't see him. Then, peering once again into the shadows beyond the campfire Dov is tending, I see Gil sitting on the ground. He is watching me, his face expressionless. I smile at him but he doesn't respond.

Against the murmur of the fire, soft conversation emerges. Someone's father is still so unreasonable about her curfew, doesn't he know she's been in the army, doesn't he know she's got her own life already? Someone's older brother has a new girlfriend. A girl with a mop of dark curly hair is laughing to herself. "My little sister spent the whole Gulf War asking our dad where babies come from. She was relentless, and my father had nowhere to escape. We sat in the sealed room, just laughing at him while he spouted euphemisms, and she shot every one down in her little five-year-old voice."

"The Gulf War," a gawky boy intones. "A family experience."

"I always thought the Gulf War was more of a lovers' war," says the girl with the guitar. "Everybody locked up like that night after night. Look at all the babies born nine months later."

"A lovers' war?" a girl named Tali echoes. "Yes, but what about all the stress, what do you think that produced? If you want to see what kind of love we got in the sealed rooms, come volunteer with me at the women's shelter. During the war our calls went sky-high."

"All right. True." The girl with the guitar stops tuning to wave in acknowledgment. "But still, lovers didn't do too badly. And not just lovers. I know whole groups of friends who had fallen out of touch. They spent the SCUD nights together, sleeping on each other's floors and catching up on life."

My hands drift around the cooling metal of my coffee cup. At the edge of the group, turned halfway toward the water, Dov is stone-faced and silent. Beyond the campfire Gil sits apart, his eyes glittering in the low light of the flames. I look from one to the other, careful to keep my eyes moving. Rina sits near me; the slight furrow between her eyebrows tells me that she and Dov have not reconciled.

Above us the stars have grown enormous. Larger daubs of white light stand out against a carpeting of smaller stars. I trace fanciful constellations between the beams of the shelter, and wait for the singing to resume.

It is Rina's low groan that draws me down from the sky and into a

growing clamor. Belatedly I become aware of the heated tone the conversation has taken. They are discussing politics. Dov's expression is
blank. Beside me, Rina is tight-lipped. Voices spin against each other and
recoil; I slouch lower over my coffee. I'm drunk with exhaustion. Maybe
Dov is right: I'm only an American girl, out of place in this gathering
of soldiers and former soldiers. Maybe I *don't* understand. I don't even
know, I realize, whether I want to.

"I can't take any more of this," Rina whispers to no one. I turn to
her, relieved, but she is looking across the group at Dov.

We can't go on the way we've been going, someone is saying.

You can't take a person's home away, another voice picks up, steady and
reasoned. *You can believe you have all the best reasons in the world, but eventually you have to compromise, or there will be poison between people forever. At
least, that's what I think. About the Palestinians.*

Other voices call out sharply now, the jumble of declarations and
objections rising through the open roof to the star-dusted sky. Heavy-
lidded, I let the sounds sail past me.

*That's what we need to make peace. We need faith even where everyone says
it's impossible.*

What, like the blacks have faith?

*Maybe. Maybe just like that, except without their intolerance. Without their
backward ideas about God-given land. We need faith just like them, only there's
no Messiah coming to save us—we have to be the Messiah ourselves. We've lived
too long in a fortress. We're strong enough to try something new.*

*You know that's shit. Faith never stopped a terrorist. Only security. Haven't
you read their charter, did you miss the bit about wiping out our country? Let
them make a home in some other country, there are plenty of Arab nations to
choose from. We have only one, why are you so eager to give it away?*

*Because maybe if you want a change you have to give up part of what you
love.*

Jerusalem?

*Jerusalem Jerusalem, why not damn Jerusalem? I won't miss half a city if we
have peace.*

Through the molten air over the low campfire, I see Gil focusing his
binoculars on one speaker after another.

*In the name of all the survivors of the Shoah. In the name of all the ones
who didn't survive, in their memory, how can you be so casual about security?*

Hamas promises another genocide if there's a peace agreement, you want to test them? At least this way we're losing lives but we're not getting wiped out. For the sake of the Six Million, this country has to remember the danger.

For their sake shouldn't we forget? Shouldn't we move forward?

Forget? You sound like the anti-Semites. Like the Nazis.

And you sound like the blacks, with their no compromise and not wanting anything in the world to change. What good is it if we remember so hard it cripples us?

You want to lose another child to a bomb? Another dozen children to bombs? How can you talk about making concessions?

"Bullshit." Gil's voice cuts across the circle.

I open my eyes.

Unified as a flock of birds wheeling to settle on a wire, the others fall silent.

"You're all full of shit," Gil says. He has lowered the binoculars.

The fire makes a soft skittering noise.

"What's that supposed to mean?" says the girl with the guitar. Her voice is familiar and I know she played a part in the argument, but I can't recall which.

"You act like it matters." Gil's words are a clanging of bells, furious and strident and hopeless. Alert, I watch the dislike taking shape in the others' postures, the fists resting loosely on hips as if readying for a fight. Looking from one keen, expectant face to another, I want to warn them: Back down. Let him be, it may pass.

"You act like your pointless opinions actually make a difference. Like a few kilometers of land here or there could change something. You act like there's hope if you just do the right thing." Gil stares the group down. "There's not going to be any peace. Not with concessions and not without concessions and not with any amount of your ridiculous faith and priggish patriotism. You believed all those scout troop songs? Then you've been sold a bill of goods. There's never going to be peace and there's never going to be security."

When he's finished, it is silent.

"So what do you suggest, my friend?" Yair speaks up from across the circle.

"I suggest nothing. I suggest stop acting so full of yourselves, because it doesn't make a difference."

Yair gives a low whistle. "Ah, wisdom from on high."

Gil is on his feet in an instant. "Go ahead and say it," he taunts. "Go ahead and say you remember me from basic training."

Slowly Yair stands. He is shorter than Gil, and compact.

"Go ahead and say, 'Why should we listen to him after what he did in the army.' "

Yair takes his time to respond. So quiet I hardly hear myself, I whisper a warning to this freckled stranger. *Don't,* I tell him.

"No need for me to say what everyone already knows," Yair is telling Gil. "You can't hide a dishonorable discharge. Or the time in *dufuk*. What did they sentence you to? I imagine it must have been at least a year."

In the dim orange glow of the firelight, Gil's face is a mask of fury. I've never seen him so enraged. At any second his anger will erupt, but Yair stands unflinching opposite him. Now, alongside my dread, I feel a strange excitement.

Yair speaks. "So be as crazy as you want. Be as lunatic as you like in the privacy of your own home, I truly don't care. Tell your American girlfriend anything you want about the rest of us, it's not my affair. But you could have killed someone that day in Gaza."

A murmur of recognition passes through the group. "So he was the one," someone says from behind Yair. "That was before I started my service. But I heard the story."

I am dizzy with bewilderment, unable to look at Dov or Rina. All I can think is that the two of them brought us to this place as their guests, and now it will be impossible for us to stay. But neither of them speaks. They are as helpless as I am to stop the scene playing out in front of us. We all wait for someone to make a next move.

"I'm not the crazy one." Gil spits the words. "Look at yourselves. Playing your soldier roles and your peacenik roles, calling yourselves hawks or doves, as if it mattered. Keeping up your damn patriotism in the face of more stupid, pointless deaths."

"So what do you suggest we do?" A thin spectacled young man calls out.

"Nothing." Gil's smile is the snarl of a cornered animal. "There's not a thing you can do."

The girl with the guitar is in tears. "You think my boyfriend's cousin got blinded because she was too patriotic? She was walking on the wrong street at the wrong time." A friend takes her by the shoulders and rocks her. "I'm just trying to make sense of things, that's all. If you think that's pointless, then leave the damn country. And good riddance."

"You think I'm just not properly Israeli, is that it? You think I just don't understand sacrifice enough to deserve to live here?" Gil's hands curl against his thighs. "I've made a bigger sacrifice than any of you. My father died for this goddamn promised land and I know things are never going to change. So if anyone here knows it's hopeless, it's me."

Beside me, Rina stands.

"Take your self-pity," someone says, "and get out of our way."

Rina is walking across the circle toward Gil. I can't see her face, only the deliberate set of her shoulders. She stops so close to him that a person watching from a distance might think she was going to embrace him.

Taut as a bow, he watches her. At any second Rina will stumble backward onto hard dry earth; I see it so clearly that I react as if it had already happened. I rise.

Standing on her toes opposite Gil, Rina extends her arms. For a second it seems she is going to embrace him after all. Instead, her knuckles brushing his chest, she lifts the strap of his binoculars and takes them from around his neck. Gil, his face inches from hers, appears immobilized. Rina turns her back on him; now I see her expression, at once fearless and grim. She walks to the end of the shelter, to the stone-lined edge of the pool. In one graceful, athletic motion, she skips forward and throws Gil's binoculars far above the water.

There is a brief silence. Then, a splash.

Gil has not moved. His mouth hangs open.

Rina faces Gil from across the circle. In a soft and clear voice she says to him, "You are the ugliest thing war can produce." Her arms rest at her sides, she is breathing hard and her green eyes are unafraid. I'm struck for the first time by how beautiful she is. "And I'm sorry about your father."

Gil has not moved. He regards Rina as though he's having trouble recalling her name. Then, with a sudden and wild energy, he turns in place, from one closed, impassive face to another. At last his eyes settle on me, and his expression clarifies to one of pure hatred.

He pivots one last time, his heel digging into the packed dirt, and leaves the shelter. His footsteps sound on rock. There is a short pause; then a slow, uneven splashing.

Everyone is watching me.

As Gil did only a moment ago, I look from one of Dov's friends to another. Some sit with dinner plates on their knees; others cradle tin cups. They're not friendly and not unfriendly. They're simply waiting for me to choose, so they will know whether to take me in or leave me be.

All except Dov. He is not looking at me, but rather staring at Rina with an incredulity I recognize as love. He speaks to her quietly, and now the others listen in silence; Dov and Rina are their tutors, this towering shelter their classroom.

"I'm tired," Dov says.

And as if the simple sentence were the permission he'd been awaiting, the thin one with the glasses begins to speak. "When I was in the West Bank, do you know what it was like?" he says to Dov. "There was a terrorist attack and we had our orders to seal the border. And just at the end of our patrol, a boy broke through. He was about eleven years old, a little slip of a kid with big gray eyes and eyelashes so long you knew other boys must have teased him. He was carrying a bundle and wouldn't give it up for inspection. And we were all shaking our heads over this latest hassle—just what we needed, a kid on our hands, in a few minutes for sure his mother will be screaming at us. My friend Dan started gibing me. 'Dudi, *you* can try sweet-talking the mother into giving over the bundle this time.' And next thing you know, the boy ran right past Dan, he was past the barriers and into the orchard in a flash. We ran through the orchard, four of us from the unit, but we couldn't find him. We looked, then we gave up and started heading back to the barrier. And all of a sudden he was behind me with a knife." Dudi shakes his head. "An eleven-year-old boy with a knife. I didn't even see him. All I heard was the shot. And Dan had to shoot. He didn't have a choice. It was one or another of us going to die." Reflections of firelight curl on Dudi's glasses as he pauses. "He lay there with his mouth open like he was going to ask us a question," he says. "What kind of question could an eleven-year-old boy have?"

There is a long silence. Dudi's palms turn up, he might be trying to weigh the starlight. He speaks deliberately to Dov—it is important that my cousin hear every syllable. "I never learned his name. I didn't want to know."

I see Rina take Dov's hand.

My cousin's head droops with fatigue, he struggles to keep his gaze from dragging to the ground. "Rafi was a peacenik," he says. "We used to argue about it all the time, and I told him he was a fool. Why should we make concessions, they wouldn't bring safety. 'Peace through security,' I told him. 'Security through territory.' " A look of wonder crosses Dov's face. "I always won the arguments, too. Rafi couldn't be as obstinate as I was, never when we were kids and never when we were in the army. And I was so sure I was right."

The breeze has settled, the night is still. The splashing from the pool has stopped.

And then, before my eyes, without speaking another word, Dov makes a promise to Rina. Tightening his hand in hers, he lays his life before her.

The circle of our bodies has drawn closer. All around me, my cousin's friends sit listening. I understand that Dov is their unspoken leader, and now that he has made a choice, something is poised among us all: a question suspended here beneath the absent roof, awaiting an answer so large it might fill the spaces between the stars.

More than anything, I want to stay. I try to shape their wondering expressions on my own face, I count the beats of my heart against the steady rhythm of their silence. But my body stiffens on its own, as if I no longer have any say in my own actions. If someone would stop me, lay a light hand on my forearm or even whisper, "Stay," I would sink to the ground and never leave this gathering again. But no one moves. I wrap my fingers around my empty cup and leave the shelter, walking in the direction where Gil disappeared.

ॐ

How bright and solemn this heat. How swift the people wandering beneath it. Honking cars, drivers curse in bold Hebrew. How unfamiliar, this city to which I have never raised questioning eyes, though years of evenings I have hurried beside its gates.

Sounds of rumbling buses, slam of doors. Hills surge upward then give way before me, pavement stings my feet.

Where are You, my salvation?

Carts selling children's socks, vegetables heaped in trays, milk spilt and sour in market gutters. Chicken heads lopped in open stalls, a tangle of voices. Bread laid on conveyor belts, women pick it into sacks and brush aside shouts of competing vendors.

I scan the faces of this market, aisle upon green-dappled aisle, but do not recognize You.

Schoolchildren move in a tight circle down the sidewalk. My legs burn with weariness. The jostling of shoulders and hips, the scowl of a mother with a stroller. How creepingly the sun vaults white sky, day hangs in balance. Stone buildings rise high and higher, my gaze is struck down by brightness. Black faces and tan flow past, street singers sing. I seek You in shadow and light my American.

Ten pitas for five shekels, the best guaranteed, hot or you don't pay.

Inside fancy glass doors, guards look me over for suspicious objects. Enjoy your shopping. *Stairs move up and up into the air, glittering colors spread below. A kingdom of rubies and pearls, plastic sling-backed shoes. I trip and grab a railing, we are moved like cattle, shunted like lice into invisible sky. I cannot get off. At the top I cling to the rail and my arm is pulled in its socket.* May I help you? *the woman says. Fresh powdered face.* Have you shopped at the Mashbir before? *Swimwear here on the second floor, women's shoes downstairs.*

Perhaps she has seen You.

American styles are on all floors, *she assures me.*

Outside, sun claps heavy on my head.

Demonstrators with placards, shouting. Share the land. *Opposite,* boys in yarmulkes. Death to the Arabs. *Thunder of airplanes, thunder of a red and white bus, thunder of a shopkeeper opening his grate to sell carrot juice. I shrink from the metal sound, flee this bustling cobblestone street. Turn from these rushing crowds this mournful air, these ancient walls this urine-soaked alley.*

Across and across, down and down. Wide streets and then narrow, twisting veins of a city. Smell of overripe fruit, crowded houses spill children onto the street, spices thicken the air. Men and women walk past in headscarves, my vision ripples with heat. Clotheslines crisscross overhead, bright alleys roil with layers of laundry. On balconies and stoops women sit, hearts burn in silence. A small thin girl watches me, suspicious. I cut my eyes at her, meanly. Then I am sorry. Perhaps she can help me find You. But she is gone. An old man at my side speaks now, his accent the accent of the rug peddler. His voice carries as from a long distance. But your eyes are bloodshot, *he tells me.* Are you certain you're all right? What's a Jewish grandmother doing wandering an Arab neighborhood, you know Jews are not quite welcome on our side of Jerusalem in these times. I'll bring you a drink, won't you sit in the shade? When you and I were children, *he says,* there were better days.

Have you seen the American.

What American? *His face locks, wary.*

The American, I tell him. My American, I cry for Her in hill and valley, She does not answer.

Old woman. *He laughs.* You'll find no Americans here, and none fond of them. Tend to your health. You shouldn't go for walks on days like today, this heat could kill a camel.

I shake loose from his arm, his voice no longer reaches me.

A shop, a wall, a jeep. Sights of a fractured city.

In a park, dogs yap at my shadow. In an alley, flies encircle me. Beside tall buildings, in shadows of clouds, I search. In trash bins I peer for Your clues, hissing cats scatter like angry sparks. I seek You in gutters and on uneven pathways, sun beating on my bare head.

The schoolchildren who gawk are nothing to me, they are released from class and race each other home, I am forgotten. My feet are swollen, I no longer feel them, my head splits with pain. I walk. Passersby stare, a soldier offers her uniformed arm but I refuse her.

Smells of cooking, windows flung open as children are summoned. American, why do You hide Yourself? You see I am a worm, less than human; You see how those who encounter me mock me. All my bones are disjointed, American; my heart melts like wax.

The city is sloping down, the city funnels toward one point. The sidewalk's cracks draw me on just a few steps farther, my knees buckle with obedience. Every path leads me into this valley, this rose-colored tan-colored sun-blasted neighborhood of stone.

Home.

I have arrived at the street where I began. Here in the byways of this neighborhood, evening awaits. Birds twitter along electric wires, their chatter mocks my journey.

And I see now what You have meant me to see.

There is no future. You will not come for me.

You will not come.

The rug peddler's calls rise, and fade away.

This engraved archway. These broad steps.

This narrow doorway.

The blacks are soaked with prayer. A fat red-cheeked one bars my path. This is the men's section of the synagogue, *he instructs.* Women go to the room on the side.

I turn as if to go.

He resumes his prayer. How he rocks with devotion. He does not know, then: You have abandoned us.

How easy it is to pass by this praying man as he sways. I am quick, I have learned; I am easily forgotten. None see.

The blacks hunch together, an ocean of nodding heads. From them rises deepest music. Chants swelling beneath the roof and trembling within these stone walls. Hear our voices, *they sing.* Answer us.

Oh Mother, how you despised them. How Father stood fierce at the parlor doorway, guarding house against his lame brother.

The blacks raise their voices to heaven, I want to tell Mother they are beautiful. I want to tell her, Mother did you not see I could not hate you? Did you not understand, if I had been dull-witted I might have hated you, but I could not.

My feet drag so heavily now. I would like to settle to the floor here, and rest awhile.

How sweet Uncle Hayyim's psalms rose, mist of tears under my window. Every word of his prayers for Halina reached me, a kneeling expectant girl. Nights of shouts and longing, how I knelt upon the sill of life.

If I sing for You, American, will You love the sound of my voice?

Zion Zion will you not ask after the welfare of your prisoners? American American can You not make these broken things whole?

I am weary.

The synagogue, an eruption of shouts. There is a woman here, I heard her sing. Voices batter these walls, assail my ears but I shall not be moved. Gesturing hands find me out, fingers point.

Hail of words, babble of voices, none shall move me.

They remove their hats and slap them at my shoulders to chase me away.

Your skullcapped heads, I tell them, are shorn close as once mine was.

They do not hear, now they bat me with seat cushions I am driven backward against my will.

The flurry has deposited me on the street. The sky is an evening purple, I make no answer to their outrage. I stand motionless on this sidewalk. They tell me Go but I do not. There is no place left to go.

Soon the blacks disappear into synagogue and there remains only one. He watches me, patient. He is not unkind. I won't leave until I see you go into the women's section, or else be on your way, Grandmother.

I draw breath. In my head a fire burns. My feet are pillows of ash. The world does not want to hear your stories, I say to him.

The world does not concern me, *he replies.* Only God. God hears all.

The world hates you, I tell him. He listens respectfully. He is a young black, he will not scorn me. You bear the past in your face, I explain. They are like Father, they look at you and see what they left behind. They live in their bright today, they want no reminder.

God will mend, *he says.*

The world hates you because you bear the past in your face, I insist. I confess to him: The world despises me as well. We are alike, you and I.

He brushes his thin beard and sighs with thought.

I turn away from him, the street blurs dim in my vision. The Messiah will come, he says from behind me. This world will be healed. I turn back. No, I tell him gently. She has not come.

God be with you, *he says.*

A darkening street, a dusty scent of flowers. A valley, a valley of ghosts.

Now a low wind rises. A mournful sound fills the air. Wail of a cat, cry of a child, voice of this breeze blowing softly about me. Into it are emptied the murmurs of Halina and Lilka, the voices of Feliks and Grandmother and Hayyim and these praying blacks. All our whispered longing, sweeping over walls and walls and walls of stone.

This dry air seals my mouth. I shall not speak again.

∽∞∽

He stands alone by the far side of the pool. He does not look at me, although he knows I am only a few paces behind him. In one hand he holds the binoculars, the strap dripping. He lifts them to his eyes; he is gazing up at the stars although surely the lenses are beaded with water. Shivering in the cooling air, I look at the sky.

"Gil."

When he walks away, I know I am meant to follow him. Away from the pool, up a low hill.

"Gil."

He walks faster; he does not turn around as he begins speaking. I rush to catch up.

"They don't have the slightest idea. Rina and her precious Intelligence job, they never sent her to put down a riot. They never sent your cousin with his fancy paratrooping uniform to patrol a village every day for a year and a half." Gil moves swiftly up the path. *"You'll never understand, either. You'll never understand what it was like there."*

At the crest of the hill he stops. He speaks as if the words taste of ash. "You're just an American girl."

The wind has risen again. It brushes my cheeks, combs my hair away from my forehead. The touch is almost human.

Once more I'm visited by a memory of the woman from downstairs. I recall now the way she gripped my arm before she turned for the stairwell. Her hold was unexpectedly strong, almost painful—I nearly cried out. I recall how she addressed me: she seemed to think me capable of anything.

"No," I tell Gil. "You're wrong."

Pebbles shift beneath his sandals. "Excuse me?"

"I *don't* understand, you're right about that." In the cooling air, my face feels naked. But I stand opposite him and I don't back down. "Still, why do you assume I can't? Why the hell"—my words grow louder—"does everyone assume I can't understand?" *Everyone except her.* Astonished by my own nerve, I instruct him, "Tell me."

He doesn't answer. He faces the shelter and holds the binoculars against his chest.

"No one has a right to insult the memory of my father." He might be addressing me, or the shadows gathered around the low smudge of firelight. "No one."

From the shelter comes an indistinct voice, then laughter.

He pulls back one foot and kicks at the ground, hard. I hear a stone tumble into the darkness.

"Do you know what the air feels like when people are burning tires?" The demand is aimed at the group beneath the shelter but is loud enough to reach only me. Gil steps closer, this time I shy back despite myself. "You want to understand, Maya? I'll tell you.

"It feels so thick and hot you can't breathe. It feels like hell come alive. It feels like hate in the air. Pure hate." He takes my wrist. "I'd see the other soldiers patrolling in that haze, and we looked just like the fiends the Palestinian boys spray-painted on the alley walls. And the adults, they made no effort to hide the truth in their faces. They wanted us dead. We weren't human, to them. No more than they were human to us. None of us human. Only figures, stumbling. Stumbling in acrid black smoke—I spent my first evening at the post throwing up.

"And when they weren't burning tires, you could feel everyone waiting for the next encounter. Every child's shout, every creaking shutter might be an attack. You'd sit on your jeep with your cigarette, and after a while you got so sick of staring into all that misery that you didn't even care. You ate your sandwich and drank your coffee, then you got up to walk your next patrol and let it all burn a hole in your stomach."

Gil's words are rough with tears, but he speaks on without concealing his distress. "And one day it was so hot, and the politicians were debating new settlements again. We didn't care about any goddamn debates, we just wanted a shower and something cold to drink. And the sun was hell and we sat on the hood of the jeep and the officer was dressing us down over the radio to show initiative." He swings my arm lightly as he repeats, *"Show initiative."*

"What did he want you to—"

"Nothing moved. Flies would land on our lips while we were talking, and the other guys wouldn't even brush them off." His revulsion is palpable. "But that afternoon, something moved."

"Gil, it sounds horrible," I murmur.

"I moved," he says. "I got up off the jeep. I held my gun in parade position, and I stepped sharp, just like they taught us in basic training. I marched to the middle of the street and I looked up for a good long time while the other guys cracked jokes at me. Then I emptied my gun into that glorious blue-and-white patriotic sky. And I reloaded." Gil is whispering. "Three cartridges. I spun around and I shouted and shouted and shouted, just to hear that thick air shake. Just to crack it open, that fucking smug sky overhead."

His laughter is soft, but proud. My mind will not take in his words; I try to slow the drumming of my pulse.

"My father died for this country." He says it like a mantra.

"And do you know what a Profile 21 discharge means in this country? Do you have any idea the hurdles and psychological tests they put you through? Not to mention the time in the military prison. But I didn't give a shit. They even hauled in my commander to interrogate me. I told him, 'I showed initiative. Didn't I?' "

My mouth takes the shape of a question. "Gil, why didn't you—" Gil is stepping forward, he doesn't wait for me to finish. He wraps an arm around my shoulder and pulls me to him as he begins to walk. His steps are long and swift. We move pressed together like lovers down the brambled hill, up a second rise.

"A family of war heroes, we are," Gil says casually, as if describing the scenery outside a car window. "Just ask my mother, sitting with the other martyrs' widows on the reserved benches at Memorial Day ceremonies."

"But your father *did* die in the war. He *is* a fallen hero."

"Yes, he did die in the war. Yes, he did." Gil's steps slow; he loses his balance on the rocky ground and I support his weight. "I never stopped believing in my father. I loved my father. No one has a right to insult him. No one has a right to dare insult him.

"But you see"—Gil speaks close to my ear—"he wasn't a war hero. He was a fuck-up. Just like me." Gil lurches forward again. "Did I tell you that I botched the psycho-technic exams on purpose? That's a lie. I didn't care about how I was going to do, but that's beside the point. I walked into that room, Maya, and I was afraid. I sat in a chair and I thought: I'm sitting inside the machinery of the army. By the time I'd answered a few questions I could almost hear the gears grinding all around me. My mind froze. I couldn't have solved the rest of the problems if I'd tried."

I realize, as he speaks, that I've won. I'm not just an American girl, the cracking of his voice tells me; I'm something more. Trusted, worthwhile. Accepted.

Terrified.

Together we angle down a slope, only our racing legs keep us from tripping into the low bushes.

"Gil, I can't hold you, you've got to stand up."

"Did you hear what I said?" His shoulder drags on mine, a crushing weight. The tin cup I clutched in my hand bounces away. "She used to pray that he would die, can you imagine that? She used to sit on the bathroom floor and take me in her lap, clasp my obedient little hands in hers and pray for him to die. 'Merciful God, let a bomb land on his head and end our suffering, so my boy and I can make a new life.' "

"I can't hold you up, Gil, please."

"It wasn't a bomb that landed on his head, in the end. It was a shell fragment. A pointless, insulting shell fragment from our own side. But the God of my mother is an economical God, and saved the big bombs for enemy tanks."

We veer up a rocky incline until momentum abandons us and we stand, teetering, on the hillside.

"Maya," he says. "I've failed. I don't understand the blacks. I knew it while I was drawing them. I never understood their faith. I wanted to simply love them for it, but I hated them for it, too. If a critic looks at those drawings and he's smart, he'll see I still don't understand them."

No, I want to tell him, *you understood one of them.* But he is talking. "Faith is for idiots," he snorts. "But I believe in you, Maya. You're the only one I believe in."

My knees give way. Together we fall. I land on sharp stones and for a few seconds I can't breathe. Gil sinks down on top of me, no strength in his long limbs.

"Gil," I say at last.

He's kissing me.

"Gil, the rocks are hurting me. I need to move."

"You're so beautiful," he says. In the starlight his face is open and filled with wonder.

"Gil—"

"We're a team, you and I. Aren't we?" His kiss on my forehead is desperate. His arms lock around my neck and he speaks into my hair, his mouth wide against my skull. "Maya, I need you."

There are more stars here than I have ever seen, crowded into the sky as if they found safety in numbers. "Gil—"

"You're my chosen one, Maya," he continues in a singsong. "My chosen American girl."

His form shifts above me, blocking my view of the stars. He reaches for my cheek. I shake my head; it is enough to dislodge his hand. He reaches again. "Maya." He kisses me. "Come closer," he says.

My body is already pressed against his.

"Closer," he breathes. I shift in vain, trying to see past him to the sky.

"It's been so long," he says.

Panic floods my veins. "Not right now."

He takes my wrists, flips them over my head in a quick motion and pins them to the dirt. "Maya," he whispers.

"Gil!" The cry doesn't carry far into the night. It doesn't loosen his grip. I twist my arms uselessly. "Let me go."

"What, in Jerusalem you wanted me, now you think I'm not good enough? A few lousy hours with your cousin's macho friends, and now *you* turn on me, too?" Holding both my wrists in one hand, he takes my jaw with the other and turns my head for a better look at my face. "You too, Maya?" Betrayal registers in his voice; he speaks with the spite of wounded authority. "You need a war hero, maybe? Like the ones back there, laughing at me?"

"No, Gil. I don't. It's just that right now isn't—"

He lets go of my jaw and slams an open palm to the ground, so hard I imagine it bloodied. "Maybe you'd rather fuck one of them instead?" I can feel the pounding of his heart. "I trusted you," he accuses. "You're my everything. I chose you, you chose me." The words threaten to choke him. When he speaks again, I am startled by the finality of his tone. "What an idiot I've been. I should have known you could never believe in me."

My mind tells me to lie as quietly as possible, but without warning I am fighting. I kick against the hard ground, jolt to one side and somehow free my arms. I strike at his shoulders and chest with my fists. Surprised, he shoves me down as easily as though I were not resisting at all.

Around us the night is quiet. There is only his breathing, and mine, and now his whispered curses. Once again some impulse races through me, and I buck beneath him. My heels scramble on the stony ground, and he grabs at my legs and misses. I am almost loose, I will run to the hilltop and down into the valley, to the safety of the group gathered beside the pool. The cool air feathers against my face, the stars are bursting with freedom.

Gil's arm lifts my hip, and I am dragged backward, my head striking nettles and stone. His other hand is already beneath my shirt and squeezing, stars flash and shudder overhead. Still no sound escapes me, I discover I am incapable of words. My knees slide on rock, my face stings with tears. He pulls down the zipper of my jeans; his hands are hard and move quickly on my skin. He doesn't bother to undress himself fully, once more he pushes me down with a fury that is like panic. "Maybe you've already picked out one of the commando boys," he is saying. Brambles circle my neck like jewelry, my back is studded with rocks. The sky is heavy with stars; Gil's weight crushes me into dust. There is a thick, lacerating pain that promises to lift me out of my body.

He has finished.

"Maya," he says.

This man's voice means nothing to me. My ears refuse it.

There is a long silence.

He cannot get me to stir. He tries to roll me onto my side, but my body is limp and will not cooperate. He kneels and stares into my face. My eyes slide past him. "Maya." He shakes me gently, then more desperately. A sob of loneliness tears out of him: "I love you. Don't you know how much I love you?"

Finally he sleeps, one arm over my bare stomach.

For what might be hours, I study the slight rise and fall of his arm that correspond to my every breath.

Later, after he stumbles toward the campground, I stand. I gather my clothing. I pull my jeans over the cut skin of my legs. Once I've started moving, I don't allow myself to stop; I know dimly that if I do, the pain will grow louder and I won't be able to move again.

I make my way over the hill. In the valley there is no movement. The sleeping forms of Dov's friends are hidden. The beams of the shelter stand watch over nothing but darkness.

The water of the pool is colder than I expected. Crouching on a rock, I scoop handfuls and spill them over my face and scratched arms. Then I remove my shirt and jeans. The water drips down my stinging legs, muddies my bare feet. Patiently I rinse, again and again. Enough water and makeup will erase the marks of this night, just as they have erased the marks of every other time Gil has raised a hand to me. In the morning I will be hollow-eyed and invisible. The others, eager to be fooled, will look at me and see nothing; I'll thank them for making my lies so much easier, and hate them as well.

I rinse my clothing piece by piece, and start to put it on wet.

It's not enough. Careful to make no sound, I take off my underwear and lower myself into the pool. The water is only waist-deep, and the bottom is rough rock. The shock of the cold on my burning skin makes me light-headed, but I wade forward.

Near the center I stop moving. Ripples spread to the stone walls, then disappear. Holding myself very still, I see that the pool is an enormous black mirror. I lay one hand on the skin of the water; the sky rocks in response.

The stars between my fingers sway more and more slowly. As they stop, I allow the truth. I allow myself to know that things will not change. That my lies can save no one.

My mother is still sick—this time I don't resist the thought. And all the pretty stories I tell won't protect her. They won't protect me, either. Because there is one other thing I know, with absolute certainty: One day Gil will kill me.

But what stuns me as I shiver in the clear water is not any of these things, for I understand that I have always known them. It is the quiet in myself. Here I stand in this pool of stars, waiting for something to jar me into action. I have spent all my strength on lies. Now, when the next step ought to be very simple, I am betrayed by my own weariness. I'm too tired to do anything about the truth.

All is quiet. One moment passes, then another, and nothing changes. These stars between my fingers are forever out of reach, but if I am patient and stand absolutely motionless, I have the illusion of closeness. The longer I stand here, the closer they seem. Soft. Spread like a lush carpet on this solemn black mirror. I lift my hand, and in a moment the portrait of the sky is intact, as if I had never been here at all.

When I find Gil on the far side of the pool, he is snoring lightly. Hesitating, I stand over his slack face.

Beside him is another sleeping bag, which he has laid out for me on a spot cleared of rocks. My teeth chattering, I slip inside.

∽

You have wandered so long, Lilka says. On this cat-scattered street she walks beside me, cool and fresh in her school uniform. You deserve to rest.

I did not find Her, I tell Lilka. I failed. I was to find the American, and She would bring us our future. But I lost Her in this city. She will not come for me. Now I have lost all of you forever.

Don't cry.

I can't stop.

Don't cry, Lilka tells me. I can't bear a crybaby.

She will not speak to me any longer. I hang my head as I pass down this narrow street.

Each step, a shooting pain.

Halina walks alongside me now. She is so hard to see, only in the corner of my vision does she appear. She strides faster and faster with her anger, I cannot keep up with her. Halina wait. She paces ahead of me, her thin hands soar. They with their stupid ambition, she is saying. Mother and Father had to climb their way to the top, they wanted to force me to marry that old man. But I would not. They could not defeat me. They cannot.

Halina, in camp the Germans used your chemicals. They used your signs and symbols and they slaughtered.

Even that Lilka Rotstein was a traitor for her own glory, Halina rages. I struggle to catch a glimpse of her face, my fury-pale sister. So Lilka had to spill secrets, had to tell on my younger sister. She wanted only the celebrity, never thought about the consequences.

Halina will you look at me? See how memory has burnt its track on my brain.

Halina covers her mouth and giggles, she is talking to a boy at University. Inviting him on an outing. My sister Shifra will be there, and she's a bit strange, Halina tells the boy. But don't let it alarm you. She's just a kid, with some harmless fancies. She's quiet a lot, and likes to make up stories. You'll grow accustomed to it.

See how memory has burnt its track.

I tried so hard, Halina. I tried to hold on to every story. I could not let you be lost, and so I saved every detail. But when the One we awaited came, I could not make Her hear.

See how memory burns.

You rush ahead of me. Halina, I call after you. Blacks stop and stare from under heavy brims but I do not care. Halina, I call. Halina we were right about Karol. He did not abandon us. After the war, after the American camps, I returned to our town. And Karol's mother heard of my arrival and came to the boardinghouse where I stayed, across the street from our old house where now a red-faced man refused to open the door. New yellow curtains hanging in our bedroom window, Halina, bright cheerful fabric. And Karol's mother, with a basket full of eggs and cheese, she pushed past the muttering crowd gathered about the boardinghouse.

My son would have wanted me to see after you, she said. How quickly she spoke, her eyes turned from me. If he had survived the war he would have made you his wife. When I took the basket from her she touched my fingers, gingerly she tested my flesh only to discover it real. You'd best be on your way, she said. I wouldn't stay on in this place if I were you. I nodded to her, I did not make her tarry, for I understood what this visit cost her. If you need anything, she said. And this time she squared herself and looked me in the eye. Then she turned and was gone.

Halina you should have seen it; we were right, Mother and Father were wrong. Eggs, eggs and balls of cheese the size of potatoes. Food I had only dreamed for years, food even the Gentiles had only dreamed.

I must tell you, Halina, though it pains me. They turned Father's shop into a storage room for feed. The Rotsteins' balcony, covered in pigeon waste and screaming children. And the faces of the crowd outside the boardinghouse, hate underneath their thick lids. They wanted to know nothing of Jews returned from the dead, wanted to know only their own survival: only their still-beating hearts and bellies wrenched with hunger, and the new houses they had inherited as reward for their own suffering. I would not wait for the red-faced man to open the shutters to our old home. A girl was going to Palestine. I let her take me.

A journey on foot, a wagon across a border by night; a train to a port city, seasons upon seasons of waiting for passage. While we waited, strangers traded news of battles, of the nation born. Then, tight-knuckled nights in a tossing ship. I will marry, a girl whispered in the ship's darkened cabin. Halina, we lay on bunks as wide as the stinking slats in camp, only each of us had her own—such a wide and smooth space it was, without the crush of shrinking bodies. The girl told a story of a man met inside DP camp. Tasting the word husband, *so unfamiliar in this hollow-eyed dark, the others around me stretched tentative fingers to the corners of their wide berths.* Perhaps a child? Laughter, *spilling from one bunk onto another. Such a thought.* A child. *Girls reached under thin covers to touch bony hips.*

They might leave you behind, Halina, but I would not. I would not embrace this new-minted country without you.

And when at last we reached the Israeli port, the others sprang from the ship as if they had not retched seasick for days, as if they were mountain goats and not the empty shells of girls. Come dancing with us. Come to the shore this afternoon, there is a picnic for the young people from Galicia. There will be men, there will be bathing in the sea. *Halina we stepped onto land and were embraced by sights and smells, by palm trees and orange groves of our sudden state. A state, they told us, only recently saved from certain death,* just as you have been.

Bright sun, brighter than the flash of a thousand newsbulbs. A joke ages in the making: Jews with a homeland. The laughter burst its confines, rang from every swaying tree. From rolls of wire, cement mixers vomiting sidewalk. And how the bus rocked along new-paved roads of our new-paved country: cracked already, and uneven. We passed beneath rippling blue and white of this Jewish sky, a sky that fluttered above swaying cypresses tall as flagpoles. The girls from the boat sang verse after verse.

Home at last, *the matron said.*

Halina, I wanted to hear only the sound of my own voice, reciting your life. The other girls from the relief agency lodgings learned quickly to move away when they saw me coming. They borrowed one another's clothing to wear to their dances and did not invite me again. Alone I walked the Haifa shore, I explained you aloud as my shoes filled with sand, with every step I sank deeper.

A position in Jerusalem was found, an apartment where I might sleep. Days passed without speech in the dressmaker's shop. Outside, a world of busy builders. Cheering and weeping, rallies and rage. Through the static on the post office radio as I waited in line, a voice calling for reason. This country must move forward from— There is only one path toward our— Accepting German reparations is the way to—

Crowds shouting betrayal in the streets. Arab eyes shuttered with rage.

Halina, I sewed at the dress shop with the others, all day we worked in the quiet sunlit shack. How many of them pretended to life and how many did not need to pretend I could not know. Each morning I knotted my kerchief tight lest memory escape. I walked and ate, I turned my head with the others as if I too answered to We. We, young and reciting stanzas of hope. We who saw only clear unblemished horizon, waves caressing the brow of the country, and children that grew and grew and were bolder than any children ever before, each would be more beautiful to make up for the lost.

And again and again was war, Halina. War in Sinai— Israeli soldiers raid enemy post at— Terrorists captured by— Battle in the Old City— *War upon war, suspicious packages must be reported; sleep tilled my head at the bus stop, my grocery bag forgotten on the ground. I stood with you, Halina, beside the river, I told you a fairy tale and you smiled. A man called out in alarm. Suspicious Object, he cried. Who owns this grocery bag? Whose is it?*

I was not We, Halina. I was yours and you were mine. I would not answer to their calls. I would stay with you, I would live with you until you were well and lived again.

The bomb workers reached the bus stop, they cleared the sidewalk. With a crowd I watched them advance upon my bag of onions and potatoes, although they hid the explosion in their metal box I saw it clearly: fragments of brown and white flesh scattered on these stones, pieces that would never fit together again.

Don't dwell on the past, the others said.

So many years I fell silent. How could I speak what no one wanted to hear? Only after they brought the man for hanging did narrow gates open on our tales, but still no day was long enough, no sky high enough to hold what must be said aloud. Eichmann, Sabras spat the name in the streets. Then boarded their buses, embraced their children, ate a next meal. We must turn our backs on what is past, the girls at the dress shop insisted. See how our roots grow strong in each other?

But I would never let you die. Halina I would not forsake you, ever. And I know that you would not leave me, only that once to keep from marrying Turkevich did you betray me and, Halina, I understand, you did not mean it. I know that you did not.

Halina, I had no will to live with the living. I carried you with me, how could I set you down? And when they fought their War of Atonement I left the dress shop and retreated to my apartment at last to hold fast to my own soul. Halina, I closed myself in my apartment to await our American with all my devotion, I trusted in Her. I had no other. Alert sirens called me to judgment but I was guilty of no crimes; I waited for my salvation chanted sun-remembering rhymes.

I made myself your keeper, tied tight my kerchief lest memory escape, and the aching of my head all those days was small price to pay. I knew if I was faithful then She would come. The American would believe in you with all Her heart, Her soul, all Her means. Every story I would tell Her, every story She would heed. So many nights and years I prepared for Her coming: our past would be redeemed, sister, the light restored to our eyes.

O American, guard us like the apple of Your eye.

Here at the building, green leaves cling to woody vines. I look up into snarled treetops, sun shears across my vision until this white unforgiving light empties the world of all else.

I did not expect the American's arm to be so soft. But it was, Halina. Flesh like a child's, easily bruised. When I squeezed I felt the bone. Still I had faith in Her power.

In my apartment the air is stale. My legs tumble beneath me, I sit.

Feliks how dare you come to me now? Fair-haired Rotstein boy in short pants, your knees bruised from mischief. You stand uncertain before me, a boy timid of truth. Your shame was never known, Feliks. I might have told tales like your elder sister Lilka, but I did not. I told none that Father beat you in the shop for seeing what you should not have seen, I told none that you made up a lie because you were frightened of him. Bruised, you became a schoolyard hero for weathering a Gentile boy's blows. Feliks you never wanted the full truth and so you did not, after all those years you did not ask me the one question you should have asked. Do you not think I knew you were in love with her, when she went to University? Do you not think I saw how you stared at her during her farewell party, how you memorized my sister in her blue dress? You never had a chance, Feliks. Halina did not love you, to her you were only a little boy. And then came war. Even in ghetto you tried to smuggle extra morsels to my sister, and when she gave only dull-eyed thanks you turned away in confusion.

You lived, Feliks. You grew and battled and came to Palestine and knew women, yet you remained a coward. After the war when your newspaper advertisement led me to you, you were grown and severe, a hero of Resistance. Yet you were afraid to ask. You cared only for your Lilka, and when I told you again and again the story of her last days in camp, it was enough for you. You did not ask me about Halina, Feliks. You could not bear to remember her again, only to lose her. So you with your fragile paper-thin love chose to forget.

It was she who jumped into the fire when the Americans were coming, Feliks. It was Halina. Her body was hollowed, already burning with fever, so many days she would not lift her head when I called her Halina. She did not care for me any longer. And when the German guards stood opposite their burning building, when the German guards stood with fear in their eyes and surveyed the burning of their burning deeds, she did not hesitate. She did not speak a word, did not look at me. She crouched, she stood, she ran with bone-cracking strength into the roaring wind of the flames. Halina who knew always what she wanted in this world, she did not look to the left or the right, but ran on stilts of legs as if toward her greatest dream.

Halina, I would never leave you, even if my own fate hung in the balance. I rose and ran after you, I would dance with you in those flames and we would be together. But before I could embrace you the stranger's bony arm wrapped my chest and held. "Americans," the woman hissed. Her eyes, sunken, flashed furious strength. "Americans are coming. Believe in Americans."

How smoke billowed to the sky, while my sister danced in those flames.

The Americans came, Halina. Before the ashes were settled, before the last of the smoke had flown, the Americans came for us. Broad-faced soldiers, pouring water from metal jugs into tin cups. Water splashing everywhere, ribbons of shining water wasted into the ground. Water, they called. We have water. We have soup, come and drink.

Mouths open in thanksgiving or weeping. Cages of bones stumbled and clung to American elbows, uniforms, pant legs. Americans collapsed in corners, staggered vomiting from the smell. Flashbulbs, in the shaky hands of journalists, pinned us to this place. We will make you well. Only an American could promise it.

In this dimming apartment I rise to my feet. In the cupboard I know I will find what I need; I take the dusty glass from the shelf. A memorial candle, given me by the blacks one Atonement Day. To keep the departed alive in your mind in this holy season, they said. So you should not forget them in the hour of judgment. What need had I, then, for their candle?

Now I take it from the cupboard and set it on the windowsill. A soft striking of this match, the reflection flares on the metal shutter. My hands tremble but the flame glows steady.

O American. I am lonely for Your eyes.

Together we might have found future. But You did not fulfill Your word. You, American. You, false messiah. Parading Yourself as salvation when all can see Your bruises. You refused to understand what I asked.

And did You imagine I did not know from the start that he beat You? Did You think I did not see bruises under face powder, hear cries at night, feel in my own body how You favored one leg as You walked? Did You think I did not lie awake listening, and understand every bit of suffering You hid from the bustling world?

I am not dull-witted.

The blacks in camp prayed ceaselessly to the east, American, and I prayed to the west. To comic books cornfields GI Garbo You.

See how memory burns. See, this steady flame rising in my windowsill.

Outside, the blacks release the last of their evening prayers. Outside, winding sun-beaten streets of Jerusalem pause before drawing breath. Daylight sinks, this city trembles expectation.

Pain grips my head, a vise of Your abandonment.

Halina. You were beautiful, your fair hair shone. When we were girls and you had the scarlet fever, you lay in our bedroom remote from me in dreams. I wished upon myself death if only the illness would spare you. You never knew. You tossed and writhed with the fever, your pillow damp with sweat. I pledged, I would sit beside you and tell you stories of things you had done and might do, stories of yourself to call you back to this world. All day I knelt beside your bed. Mother could not keep me from you, she would take me to the parlor couch at night and I would appear again beside you, no gate or barricade could stop me. Tale upon tale, my voice chanted to your sleeping ears. On the third morning I touched your forehead and the fever was gone. You cracked your dry lips and smiled, an innocent smile that said you were well rested from your long journey far from home. You opened your eyes, and healed me.

Wrenching metal from its cradle of stone, I throw open these shutters. Outside, the maddened sun, weary of its own burning, tumbles. Sunset spreads over this gold and copper city, transforms each antenna and glinting rooftop tank to another shining flame. I listen until the cry of the rug peddler winds into the call of the muezzin, men sing a prayer in this kindling city.

And how this candle flares, the cloth curtain above hangs blessedly near.

O American, spread upon us the tabernacle of Your peace.

A ray of sun stretches to touch this window, soft wind billows the cur-

tain. I chant encouragement. Sunset blurs my vision but still I see the candle dance in greeting.

With a small sigh of air, the curtain lights.

Fire. Yes, Halina, at last it is on fire.

Through this flame-lit pane I see our city. I see the blacks moving beneath their signs, I see the rug peddler disappear around the corner. Figures hoping hammering toiling for redemption, framed in fire. Words lost beneath the hissing crackling sound of these curtains.

O American.

Fire, climbing. Fire stretching before me at last. Halina, you were right. They cannot save us, there will be no future. Fire, and wind. Fire, and smoke, and such terrible pain in my chest. Smoke obscures the city now, Halina your cries rise in plumes. Karol is gone, no one will ever believe I was so loved. For he could not bear that I should strain to reach him, so he bent his towering frame and kissed me. These shards, fragments, cannot be made whole. Lilka weeps, her hat and dress soiled with ghetto mud. O Americans, bend the sky and come. But Halina, you understood what I could not see. There would be no salvation.

The American is lost, Halina. The American has honey-blond hair and eyes filled with confusion. She steps fearful among those She admires and cannot seek Her own salvation. Her boyfriend dons his rage and She has fallen, silenced.

Pain, blotting out thought. Pain come at last, I am bent to the floor, twisting I search for the chute of sky above but all I see is smoke.

From the depths I cry to You, American. Who will put out this fire?

Once when I was a young woman I gave a party in the middle of a hailstorm.

Halina, all the guests came.

And now I hear it, through the crackling of the fire: the sound of the palm tree's gentle rain.

Water.

Water rushing over me, water soothing, water whispering its lullaby. Water at last, come to ease this burning. At last this fire in my brain will be quenched. I have waited so long for release, now I am stunned by its sudden beauty. I fall to my knees, there is no more strength in my two hands. O Lilka O Karol O my beloved Halina, now at last the past will die with me and we will be set free. Redemption has come after all, for look, *the pain is gone. My mind, after days upon nights, my mind no longer burns. How gentle, this soft breeze. I have no strength to lift this weary head and so I cradle it in my own arms. I have stayed faithful to you, my sister, I have guarded your memory these endless years. I did not forsake you. Now stay with me in this blessed hush and do not leave me, ever.*

∞ 15 ∞

Morning. Brightness seeps through the pores of cloth over my face. I push the flap of the sleeping bag aside.

Although it can't be long since dawn, the campgrounds are bleached with daylight. High above, the sky's blue is thin and hard; a person could scrape it with a fingernail and leave a streak of dusty white.

Gil's sleeping bag lies empty beside mine. I see him across the pool, apart from the others. He is gathering food from a picnic table.

I stand. Immediately the light bounds through my head, I raise both hands to my temples and press. But it brings no relief. My jaw feels swollen. My legs are tattooed with scratches, and threaten to buckle under me.

"My God, what happened?"

Here beside me, so quiet I didn't detect her presence until she spoke, Rina stares with undisguised horror.

I lower my hands. I press my lips together against the pain and stare back. If I don't answer, I'm convinced, I will become invisible to her. She will forget about me and leave.

She doesn't move.

A faint hope rises in my chest. I try to quell it.

My cousin's girlfriend gestures mutely at my face and waits for an explanation.

I won't give it to her. She knows the answer, why does she need me to say it?

"Maya," she urges.

"Help me," I say.

"Oh God, you poor thing." She steps forward but stops a few paces away. "How could he do this to you? How badly are you hurt?"

I see she's afraid to touch me. I see I'm incomprehensible to her; I'm pathetic.

It takes only a second for my shame to turn to hatred. At least Gil doesn't look at me with that insulting pity, erasing anything about me that's worthwhile. Gil knows who I am, he knows exactly how weak and uncertain, and he wants to be with me all the same. To him, I'm more than just an American girl. To him I'm special.

A deep breath, then Rina formulates her plan. "I'll get the others to keep him away from you. Dov can handle him, and Yair will help. We'll drive him to Eilat and put him on a bus for Jerusalem. Then, when we go back to Jerusalem, we can all help get you out of the apartment."

I let her finish. Then I shake my head. I touch my cheek. "Help me."

She stands perfectly still, uncomprehending. Then disgust floods her face. "I don't have any makeup," she tells me coldly.

I turn away, uninterested. I have no use for her, this girlfriend of my cousin's. I wait for her to go away.

How long she stands there.

At last I hear her leave. But before I've had the chance to search my own backpack for cover-up, she returns with a wet washcloth dripping a chain of dark spots on the packed earth. Her motions are angry, she barely pauses when I wince. When she has finished, she gives me a towel and I dry my face without a word. With an angry turn of her wrist she opens a jar of tinted face cream; she found it in one of the other girls' packs, she mutters. The cream is cool on my skin and her finger is not gentle. Only when she's finished does she look into my eyes. She bites her lip. Compassion and hostility clash in her eyes. When she speaks, each word is clipped. "I'm going to talk to Dov," is all she says. Then she's gone.

The sky quivers with heat waiting to pour through. My face burns from Rina's touch. Gil is coming with my breakfast; I wave him back to the shelter, pointing to indicate that I'm coming soon.

Gingerly I step around the pool and make my way toward the shelter. Neither Rina nor Dov is anywhere to be seen. The others stand munching cucumbers and pita. They glance at me curiously as I near, but I turn my face toward the ground. Training is everything. I know from years of dance how to hold myself as if I have far more energy than I put into each step. As if I have energy to spare.

Gil's hands are before me, he offers me food and I take it without looking at him. I eat facing away from the others, pretending absorption in the spectacle of the hills. Gil sits behind me. Once, he reaches out a hand and massages my shoulder. I don't move. I know what he does not: In a few moments, Dov and Yair and all the others will be alerted. I don't know whether they will do anything. I don't seem to care. I don't feel any obligation to warn Gil, I don't wish Dov and Rina success. My mind is as still as the hills before me.

In a few minutes I hear Dov and Rina's purposeful footsteps. I hear Rina summon Tali, and I realize without turning my head that this is the girl who spoke last night about the women's shelter. Out of the corner of my eye I see Dov speaking to Yair at the near edge of the pool.

Gil tears a pita in two and offers me the larger piece. As I shake my head, he catches my chin with his fingertips. He examines my face.

Some time passes before I raise my eyes. Gil still holds my chin, but he has drawn back in confusion. He looks shocked by the work of his own hands. Then frightened. The question is plain on his face: *Did I do this?*

I turn to the group behind us. Rina and Tali, Dov and Yair stand in quiet conversation; the others, though ignorant of what's going on, have fallen silent. They are alert to some disturbance, their gazes rove the shelter.

Something about the scene distracts Gil; a thin film of normalcy settles over his face. He cracks his knuckles, once and then again. He wanders off to rummage in his pack.

Tali approaches a couple seated on one of the low benches, and within minutes the whispers have begun. I watch the alarm spread; I see the news register in the eyes of each neighbor in turn. *Violence among us.* In face after face I read disbelief. These bold Israelis, whom I have so long admired, sit paralyzed with confusion. They lift uncertain gazes to me, all holding the same message. *That's not us, is it?*

For the first time since I arrived in this country, the Israelis around me seem as vulnerable as I. *More* vulnerable, I tell myself. Because they're surprised. *Fools,* I address them silently. *It was here all along, you just didn't want to see it.*

When it's become plain to them that I'm going to offer no response, I feel their attention shift gradually from me to Gil.

Gil, his back to the group, is relacing his boots. From the tightness of his shoulders I can tell he is aware of being watched.

The sun rides higher in the sky. Breakfast is finished, but no one moves to begin the morning's hike. The shadows cast against the ground by the wooden beams become razor-sharp. Perched on a rock, I watch the still surface of the pool. Behind me there is subdued activity, a half-hearted attempt to pack food and prepare water bottles. I feel everyone watching the distance between my body and Gil's.

It is his alteration of this distance that starts it. He calls my name; when I don't respond, his steady tread approaches over the hard ground.

Before he has reached me, Yair is blocking his path.

"How could you?" Yair speaks softly, but there is no one under this shelter who does not hear.

Gil's footsteps stop. He says nothing.

I am not listening. I want to tell Tali and Rina and the others: I'm not the pathetic person you think I am. I'm not like those women in shelters. I'm not one of those eternal victims my mother fights to save.

"You're sick," Yair says, only a few yards behind me.

Staring at the water, I can picture the pallor of Gil's face. He wants to make amends with me; Yair is merely a distraction. Right now, if he thought it would absolve him in my eyes, Gil would lay his neck before them all.

"Get away from her," Yair says.

I turn.

Gil hasn't moved. His head low, he waits to resume his path to me. To the others he must appear obstinate; only I know that his head is hung in grief.

When Yair shoves him, Gil stumbles a few steps but does not look up.

The back of Yair's neck is a dull red. "None of us wants any part of you, do you understand?"

Dov approaches; he sets a hand on Yair's shoulder. Then he speaks to Gil in a steady and quiet tone that catches me off guard. "This is what you need to know, so listen closely, because I won't say it more than once. If you ever set a hand on my cousin again, you will regret it for the rest of your life."

Gil and I and the others under the shelter are transfixed. But Yair cannot be quieted. "We fight so damn hard to make it safe in this place. This isn't who we are." He steps away from Dov's restraining hand. "I swear," he says, "I could kill you this minute." Then he swivels to me, his eyes shining with outrage and hurt. "Just say the word, Maya. Just tell me to knock the bastard down and I will."

"Yair," Dov calls. He is shaking his head sadly, and he waits until he has his friend's attention before continuing. "Don't make it worse for her."

Gil looks up. He gives a feeble hoot. "Is that what you're all on about? I didn't hit her. She fell, that's all." He turns to me for confirmation. We're a team, I can almost hear him say. The sunlight slants across his face, there is no seeing past the brightness.

The others wait, rapt.

I swallow hard against a tide of nausea that threatens to pitch me forward off the rock where I sit, and then I do something that startles me and leaves the Israelis looking stricken: I laugh at them all.

Noon has become a standoff that, I am convinced, will never end. I sit on the rim of the pool; Gil broods beside the picnic table. Dov and Yair are stationed between. Behind me, Rina and Tali wait for me to change my mind. "Come to the women's shelter," Tali repeats. "Just for a counseling session." The others have left for their hike.

"No one has to know," Tali insists.

Again my mind turns over the possibilities. Maybe I could go, just once, to hear what the people there have to say? The possibility of help overwhelms me. I can hardly bear to consider it; I blink back tears.

Still, I know no one can sweep me up, erase the marks of Gil's hands, or convince me that I'm worthy of anything other than this. Tali and Rina don't understand the least thing about me. They don't really care for me, I'm just a problem they want solved.

Gil is the only one who will stick with me no matter what. I know he'll never leave me.

Once more, I try to review my choices. I'm not thinking clearly.

I see that what paralyzes me, more than anything else, is fear of losing the one thing I have left: my mother's trust in me. A thought comes sailing into my mind: *I came to this country to save* her. *I'm not supposed to need saving.*

I am not aware of the sound of the motor. But as the car pulls up beside the steps, I hear, above other shouts of recognition, Dov's voice rising in alarm. "What are you doing here?" he barks. I turn my head. I am met with the sight of this suntanned soldier, my moody terse cousin, racing toward the steps as if everything in his life and training had prepared him for this moment.

The car door opens; Nachum gets out.

Dov reaches the car and stands before his father. Ariela has squirmed out of the backseat to hug Dov's waist, and Dov reaches automatically to stroke her hair. Inside the car I see Tami.

Nachum lifts his chin and clasps a firm hand to his son's shoulder. The gesture says, Not this time—all of us are safe. The two men face each other. Then they move off, Dov lifting Ariela to his shoulders, Nachum stepping toward the shelter.

Nachum passes among Dov's three friends, extending his hand in greeting to each. Then he glances around and comes to me.

There is no way to avoid it. I face him. Nachum blinks as if noticing something peculiar about my appearance. Then he clears his throat and speaks, his eyes apologizing into mine. "Your mother needs you in America," he says. "One of her co-workers sent for you."

∞ 16 ∞

The trip to Jerusalem is a silent passage through sharp, clear light. My mind is empty of thought. Nachum navigates the hills steadily. Gil and I sit in the backseat, jolted together from time to time. The desert spins below us, but I look only at the bright empty sky. Gil searches me with his eyes.

Our departure from the nature preserve was rushed. No sooner had Nachum spoken to me than Tami made her way between Dov's friends to remind him that time was short. The Shachars had placed me on standby for a night flight and we needed to get under way.

Within five minutes of the Shachars' arrival, I'd gathered my belongings.

"Maya looks bad," Ariela announced as I zipped my backpack.

Nachum knelt to explain. "Her mother is very sick. Sometimes when people are sad and cry very hard, their eyes get a little bit puffy."

Dov's friends were relieved I was going, I knew it. Rina stood apart from Tali and Yair, and stepped forward only when Dov hoisted my bag into the trunk of the Shachars' car. "Good luck," she said. Then she touched my shoulder. "Please, Maya. Will you think about it?"

As Rina retreated, I watched Gil throw his knapsack and our sleeping bags into the trunk and climb into the backseat. No one spoke to him.

Dov intercepted Nachum and Tami as they headed for the car. "I need to talk with you."

Nachum, in a gesture clearly foreign to him, looked at his watch. Impotent, he raised his hands. "We can't miss her flight, and she needs time to pack. But we'll be back from the airport tonight. Can it wait until then, maybe you can drive to a phone in Eilat and call?"

Dov frowned. "No. I'll get my gear together and I'll drive back today. I'll meet you in Jerusalem and we can talk."

"Aren't you supposed to stay another two days?" Tami asked.

Dov made a dismissive gesture. Then he made another gesture, a simple sweep of his hand that seemed to include me in his circle of responsibility. Before I ducked to enter the car, I paused to take in this new appraisal of me: family. "Look after Maya," Dov said.

Nachum opened his mouth to reply. Then, glancing in bewilderment at his watch once more, he got in the car.

Tami lingered to consider her son. "I will," she told him solemnly.

For hours we drive, past hills and goats and Bedouin women in black. Near some power cables, two men squat on the ground outside a tent, watching a small television set propped on a pile of rocks. The desert rolls on.

The Shachars know nothing, yet. But they will, before the night is out. I wait, with the certainty of a convicted criminal, for the charges against me to be made public. I am convinced that if they tell my mother, she won't want to see me.

Patting the makeup in the hollows beneath my eyes, I recall how hard I tried to conceal all those long-ago nights in the dance studio.

She won't need the Shachars' help to figure it out.

In the car, only Nachum speaks. In respectful tones he provides answers to questions before I can ask them; he offers details of the flight,
assures me that my ticket will be waiting for me at the terminal, and
seems eager to avert my every need for speech. I watch him move delicately around my silence, afraid to upset a basket piled high with feelings. It is not hard to recognize the baffled caution with which he
navigates his wife's moods.

On a steep incline Nachum pulls to the side of the road and demon-
strates an optical illusion for Ariela. "If we release the brake here, it
looks like we're rolling uphill. Watch the rocks slide by. Magic, Ariela."
Ariela's giggles fill the car, gravity appears to drag us uphill. Forward
and backward roll into each other in this hard dry place. I look to
the sky.

It is late afternoon when we reach Jerusalem, and traffic is heavy on
the city's main streets. The Shachars let Gil and me off in front of our
building and promise to come back for me in an hour. They have been
driving since the seven-a.m. telephone call from New York, and
Nachum wants to sleep before taking me to the airport. Tami turns in
her seat as we leave the car. "See you at six," she says. She looks into my
face. I have no idea what she sees.

Just inside the building entrance, Gil and I pass a black-hatted student taping notices to the wall. We climb the stairs. As we near the second floor, I see that the door of my downstairs neighbor's apartment is
wide open. The sight triggers a distant alarm, but I have something
more pressing to think about. One foot, then the other. My legs cramp
in protest. The hours in the car have knotted my aching muscles; at each
step I fight the desire to rest.

A young, heavyset black appears in the second-floor doorway and
watches us approach, as though, from this vantage point, spying is only
natural. He inclines his head toward Gil, who is in front of me, and
through a heavy lisp informs him, "We need a tenth for a minyan." But
Gil moves on.

In the apartment Gil sets down his things, then lifts my backpack
from my shoulder and lays it on the floor as well. "You're going to
America," he says, dully. "Your mother will get well and you'll be happy
with your American friends and you'll want to stay. You'll run away

from me because I haven't been good to you." Fear has drawn his arms across his chest.

It's only now that the pages on the bulletin board downstairs, the open door, and the blacks assembling men for prayers add up in my mind.

"Just a minute," I stammer. Gil looks puzzled, then uneasy. "I'll be right back," I tell him. I walk down the stairs as fast as my buckling knees will carry me. At the bottom of the stairwell I read the bereavement notices, one after another; I read each and every one, although they all carry an identical message: *Shifra Feldstein, of blessed memory. Died the 19th of Elul 5753. May God comfort her mourners along with the other mourners of Zion and Jerusalem.*

I step into the garden. The trunk of the palm tree is thick and scarred; I rest a hand against it. *Shifra.* I turn her name over and over in my mouth, it feels like the first word I have spoken in weeks.

"She was gathered to her forefathers last night," a voice says from behind me. I turn to see the same black who spoke to Gil upstairs. He stands against the wall beside the entryway, half shaded by the stout trunk of the palm tree. I'm amazed that he speaks to me at all, in my short-sleeved shirt and jeans. But he doesn't seem troubled; he keeps his blue eyes fixed on a point beyond my head, so that he won't see my immodestly exposed elbows. He doesn't so much as glance at my slumping body or swollen face. I am acutely grateful—this courtesy might have been designed especially for me.

"I have relatives in Queens, I visit. I studied also once at yeshiva in America, two years I studied there. Crown Heights. So I know from there my English."

Only as he says this do I realize that he has, indeed, been speaking to me in English, his lisp even more pronounced beneath that heavy accent.

He fishes in one pocket for a cigarette, then lights it with a match from a tattered book dug from another pocket.

"You're the upstairs neighbor," he tells me. "American."

I nod.

He nods as well, staring off into space. "There's no need to worry. All was done properly."

I hesitate, unsure how much he'll be willing to tell me. But I need to know more, and in English I'm bold. "Did any family come for her?"

"We came."

"Who do you mean, 'we'?"

"*Chevra kaddisha.*"

"*Chevra kaddisha?*"

My ignorance elicits a sour expression, but his gaze doesn't waver from its focus. "The burial society." He indicates the upstairs apartment with a motion of his chin. "That's who arranged shiva. She herself had no family. But no one"—he takes a deep drag on his cigarette—"is without family in the house of Israel." He exhales smoke, then speaks through a cough. "We accompanied the body to its resting place."

"What happened to her?" I find I'm looking past him as well; our words float ownerless in this quiet garden.

"What happened? She was gathered to her forefathers."

"What I mean is, how did she die?"

"I know what you mean," he responds. "But what matters how? She went to her creator." He draws on his cigarette again, then seems to tire of his own self-satisfaction. Dropping his voice to a level suitable for mildly illicit gossip, he continues. "Her curtains caught fire. From the flame of a memorial candle she lit." He sighs. "Careless. She put the fire out herself, she tore down the curtains and put out every last flame, but she had a heart attack. Our coroner said exhaustion from heat was what did it."

She's dead, that's all I can think. But that can't be so. Obstinate, I shake my head. There was more we had to say to each other. There was a question she wanted me to answer. And something she had to tell me, I'm sure of it now.

"Can you tell me about her?" I ask.

I half expect him to inform me once more that she was gathered to her forefathers. Instead he twists his free hand meditatively in his beard. "She was a survivor. Of the Shoah." He taps ash onto the dirt path and grinds it with the toe of one shoe. "Neighbors say she came here after the war, she worked textiles until she got too old or strange and they retired her on pension. She used to have couple of visitors every year, Polish maybe, or Hungarian, who knows. Friends, or just charity workers. But whoever it was, they stopped coming. The children here were scared of her, that's what people say. She wore a kerchief like a God-fearing woman, but her eyes were crazy. And when they found her, her hair was matted. Like she never once in fifty years combed it. Like she never noticed the war was over and she was still living. She was one of the strangest, this one, may-her-memory-be-blessed." He shrugs. "Still, she's gone to God's kingdom, same as others. It goes this way lately— so many of them dead or dying. We see it every week in our work, the generation of survivors is leaving this world. God is gathering his most deserving crop. We must cherish their memory."

The garden is dappled with light, birds flit past the wall where this man stands. "No," I say to a spot above his head. "She didn't believe that. She didn't believe she was special because she'd suffered. And she wasn't just interested in being remembered, she wanted something else. Something more complicated than that."

"But you're wrong," he tells the air behind me. "There is meaning to suffering. Our souls are tested, strengthened. We must understand, the survivors are proof of God's will to sanctify us."

"No." My voice rises. I steal a glimpse at him, but he still isn't looking at me. The anonymity frees me to say whatever comes to mind. "Survivors aren't proof of anything. She wasn't just some symbol, some evidence of God's plan. She was a *person.* You know, you're as bad as that damn art critic who was so determined to figure out what *you* symbolized."

"Pardon?"

Now it's my turn to be smug. "Never mind."

He puffs on his cigarette. For several minutes he chooses to ignore me. Then he speaks once again. "The interesting thing is, it wasn't one of the faithful who found the body. It was a woman from outside." With a careless circle of his cigarette he indicates the entire city beyond this street. "A fancy lady," he adds with disdain, and then explains: "Perfume."

He blows a stream of smoke. Together we watch it form a small cloud, then disappear.

"A very strange thing. This lady said she wasn't a relative, she said she'd only met the dead woman yesterday. She said the dead one left something at her apartment. A suitcase. This lady carried it all the way back across Jerusalem just to finish an argument. She wanted to *quarrel* with the dead woman. She wanted to throw the suitcase back in her face." Quietly he chuckles. *"God in heaven.* When I arrived at the apartment—I was the first *chevra kaddisha* member to come, after somebody on the first floor called—the fancy lady actually ordered me away. Can you believe it? She wanted me to take the suitcase with me as well, said she didn't want it in her sight. Said it was a filthy thing." The man shakes ash into the garden. *"Lunatic.* All what was in the suitcase was a worn old dress and shoes, some dry crackers, three teabags, and a dirty old hairbrush that looked like it hadn't been used since maybe the days of the Temple, may-it-be-speedily-rebuilt. But the lady insisted I get rid of it all. She sat beside the dead one talking insults. She said she would have nothing to do with this woman, she couldn't stand her.

"But when the others from *chevra kaddisha* arrived, she cursed us with such as I never heard from the mouth of a woman. She didn't want us to take the body away. Guarded that woman like it was her own best friend who had died." Ruefully he shrugs. With his heavy side-locks and lisp, there's something almost likable about him. "All right, so she made it clear she doesn't like religious people, and especially *chevra kaddisha.* We had to send some of our women to coax her out of the apartment. They said that at the last moment before she left, this mad-woman cried over the body. And then she went and hasn't been back since. Not for burial this morning, not for shiva." He stubs out his cig-arette against the side of the building, leaving a dark smudge. "Fickle," he pronounces.

From the second-floor window comes the sound of soft chanting.

"Still," he considers, "she sat with the dead, which is a mitzvah. The Lord puts good deeds even in the paths of those who stray."

I have no idea what to make of this story. So instead I imagine the funeral. I picture a cluster of men in black hats and coats, watching while a group of kerchiefed women carry an insignificant, cloth-wrapped body down the stairs. And in the cemetery, a circle of religious men and women around her grave, rending their clothing because there are no family members to do it. A Jerusalem burial, a shadeless plot of earth, voices lifted in prayer. Psalms working the hard earth, softening it to receive her.

My companion's gaze has wandered to a banner hanging low out-side the garden. "The Messiah is coming at any moment," he says. "We are waiting, we all wait patiently, and endure. We do what we can to has-ten Redemption." He smiles as at some private joke. "Even *you* wait. Even *you* live balanced on the innermost fence of Redemption. That's what it means to be God's chosen."

"Then how do we get unchosen?" I don't know why suddenly I should be so enraged. "Shifra, my neighbor, she was looking for a way out of your precious holy suffering. There has to have been a way out for her."

He lowers his gaze and looks at me directly for the first time. His eyelids crinkle with amusement. *"Americans,"* he says. He makes a soft tutting sound. Then he steps forward. "May God comfort you along with the other mourners of Zion and Jerusalem." With a motion he indicates that I must step aside so he can pass without touching me. Then he walks down the path toward the street. He walks out of sight under swaying signs that have faded to pale yellow, their once bold lettering almost invisible against the sun-bleached background.

A three-legged cat picks its way along the top of a stone wall edging the garden and leaps onto a dumpster. I watch its tail wave high in the air.

In the building behind me a window opens. "I've got some sandwiches ready for us," Gil is calling. His voice is kind.

When I don't move, he taps on the shutters. "Maya," he cajoles.

My chest heaves: a labored exhalation. All around me, the sun burns pale-veined buildings. The blacks' signs sway along the street, the heat makes my eyes tear. Gasping like a fish, I make my way toward the forgiving darkness of the overhang. I lean back against the rough plaster wall and try to drive the sun from my mind. I think cool water thoughts.

"Food's ready," Gil announces from above.

He is waiting in the kitchen. He's laid the table with care. When I've finished my sandwich, he brings out sliced fruit and watches me eat. I spoon the pieces to my mouth one by one. I nudge the empty bowl away; Gil looks encouraged. He stands and moves behind me. Placing a firm hand on each of my shoulders, he squeezes as if to anchor me in place.

"Maya," he says, "I know I haven't given you much reason to trust me."

Gently he massages. "But I love you."

My head feels as if it's in a vise.

"Now you know everything there is to know about me. I've told you my secrets, you've seen me at my worst. When your mother is well, come home to me and I'll do things right."

"My mother won't get well," I tell him.

He kisses the crown of my head. "I know you're worried. You're so close to her. You say you two have problems, but I see you writing to her all the time. I see how hard you try."

I listen attentively, aching for his understanding.

"I'm certain she loves you, too," he tells me. His voice is raw. "It's just that sometimes love can be hard."

"I'm afraid to go back to America," I whisper.

He leans closer; my head rests on his chest. His heart is racing. "No matter what, I'll be here waiting for you. No matter what it takes, I want you here with me." From his position he can't see my face; his hands travel my shoulders and neck and avoid my swollen jaw. "Just say you'll come back and stay with me. Say you'll marry me."

He is clasping my shoulders so solidly, I know that his love will never falter. "I promise," I tell him. I stare at the wall ahead of me. And as he moves forward to kiss me, as he thanks me wholeheartedly with every touch, I wonder whether it's me making this promise, or someone who can be trusted to tell the truth.

Twenty minutes later, Tami picks me up in front of my building. Nachum had to see to some things in the shop, she tells me, as I lay my suitcase in the trunk; now he's showering, we'll leave from their apartment when he's ready.

Traffic is still heavy, though brisk, and as we wait at a light the hourly news signal beeps from open car windows all around us. The light turns green; Tami drives on in silence, peering stiffly into intersections as if mystified by the choices of the other drivers.

After we park on Wolfson Street, Tami sits for a minute before removing the key from the ignition. She appears to be on the verge of speech.

I follow her along the stone path. With a jangling of keys, she unlocks the building's main door. We cross the dark foyer. On the second-floor landing she pauses and turns to me. "I hope everything is all right with your mother," she says. She seems uncertain what comes next.

"Thank you," I say.

We climb to the apartment. As soon as Tami opens the door, Nachum is calling to me from the back bedroom so cheerfully he might have forgotten the purpose of my trip. "I'll be there in only a minute, in only a few minutes," he promises. "I'm already there." He continues to broadcast the state of his preparedness while Tami and I head to the kitchen. "I called the airport. They said we needed to get there two hours in advance." Briefly there is quiet; then he reports, with clear pride as well as a trace of astonishment, "But I'm making sure to get us there three hours ahead."

In the kitchen we find Fanya and Shmuel Roseman, Fanya's gentle-man friend from the concert. He remembers my name, and takes my hand in his. "I'm hoping all will go well with your mother," he says.

"Thank you." I glance at Fanya, who smiles a greeting distractedly. She appears to be deep in thought, but she rouses herself to speak.

"I hope the same. Your mother is a lovely woman." With uncharac-teristic awkwardness, Fanya fingers the knob of her wristwatch. "This must be very hard for you," she says.

Across the room, Tami whirls in surprise. In an instant her whole de-meanor has changed, her attention is riveted on her mother.

Fanya goes on. "I remember how frightened I was when my hus-band Daniel fell ill." She seems almost shy, unprepared for her own words. "It was the most terrible thing I'd ever gone through. I hope your mother gets well."

I nod my thanks. And then Fanya does something I do not expect. She rises and, before leaving the room, lays a hand on my head.

Tami's cheeks are flushed with concentration. She watches her mother disappear. Then her eyes, glittering strangely, fix on me. Her thin face radiates pure jealousy. She leaves the kitchen.

Shmuel sits opposite me, his arms folded on the tabletop. Pretend-ing not to have noticed Tami's baleful stare, I consider first the pepper shaker, then the salt.

But all at once, the lengthening of Nachum's delay, the quiet of this apartment, the throbbing of my legs and head are more than I can bear. I am overcome with resentment of Tami's selfishness. Before I know it, I'm crying in self-pity, patting my cheeks with wet fingers to keep my painstakingly applied makeup from running. Without intending to, I say aloud what I've been trying not to think. "My mother isn't going to want me there."

Shmuel raises his eyebrows. "Why do you think that?"

Already I regret speaking, but the tears are coming thick and fast.

"She and I don't exactly have a history of getting along well." My voice trips over resentful laughter. Seeking a quick end to the subject, I tell Shmuel, "Just the usual mother-daughter stuff. She doesn't exactly *get* my life, you know?"

Shmuel purses his lips. He nods. "I see." Slowly he settles back in his chair, uncrossing his arms. "That's very difficult."

On the soft wrinkled skin of his forearm I notice it immediately: a number tattooed in faint blue.

He sees me notice. Leaning forward once more, he reaches across the table and squeezes my hand. *Yes,* the gesture says. *I also.*

"You can't let what happened yesterday paralyze you today," he says. I look up at him.

"I mean with your mother. You can't let whatever happened in the past make you afraid to talk with her today."

"But you don't understand," I blurt. "She'll be so disgusted with me she won't want anything to do with me. I've told her lies, I've been terrible."

"Terrible?" He inclines his head slightly, as if the word holds no meaning for him. "What's 'terrible'?" I see he's reprimanding me, but without anger. Resting his elbows on the table, Shmuel waves the fingertips of one hand. "Whatever happened yesterday, however bad it was, isn't as important as what can still happen. The most important yesterday isn't as important as tomorrow." From another room comes the sound of Tami slamming one bureau drawer, then another. "I'm not saying you should forget what happened," Shmuel says above the noise. "You and your mother ought to maybe talk a little bit about all this 'terrible.' But, listen to an old man's advice, if you let yesterday be bigger than tomorrow"—he pronounces his conclusion deliberately—"then there's no hope for nothing." He nods, pleased with himself, and burps softly. "Yesterday *plus* today, even, both of them added up, are never as big as tomorrow." There is a short silence. Then Shmuel winks, and with a motion of his chin indicates the doorway where Fanya vanished moments ago. "Trust me." A mischievous glint lights his eyes. "There's always tomorrow. I'm counting on it."

I wipe my face with the backs of both hands.

"Talk to your mother." He nods encouragement. "Be optimistic."

Leading Ariela and carrying a small cushion, Fanya comes back into the kitchen. With a grave smile, Shmuel reaches across the table. For what might be only a few seconds, he cups my aching jaw with a warm palm. His face registers pure compassion. I'm certain that my tears will begin again, and never stop. Then Shmuel pats my wrist and turns in his seat to look at Fanya.

Settling on a chair, Fanya drops the cushion on the floor. She signals for Ariela to kneel, then begins braiding pink and purple ribbons into the girl's hair so that the colors alternate evenly.

There's a lively knock on the door jamb, and Nachum's towel-draped head appears from around the corner. "Two minutes," he calls. "I'm already there." Ariela giggles as her father disappears, and Fanya steadies the girl with a hand on her shoulder. The banging from down the hall continues. Working the last bit of ribbon into Ariela's hair, Fanya chatters to Shmuel about the lack of variety in the upcoming chamber music programs.

Something is building in the apartment—a tension so obvious I wonder that anyone can ignore it. Tami is out of view, but every sound from the hallway announces her ill humor. Soon she comes into the kitchen with a washcloth and wrings it noisily into the sink. I've never seen her so animated. Her cheeks are red, as if she'd been slapped. No one else seems to pay her any attention; I watch Fanya, without interrupting her own sentence and without even a glance at her daughter, move her legs to allow Tami to pass. The two of them are like combatants pacing a ring before their match begins.

Or perhaps only Tami is. Fanya speaks on—she doesn't see Tami's agitation, or doesn't care. Briefly I muster the concentration to feel annoyed at them both. Then it seems to me that I don't care, either.

Nachum's banter cuts the tension. "Nu, let's go, why's everyone sitting around?" He bends, tweaks Ariela's chin, and teases as she reaches to touch his damp hair. "I've been waiting and waiting for you, what took you so long to get ready?" Flirting and coaxing, Nachum leads us down the stairs.

The air is cool, and the street has taken on the golden cast of evening.

"Drive safe," Shmuel chides through the open window of the car, as if Nachum were a teenager embarking on his first independent outing. Nachum responds with a mocking salute, which Shmuel ignores as he pats the side of the car in farewell. He has refused Nachum's offer of a ride back to his apartment over the jewelry shop. Now he stands on the sidewalk and waves while Nachum eases the car out of its spot. As we pull away, I twist in my seat to watch him. It is with an unexpectedly light step that he turns and sets off down the street. I picture him laboring well into the night, seated patiently at his watchmaker's bench. Squinting through a single magnifying lens, he is mending what can be mended; restoring the ticking of precious seconds and hours to silenced faces and stilled hands.

Seated in the back of the car with Ariela and Fanya, I watch the streets of Jerusalem broaden and give out to highway. On the radio a group of men and women trade contradictory rumors of progress and catastrophe in the peace negotiations. After a while Nachum turns off the program. He whistles as he drives, one elbow propped on the windowsill. From the passenger seat Tami stares out one window; from the backseat Fanya gazes out another. The two mirror each other unconsciously, a matched set.

I try to imagine what I will say to my mother when I arrive at the hospital. I can't think of anything.

We are more than halfway to Tel Aviv when it begins.

Nachum has been speaking about a competitor of his, the owner of a shop in Katamon. Although he gossips enthusiastically about the man's bungled business, he draws a firm line at repeating the stories he's heard about the competitor's divorce. "I won't kick a fellow for his misfortune. They say she's giving him a terrible time in a thousand different ways."

"And what do they say her complaint is?" Fanya prods.

Nachum chuckles. "Who knows? You've got to pity the fellow, maybe all she wants is someone who doesn't turn gold into shit every time he opens the cash register, excuse my language."

"Nonsense. If she loved him then she wouldn't care about that. It's all about love."

"So," Tami says tartly, her eyes still glued to the view outside the window. "Listen to the expert."

Fanya makes a self-deprecating noise, but her face shows surprise. "Well," she says, "I think I'm allowed to have an opinion about love. After all, I've seen a thing or two."

"Oh," Tami says. "And I don't know anything about the subject? You think I don't know anything about love? You should talk. You'll never really care about anyone. You're not capable of it. You just string people along for your own satisfaction."

"Tami!" Nachum glances at his wife, but Tami does not pay him any attention. He checks my reflection in the mirror. He looks like he wants to apologize to me but doesn't know what to say.

"What does that mean?" Fanya asks. There is genuine hurt in her voice. If it were possible, I might think Fanya had never noticed Tami's loneliness, or the discontent with which she drifts at the edge of every gathering.

"Fanya, the expert on love." Tami all but spits the final word. Then she laughs harshly and says nothing more.

Fanya sits perfectly still. Her healthy face is ashen. The wind whips her hair.

Nachum is holding the wheel with both hands—perhaps the steadier grip will help him comprehend what is taking place in the car he steers. After a moment Fanya purses her lips. I recognize the haughty look she levels at the back of her daughter's head. She has decided to dismiss Tami's behavior as self-indulgent.

"Can you roll the window up further?" she asks Nachum.

He rolls the window halfway.

At one and the same time, Tami and Fanya speak. "More," they say.

Hurriedly, Nachum shuts the window. We ride in silence.

Then, as though thinking better of her decision, Fanya speaks. Her voice is as smooth as it is venomous. "At least I have people who care about me. At least I'm not so unpleasant to be with that people stop issuing invitations because they can't stand my sour face."

Tami seems to grow smaller in her seat. She shrugs, as if her mother's words don't matter to her.

But Fanya is not finished. "You always were a bitter girl," she says. "Now you're a bitter woman."

Without looking at me, Ariela knots her moist hand into the fabric of my T-shirt. I clasp the cloth-wrapped fist and squeeze.

Tami watches the view. She is a woman emptied of everything, barren of wishes.

There is nothing left to say. We pass dark green fields, orchards of low trees.

Then Tami speaks. "Sometimes I feel like I don't even matter." Her voice is hollow. "Like I might as well be invisible, like nothing I do or say makes any difference."

"I don't understand you when you talk such nonsense." Fanya turns to me. "Maya, I do apologize."

I nod my acceptance, but keep my face averted; all I want is to avoid scrutiny between here and the airport.

Tami gives a despondent laugh. Then, with peculiar brightness, she speaks. "Of course you don't understand. You don't understand your bitter daughter because you never loved me enough. Or anyone else."

Fanya looks out the window, tight-lipped.

"Like Shmuel Roseman," Tami charges. "Like him. When will you admit it? You don't care about him, but you let him follow you everywhere."

"What sort of heartless person do you think I am?" Fanya retorts.

Now it is Tami who says nothing. Nachum's fists are balled tight around the wheel. Ariela and I stare straight ahead.

"Do you think I'm so very selfish?" Fanya insists.

"Listen to me, Mother." Tami releases her seat belt and turns to face Fanya. "For once you're going to listen to me. I am sick of you charming everyone to pieces. Everyone believes you're the most gracious, kindhearted person in the world, and they adore you for it. Only I know it's not true. I know that the minute someone really needs you, you'll turn your back. You'll tell them not to take things so *seriously.*"

"When did I ever—"

"When? What about when Rafi died? What about a thousand other times? What about my miscarriages, you came from Tel Aviv and you couldn't even say—"

"What did you *want* me to say?"

"Anything! *Anything,* Mother. *Anything* would have done. It didn't even have to be 'Are you all right?' Do you know what perfect strangers said when they discovered I had only one child and I'd miscarried? They said, 'For heaven's sake don't give up trying, what if you lose your first to war?' They cared enough to say that. You could have barged in, the way normal mothers and grandmothers do: 'Try again, have another, help make up for the lost. The Germans may have had the final solution, but they won't have the last word.' You could have said anything, Mother. Instead of blowing everyone kisses and getting back on the bus. You could have stayed with me." Tami's words threaten to choke her but she continues. "I may be a bitter woman. But at least I don't lie about what I am."

"Tami." Fanya pronounces her daughter's name with bewilderment. "I gave you the best gift in the world. I showed you how not to sink yourself in mourning." Her hands rise to her cheeks. "You were there, Tami. All those years, you were there, you saw what I saw. What else would you have had me do?"

I am aware of my own held breath, and Nachum's and Ariela's. The argument has turned a corner that only Tami and Fanya understand; no one else utters a sound. Tami glances up at her mother's reflection as if she might be sorry, but there is no stopping the stream of words that comes from her mother now.

"Do you think I'm heartless? Is that it? Well, I'll remind you of something. In case you've forgotten, I'll remind you." Fanya's voice is ragged. "Do you recall what it was like when you were small? Refugees coming in like cattle. Like fleas, lice. They were . . . they were *horrible,* those people. Do you remember what a broken human being looks like, before he finds strength to start a new life?

"So many of them." Fanya shakes her head; she might be trying to rid herself of a lingering dream. "So many. Their eyes empty. Or worse, their eyes full of what they'd seen. And your father, Tami, your father needed to give a hand to everyone. He couldn't stand to see their pain without helping. All day long distributing food, all day long translating for refugees, all day long assisting their dolorous searches for people who were long since nothing but ashes. He sought out news of the friends we'd left behind in Amsterdam, too. He couldn't get over the things he heard. Do you understand me, Tami? All day long your father took in what had happened in Europe, every day more. And when he came home, his eyes were empty, too. He was theirs, every waking moment. He was a softhearted man. And a softhearted man couldn't withstand a thing like that."

Fanya lifts her chin. "Every evening when he was due home, I dressed up in my best. Yes, that's right, perfume in Israel in 1950. I ordered it from Europe and I didn't care what anyone said. I even ordered it from Austria, let the gossips go to hell. I made a candlelight dinner, I didn't care how I had to scrape or go without during the day. You have no idea how hard it was to find decent food in this country in those times." She lets out a sour laugh. "Israel, home of the ingathered exiles." For a moment she falls silent. Then she continues, her voice softened to a murmur. "Their sorrow almost broke him. He, with his guilt at escaping while his whole family perished behind him.

"Only I, I made sure he didn't come home to a sorrowful house. Or to the least bit of ugliness. Or to a crying child." She gazes blankly at Tami. "I was his bride," she says.

Outside the car windows, farms line the highway on either side. The low sun flashes along ruler-straight lines of trees. I glimpse small tractors and pickup trucks, parked between the rows for the night.

"I married a softhearted man," Fanya says. "Because of the way he used his hands, so carefully. Because of the way he looked up from under his eyelids when he spoke—begging my permission to tell me his thoughts. That was your father, Tami." She closes her own eyes. "I never understood him. But I loved him."

For several minutes Fanya sits motionless; the sound of the car's engine asserts itself and lulls me half to sleep before she speaks again. "After he died," she says, "there was such darkness. You were in high school, Tami, I'm sure you didn't notice."

Tami is speechless.

Fanya opens her eyes. She straightens sharply, as if roused mid-argument. "And would I have been more noble if I'd sacrificed my life to patching sorrows that are too big to be patched? Mourning the dead, mourning your father, mourning every bit of life that was taken from me? What kind of living is that? So Yad Vashem wants a mother to shed tears for her children until there are only stones left?" Fanya's jaw is tight. "No, Tami. No, I will not let them take my life away from me. Do you understand? I will not let them take life away. I refuse to be anyone's monument to tragedy. Like that"—Fanya tastes the word—"that *black* woman who came looking for Maya. I'm not like her. She wasn't even a woman anymore, not even a person, she was a *thing*, Tami. A thing. A broken-off, dried-up shard of a person."

"I don't know who you're talking about," Tami inserts dully.

"She wasn't religious," I whisper, but no one hears me.

"Life is for laughter," Fanya says.

Looking across Ariela's smooth ribboned braids, I try to see in Fanya the wild weeping stranger of the *chevra kaddisha* man's story.

"But I wasn't *trying* to make you unhappy." Tami's words are a plea without hope. "I'm sorry if I was always too serious."

"What?"

"Maybe I was always in your way with the things I needed, but I couldn't help it. I'm sorry if I was too serious and you couldn't stand it. I'm sorry if you always had to get away from me to do happy things. I wasn't trying to take away your life."

Quizzically Fanya raises her eyebrows. Then speaks with annoyance. "Who ever said it was your fault, Tami? This has nothing to do with you. Why would you think such a thing?"

I wait for Tami's reply, but none comes. After a time she settles back into her seat, her mouth fallen open like a child's.

"Fanya." Nachum speaks up. "Couldn't you have returned to Europe, if being here in Israel was so terrible? Amsterdam was your home, after all. Did you ever think of going back and starting a new life there?"

Fanya holds her head very high and says nothing.

Nachum watches her in the rearview mirror. He gives a low whistle. "All these years of talking about Europe, and you've never even been back to visit, have you?"

Fanya speaks slowly and with enormous dignity. "I could never go back to Europe after the war. Maybe if I had had Daniel with me, but we never did go. He said Europe was dead for him. And after Daniel died, I never wanted to go alone." Her shoulders back, she meets Nachum's gaze squarely in the rearview mirror. "I want to remember Europe the way I choose. They can't take that from me."

There is a long silence. The sun has set without my noticing; the roadside groves fade steadily into darkness. We pass down the highway at what feels like a tremendous speed.

It is Fanya who breaks the silence. "This morning Shmuel asked me to marry him."

Nachum snorts with laughter. "Another proposal for Fanya? And it's not the first from Shmuel, either. You've got to give him credit for being persistent."

Fanya is looking out into the twilit fields. "I said yes."

It takes a few seconds for Tami to speak. When she does, her voice cracks with incredulity. "But why?" is all she says.

"Because," Fanya says. "Because it's time. I don't know if I'll ever love him as much as he loves me, but it's time to try again." She chuckles to herself, then looks nakedly out the window. "I'm not getting younger, you know. *Not* that I'm about to roll over and give in to crow's-feet, mind you. Still, be that as it may."

All of us watch the darkening fields pass. Nachum, steering down the dim highway, lays a hand on Tami's knee without a word.

At the airport Nachum unloads my bag, and we all walk together to the check-in area. The lines stretch back almost as far as the concession shops. Luggage carts trundle past, missing each other narrowly. For the past ten minutes Ariela has been complaining that she is hungry. Now she says she wants to go to bed, and when no one pays her any attention she starts to whimper.

"Stop it," Tami says wearily.

Fanya, who has been silent since leaving the car, occupies herself with looking for the proper line.

"Stop it," Tami says again after a moment. Then, abruptly, she stops walking, causing a man with a luggage cart to veer and nearly upset his load. She spins and, instead of facing Fanya as I expect, turns on Nachum. "I can't stand it. You don't care about me. No one cares about me. The only one who even notices me is Ariela, and she'd forget me if I were gone, too."

"Tami, you know that's not true."

"You don't even care," Tami whispers. She takes a heavy step away, her body slouched in defeat. "Just let me be." A second step, then a third. Then she is running. Dodging through the crowd, she weaves farther and farther away from us.

Nachum stands blinking, at a loss as to which to do: follow his wife, or do as she asks. And then, I see that Nachum is not lost, after all. I watch him spring into the crowd, shoving his way between carts and surprised tourists. As he disappears, I understand that Nachum is the one person who has not given up on Tami. He has only been waiting, all this time he has been waiting, for a chance to break down the doors and come looking for her.

Part Five

⋙ 17 ⋘

"Well, it's not as painful as it looks," she tells me as I enter. Her face is sharp, her eyes dark against ashy skin. An IV line feeds into the crook of her arm. Under thin white covers, her figure lies still.

She is smiling, a luminous frightened smile.

All this time, I've forgotten how beautiful my mother is.

"Come in." Her voice rattles loose in her chest. "Sit." As if we've simply been interrupted mid-conversation. She waves at the IV apparatus beside the bed. Ignore this, the gesture says.

The patch of sun between the window and my mother's bed is a spotlight. I tell myself I don't need to worry; I spent fifteen minutes checking and rechecking my makeup in the hospital's first-floor bathroom. But I skirt the brightly lit area as I make my way to her.

Her cheek feels dry and papery under my kiss. The smell is a hospital smell, not hers. "Thank you for coming, Maya," she says. Her body is slight; even through the covers I see the bony ridge of a hip. I look at her long, tapered fingers. At the short, tidy fingernails. Then back up, at the deep-set eyes, the cheekbones I've always envied—the face people have always remarked on. *Classic. Timeless. If I had a face like that, maybe I wouldn't wear makeup, either.*

Her hair, usually dark and shiny, now paler and brittle, is gathered in a knot on top of her head. She likes the movie *Good Morning, Vietnam,* I recall for no reason. She likes Etta James. I want to step nearer. I want to kiss her again, or hug her. My mother hates peanut butter. She won't wear high heels, she mocks people who spend three months in England

and return with British accents. I want to sit on the edge of that narrow bed. I wonder what she would do if I climbed in.

I don't move. I stand before her, clutching my suitcase.

"Faye is managing," she assures me. "Her husband is helping at the Center. And the volunteers are doing just fine in my absence."

I nod, as if the welfare of the Center were paramount in my mind.

A drop moves down from the IV bag. Another forms at the base, quivers there, then falls to the small plastic chamber that feeds the line. It appears to me that my mother is mulling something over. Then I understand she is only gathering strength to speak again.

I follow the line to the tender bruised patch on the inside of her left elbow, where it disappears beneath a strip of white tape. I see that the tape has pulled fine taut lines in the surface of her skin.

She takes a deep breath. "They paid for the private room," she accuses. "Everybody at the Center, Maya. They held a fund-raiser. I told them not to, but they insisted. I've had my own room for three days now." She makes a slight agitated motion with her right hand. I am mesmerized by the number of veins and tendons I see. "It's a waste of their precious dollars."

She waits; she seems to expect that this information will prompt me to immediate, outraged action.

"They wouldn't even tell me how much it costs. But I found out." She draws breath again, carefully, coaching the air on its journey to the bottom of her lungs. "From the nurses. I told Faye, It's criminal. It's a criminal waste of the Center's money. After all my years of working to help."

As my mother speaks, I touch my own face with my free hand. Pretending it's an idle gesture, I brush my forehead, cheek, and chin; I recall my long-ago outrage when strangers assumed she and I weren't related. Compared with her olive skin and purposeful jaw, my own features feel weak. Why would I ever have thought strangers would guess us to be mother and daughter?

But just as I tell myself we are nothing alike—just as I tell myself there has never been any golden thread connecting us—I see something. I see my mother's bony hands tremble, then steady themselves. In the instant's effort are mirrored all the months I've spent lying for her sake.

She looks at me hungrily. She seems helpless to leave the topic she has chosen. "A lot of good that did, telling them not to waste the money. Faye wouldn't listen." Tears of frustration brim over her lower lids. "Promise me you'll talk to her now that you're here."

"I'll talk to her," I say.

"Call her today."

"I will."

I set my suitcase gently on the floor.

At the hallway station, the nurse, a small woman with obviously dyed blond hair, reaches up with both hands to release a barrette. "There's been a vigil," she informs me as her hair falls over her ears. "People here from Brooklyn every day. *Every single day.* For the entire two weeks. And from their part of Brooklyn it's quite a trek to get to the Bronx."

I stand against the chest-high gray counter. *Two weeks?*

Refastening the barrette, she continues in the admiring tones so familiar to me. "Whatever your mother does in Brooklyn, she's got a fan club. They show up for a day or two at a time." She adds with a hint of surprise, "They're very polite."

I follow her gaze. There in the hall, a brown-skinned woman sits perfectly still, her hands folded in her lap as if she were in a church. I didn't see her earlier, although she must have been in plain view when I exited the elevator. Surely she must hear, but she doesn't look up when the nurse mentions her. It takes a moment for me to recognize her as the Jamaican woman from last Thanksgiving, the one who waited indifferently while my mother stalled her guests.

"Everyone wanted to contact you earlier," the nurse explains. "But your mother refused. She insisted that you not be disturbed. Nothing we said could budge her. Your mother's a stubborn lady, in case you didn't know."

I don't bother to respond. T he nurse goes on apologetically; I can tell she's afraid she's overstepped.

"Sunday she woke up in the middle of a storm, she was terrified. I answered her call, and it took a while to calm her. I think she was disoriented by the noise of the wind. After I'd sat with her a minute, she had me crank up the bed so she could watch the storm. I left her like that—just sitting in the dark. And who knows what convinced her, but later she handed one of the Brooklyn women a piece of paper with a telephone number on it. Then she couldn't stop asking us when your flight was arriving."

With the pads of her fingers the nurse pats her temples. Fine lines spread from the corners of her eyes and stretch over her cheekbones, a faint web of fatigue. She looks at me with a swift and vague pity.

"You must be tired," my mother tells me.

"I'm fine," I say. I'm trying to make sense of what the nurse told me. I've never seen my mother terrified. I've never seen her afraid of anything.

"Why don't you go wash up, and rest? The nurses will have whatever you need. I'm not going anywhere." The joke is hurried; in the few minutes I've been at the nurses' station, exhaustion has blunted her features. Now it occurs to me that she wants me to leave before I notice. "When you're rested you can come back. Then we'll have time to talk properly."

Gingerly, I kiss her cheek. Then I lift my suitcase and go. She doesn't close her eyes until she sees I've reached the door.

As I pass down the hall, I nod to the Jamaican woman. She looks at me, then through me.

The nurse tells me I can sleep in a spare conference room; I go to the door she indicates. I enter and shut the door behind me. Setting down my suitcase, I allow myself to draw a deep breath.

Even in this hospital with its antiseptic smells, it is impossible to miss the difference. I felt it the instant I stepped off the plane: the air here is thick, soft. I draw another deep breath, and the air in my lungs seems to promise miracles. *American* air.

My mother may get well. Anything, I tell myself, is possible.

Light enters the dusty pane above the sofa, and dances on the floor. Five stories below is Morris Park Avenue, a wide river of pavement marked by cavernous underpasses and weedy lots. I watch a bus start up at a light; exhaust stirs the trash. Discarded wrappers and loose papers wave like flags, welcoming me home.

The book of psalms is at the bottom of my suitcase. When I retrieve it, the cracked binding under my fingertips is a small comfort. I settle on the sofa. I open the book and read silently. "From the depths of my despair I cry to You O Lord." I repeat the words aloud, but they fall from my lips without a destination. *O Lord?* I don't know how to pray. Instead I press a hand to the greasy window and watch America blur between my fingers.

I fall asleep with the book open on my chest.

The nurse who stops me in the corridor indicates the bottle of orange juice and plastic-wrapped oatmeal cookie I hold. "She's not eating, you know."

I nod, and step along with a knowledgeable smile that does not falter until my back is to the nurse. Ignoring the thumping of my heart, I pretend that the snack cradled in my sweating hands was for me. The woman from the Center, still on the bench, watches me pass. This time I'm the one who won't meet *her* eyes.

My mother is waiting for me, and turns pertly as I enter. She is wearing a fresh white nightgown. Faint pink lipstick shines on her lips, there is color in her cheeks. I glance around the stark room; she must have hidden the makeup. I didn't know she knew how to put makeup on.

She's trying to make this easier on me.

Dizziness swallows me. I sit. Yes, I'm well rested now. Yes, the flight was fine. I bought a snack, is it all right if I eat in here? I inch the orange plastic chair as far from the window as I dare. I'm certain that the shadows on my face are well disguised; I've checked in every bathroom mirror between the cafeteria and here. But before her steady, almost black eyes, I feel a twist in the pit of my stomach. Immediately I recognize this nausea; it's as familiar as my own name. I've failed her and I'm about to be found out.

I stand. I have to look adult, purposeful. I have to show her I'm the new, trusted Maya, so different since she went to Israel. I cross to the window and try in vain to open it. I mumble something about getting a little more air.

"Maya," she says.

In this stark, clean room there are only a few distractions: the spare rail of the IV, with its knobby, indifferent wheels; the small stack of mail on a shelf behind the headboard; the chair on which I sit. And my mother's travel bag, set just inside a half-open locker, awaiting some imminent departure.

"Yes?" I can't stifle the anguish in my voice.

Her eyes take me in. I try to meet her gaze. At last she says, "I've longed to see you."

The confession stretches like a soft broad carpet between us. I sit motionless, amazed. Then, without meaning to, I start forward in my chair. I will cross the space between us to touch her thin hands—will they still feel familiar after all these years? Will the large-pored skin of her face be warm under my wandering fingertips? Surely if I curl my fists into hers, if I lie beside her in the bed and breathe her breath, I'll grow warm and sleepy like a child.

She is talking. Her rasping voice searches for purchase in the bright room. "Tell me, how are the Shachars?" Her eyes glint eagerly in their hollows.

I don't know what it is she's yearning for. But I settle back in my seat to try to give it to her.

I've promised myself that I won't tell my mother any lies. So I tell her about Ariela's dolls and Dov's girlfriend Rina. I tell her about Shmuel, the grace of his thick hands. Although I'm uncertain how she will receive Nachum's crudeness, I repeat some of his anecdotes. She laughs. Encouraged, I tell her more safe stories, stories with beginning, middle, and end. "Last week I went traveling in the south. Gil and I camped out with a group of people, Dov's friends." I talk about the wadi, about the scenery; I even relate Dov and Rina's arguments about his army career, omitting Gil's role and mine in their exchanges. We travel the desert, I spread the view of the rising hills before my mother's grateful eyes.

Still, listening to my own words, I feel seasick. Lying has become such a habit that the truth is only one among many stories I choose from. Nothing more.

After a while I've run out of truth. In my confusion I find myself hesitating longer and longer between sentences, trying to come up with a next anecdote. I can't remember anymore whether what I'm saying is what actually happened, or only what might have.

But my mother is still waiting, alert to my every word.

I strike out from shore. I show her the sights I saw with Dov's friends after leaving the nature preserve: the swaying green of towering trees at Ein Ovdat, the sudden blue of the Red Sea after hours of tawny stone. I describe the snake path and the ruins at Masada; I know these places so well from the tourist brochures that I half believe I've been there. I speak on, swallowing the terrible freedom of lies. Why tell the truth, I argue to myself, if it won't make anyone happy? The excursion I describe to my mother ends with a beach barbecue in Eilat. We return peaceably to Jerusalem, there is no interruption of our trip. There is only a telephone call to me at home from Tami, letting me know my mother is in the hospital.

I stop, daring her to admit this one truth I have named.

She closes her eyes. Her hands are folded on the blanket. How thin the fingers are, bones shedding disguise. I recall her standing in the entryway of the Center, wrapping her long hair swiftly into a bun. And I remember the volunteer who paused, children in tow, to admire: "If I had your shiny black hair I'd wear it down at my waist every day." My mother hardly smiled at the compliment. "No time for vanity," she countered. And then, perhaps to mask her embarrassment at the attention, she checked her wristwatch—set exactly on time because she didn't need to trick herself into promptness. I can picture her just as she appeared that morning: nails efficiently short; skirt severe; low artificial-leather pumps only slightly scuffed. She bent to collect her briefcase and left with only a nod; such a slender back for such an iron will. The volunteer and I traded exasperated looks.

As my mother rests now in this bare hospital room, I imagine an outing to Coney Island. I imagine my mother trailing behind the line of children on the rain-pocked sand. Someone produces a camera and she shies away from the pallid flash; the chemo has failed to do its work, her regrowing hair is wrapped in a kerchief and she does, after all, have enough vanity, this once, to stay out of the camera's view. The photograph will turn out well and she will send it to me, as if the children, sharp and energetic against the heavy sky, might distract me from noticing her absence. As if the image might prevent me from noticing that she wasn't going to be around to run the new day-care facility she and Faye fought so hard to secure. That there was never going to be a hiking trip to Bear Mountain with the children—not for my mother.

Finally I understand that her letters have been as full of lies as mine.

The drops of fluid fall to the chamber, become a thin line of liquid, disappear into her arm. I see now that these were our final months together, and we spent them sending coded messages across oceans. My mother has aged ten years in these six months, while I've stood still halfway around the world, listening to my own heartbeat.

_____

Day merges with night, there is no sense to the numbers on the hospital clock. People from the Center come and go with respectful nods to me, the Jamaican woman returning most frequently.

My mother's voice is rough with excitement, and a patch of real pink glows in each cheek. "Your father would have hated that drive into the desert." She laughs. "Heights made him dizzy."

"Mom." I face her stubbornly. "Does Dad know?"

She huffs in practiced disgust. *"Your father.* I didn't tell him I was here, but some of my *colleagues"*—she rolls her eyes—"decided he had to know. I suppose it isn't surprising that they tracked him down—they had no way of knowing how he gets when anything frightens him. It was a long, long telephone conversation, Maya. Good thing he can afford that kind of phone bill, I kept telling him. He told me to be quiet about the bill, couldn't I stop being practical just once?

"So, you see, it was just like old times between us." Bitterness salts her laughter. "He kept asking did I need anything, I said no. He said I should know he stood ready to jump on a flight that minute." She lifts one hand, drops it to the covers. "Mr. Romantic. He always *was* good at the extravagant offer. I said he could fly to New York if he liked, but I didn't need anything and he'd be wasting his money. 'Make a donation instead,' I told him. I knew that would set him off. He gave me the usual hard time for a while, about how I never did let anyone help." She falls silent. A moment later, she adds, "And why should I let people help, when I know they'll just screw everything up?" She winks. I know what she means, don't I? But her eyes are wet. She looks confused.

Dread prompts me into speech; I'm afraid that my mother is going to ask me for advice. After all these years of asking help from no one, she'll relinquish her authority and lay it in my hands. And if she does, I'll know she's decided to die. I rush to reassure her before she can doubt herself. "I know just what you mean," I say.

My mother pats her hands together. Then, heavily, she sighs. "So we hung up. And if I know anything about your father, I know he was relieved. He didn't have the nerve to come. Your father never had the nerve."

A loud swish of wind rattles the windowpane; we both look at the sturdy glass.

"I never stopped loving your father," she says.

I turn away from the window, but she is still staring through the glass.

"It's true. It was just that neither of us could quite manage to live with the other. So he went off to a more comfortable life, and I followed my heart and stayed with my work. But I didn't ever fall out of love with him. Don't ask me why." There is perplexity in her voice. She glances at me, acknowledging what we both know: She's never confided in me this way.

"After the divorce, I think I gave up on some notion of happiness. So maybe that's why I took risks with my own safety, maybe that's why I did things other people weren't willing to do. Because once you stop caring for your own happiness, you can do those things." She worries the single button at her throat. Then, with a faint smile, she addresses me. "It's no matter, Maya. There are worse tragedies in people's lives than love that doesn't work. Maybe you haven't seen that yet, but you will."

"Mom, maybe I should call Dad again. He'd come."

"No." She pronounces the word firmly. She isn't confused or in need of advice, after all. "I don't want that, Maya. Your father and I have gone our separate ways. I may love him, but I've learned how to be without him."

The long speech has exhausted her. The shadows under her eyes have deepened and she breathes shallowly. "Tell me more," she says.

I cast about for a subject. I can't think of anything new, fact or fiction, to tell her about the desert. But the silence is lengthening, so I begin. "Tami and Fanya had a fight." Without embellishing or masking a single detail, I relate the conversation on the way to the airport. When I conclude with news of Fanya's engagement, my mother doesn't respond. Thinking she might need more time to rest, I tell her about Nachum racing after his wife in the crowded airport. And about how, when at long last I turned from checking my bag, Fanya stood beside the counter waiting for me. She was holding her granddaughter tight against her, and Ariela was snoring lightly, her head tilted back against her grandmother's belly. Beside them stood Nachum, with his arm firmly around Tami. Tami's cheeks were streaked with tears, but her head was nested in Nachum's chest. "It's all right," he was saying. He reached out his free hand and laid it on Fanya's shoulder, but it was Tami he was speaking to when he repeated, "It's going to be all right."

I am aware of setting this picture before my mother as evidence, although I can't say what exactly it is I'm trying to prove.

The door swings with hardly a sound, a nurse enters, and my mother's eyes lift gratefully to the wall clock. The nurse steps forward, holding a syringe of what I guess to be pain medication. A slight nod of my mother's head tells me I'm to leave.

The hall is empty now, even the Jamaican woman is gone. I sit on the low bench and fold my hands in my lap. I choose not to think about the flat littered streets outside this hospital; I skip over the breeze stained with the smell of damp cigarette butts and exhaust, bypass the traffic and graffiti, and I think, instead, of clouds mercifully blurring the horizon. I think of trees and rain. On my tongue I taste soft American air. She will get better, I tell myself. Nothing can go wrong here that cannot be fixed.

American promises. The disapproving phrase comes, from nowhere, into my head.

"She'll rest now," the nurse says beside me. She's appeared from my mother's room noiselessly, as if she takes special pleasure in making the hospital feel like a funeral parlor.

I nod; then, with the most professional air I can muster, I ask, "What's the next step in my mother's treatment?"

"Honey"—she looks down at me with a sympathy so thick it's suffocating—"this is a hospital for terminal patients. Your mother has decided not to pursue any more treatments."

I sit very still, and soon she's gone.

It might be an hour that passes, or two. I don't move. I spend the time trying to breathe. All the air has gone out of this corridor.

The thoughts come at intervals, logic operating at a glacial pace. I realize: My mother isn't going to call me to account. She isn't going to see through my makeup and my lies. She's too tired.

I don't, in fact, need to worry about being found out at all. The Shachars won't telephone my mother.

Because she's dying.

And I knew it all along, even if I never admitted it. I knew it well enough, last fall, to act. I pulled one loose thread from my mother's life: *She never moved to Israel.* And out of it, out of this one fiber with which she might possibly have accepted a daughter's help, I wove a cloth of stories big enough to wrap both of us.

Now, though, I see that it is necessary to unravel what I've spent so long creating. It is necessary to throw away my mother's approval once and for all. I remember my high school lab partner turning to me in sympathy when she saw my chemistry grade. "Your mom is gonna flay you." I tell myself: It won't be so bad, being that disappointing daughter again. I'll show her the truth. Tears stinging my eyes, I imagine my mother rising out of the bed in fury at my lies and my weakness. Disowning me, saving herself.

I wash my face in the bathroom adjoining the conference room. Meticulously I remove every trace of makeup. Then I turn off the fluorescent lights, so the room is lit only by the single window. I lie down on the sofa and try to sleep.

I dream of the woman from the apartment downstairs. She beckons to me with surprising grace; she speaks and I can't make out her words.

Waking, I try to chase the dream from my mind. I never understood what my neighbor wanted—all I know is that I failed her. She's dead, I remind myself. What's the use of dreaming she might help me?

In the grainy light, I sit against the low arm of the sofa. I pull my suitcase toward me and take out the photograph. The revelers, crowded together on their European porch, are gathered for a celebration I'll never understand. Yet as I look at the expressions frozen on their faces, I allow myself this prayer: May the waif poised at the edge of this gathering fly into the air. May she defy logic, gravity, and the two dour adults behind her. May she sail over the heads of the others and into the sky and, freed from this picture at last, speak to me.

Shifra.

"I'm sorry you had to come," she says. The medication has eased the sharp lines of her face. Her lids hover in near-sleep, but she seems determined to speak. "I hope you didn't ruin any plans on my account."

"It's all right," I say.

A hospital cart trundles down the hall.

My throat is so tight it threatens to choke the words. In a few sentences I will strike myself down, throw away her love forever. And— I believe this with all my strength—she will rise.

But before I can begin, she speaks in a ponderous Hebrew. "It is so long since I spoke this language. I almost forgot how."

My whole body feels weak. *"Ani edaber itach,"* I answer. I'll speak with you.

She nods.

The truth floats in my mind—half in Hebrew, half in English. I struggle to shape a first sentence, telling myself that once I do, the rest will come easily. My body aches with the effort. This time I don't imagine joining her in the narrow hospital bed; I imagine taking her place.

"Maya." The Hebrew makes her shy. "Exciting, isn't it? All the things you are doing in Israel. I am glad." Her gaze slips to one side, she permits herself a few seconds' rest before continuing in English. "I gripped the world with both hands when I was young, too."

Her eyes are closed, she speaks on unevenly. "Not that I ever did as much as you. I wasn't brave about exploring new places. Meeting people. I used to wish I had that kind of nerve, but I was a bookworm. I had to fight that bashfulness so hard, when I got political. Maybe you never knew that, Maya?" She swallows. It seems to take forever. "Bravery came later. When I was so angry about what I was seeing, I didn't care anymore what anyone thought of me." She raises her lids, then closes her eyes again, satisfied that I'm listening. "That was when your father and I started to fall apart."

And now, in English as stumbling as her Hebrew, my mother begins to unburden herself.

"It was when I was your age, and my parents didn't want me to get involved with the Freedom Riders, that things got bad. Of course I went to Mississippi against their orders. And they were furious." She sighs, and is quiet for a while before continuing. "My parents just wanted me safe. They didn't understand why I needed to do this. But I had to. Just like you need to be in Israel, Maya. And so I never argued with you for a second, even though the news from that part of the world makes me worry."

"Worry?" I echo, unbelieving. For an instant I wonder whether the medication might be affecting her mind. "You've worried about my safety?"

"I never show it." Without opening her eyes, she raises her eyebrows: a single gesture of satisfaction. "I tell myself, 'I took my own risks for what I loved, Maya will take hers.' And see? You're fine." She laughs.

"See, you never knew I worried. I always promised myself I'd never crowd my child the way my parents did me."

Her lids flutter; she looks up at me as if she expects thanks.

I say nothing.

"Sometimes," she confesses, "in darker moments, I wonder whether resisting my parents was the reason I never did get on that boat to Haifa."

I can't keep the panic out of my voice. "I thought you didn't move to Israel because of the movement. And later because of Dad. But you always wanted to."

"Yes." She shakes her head. "I know I said that. And believed it. But quite possibly another reason I didn't go to Israel is that if I'd gone, my parents would have *accepted* it. They supported Israel—it was the only thing we agreed on. They were the ones who sent me to Hebrew classes and youth meetings in the first place. Of course, their version of Zionism was giving money to plant forests in Jerusalem. All they knew about youth meetings was that I'd meet Jewish boys. They would have been horrified by my fascination with the socialist kibbutzim.

"By the time I started college I was so angry with them." She pauses to catch her breath; an old resentment crosses her face. "You never knew your grandparents, you never knew how difficult they could be. Still, they were good people. I should have been more of a grown-up. I should have tried to understand their point of view. But the movement was overwhelming, Maya, there's no way to explain. It just took you in like a family, only better than your own family, and you could put everything into it and still wish you had more to give. And then of course I met your father. I met him on the bus. We were already family, all we had left to do was fall in love.

"Marrying a non-Jewish man—it drove my parents wild. Which gave me a certain satisfaction. So maybe *that's* why I never moved to Israel—I couldn't stand to concede an inch of my life to them."

I want to plug my ears. I've wished for so long that my mother would explain herself to me, but now I don't want to hear anything else that will turn the world on its head. I don't want to accept her confession, these stories she passes to me, relieved to place them, at last, into steadier hands.

"I'm sorry your grandparents didn't live to meet you. That might have softened their position on my choices. And maybe I would have been grown-up enough by then to admit some of my own bullhead-edness. I never really did, you know, before they died." Her voice is shaking. "Maya, your coming to me now, our talking like this . . . it's more than I deserve."

Embarrassed by her own tears, she wipes at them with one palm. As they slow, she gazes at me with open longing.

I have no idea what she notices as she teeters between pain and medicated drowsiness. Does she see the dark bruise that has emerged on my jaw, does she see my shadowed eyes? Or only a thriving daughter whose friendship she's won by hiding her worry?

I know that I can't tell her the truth.

From her expression I can see that the pain has taken hold once more. She settles her head on the pillow and blinks at the ceiling. "Talk," she says.

There is a moment when I try to speak but cannot. Words in two languages collide in my throat. Then I fill the room with stories.

She doesn't object when I repeat things or contradict myself; she dozes, wakes, and dozes again. The afternoon light softens, evening rush hour arrives. Below the window the sidewalks are crowded and cars wait at a traffic light. Still I talk, shaping a Jerusalem again and again in this sterile white room.

By the time my mother stirs, my throat is sore from speaking. "Maya," she says. "Will you go back to Israel?"

I turn from the window. "I'm staying here to take care of you."

"After," she says.

"After you're better." I lean against the pane, my back to the cool glass. "Of course. Of course I'll go, I'll spend the fall semester there and maybe stay longer." I search her face for clues: Is this what she wants to hear?

We listen while a doctor is paged over the P.A.

"Talk to Faye about getting me out of this room," my mother tells me. "It may only be a few more days, but even a few more days will cost them a fortune." She attempts a laugh. "If there's anyone in the world who knows I like to economize, it's Faye. Ask her. Ask her, Is she try-ing to hurry me out of this world?"

I listen to the blowing of the hospital ventilation system. I try to feel some movement of the room's tepid air against my skin, but I can't.

"Gil and I are talking about getting married."

The happiness blooms slowly on her face. "That's wonderful, Maya."

"So we'll need you well for the wedding."

She says nothing. Her smile is a wrought-iron rose, dark and delicate and thorned.

In the corridor, lights assault at every corner. I reach the merciful darkness of the telephone booth and use both hands to make sense of the smooth shallow buttons.

I've woken Gil, but he tells me he doesn't mind. He tells me he misses me. His questions about my mother are detailed and careful. "Good luck," he says. "I'll be waiting right here for you." The connection is bad and sometimes his words are indistinct, but I cling to them. His steady voice is a lifeline reaching me from afar. Wrapping me firmly under the arms, while all else dissolves. I keep him on the telephone for a long time.

"That was the year of the moon landing," she continues. "Everyone was crazy for the news. Your father was in an argument with an old boyfriend of mine. . . ." Old boyfriends, best friends, rallies, disappointment: my mother dips a ladle into the vast well of everything she's never said to me, and spills stories over my open hands. Because I've fooled her into thinking I can be trusted.

The day King was assassinated, the demonstrations on campus. Hurrying along a tightrope between sleep and pain, my mother sheds the months and years she has accumulated—lightening her load for a journey. Quietly she confesses dreams, and shortcomings. "Maya, maybe those sacrifices I made drove us apart. I didn't know how to talk to you, for so many years. I always found it easier to know the right thing to do at the Center."

Her stories race between my fingers. I try to hold them all but there are too many.

Don't die.

"There have been times," she tells me, "when I've felt lost. Times I've looked out my barred window onto fields of broken glass. And I've felt abandoned by everyone. By the country, Maya, and by its promises. I've had doubts. I've asked myself, Why keep trying? Sometimes I'm afraid that for all we do, we're just going backward faster and faster. Into despair and hate and division."

That cannot be. The words pop into my mind. *America cannot be burning.*

"I've been lonely," she says.

Outside the window, streetlights begin to glow. I lean against this un-openable window and listen to my mother's soft breathing. While she rests, I begin another description of my neighborhood.

" 'Prepare for the coming of the Messiah'?" She interrupts in a whisper.

"Yes." In the dusk the room is blurred and dim, like a frame in an old film. "The signs are all over the place."

"I've seen those here, too. In Crown Heights." She reaches for the metal rails on the sides of her bed and straightens herself on the mattress. The effort drains her and she waits to recover her strength. "I suppose if they want to prepare for the Messiah, it doesn't hurt anyone."

The room is getting darker.

"No," she says. "That's not what I mean. What I mean is, it doesn't hurt if they believe in a redeemer, so long as they also believe we need to work to fix the world. And fix it for everyone, not just Jews. The people I work with live in the worst of conditions. They might or might not believe in redemption, but they certainly aren't waiting around idly. Black, white, brown—it doesn't matter, they know we've got to do at least half the work of the Messiah."

She signals me to turn on the light. "Tell me more about your trip to Tiberias."

I flip the switch and the room is abruptly, unnaturally bright. As I speak my mother brushes the fingers of her right hand drowsily up and down the inside of her left wrist. "I thought of you a lot during that Tiberias trip," I say, "because I know you always wanted to travel there."

Something in my words catches her attention. "What does that have to do with you?"

"Nothing. I just mean it's something you never did."

She looks me over. "There are a lot of things I never did, Maya. But everyone has plenty of things they don't do. What does my unfinished business have to do with where you travel?"

I shrug. "Nothing. The trip to Tiberias was terrific. After we got back to Jerusalem I thought I'd need to rest for a week from all the walking, and Gil kept saying he wanted to go back and adopt one of the stray dogs for a pet. I told him—"

"Maya."

I wait. She breathes hard.

"Maya, is that why you went to Israel? Because of me?"

"Of course not."

Her body is tense with watchfulness.

My hand, unbidden, rises to my cheek; her eyes narrow with suspicion. She makes the barest of gestures. Obediently I drop my hand.

"What's happened to your face?" she says.

"What do you mean?"

Her lips press together, a thin, precise line. She doesn't waste the strength to say, Don't play games with me.

Tears are running down my cheeks. I wipe at them hurriedly. "What? There's nothing wrong with my face. Except maybe I lost a little beauty rest from jet lag. You're saying I'm ugly?" I try to laugh. "So I've got circles under my eyes, maybe."

My mother is struggling to sit.

"I lost a little beauty rest, that's all, when the Shachars came to find me."

"Came to find you? I thought you were back in Jerusalem already when they called you."

"I mean came to my apartment to find me."

She is sitting, her knuckles sharp on the bed's railing.

"Maya. Look at me."

I can't look at her.

"Look at me. God damn it, look at me." Her voice is frantic, clawing at the walls of my silence; it would be a bellow, were it not hollowed by weakness. "Maya, there's something going on. Tell me."

I lift my head and meet her stare.

My mother's eyes are a fierce, reflectionless black in the severe pallor of her face; shadows dark as bruises have stationed themselves beneath. She never wrote to me about a turn for the worse. She never told me about deciding to give up on treatment. And I chose, for months on end, not to know. My own stupid blindness makes me furious. "You lied to me in your letters," I accuse. "You didn't tell me the treatment didn't work. You didn't tell me—" I can't bring myself to say it. I gesture weakly at the IV. "Why didn't you tell me you were getting sicker?"

Her reply is clipped: the answer is so obvious it shouldn't need to be spoken. "I didn't want to burden you."

"And now I'm not burdened?" The sarcasm of my reply is not what I intended.

She blinks at me—at the end of some long and exhaustive argument, I've unexpectedly stumped her.

My fingernails have carved painful indentations in my damp palms. *Stop,* I tell myself. But since arriving here I've determinedly filled my mother's silences with words. Now, when I should stop speaking, I can't. "Why do you shut yourself off from everyone?" I demand. "You've always got to be the heroine of the story. You've always got to be crusading for something, sacrificing more than anyone else. Maybe you could have given me the chance, stopped controlling everything for once in your damn perfect life and let me know you were getting sicker. But you can't, you never let anyone help you." I spit out the words without thinking. "Dad was right."

She doesn't move and doesn't answer.

All around us, the hospital is silent. "I'm sorry," I say.

She doesn't move.

"I'm sorry."

She is looking at the wall as if, with enough perseverance, she could see through it to the street below. "I wanted you to be happy."

Soft laughter comes from the nurses' station down the hall. Somewhere nearby, a door bangs. Footsteps recede.

"And you're happy in Israel," she says. "If I had told you, you would have worried and come home. I gave you six happy months. I did that. Didn't I?"

I'm not in control of the muscles of my face.

"Besides. What on earth do you think you could have done, Maya? What could you have done if you'd known? Swoop down and save me?" Her mouth twists humorlessly; she shakes her head. Then she stops.

My lips won't form words.

I can tell she's afraid she's been too harsh. Sitting back against her pillow, she begins to say something, then changes her mind. "Maya." She waves a hand in apology. "Let's not argue now. It's not your fault." She watches me evenly, then continues in a businesslike manner. "Now tell me what's happened."

The pain in my palms nauseates me. The darkening world swoons outside the window; in this room, under the bright fluorescent bulb, my mother is near the end of her strength. For a moment her death flashes before me. I can see this room, this chair. The hospital bed, empty.

"It's nothing, Mom," I tell her. "Why don't you get some rest?"

Doubt enters her eyes. "Maya?" She calls out my name and I understand she is asking me to tell her I'm all right. Thoughts pass like clouds across her face. Without words she shows me: She has ached to have me here. She has denied herself my presence fastidiously, hour after hour, in order to give me the gift of another day; now she pleads my forgiveness for not summoning me earlier. She asks humbly that I confirm her reward, the fruit of this last sacrifice in a life of sacrifices—my well-being.

She is exhausted. And something more: She is afraid—for me, and also for herself. From her bed she searches my expression; I am the sum of her lifetime of good intentions, the final verdict on a difficult course she has struggled to navigate for years. Should she have failed, she is too tired to make amends. If I lie to her, her eyes show me, she will choose to believe.

I step forward. I cross to the bed, place a scored and damp palm on her forehead. "I'm fine. I'll feel better when I know you're resting, though."

I watch the relief spill over her face: a quiet, final peace. She draws a long breath, then smiles faintly. At last, she can set down her long task. In the descent of her lids is a heavy satisfaction.

"A few more minutes," she says. "I'm tired but I don't want to sleep yet."

"Do you want me to tell you more about Israel?"

"No." With great care, she arranges the covers around her waist. "Maya," she says, "don't you be afraid of my dying."

"You're not going to die," I recite weakly.

"Yes I am." Each word is a stepping-stone on which she rests her full weight. "Yes I am. And I know it's hard. But I also know that you'll manage without me."

I say nothing.

"You will, Maya."

"No," I refuse her. "I'm not strong. Not like you."

Her face flickers with surprise. Then annoyance; I've stumbled upon some buried pet peeve. "There's no such thing as a strong person," she says.

"*You're* a strong person."

Scowling primly, my mother lays her palms flat on the blanket. "This is important, Maya. So I expect you to listen." And one last time, as I stand with my fists clenched at my sides, she lectures me. "People aren't strong or weak. That's a myth. *Actions* are strong or weak. Calling someone strong is just a cop-out, an excuse people use to stand behind the barricade and let someone else go out front. But courage isn't something you test for at birth. Maybe I've done strong things, Maya, but anyone can. I don't care if you're eighty-five and you've never done a bold thing in your life—that's no excuse. There's never been any such thing as a strong person. There are only strong actions, and any of us can take them at any time."

After a moment's silence, she opens her hands to me. "Don't you know that?" We listen to the tread of strangers passing down the hall. Her eyes begin to close once more. "Don't you know, Maya?" She seems to be singing herself to sleep. "My Maya. I loved you more than anyone."

The minute I lie down on the conference room sofa, I am arrested by the image of an old woman with her head wrapped in a kerchief. She stands alert before me, her face bright with intelligence. Her every shifting expression is as luminous as a stained-glass window. *Hear me,* her swaying form directs.

I watch it happen, as heart-stopping as the first time, and now, as then, there is nothing I can do to prevent it. Her water glass crashes to the floor. My eyes tear at the sight of the shards, she turns away from me and her final question rings in the empty stairwell. *And who if not you will put out this fire?* The heightened color has vanished from her cheeks; the one she has believed in will not rise to right the universe. *Who if not you?* I watch her slump as hope drains from her dry bones, leaving her frail and alone in a tottering world.

She turns. I want to pull her back, but I'm unable to move. I listen to her descent, slow at first, then more rapid, until it seems she is running down an endless stairwell that echoes her footfalls to the roof and waiting sky.

Trembling, I stand. I leave the conference room and walk down the hall, afraid of what I will find.

Mom, I whisper.

In my ears, faint but stubborn, I hear my own pulse.

And like my neighbors in their cool stone synagogues, I sway before my mother's silent form. *I offer you all the magic of my suffering.* My arms wrap my chest.

But there is no magic. My hands discover the ridges of my ribs, my thin bruised arms, and I'm ashamed at this shape my body has taken. There is nothing redemptive about standing here broken while she fades before me. There has been no purpose, after all, in the path I've chosen. It has saved no one.

My mother is sleeping. I say it aloud: "I tried."

She doesn't stir.

My pulse has slowed and grown faint, I am no longer certain of it.

Below the window, people walk holding grocery bags and briefcases. They sit on benches and squint up idly at the streetlights; they are unaware of anyone watching them. Standing here on the fifth floor of this drab brick building, I see that I have at last succeeded in becoming just another ghost, sacrificed for nothing, my voice speaking in a register no one can hear.

I am alone.

You will not be alone. The words come to me out of nowhere, but they make no sense and I lay them aside.

I try to imagine tomorrow, or next week, but I can't. In my picture of the future only Gil stands beside me, and suddenly I can think of nothing but how much I miss him.

Once more my mother wakes, and again sleeps. She is quiet now, in no more pain. *Be good, Maya,* she says. Through her weariness, she smiles.

I take her hand.

She closes her eyes then, and is silent for a long while.

Wake, I whisper carefully at her silent form. And then, more forcefully. *Wake.*

I don't know how long I sit without moving. Nurses come to the door of the conference room and try to engage me in conversation. But I won't speak. I'm not hungry. I'm not tired. I don't know what's next.

The book of psalms lies untouched in my suitcase; words float through my mind. *See how Your heart melts like wax*. I don't understand them. *I am Your right hand, You are my strength*. I let them slip away.

Outside the door there is a stirring. Footsteps converge in the hallway. A nurse huffs as she reaches to twist the television knob. "It's starting," she calls.

Her words fall against my ears, meaningless. The steady beat of a newsman's voice breaks, then rises. Through the crack beneath the door, flashes and shadows from the television screen invade my darkened room.

Wake. The papery whisper is not my own.

The cafeteria is an echoing, crashing place. The distance from register to table is so vast, I'm surprised to discover I've crossed it. I don't know why I'm here. The nurse who sent me said she would help me make some telephone calls. But first, she said, I had to eat.

In the corner, a wall-mounted television shoots images and snatches them away. Through a doorway, I see a man unloading trays from a dishwasher in the kitchen. Steam wreathes his shoulders. I stand in line for dried-out noodles, scooped from a tub edged with cracked bits of red sauce. The people sitting singly or clustered at the red plastic tables are too colorful, larger and louder than is reasonable. The music in the background has too rapid a beat, my head aches. An overweight woman in a food-service uniform motions me toward a basket of pale puffed dinner rolls.

Someone turns off the music. The television becomes audible, and a few people stop speaking to listen. Glancing up, I recognize that the picture is of Israel. "Hebron," the announcer announces. The picture shifts; atop a roof in Hebron, a reporter stands. I wonder whether it is the same reporter who stood on Tel Aviv rooftops during the Gulf War. This time the filming is surer; the camera steadily pans the neighborhood behind the man, revealing flag after flag of green, red, black, and white. "Today is a day of celebration for many Palestinians and Israelis," the reporter intones. "But in the meanwhile, others are not so confident." The camera cuts to Jerusalem; I recognize Ben Yehuda Street. A thin man wags his head, his hands fly with conviction. "If the Arabs are given a state," he assures the camera, "there will be another Holocaust."

The reporter on the rooftop is back. "Today America helps usher in a new future for two long-suffering peoples." He paces his words solemnly, as if trying to meet a time requirement.

I stare at the television. I can't make sense of the images. I arrange my food on its cardboard tray and leave.

In the elevator I watch the numeral light for each floor. I clutch my tray. After the doors slide open, it is a few seconds before I remember to step out. The nurses look up as I approach. I wonder whether they see it written on my face: I don't want to go on from here.

I set my tray down at the nurses' station and hear the low murmur of the television above the desk.

"Look at that, Tracy," the blond nurse calls.

Holding her place in a thick file, a second nurse looks up.

"They're going to shake hands," the blond nurse says.

The three of us watch the screen. At first, the slow-moving collage of colors means nothing to me. Only after a few minutes have passed do I begin to make sense of what I'm seeing.

Heavily the old general rises, then turns. The two men approach each other: Israeli and Palestinian.

The nurse telephones Faye, puts me on the line; I answer Faye's questions mechanically. As soon as I set down the receiver, I retreat to the conference room.

I lie on the sofa. My mind is washed clean; all I know is that the details of the funeral planning escape me. Soon I will be on a bus to the Center, where my mother's co-workers will be waiting. I wish my mother were with me. I wish I hadn't waited to tell her the truth until it was too late. I wish I could hear her, competent and straightforward, telling me what to do.

Listen, I imagine her instructing me.

For what might be hours, I sit without moving or thinking. Then I take the photograph out of my suitcase and set it on the center of the low table in front of me. The book of psalms I lay in one corner, the scraps of newspaper in another.

I call my neighbor by her name. This time I don't wait for her image to present itself; I summon her from her apartment, beckon her up the stairs. In my mind, I show her to the sofa.

I thank her for visiting me. My speech comes haltingly, but I continue all the same; I tell her I'm grateful for her gifts. Quietly, drawing words and rhymes from thin air, I sing praises of her courage. With cocked head, she listens. *You are the only one,* I tell her, *who was never afraid of the truth.* She gives a single nod. *You are the only one,* I say, *who knew what was happening with Gil and still trusted me.* As she nods once more, I utter the question that has nagged at me since Gil and I left for the desert. *Why?*

∞

O American
  Matchstick rock salvation

∞

Her chant, steady and barely audible, grows around me as thick as smoke, until I am enveloped in sound. I take her bony, hard hands in mine.

∞

O my sky my cloud my trash heap my salvation
  My taper my oil
  My tombstone throne my shield my stone
  Hills brim oceans leap o rock o redeemer, my vision my plea my new
  My hope beyond hope
  My prayer.
  Heed my cry. Here in this dark Your hands spill with sorrow, Your heart melts like wax. In Your letters You have written a land of milk and

honey; in Your days and nights You have lived this land of fists and barbs. Now because You do not understand You sit eyes shut; You breathe fear.

O American, how can You, of us all, fear the future?

But I am Your right hand. And You, American, are my strength. Listen to my voice and do not falter.

American, heed Your own cry and wake.

∞

My neighbor's chant blurs, her words are, once again, incomprehensible to me. Yet I think I understand all I need to at this moment. She believed in me. I don't know who this woman was. I'll never know her story. But I know that her spirit held on under the hot sun. I know she didn't give up—she tried and tried to talk to me, even though I failed her. And if she could keep going despite all she survived, surely I can weather whatever comes next.

I confide in her, *I don't know how to begin telling the truth.* And then I see that if she could speak of what she had endured, surely I can find the strength to tell my own small story. *I don't know how to go on,* I confess. Sitting on the couch in this dim conference room, I am humble before her trusting eyes. I know that I will whisper my every secret to her, until nothing is left untold. But first I offer her an apology, and a promise. I tell her, *I don't know what you saw that made you look at me with such love, but I won't let it die.*

∞

Your voice is my voice Your breath is my breath my soul my tear-blinded eyes, American I am the wind in Your hair. Only heed my cry, give ear to my words.

Do not follow where I have gone.

For we arrived in the port they said was Haifa in the new country Israel, our hearts buzzed with a seasickness greater than any known aboard a ship. And we learned to tread cities, farms, streets newly hewn but lined all the same with rubble, each stone a memory. How sharp the stones. Along each road I peered into construction sites to see the bright hope others sang of. I saw only a film of ash. My eyes strained after the bright future but saw instead smoke, clouding every horizon.

O American, I stepped from the boat in the port they said was Haifa and stumbled. I held the hard-shelled suitcase, worn and secondhand then but not yet old; I felt a breeze against my arms and calves, now fattened enough to be called slender. From beneath my kerchief a bead of sweat caressed my neck, I wiped it with a hand that was smooth and I saw I was young and could not understand.

And in this land men with hearts of stone shouted for death. And in cities and fields, stones with hearts of men ached, not a pebble was spared in the grief. I dwelt in my woods and my farms, my hands brimmed in their emptiness I shut my ears against the clamor outside.

American, I have bared my heart to You. Now listen to my voice.

Ask after the welfare of Jerusalem and see this riven city. On the street debates rage, some stand with placards some shout death to the enemy and others weep. Outside the marketplace women hail the Arab peddler, Alte zachen *they shout—old junk. He turns at the cry, his eyes a tale of fruit dropping ungathered, orchards forbidden. And see how soldiers blink against loneliness, weigh choices with battered scales.*

Suicide attacker sends schoolbus into ravine— Release of victims' names pending— Families being informed— *An explosion of dreams bounces sharpest echoes across the wadi, because stones tumble slower than lives they will build a monument to the children.*

Zion spreads out her hands, she has none to comfort her.

I could not bear the company of the living so I kept my counsel with the lost, I sat in my apartment and explained each war to Halina to Lilka to Karol Mother Father. I sat in my apartment and explained six wars. I tended every story, I waited for You to bring redemption. See, Halina, we have gathered mushrooms enough. And do you recall, my sister, one Sunday? Mother slipped cubes of sugar into our pockets as we walked beside the river, for we were so loved.

I have planted a garden of memory.

Nineteen killed in suicide bombing— Borders closed, memorial service planned— Families have been notified—

My garden bears thorns.

ॐ

I sleep deeply. And when I rise, I know what the woman downstairs wanted.

It is so plain I'm ashamed not to have understood from the beginning. My heart floats up with the simplicity of it. She didn't need me to remember every detail of her story; that would have mended nothing. Nor did she want me to forget where she'd been. She wanted only that the past be redeemed. But there is no fixing the past.

Only the future.

The lobby is an ocean of sound and movement. As fluidly as if I'd choreographed it in advance, I weave between groups of visitors and patients. My limbs feel loose, and—despite the bags I carry—frighteningly weightless. There is no one watching this dance. no one to save, to resent, to stage my life for. I understand that I hardly knew my mother; I will spend a lifetime learning who it is I am missing.

Near the glass doors, I hesitate. Outside, the sky is heavy.

A woman standing beside me digs into an enormous handbag, at last pulling out a clear plastic rain bonnet. She settles it over her iron-gray hair. As she ties the crinkling strips under her chin, I realize she's the woman from the vigil.

Without introduction or pleasantry she addresses me. She says nothing of loss or consolation. Instead, she fingers the small gold cross at the base of her creased neck. "I hear you people are making peace over there in that Israel."

I face her and show her my uncertainty. "I hope so. We're still so far from peace."

She considers this, then fixes me with a determined stare. "Even so," she tells me.

She pushes open the heavy front door and leaves.

I stand outside the hospital's main entrance: a wide skirt of semi-circular steps descending to an unswept courtyard. A blunt wind blows, flinging leaves and debris against the building. The fine mist on my cheeks confuses me. Then the wind rises, with a sound so familiar I close my eyes to listen. In this concrete American city, I think of the palm tree outside my window. I think of a breezy Jerusalem night under a bottomless sky.

I set down my mother's bag, then mine.

In my hands I hold a second thread drawn from my mother's life. It's only a slim filament, a tiny portion of the conviction that drove her all these years. But enough, I tell myself, to weave a new cloth.

When the funeral is over, when Faye and the others at the Center have sorted the last of my mother's belongings for sale in accordance with her detailed instructions, I will return. The flight will be a long night's passage through darkness, the steady noise of the engine lulling me.

In Jerusalem, the streets of my neighborhood will be waiting. Balconies and electric poles and cypress trees will cast their shadows. The yellow signs will hang motionless, expectant under the golden autumn sun.

As I round the stairs to the second floor, the dust will coat my sandals and make a film between my toes. No one will have moved, yet, into her apartment. On her door will flutter a single remaining bereavement notice, and something else: a crooked yellow sign. "Prepare for the coming of the Messiah," I will read aloud. Carefully, then, I will take the sign down and lean it against the wall. *You misunderstand,* I will imagine telling the black-hatted man who addressed me in the garden. *She believed our Messiah had already come. She believed the Messiah lived in your neighborhood. In your building,* I would explain to him. *In your apartment. In all our apartments.*

Dov, his mother, and his grandmother will wait respectfully at the foot of the stairs until I start climbing once more.

In the apartment, Gil's confusion will shine in his eyes. Tami and Fanya will stand side by side in the doorway, their gaze almost palpable on my back. Dov will wait on the steps. And Gil's face, wavering between wonder and haughtiness and desolation, will crumple. Then harden.

My books. My clothing. Gil talking, talking. *Maya give us a chance. Maya how could you. Maya I need you.* He will trail after me through the apartment, to and from the bedroom, in and out of the living room. At last he will sit quietly on the bed, watching me pack. The apartment echoes more firmly with every empty drawer I shut.

"You won't make it without me," he warns. "You've never been able to do anything on your own. Your mother knew it, too."

I pack.

"When my father died I didn't just run away from home like you're doing. I shouldered my responsibility." He bites back tears, but he can't help the tremor that shakes first his voice, then his entire body. "I stayed. Just as I'm offering to stay with you now, Maya. Even in spite of this stupidity of yours. I'll stay with you if you wise up. If you stop packing, right now."

I'm through with the bedroom. The kitchen takes longer; I finally choose to abandon most of what Gil and I bought together.

The last things I must retrieve are in the living room, where white curtains billow toward the balcony. Gil sits with his head down, fingertips dug into the wells beneath his eyes. When he looks up he gazes not at me but at a few sheets of white paper hanging above him—spare sketches, rejected in his preparations for the exhibit. He's hung them during my absence, perhaps to keep himself company. His face, pale beneath its freckles, is a portrait of suffering more naked than any of those he's drawn.

I don't know what reply I expect, but I accuse him all the same. "I believed in you."

He lowers his gaze, and the anguish with which he watches me almost pulls me forward to touch him. "Don't you know?" he explains to me gently. "This is love."

I take my last bag and walk away. Out of the room, out of the apartment. Past Tami, who turns to follow me; past Fanya, who lingers; and past Dov, his eyes politely averted. Down the stairs, past the closed door on the second floor, down to the first floor, and into the freshness of late morning.

From the open kitchen window, Fanya's words drift over the garden. "I don't know a thing about you," she is telling Gil. "And I don't plan to." At the bottom of the stairs, Dov nods approval at each pronouncement. "Don't call her," Fanya says. "Don't even try to see her. We'll call the police. And don't think you can just go looking for her at the university, because my grandson and his friends will be watching for you."

Gil's low reply reaches the shaded spot beneath the palm tree where I stand. "You think she can leave me so easily?" His words trail me as I walk to the street. "She'll be back."

I stand beside the car until the others arrive. "And do you know what he had the nerve to tell me?" Fanya is saying as she reaches the street. "He said I couldn't possibly understand what it means to love the way he does." Beneath her indignation, she sounds hurt.

After a few seconds Tami, quiet until now, makes a soothing sound in the back of her throat.

I wait in the car with Fanya while Dov arranges my things in the trunk. In the side mirror I see Tami lose her balance as she swings a last bag off the curb. And although she has already regained her footing by the time Dov looks up, still she allows his clumsy steadying hand on her back. With an awkward nod, then, Dov takes the bag from her and puts it in with the others. He slams the trunk, making the Subaru shudder. As his mother lowers herself into the car, he stands at the curb, hands loose at his sides, an uncertain tenderness on his face. I turn from the mirror to allow him privacy.

Tami has settled beside me in the backseat; Dov drops into the driver's seat and closes his door. He rests one wrist on the steering wheel and surveys the neighborhood. In the shade of a bent olive tree, two white-bearded men lean on wooden canes. They seem engaged in a gentle argument of great duration. Farther along, black-hatted boys cluster on the sidewalk. One turns with a sudden and violent gesture, and glares at us openly. Dov scans this black-and-stone horizon—perhaps he's trying to fathom what it is they are all waiting for here on this mild, still morning. Then he starts the engine, and we leave the street: a vanishing blur of stone and branches and grass, a quiet circle of black that closes behind us.

The Shachars' apartment is sunlit. From the radio, tidings of peace arrive tentatively in the kitchen. "Who knows what this country is going to look like in five years," Nachum murmurs to Moti, who listens, transfixed, to the broadcast. "Who knows whether we'll be able to pull it off."

Dov sets the last of my bags on the living room floor; Tami pours milk into a glass of black coffee, muddying it to a pale brown. She sets the glass before me, then prepares another for Moti, who eyes it without enthusiasm.

"Who knows whether we'll pull it off," Tami echoes. Then, forcing a blunt knife through a dry tart, she continues. "But it's right to try. To really try." Finally she manages to cut a slice, which she sets on a plate before Moti. He does not appear eager to claim it.

The kitchen clock reads eleven-thirty, the second hand sweeps evenly around the dial. I hear Shmuel lay down his newspaper in the living room. When he appears in the kitchen doorway, his face is weighted with sympathy. "I'm very sorry to hear about your mother, Maya," he says. "If there's anything I can do . . ." Gradually, his meditative expression softens. He nods, as if in agreement with something I have proposed. "Welcome back," he says. Then he leaves the kitchen, and Fanya goes to join him.

"Hey," Moti says. It's clear he's keen to do the right thing, too, but now that he has my attention he fumbles for words.

Then his face brightens with inspiration; I watch the joke take hold in his mind until he can't contain his grin. He points at the dry wedge of tart on his plate. "Suspicious object!" he calls out. "Everybody clear the area!"

Tami glares.

Satisfied that he's made me smile, Moti laughs heartily. Then he dares a glance at Tami. Quickly he reaches for the tart to make amends.

But Nachum is quicker. Before Moti can touch it, Nachum grabs the edge of the plate and spins it to his own side of the table. "Sorry, my friend," he tells Moti, and stabs his fork into the tart. "Security check." After chewing his one bite for a long while, he swallows and grins at Tami. "Delicious," he declares.

Tami, standing at the counter, says nothing. Then, dropping the knife with a terrible clatter into the sink, she crosses to Nachum's chair and punches him heavily on the shoulder. "Liar!"

There is a short silence. No one moves. Then Nachum hollers and grabs his wife by the waist. As his chair screeches against the floor, an explosion of high-pitched laughter behind me lets me know Ariela has been watching. With his face buried in Tami's side, Nachum is shouting for a medic, and Tami, bent over him, is shaking with silent laughter, her face blotched with red.

Until I'm ready to move back into the dorm, Dov's room will be mine. He won't need it for another few months, until he's finished his last army obligations; then he'll work at his father's shop until he can begin his engineering courses at the university.

In a few weeks' time, on the first morning of classes, Orit will meet me at the university bus stop. As soon as Rina contacted her on my behalf, she set to enlisting her friends to keep Gil away from me. On the telephone, Orit promises to help me choose my courses. "Only tell me," she asks, "why did you decide to return to Israel?"

At first I don't know how to explain that I have more to do here before going back to pick up my life in America. Then I do. "This is a beautiful country," I tell Orit. "I'd like to see it."

It's late afternoon. While Dov emptied his belongings into a hallway closet, I napped on the living room sofa. Now Dov leads me into his room. Here is a towel, here is a drawer for shirts. Lingering over obvious explanations, he is solicitous and embarrassed by his own generosity. Finally he disappears down the hall.

By this hour the sun should be heavy on the trees outside. But the light is strangely muted, and deposits only a faint glow on the tile floor. The window holds a picture of the world beyond this room, framed in dull gray tape and as unreal as if viewed through the wrong end of a telescope.

I set the house key Dov has given me on the dresser; I lay my knapsack on the bed. And with both hands I take hold of a corner and rip the tape from the window over the bed. Paint chips and bits of plaster scatter on the bedspread and the floor as I tear: up, over, across. The sound is loud in the quiet room, white flecks shower my hair. But I continue, my arms aching with the effort.

The window is left bare, framed only by a ragged track of plaster as naked and unprotected as flesh. I turn the metal handle, and push.

Outside, in the surprisingly cool air, a world. An ordinary, flawed world, no larger than life. Cars move slowly down the street, a girl shouts as she runs after a soccer ball. The air is soft to the touch and gives a feeling of depth. It seems to hold its own faint light, which flows along the street to illuminate each chiseled facet of stone. A breeze brings the perfume of the building's gardens, and with it, something else: a smell that reminds me of childhood.

"Do you smell that?" Tami speaks from the doorway. Her voice is hesitant and full of wonder.

She walks into the room. She says nothing about the balled-up tape or the paint-littered bed. Her expression is rapt and dreamy—she hardly trusts her own senses. I stand aside as she places one cautious hand on the paintless track ringing the window and then, kneeling on the bed like a girl, looks out.

I kneel beside her, our shoulders brushing. What I smell is earth, the dust turning up its face in greeting. Small puffs like smoke rise along the narrow garden footpath; the pale dirt is speckled with dark spots.

A fine rain is falling, so fine it is only a shimmer in the air, a vague distortion marking the distance to the monastery in the valley, the Knesset building, the road climbing the hill to the museum. Between here and there, between here and everywhere, the air is in motion. From this window it appears that all of Jerusalem is afoot, dressed in the brushstrokes of an impressionist painting.

"The first rain of the year," Tami says. I expect her to add some practical comment: The country needs the rain, the farmers will be pleased. But she does not.

"The first rain of the year," I agree.

We watch the world outside. People the size of people, taxicabs the size of taxicabs. Sounds reach us in their proper proportion: the slam of a car door, a man hailing a friend from across the street. Somewhere on the hill, a car backfires. It's a car, not a bomb or a gun, yet it takes an effort not to start from my perch. My heart hammering, I plant my elbows on the sill. I glance at Tami and read the question on her face: *Who knows whether any of this will work?*

Our elbows rest lightly against each other on the windowsill, two cornerstones propping up the world. Who knows whether we'll make it here in this silvery new afternoon, the trembling leaves heavy with their half-year's coating of dust.

I picture the raindrops falling between the leaves, softening hard-packed dirt, forming rivulets. I picture them flowing through crevices in these streets, through paths and gardens and soccer fields, until they join a current of water rushing far beyond the limits of this city. When at last the water bursts into the desert, it has a force I could not imagine had I not seen the proof: smashed rock, twisted metal, layer upon layer of violence carved into the walls of the wadi.

And then, after the winter's rains have spread and stilled, the desert will bloom. Against all odds, it can bloom. It's something I've never seen.

We will stay like this, elbows propped on the sill, for a long time. The breeze, ruffling the highest branches of the trees as it moves up from the valley, will carry a hushing sound through the neighborhood, and it is under this canopy that Tami will turn to me. Her words will fall quietly into the garden, as buses pass with a glitter of windshield wipers and the muezzin's call makes its way from the Old City walls. She will address me in a voice as silvery as that of the rain itself, and as simple. Whispering down on the green tops of palm trees, on bulb-lit grocery stands and uneven sidewalks, and forgotten bicycles leaned hurriedly against gates.

Here in the Bronx it is raining already. The sky is dark, the wind wraps the steps of the hospital. The litter that was blowing against the building is now flat and sodden in the gutters. I stand beneath the overhang, watching the downpour grow until rain pummels the circular drive of the hospital and parades in sheets across the pavement. Twisting ropes of water spill from the overhang; even with its protection a sharp spray stings my face, daring me to retreat to the safety of the lobby.

I think of the telephone call I made only a few minutes ago, knowing it was already late night in Jerusalem but dialing the long chain of numbers all the same.

"I'm coming back," I told Tami.

She did not hesitate. Dov, I knew, would have told his parents what he'd seen of Gil. "You're welcome to stay with us." She spoke the promise firmly.

Without realizing it, I've moved beyond the protection of the overhang. The pitted concrete stairs of the hospital have become a polished waterfall. Drops hit my face and roll down my neck; the water entering my shoes sparks my feet with cold. My hair is plastered to my head, and as I draw a wet forearm across my cheek, I discover I'm fighting to breathe. Even with the rain drowning out the worst of the ache, I can barely stand. This city, this world, is anchorless, and now I panic—if I leave this place, will I forget what little I ever knew about her?

I fight the impulse to turn back, and after a moment my mind offers a first recollection: My mother was the one who knew it wasn't a valley of ghosts.

The sturdy phrases of her letters come back to me. Beneath the sound of the rain I hear them, one upon another, in her low, steady voice. Only this time, what I hear is not challenge but forgiveness. We didn't understand each other; still, we loved enough to lie to each other. And had she known the truth, I am now convinced, she would have insisted with all the strength she possessed on my happiness. She would have stood by the petitioning of the woman downstairs, charged me to take hold of my future with both hands and refuse to be cowed.

I start down the broad stairs. Water streams cold along my neck, and into the hollow between my breasts. I pass into the puddled courtyard; rain chills my belly and my sides, my back and my legs down to the ankles and every part of me. I walk on, my clothing soaked. I cross the courtyard, one foot in front of the other, until I am shivering and washed clean.

At the corner I see Faye, waving from beneath a red umbrella. She hurries toward me. "Didn't want you to make the trip alone," she says when she is near enough to speak. "Look at you, you're soaked."

As she takes a bag from me, I tell her. "Faye, there's something my mother never knew about."

She is nodding. "I thought maybe we could spend some time talking. A woman at the vigil told me that she was worried about you. She said I should make sure you were all right." Faye takes a folded tissue from her pocket and, tending to me as naturally as she would a rain-soaked child at the Center, pats my forehead and cheeks. Assessing my still-dripping face with concern, she directs me toward the shelter, where, she explains, we will meet our bus.

☙

O American my American, I will sing to You a new song. It is a song of hope, will You learn this new anthem?

For You have revealed Yourself, mountains tumble. You have called upon the heavens they bring forth joy.

Time flows free through my fingers, hope rises in my heart.

I did not leave my sister, ever. Now do not forget me, do not forsake me but carry me with You all the days of Your life. For in You the lost live; You are my psalm and my anthem. And danger will never leave You, You will believe You are moving forward only to find You are dragged back, You will fear. Despair will nip Your heels, he will wait for You in his airless apartment. Only You must remember why You have come among us, You must remember: Water spreads at last in the middle of the desert. Words soak soil there is peace.

Do not fear from sudden terror, nor from the rise of the wicked should it come, only let Your heart abide in our valley. Our valley, this valley of giants.

And You will not be alone.

I will sing to You a new song, sing a hymn to You with a ten-stringed harp and You will not be alone.

Long after the war is over they curl together beneath this thin sheet, between these thin walls in this breezy night. They love in darkness, hush themselves that the girl sleeping so near in her bedroom not be frightened from her dreams. They are filled with wonder: this woman blinking into moon-shadowed night, this man reaching to finger her hair.

You know them well but You may never see their affection in day-

light. They are like first lovers perhaps or like night-animals, shy of regard.

She, reaching. He, blinking into dark. So many nights she has lain beside this man, she has braved a life with him and hardly seen years pass: one son, a soldier, gone to battle and returned with questions breaking in his mouth. The other child, sleeping girl, is the mystery none have fathomed. So quiet she is unnoticed, the girl is not dull-witted at all but sees every flash of rage and joy, every gesture caress and deed. In sleep behind closed lids she spins tale upon tale of possibility, as they dream down the hall of her future.

In silence this woman reaches, and touches: his face. The prickle of stubble, mowed grass on a field. The heat of his skin, moonlit progress of his breath. The sweet smell of his chest.

May the words of my mouth and the prayer of my heart be with You always. You are my rock my redeemer and I will not leave You, ever, but watch over You all the days of Your life. For the One we have awaited lives in Your house, sleeps in Your bed. Breathes as You breathe.

I believe in You.